> "Like good whiskey, Bond seems to just get smoother with age."
> —*The Cincinnati Post*

A voice broke the silence. "Here we are again, Mr. Bond. We seem to meet under the most unusual circumstances."

Bond shot toward the voice, but then he heard laughter behind him. Bond twisted again and fired. There was silence and then the voice came from yet another place in the dark.

"You're in my habitat now, Mr. Bond," Cesari said. "You can't see a thing, can you?"

Bond could hear the voice moving. He fired the gun into the darkness again, but the laugh came from a different direction.

Then a club struck him hard on the right shoulder blade.

"Have you had any strange dreams lately, Mr. Bond?" the voice asked as Bond fell to the ground in agony. "You know what they say . . . Never dream of dying. It might just come true."

More praise for Benson's Bond . . .

"A perfect read."   —*Chicago Tribune*

"Fast and furious."   —*Publishers Weekly*

"Lively, imaginative . . . should elate Bond addicts."
                              —*The Buffalo News*

Also by Raymond Benson

NEVER DREAM OF DYING

Raymond Benson

JOVE BOOKS, NEW YORK

NEVER DREAM OF DYING

A Jove Book / published by arrangement with
Ian Fleming (Glidrose) Publications, Ltd.

PRINTING HISTORY
G. P. Putnam's Sons edition / June 2001
Jove edition / May 2002

For information address: The Berkley Publishing Group,
a division of Penguin Putnam Inc.,
375 Hudson Street, New York, New York 10014.

Visit our website at
www.penguinputnam.com

ISBN: 0-515-13307-8

A JOVE BOOK®
Jove Books are published by The Berkley Publishing Group,
a division of Penguin Putnam Inc.,
375 Hudson Street, New York, New York 10014.
JOVE and the "J" design
are trademarks belonging to Penguin Putnam Inc.

PRINTED IN THE UNITED STATES OF AMERICA

10 9 8 7 6 5 4 3 2 1

For Max

Acknowledgments

The author and publisher thank the following individuals and organizations for their help in the preparation of this book.

In Corsica: Antenne Médicale d'Urgence (Calvi); Taverne Astalla (Calvi); Jean Philippe Di Grazia, Agence du Tourisme de la Corse; Le Goulet restaurant (Bonifacio).

In London: Carolyn Caughey; Samantha Evans; Peter Janson-Smith; Corinne Turner; Zoë Watkins; the Heirs of the late Ian Lancaster Fleming.

In Monaco: William Ray, Casino de Monte Carlo.

In Paris: Blandine Bideau, France Télévision; Pascal Boissel, Grand Hôtel Inter-continental; François-Xavier Busnel; Kevin Collette; Le Petit Mâchon restaurant; Laurent Perriot; Daniel Pont, Musée de la Police.

In Nice: Christian Duc, Riviera Studios; Sandra Jurinic, Office du Tourisme et des Congrès; Palais Maeterlinck; Pierre Rodiac.

In the United States: Paul Baack; Gaz Cooper; Paul F. Dantuono; Fountain Powerboats; Dr. Ira Garoon; Dr. Rob Gerowitz; Isabelle Grasset-Lapiere, French Government Tourist Office; Sandy Groark, Bannockburn Travel; Tylyn John; David Knox; James McMahon; Gary Rosenfeld; and my wonderful wife, Randi.

Contents

1

The New War

A tiny bead of sweat appeared at the commandant's right temple and lingered there, waiting for the moment when it would drop off and trickle down the man's high, scarred cheekbone.

James Bond knew that the French commandant was nervous. He empathised with the man, for he, too, never went into a situation such as this one without feeling some amount of anxiety. It was normal. It was healthy. It kept one sharp.

They peered around the edge of the carpenter's shop. It was night and the studio had kept the buildings' exterior lights on. Besides providing plenty of illumination, this created the illusion that the film studio lot was in reality another village with its own paved roads, buildings, and community. The palm trees, standing like sentinels around the property, tended to further perpetuate the notion that this was a Hollywood-style studio, even though it was located in the south of France. The trees, Bond had heard, were not indigenous to the country. They had been imported from Africa by Napoleon in the nineteenth century.

Bond focused his attention on the two bungalows near the soundstage. The lights in the windows had not changed.

"Are you absolutely sure that they're in there?" Bond

asked Commandant Malherbe in French. "They might have left."

"We have been watching them all day and never saw them leave," Malherbe whispered, taking a moment to wipe his forehead with his sleeve. It was a mild January day, nothing unusual for the Riviera at this time of year.

Bond surveyed the scene once again. The two bungalows, used by the studio as dressing rooms, stood quietly at the dead end of a road between two soundstages. One of the soundstages was currently in use, even at 9:45 in the evening. According to the French police's sources, a television movie was being filmed and was behind schedule. They were making up for lost time. Every once in a while, a technician or actor stepped outside the stage door for a cigarette. Signs of use were everywhere—several cars were parked nearby and a good deal of equipment had been stacked near the loading doors—crates, boxes, and petrol drums. For special effects, perhaps?

There were no vehicles in front of the bungalows. Bond was still not convinced that the Union thugs inside were planning to move the arms tonight. If there really *were* arms.

Bond felt compelled to speak. "As an official observer for the United Kingdom, I have to give you my recommendation not to carry out this raid. There are too many civilians about, in my opinion."

"Noted, but I have my orders, Commander Bond," Malherbe said. "We are not to let them leave. We are to catch them with their hands dirty. They've got millions of francs' worth of guns in there. Do you really want them to get away with that? Surely you must have a rather personal score to settle with the Union yourself?"

Bond chose not to answer him, but merely nodded grimly and moved back around the empty building to where Mathis and the others were huddled.

Bond's longtime French colleague and friend, René

Mathis, was quite happy to observe from the sidelines and let the French RAID officers do their jobs. Mathis thought that they looked much too young for this sort of job, but then again, nearly everyone in this business was younger than he was.

Bond crouched beside him and said, "René, I have a bad feeling about this."

Mathis hesitated a moment and then said, "Me too."

"Call it off."

"I can't."

"Your information could be wrong."

"It often is."

Mathis looked hard into Bond's eyes and then grinned with a sardonic gleam in his eyes. Bond's old friend was being stubborn.

Bond studied Mathis's eyes. He and Mathis had a long history together. The Frenchman had even saved his life once. He owed the man a lot. Bond had to trust him and his organisation.

The logic behind the plan seemed sound enough. For some time, Mathis's outfit, the D.G.S.E., which had swallowed up the old Deuxième Bureau years ago, had been gathering reliable intelligence on the whereabouts of Union arms depots ever since France had been the target of a Union bombing spree. No doubt the criminal organisation had been funded by one of the country's independently minded terrorist groups, for the Union purportedly never took political sides. They were only in it for the money.

And made money they had. In the last three years, they had grown from a small group of terrorists and mercenaries based in Morocco to an international network of criminal enterprise. The Union's mysterious leader, *Le Gérant*, remained an enigma and his location was unknown. The organisation had moved its headquarters out of Morocco over a year ago; discovering its current location was the priority of several nations' law enforcement divisions. The

CIA, FBI, SIS, D.G.S.E., and Mossad had declared the Union to be the world's most dangerous threat.

It was true that Bond had no small reason to hate the Union. He had been involved in two of the syndicate's more dangerous schemes and had personally been the target of one of them. The Union had been responsible for the deaths of several people Bond had been close to. He had seen the organisation stop at nothing to invest time, energy, and manpower into seemingly impossible stratagems that ultimately ended in the destruction of its target and the immediate satisfaction of its current employer.

At SIS it was known as "the New War," meaning that the conflict between the Union and the world's law enforcement and intelligence agencies had become akin to a war with an unfriendly foreign power. As in a real war, guerrilla tactics were used to gain information and strike at the enemy. Known safe houses all over the world, for both sides, were bombed. Lives were lost. But money talked and agents were turned. Retaliations were frequent. In seven months the New War had reached a stalemate.

Finally, word had come from René Mathis. When Bond had learned in Morocco that *Le Gérant* might possess a Corsican surname, all investigations had focused on France and her headstrong island in the Mediterranean. Bond reestablished contact with Mathis, who normally worked out of Paris. As it happened, the D.G.S.E. had placed Mathis, once the head of the Deuxième Bureau, on its own Union task force; thus the two old friends were able to share information.

One of Mathis's agents had been following the trail of Julius Wilcox, known to be one of *Le Gérant*'s top lieutenants, or "commandants," as they were called in the Union's inner circle. Wilcox had the reputation of being a killer with no mercy for any victim unlucky enough to get in his way.

He was reportedly working with Union arms dealers operating through Western Europe. He had been sighted several times in the Côte d'Azur, mostly around Nice and Cannes, and occasionally in Monaco. When his movements were traced to the old Bisset film studios in west Nice, the D.G.S.E. convinced SIS and the CIA that the Union was storing illegal arms there.

Until recently, the film studios were only partially in use. They had been constructed in 1927, and many famous motion pictures had been made there. But after their heyday, in the sixties, the studio facilities fell into disrepair; they were now terribly outdated. Most of the buildings, long abandoned, stood rotting on the lot. Only areas essential to the small films currently in production were kept functional.

A well-known French film producer and director had purchased the studio a month ago. Mathis had told Bond that although the man was a celebrity, the D.G.S.E. were keeping their eyes on him. An influential but controversial figure in French cinema, Léon Essinger had a rather shady past. Mathis had spent some time attempting to link Essinger to the Union, but he came up empty-handed. At any rate, with Essinger's purchase, the film studios, now renamed Côte d'Azur Studios, were scheduled to see a vast facelift within two years.

Commandant Malherbe appeared, and whispered to Bond and Mathis: "I have the go-ahead. This is it, gentlemen. Are your vests secure?"

Bond tugged at his bulletproof vest and replied, "Mine's secure, but I'm just an observer, remember?" He smiled at the French officer.

Mathis said, "Commander Bond is concerned about the number of innocent civilians about, and I agree with him."

"We'll do the best we can," Malherbe said. "But if we wait any longer, they may attempt a getaway. That could create chaos all over the studio grounds, and that's infinitely more dangerous. At least we can control a raid ourselves." The commandant adjusted the microphone on his headset and spoke into it. "Lieutenant Busnel? Are you ready?"

The French officer listened and then gave a thumbs-up sign. He turned to a sergeant at his side and barked an order. Four men picked up a metal battering ram and prepared to rush forward. Malherbe directed other men to their positions, guns drawn.

Bond felt helpless as he crouched beside Mathis. He had his Walther on him, but technically he was prohibited from using it here. This was a French government operation. To hell with that, he thought. He would damn well use it if he had to.

The commandant gave the order and the four men with the battering ram rushed toward the door of the bungalow on the right.

Later, survivors would swear that the four men were instantly vaporised by the fireball that suddenly engulfed the area. It was a tremendous explosion, one that rocked the ground and shook the buildings. The noise was deafening.

Bond pulled Mathis to the tarmac as waves of searing heat passed over his head. He could hear shouts of pain and terror from the men near him. Then came the gunfire. Bond looked around the corner. Through the smoke, he could vaguely see men on the roof of the soundstage. They were firing at the RAID officers.

It had been a trap. A typical Union trap.

"Roll over to the edge of the building!" Bond shouted at Mathis. The Frenchman was cursing and drawing his own gun, a 9mm Smith & Wesson, but he managed to do as he was told. Bond rolled with him, ultimately pushing himself against the side of the building. He crawled slowly on his belly so that he could get a better view around the edge of the building at the mayhem in the street between soundstages.

There was nothing left of the first bungalow, and the

other bungalow was on fire. Both had obviously been empty. Several RAID men were lying facedown on the street. The others still alive were scrambling for cover as bullets sprayed the area from above. RAID men were falling left and right. The assault was a disaster.

Bond rotated his body so that he could get a clearer view of the soundstage roof. There were three men with machine guns, blasting at anything that moved on the ground. Bond drew the Walther, took a bead on one of the killers, and squeezed the trigger. The man's head jerked and then his body rolled forward and sailed smoothly off the roof. The other two men looked around, trying to determine where the shot had come from. One of them spotted Bond and pointed. Bond jackknifed to his feet, scrambled across the road so that he was beneath the shooters, and hugged the wall. Unfortunately, there were three more men with machine guns on the roof of the building he had just left. They began to fire at him. Bond leaped for cover behind a large crate, but a bullet seared the top of his thigh and sent a burning shot of pain down his leg. Once under cover, he examined the wound and saw that it was superficial, but it hurt like hell.

The noise and chaos had attracted the attention of the production people inside the soundstage. A stage manager stuck his head out the door, saw the horror, and immediately slammed the door shut. Alarms sounded.

Bond noticed two RAID men pinned down behind crates twenty feet along the wall to his left, unable to move away from the gunfire. He aimed at the men on the roof and fired. Both of them spun around and fell. The two RAID men waved at him and emerged from behind the crates, firing their guns.

A white van tore around the corner and sped down the street toward the burning bungalow. As it screeched to a stop, the back doors opened. Two more men with submachine guns jumped out and sprayed the area with bullets.

The remaining Union men on the roofs jumped onto the crates, then slipped off to their feet—obviously professionally trained for such stunts. They ran and climbed inside the back of the van as the two shooters continued to spray the road.

Bond looked around frantically for a better weapon. One of the RAID men lay dead in the road about ten feet away from him. An MPL submachine gun was by his feet. Bond tempted fate and simply bolted out into the rain of gunfire. He hit the tarmac hard and rolled like a log towards the body. He grabbed the MPL and, on his belly, aimed it at the men by the van. The machine gun vibrated hard in his arms as the bullets found their targets. The men slammed back against the van and fell to the ground. The others inside the vehicle attempted to close the doors, but some of Bond's bullets penetrated the metal. One of the men fell out as the van began to move backwards. The vehicle turned and backed up against the soundstage, near the barrels of petrol. The driver was attempting to turn around so that they could speed out of the studio lot.

Thinking quickly, Bond aimed his gun at the petrol drums and fired. The bullets pierced the metal and ignited the petrol. The van was sent flying in the ensuing explosion. It rolled twice and settled on its side as the passengers scrambled to get out. But they were too late. . . . The van's petrol tank exploded, killing them all.

Bond got to his feet as three RAID men ran toward the soundstage. The exploding petrol barrels had set the building on fire. Mathis, out of breath, ran to Bond and said, "We have to get those people out of there!"

The wooden building was very old, and the fire spread quickly. Burning support beams collapsed and covered the door, trapping the people inside. The burning van was pushed up against the loading doors, eliminating that as a possible exit.

"Is there another way out?" Bond shouted.

"God, I hope so," Mathis said.

Bond ran down the road to circle the soundstage. On another side of the building, black smoke was pouring out of a broken first-floor window. He could see a woman there, her face frozen in terror. He called to her in French to jump, but she couldn't bring herself to do it.

He had never seen a fire spread so quickly. These studio buildings were fires waiting to happen. They probably should have been condemned and flattened years ago, he thought.

More frightened faces appeared at the broken window. One man did jump, landing hard on his ankle. He cried out in pain, but he was alive. Bond ran and helped him away just as the RAID men ran forward with a steel ladder. They propped it near the window and beckoned for the people to descend. The first woman finally found the courage to step through the broken glass and climb onto the ladder. She was followed by another woman, who nearly slipped off the first rung, then managed to regain her balance after several tense seconds. At this rate, evacuating the victims would take forever.

Bond continued his survey of the other sides of the soundstage. The fire must have spread rapidly inside, probably igniting the flammable paints and canvas used to make scenery flats. Curtains on stages were notorious fire hazards. Old ones might not have had the asbestos treatment used in later structures.

He heard glass breaking above him. A man and a woman were at another high window, crying for help. The black smoke billowed out around them. Bond looked around him and noticed a pile of metal piping with pieces of varying lengths and a stack of bricks lying next to them. He quickly rummaged through the piping and found a piece that might just be long enough to reach the window. It wasn't terribly heavy, so he took it along with two bricks and ran with them back to the side of the building.

He called in French to the man in the window, "Secure the end if you can!" Bond used his foot to hold one end of the pipe on the ground and then levered it up until the other end was near the window. The man grabbed the pipe, tore off his shirt, and used it to tie the pipe to the window sash. Bond placed the bricks in such a way that they would prevent the pipe from slipping on the tarmac. He signalled to the man that he was ready and held on to the pipe. The man pushed the frightened woman out of the window first. She tentatively climbed out onto the pipe, held on to it like a firefighter, then slid down the pole. Bond caught her as she landed.

"Merci!" she cried.

The man was next. He climbed out onto the pole and slid to the ground after calling to others behind him.

Bond could see a procession of other panicked people in the window, waiting their turn. He turned the job of holding the pole over to the man, said, "Good luck," and ran back around to the other side of the soundstage to find Mathis.

Sirens grew louder. At least the firefighters were on the way. They would know what to do.

Mathis was bending next to Commandant Malherbe, who was lying against a crate with a bloody wound to his head. The blaze on the soundstage was reaching inferno proportions.

"We have to get these men out of here!" Bond shouted, waving his arm at a couple of other wounded RAID men lying on the road.

Mathis said, "Help me!"

Together they dragged Malherbe away and down the road to a place of safety. He had been hit at least three times and was bleeding profusely. They went back for the other men just as two fire engines roared onto the scene, followed quickly by an ambulance.

"Better tell them they'll need a few more ambulances,"

Bond said to Mathis. Mathis sprinted toward the emergency vehicles, ready to take charge.

Bond, covered in grime and sweat, backed away from the smoke and heat as the roof of the soundstage completely collapsed. He moved to a safe distance, sat on the ground, and watched the catastrophe unfold. He knew that there was nothing else he could do. People were dying inside the burning hellhole. Had it been his fault? If he hadn't shot the petrol barrels, this wouldn't have happened. But then, the van full of Union killers would have escaped.

As a result of the failed raid, nineteen people died inside the destroyed soundstage, including two women and an eight-year-old child actress. At least twenty others were injured, some seriously. They were all innocent professionals working on the television film—actors, technicians, stagehands, designers, grips . . . The building itself was completely ruined and had to be levelled after the city had made its investigation into the fire. The media had a field day, blaming the tragedy on the French police, the D.G.S.E., and "unknown foreign intelligence officers" who had been present.

Léon Essinger, the new owner of the studios, was outraged. A flamboyant character, he appeared on national French television and expressed his anger at the authorities. He was mortified that accusations had been made claiming that a criminal organisation was using the studio as a storehouse for illegal arms. "The notion is ridiculous," he said. "All these allegations turned out to be completely false." When asked who the men were that attacked the assault team, Essinger started to bluster. "It has not been proven that there *was* a group of attackers. I think the government made them up to justify its actions!" He vowed to get to the bottom of the incident and make sure that "those responsible would pay."

The raid did not go down well with the French government, either. Fingers were pointed in every direction. The French police blamed the D.G.S.E., and vice versa. René Mathis was given two months' suspension from duty, even though it wasn't his fault that the intelligence he had been given was incorrect. Nevertheless, Mathis vowed to continue his pursuit of the Union on his own, pay or no pay. Bond told Mathis to keep him informed and he promised to help if needed. They put together an informal method for communicating with each other about the case and bid each other *Au revoir* and *Bonne chance*.

James Bond was recalled to London. SIS was formally ordered by the D.G.S.E. to back off. They would handle the case and keep other agencies informed from then on. Bond not only understood the firm's embarrassment, but he shared much of the guilt. Over the next few nights, he relived his shooting at the petrol barrels in his dreams. Each time he lifted the gun and aimed at those barrels, an inner voice warned him that lives would be lost. And each time, Bond ignored the warning and squeezed the trigger. The noise of the explosion was always overshadowed by the screams of the people inside the soundstage. The cacophony of horror and death never failed to wake him with a jolt.

Bond was quite accustomed to guilt. It was part of his profession. In his business people lived or they died. It was that simple. His actions always had consequences, and bearing the weight of those repercussions was just another part of the job.

The trick was learning to live with it.

2
The Blind Man

Approximately four months later, René Mathis finished his cup of café au lait in the Louis XV restaurant, which adjoined the opulent Hôtel de Paris in the proud, tiny principality of Monaco.

Mathis had always found Monaco an anomaly. Located on a beautiful piece of shoreline on the Côte d'Azur covering just under two square kilometres, it is surrounded and protected by France, yet it remains fiercely independent. Its roughly five thousand citizens never pay taxes, and they have their own flag and traditional dialect. Monaco even looks different from France. The buildings, when seen from a distance, look an ochre colour immediately distinguishing them from the structures in, say, Nice. Mathis likened the architecture to Lego blocks, as if a child had assembled the buildings with preexisting pieces so that they appeared jagged and irregular. Since there was no room to expand the principality by land, buildings were built high and even below ground. Despite the seemingly haphazard construction of the community, it was beautiful to look at. Mathis enjoyed coming to Monaco every once in a while to gamble in its famous casino. Tonight, however, he was in the principality on important business.

Mathis raised his hand at the waiter and said, *"L'addi-*

tion, s'il vous plaît." He paid the bill and walked out of the restaurant into the Place du Casino. The magnificent casino was brightly lit. It was still early: the place wouldn't be buzzing until after midnight.

Mathis went inside, presented his identification for entry, and stepped into the luxurious palace that was designed by Charles Garnier, the same man who had created the Paris Opera House. The gold inlay and marble pillars presented the impression that this was indeed a royal castle from the nineteenth century. The beauty of the interior, the high-class ambience, and the sight of beautiful women in designer evening gowns always impressed Mathis.

He made his way into the *Salon Privé,* which was separate from the main centre of the casino where most of the tourists gambled. Only those well known by the casino staff or players who have given proof of a serious intention to play for high stakes were allowed inside. Luckily, Mathis had an informant at the casino, and Dominic was at his usual place by the door.

"Bonjour, Dominic," Mathis said.

"Bonjour, Monsieur Mathis," the young man said.

"Is our party here as scheduled?"

"Monsieur Rodiac arrived ten minutes ago. I'm sure he's at the table now."

"Merci." Mathis went past Dominic and made his way to the little crowd around the *chemin de fer* table where the blind man liked to play.

He was an interesting-looking man, and it was very difficult to tell what nationality he might be. There were definitely swarthy Arabic features, perhaps Berber, but there was also a European softness about him. He wore a fashionable dinner jacket and dark sunglasses, and he smoked what appeared to be an American brand of cigarette that he kept in a case inlaid with ivory. The usual goons were around him: His helper was sitting to his right, and two bodyguards who looked like professional wrestlers stood behind him. As the man was blind, his helper would whisper into the man's ear and tell him what was on the cards. The man would then make the appropriate bets, ask for a card, or whatever.

He always seemed to win.

"Ten minutes. He is already doing well," Dominic said as he slipped beside Mathis.

Mathis grunted affirmatively as he watched the blind man, who went by the name of Pierre Rodiac, play various challengers around the *chemin de fer* table.

It was a relatively simple game, a cousin to baccarat, except that the house served as "referee" instead of as banker. The casino supplied the room, the equipment, and personnel, for which it charged a five-percent commission on the winnings of the bank hands. The banker-dealer was whoever could put up the highest amount of money. He had to relinquish the deal to the player on his right if he lost a hand; otherwise he could quit at any time. All other players at the table bet against the bank. One hand was dealt to the "player," the cards usually controlled by whichever player had put up the highest bet against the bank. If the banker won the hand, the amount of money in the bank could be doubled, creating a good deal of suspense for the players who wanted to continue the game.

Pierre Rodiac was the banker after having initially secured the position by putting up 250,000 francs as the opening bank. After winning five hands, the bank now totalled 8 million francs. The other players were a little more hesitant to cry *"Banco,"* which meant that one of them would cover the entire bank. Instead, the players might be more willing to bet against a portion of the bank—one might bet against 100,000 francs, another might bet against 500,000, and so on, until the entire bank was covered, or not. Only the amount of the bank that was bet against would be at risk.

Mathis watched carefully as an Englishman, after consulting with the woman sitting next to him, presumably his wife, called, *"Banco."* Rodiac didn't flinch. The croupier repeated the amount of the bank as the Englishman slid chips totalling 8 million francs onto the "Player" space on the table. Rodiac slipped a card out of the sabot. The croupier used the paddle to scoop it up and swing it over to the Englishman. The blind man then dealt a card for himself, then another for his opponent. Once the two cards were in front of him, the Englishman peeked under the corners to see what he had. He needed to get as close to nine as possible. Court cards were valueless and an ace counted as one. Rodiac's helper glanced at the faces of the banker's two cards and whispered in the blind man's ear. The Englishman indicated that he would take a card. Rodiac dealt it and the croupier turned it faceup—a nine. According to the official rules, the banker had the option of drawing a third card if his total was three and he had just dealt a nine to the player. Rodiac hesitated, then dealt himself a card— an ace. Both hands were revealed. The player's total was three. Rodiac's total was four.

Everyone at the table gasped and murmured. As for the blind man, he registered no emotion. He simply kept his head straight, as if he were staring through the croupier at the wall.

Mathis wondered the same thing that they all did. Had the blind man simply made a good guess in choosing to draw a card? Was it a lucky gamble? Or had it been some sort of trick? Had he known that the next card would be an ace? Mathis had indeed detected something before Rodiac had drawn the card. There had been something in the man's body language. He had *known* the card was good. But how?

Mathis carefully reached down to his belt buckle and activated a miniature camera that he kept there. He flicked the shutter twice in Rodiac's direction. With any luck, he would get a couple of good shots of the man.

"He seems to have a sixth sense about this game," Dominic said, shaking his head.

"I'm going to have a drink," Mathis said. They left the room and found the bar. Mathis got a Scotch and soda and went into the buffet room, which was relatively empty. The buffet room amused him because there was a painting on the ceiling that depicted a heavenly scene in which naked cherubs and angels were all smoking cigars. The room had once been the smoking area.

Dominic sat down with him and said, "I can't stay long. I must get back to my post."

"I understand."

"Monsieur Rodiac hasn't missed a Thursday night. He apparently comes in on his yacht and leaves it at the harbour. According to his identity papers, he lives in Corsica. His business address is in the town of Sartène. I haven't been able to find out exactly where he lives."

"Sartène?" Mathis asked. "Why, there's nothing there but devout Catholics and fervid penitents!"

"There are some vineyards in the area, sir."

Mathis raised his eyebrows, indicating scepticism. "Why would he want to live in such a remote area? He's obviously got a lot of money. If he wanted to be in Corsica, why not Bonifacio, Ajaccio, Porto Vecchio—one of the *nice* places?"

"I can't say, sir," Dominic replied. "I must get back."

"Very well." Mathis dismissed him with a wave of his hand and sipped his drink.

It had been a difficult four months. After his suspension he had been reinstated at the D.G.S.E., and during the interim he had learned a thing or two.

To start with, the arms that had supposedly been stored at the Côte d'Azur Studios in Nice had actually been there. They had been moved out a day before the disastrous raid. Mathis hadn't been able to prove this to his superiors, but he knew it to be true. Second, he was becoming more and more suspicious of the studios' new owner, Léon Essinger. The man had made a lot of money from the fire insurance. He had to have ties with the Union.

More important, Mathis had discovered evidence suggesting that the Union was operating on a large scale in the south of France and in Corsica. Perhaps this meant that the current Union headquarters was somewhere in the area. Could it be on that mysterious little island in the Mediterranean that had more ties with Italy than with France? Corsica—the birthplace of Napoleon and the source of the concept of "vendetta"—it wouldn't surprise him if the Union had a base down there.

After Mathis went back to work in Paris, he had immediately been put on a new assignment that he believed to be Union-related.

The Americans had been experimenting with a new explosive material called CL-20. Supposedly, it was the most powerful non-nuclear explosive ever made. Described as a high-energy, high-density ingredient for both propellants and explosives, CL-20 looked like granulated sugar. When ignited by a detonator, it produced a massive explosion capable of levelling a building using a single warhead the size of a household fire extinguisher.

The U.S. Air Force had loaned a supply of CL-20 to the French on a trial basis. It was being stored at the air force base in Solenzara, on the east coast of Corsica. A major strategic centre for the French, Solenzara was a staging point during the Kosovo conflict.

The CL-20 had mysteriously disappeared under the very noses of the base commanders. It had somehow been smuggled off the base with the help of an insider, a lieutenant who had been in charge of the stockpile. When investigators arrived at the base to question him, the lieutenant was found dead in the barracks. His throat had been slashed, ear to ear, in the style of the Union. Working with the French military police, Mathis pieced together a possible scenario: The lieutenant had probably been bribed to pack the CL-20 in something innocuous, like laundry vehicles, or food vending lorries, then they were transported off the base to points unknown. Afterwards, he had been killed simply to silence him.

Mathis had followed the trail of money, but it led back to unidentified sources in Switzerland. The job had obviously been instigated by a superior organisation. Mathis would have bet his life that the Union was behind it.

Where did the CL-20 go? He had spent the last two months pursuing every lead. He had turned Corsica upside down and found nothing. If anyone knew anything, they weren't talking. It was a strange country. Corsicans were rarely forthcoming when it came to secrets. Although the island was French, Corsicans firmly believed in their independence and considered themselves "separate" from the mainland. Being French, and an intelligence officer, Mathis was naturally treated with suspicion. It was difficult to get anything out of those people.

Mathis continued the investigation in the south of France. He thought that he might be on the verge of uncovering something when he got word from his man in Monaco. The report stated that a mysterious blind man from Corsica had begun appearing at the casino on Thursday nights and was making a killing. Casino authorities were perplexed by the man's good fortune. They couldn't spot any way that he was possibly cheating. Some people who had observed the blind man claimed that he had some kind of psychic ability. This was demonstrated when, one evening, the man held a total of three in his hand. He was expected to draw a third card and was about to when he stopped suddenly. "No," he said, waving away the third card. It was as if he had received some divine message in his head. Sure enough, he won the hand—his three against his opponent's two. The next card was revealed to be an eight, which would have given the blind man a total of one, and he would have lost.

Once Mathis learned about this blind man, this "Pierre Rodiac," he put the investigation of the CL-20 theft on the back burner and proceeded to unearth what he could about the stranger. His yacht, a superb Princess 20M, made the trip to Monaco every Thursday night, and back to Calvi, a port on Corsica's northwest shore. A black Rolls-Royce would then take Rodiac south, into the mountains. Where he went from there was still a mystery.

But when he reported all of this to his superiors at the D.G.S.E., they admonished him and warned him not to pursue it any further. After the tragedy in Nice, they wanted no part of any "speculations about Union schemes." Mathis became angry and walked away, taking an indefinite leave of absence from his job. He decided to look into the matter on his own.

Mathis finished his drink and strolled back into the *Salon Privé*. Rodiac was still playing, and his pile of chips had tripled in size. Mathis shook his head, said goodbye to Dominic, then left the casino. He walked to the gardens behind the building and followed the path to the lift that would take him down to the harbour.

The smell of the sea was strong at this time of night. Seagulls were still out in force, crying loudly, looking for food in the water.

Rodiac's Princess 20M, a sleek, white modern motor yacht built by a British company, Marine Projects, looked to be about seventy feet long and probably came with all the modern amenities.

"She's a beauty, isn't she?" came a voice behind Mathis. It was the harbour manager, a salty Monégasque in his fifties with sea-brine white hair.

"Oui," Mathis replied. "Who owns her?"

"A blind man, he comes here every Thursday. He's up at

the casino now," the man said. "He must be a wealthy bastard."

"May I ask where the boat is registered?"

The man frowned. "I'm not allowed to give away that kind of information, you know."

Mathis pulled out a five-hundred-franc bill. "I'll pay for it."

The man scratched his chin. "Make it a thousand?"

Mathis slipped out another bill and handed it over. The man gestured for Mathis to follow him into the little office on the dock. He found and opened his notebook, then began to look through the pages.

"Here it is," he said. "It's registered in Calvi. Owned by a man named Cirendini."

"May I see?" Mathis asked, feeling his heart skip a beat when he heard the name. The man turned the book toward him. Sure enough, there it was. The yacht was registered to Emile Cirendini.

"Merci," Mathis said. He left the office and walked back across the dock to the steps leading back up to the lift.

Well, well! he thought. Emile Cirendini . . . one of the most senior members of the old Corsican mafia—the legendary Union Corse! While the name "Union Corse" was no longer fashionable, the Corsican mafia was still very much alive, operating mostly in France and the Mediterranean. In the old days of the Deuxième, the Union Corse was the equivalent of the Sicilian mafia, specialising in drug smuggling, prostitution, racketeering, arms sales, and gambling.

Cirendini had been in and out of prison on various racketeering charges but always managed to produce sharp lawyers and a lot of money. He never stayed in jail long. Now he ran a supposedly legitimate shipping business out of Corsica.

So . . . the blind man Pierre Rodiac was using a yacht

owned by Emile Cirendini! This was *very* interesting indeed.

Mathis decided there and then that he would make arrangements to follow the Princess 20M to Corsica—if not tonight, then next Thursday. From there, he would do his best to track Rodiac to his home and find out for certain if the man was who Mathis thought he was.

If it was true, then Pierre Rodiac was in fact none other than Olivier Cesari, the man at the top of the Union, the man they called *Le Gérant*.

3

The Filmmaker

The cocaine burned the inside of his nostrils as Léon Essinger snorted and jerked his head back to savour the full effects of the drug.

He looked in the bathroom mirror at his shiny white teeth to make sure that none of his lunch was caught between them. As his heartbeat accelerated, he stared at his reflection. Not bad, he thought. His wavy brown hair, high forehead, dark eyes, and full lips gave him a ruddy, Mediterranean look; he had been told that he resembled a famous rock star. At fifty-two, he was still considered good-looking. Women still came on to him, especially after his separation from Tylyn. He had everything going for him now.

Then why the hell was he so unhappy? Why did everything seem like a disaster waiting to happen?

Essinger was sure that Wilcox was wondering what could be keeping him. He said quietly, to himself, "You can wait, you American bastard."

He straightened his tie, stepped out of the bathroom, and walked back through the corridor and out onto the bright terrace of the sumptuous Palais Maeterlinck restaurant in Nice. Most of the lunch crowd was still there. Sure enough, Wilcox was impatiently looking at his watch.

Essinger sat at the table. The lunch plates had not yet been removed.

"The reason you don't have any money is you spend it all on that crap," Wilcox said, pointing to his nose.

Essinger didn't like Julius Wilcox. The man gave him the creeps. He was terribly ugly, what with that awful scar over the right eye, the hawk nose, and greasy, slicked-back grey hair. He always appeared in a suit, but over that he wore a long duster, the kind of coat worn by outlaws in the American Wild West. It was an odd combination, thought Essinger, but it worked. The man oozed menace, and Essinger could perceive that Wilcox had little regard for him. Wilcox was being cordial because he was following orders.

Essinger decided to ignore him and gaze at the Mediterranean. It was always a pleasure to come to the Maeterlinck when he was in Nice. It had a most interesting history. Originally conceived as a casino in the 1920s, the project was abandoned and later purchased by the author Maurice Maeterlinck. Recently restored and fashioned into a luxury hotel and restaurant, the Maeterlinck was the chic place to be in Nice, where Hollywood stars stayed when they were in town, where scenes from movies have been shot, and where they served the best truffles stuffed with lobster. Essinger felt *important* dining there.

"We should be hearing from our man in L.A. any minute now," Wilcox said.

Essinger nodded. They had been there for nearly two hours. He had met Wilcox for lunch and they had completed the meal half an hour ago. At any rate, if the call came through there would be some consolation, Essinger thought. Perrin and Weil were thorns in his side that had to be extracted as soon as possible. The two rival producers had slapped a multimillion-dollar lawsuit on him recently for breach of contract. The litigation was holding up funding from an American studio for Essinger's latest picture.

They had told him that the money would not be forthcoming until the suit was settled.

Sometimes Essinger wished that he were in another business. The motion picture industry had certainly made him what he was today, but it had also corrupted him, turned him into a less-than-moral person. He admitted it, but he had few regrets. His successes were sweet enough to combat his failures. Unfortunately, lately he had experienced more failures and setbacks than successes.

As he took another sip of the *vin de table,* Essinger pondered the last ten years of his life. It had been a rapid rise to stardom. His early French films as a producer/director had established him as an *auteur* to be reckoned with, and he had spent nearly twenty years of his life making small films in Europe. Receiving the Palme d'Or at the Cannes Film Festival at the age of twenty-eight had boosted his career considerably. As an experiment, he tried doing an action film when he turned forty and it was a major international success—one of those small-budget, big-business anomalies that are legendary in the motion picture industry. It wasn't long before Hollywood came calling, so Essinger packed his bags and left Europe. After moving to California and making two big-budget blockbusters for major studios there, Léon Essinger's fortune was secured. The first film featured a popular American actor in an action role that the public simply couldn't get enough of. Essinger quickly found that more money was to be made with that kind of pulp fiction than with art films. Some of the critics said that he had "sold his soul to Hollywood," but he didn't care. He was laughing all the way to the bank.

The second film built upon the success of the first one, and it nearly doubled the former's business worldwide. This film was even more significant in that it featured Essinger's wife, model Tylyn Mignonne, in her first starring role. She had caused a minor sensation and, in the process, created a new career for herself.

The credit "A Léon Essinger Film" above the title began to mean something. He formed his own production company and produced other pictures under his banner. Some were profitable, others were *very* profitable. For ten years he lived the life of a Hollywood mogul, but it had cost him.

For Léon Essinger had a dark side. There was the cocaine bust that didn't help his standing in the Hollywood community. He also had a reputation for losing his temper in public, of throwing bottle-breaking fits in restaurants, exhibiting road rage, getting into scuffles, and of beating his beautiful wife.

What nonsense, he thought. After Tylyn had left him, a ridiculous story came out that he had hit her!

But it was the special-effects accident that had really turned his life upside down.

He was in the middle of filming his third action picture in Hollywood and had decided to cut costs by using a less-than-adequate scenic material to absorb the heat of explosions on a set. The ensuing accident caused the death of a major Hollywood star and three young extras. The SFX man had been fired, but that didn't keep him from telling the press that he had warned Essinger about the poor protection. A month later, Essinger faced criminal prosecution. In response he did probably the worst thing possible—he fled the States and returned to France. As long as he remained in his native country and continued to work there, he would be fine. But he could never return to America, which was unfortunate.

However, it wasn't long before he perceived that Hollywood had more or less turned its back on him. He found it more difficult to obtain studio funding. The calls stopped. He had been all but blacklisted by most of the major studios. Essinger had to rely on a small, independent art house, EuroClassics, to finance his last picture and the upcoming one. Unfortunately, he had made a mistake the night he had returned to Paris. Totally drunk and high on cocaine while dining at Maxim's, he made a deal with Joe Perrin and Craig Weil, two Hollywood fast-talkers who owned a company that made B movies and teen horror and sexploitation comedies. They talked him into a contract that basically kept him prisoner to their company for life. He was forbidden to make any other deals.

When Essinger got funding for *Tsunami Rising* from EuroClassics, Perrin and Weil sued. EuroClassics withheld the money for his next proposed blockbuster, another action film starring international star Stuart Laurence. It was dead in the water until the lawsuit could be settled. Essinger had high hopes for the new picture, for *Tsunami Rising,* also starring Laurence, was scheduled to premiere at the Cannes Film Festival. Shooting on the new film, a sea epic called *Pirate Island,* was supposed to begin shortly in Corsica and on the Mediterranean. If production didn't begin on time, he could stand to lose what little money he had left.

When his wife left him things really began to turn sour. And to think that he had already cast her in *Pirate Island*! he considered grimly. He wished that he could fire her, but he couldn't. She was good for the box office.

The waiter asked if there might be anything else. Wilcox ordered a *café au lait.* Essinger waved the man away.

Essinger hated waiting.

Nine time zones to the west, the sun was not quite shining on Los Angeles. It was a kind of witching hour in the city—when it wasn't quite dark and wasn't quite light. It was the time of night when people are at their most vulnerable and unprepared.

The killer from the Bronx known only as Schenkman emerged from his discreet Volkswagen bug at the bottom of the hill where Maltman Street emptied into Sunset Boulevard. Traffic on the streets was light. Practically no one was about this early. Silverlake was unusually quiet.

He walked up the steep pavement, following the street as it curved up and around and met another hilly road called Larissa. Schenkman turned left and walked to the edge of a brown stucco house that had been built in the thirties. He checked to make sure the two BMWs were parked in the drive, then paused to pull a 9mm Browning High Power from underneath his black leather jacket. Another hand brought out a suppressor seemingly from nowhere and attached it to the semiautomatic.

Light shone through two bedroom windows. Schenkman could hear music through the walls. The party was still going on.

Although they were based in New York, Joe Perrin and Craig Weil were native Hollywood players who kept a two-bedroom hideaway in Silverlake for business purposes. It was nothing fancy, but it was quiet and discreet. They also had flats in London and Paris. The apartments were the perfect havens for script meetings, deal making, and orgies. They liked to travel often to get away from their wives.

They had arrived late the night before, immediately called their favourite escort agency, and proceeded to indulge in some serious partying. The festivities had begun around one o'clock in the morning and showed no signs of stopping.

When the buzzer rang, Joe Perrin had just turned over on his back so that the nineteen-year-old hooker could straddle his potbelly and get more leverage to move.

"Who the hell could that be?" he muttered. He called into the other room. "Craig? Are you expecting someone?"

Craig Weil was also in a compromising position. The girl with him was older, probably thirty, not as pretty, but she was definitely more experienced.

What the hell, this isn't supposed to happen, Weil thought.

"I'm not expectin' anyone," Weil shouted back.

"I dunno," Perrin said.

"Well, go answer it!" Weil shouted.

"You answer it!"

"Like hell I will!"

Perrin cursed and said to the girl, "Sorry, honey, you gotta get off," and pushed her roughly over on the bed. She said, "Hey!" as he got up, naked, and staggered to the bedroom door. He was quite drunk.

The buzzer sounded again.

"All right, damn it," Perrin called as he walked through the living room. "Who the hell is it?"

"Urgent legal papers from Europe, sir," Schenkman called from outside.

"It's kinda early, ain't it?" Perrin asked.

"I must have your signature, sir."

Perrin forgot that he was naked. He cursed again, unlocked the door, and threw it open.

Phht!

The bullet caught Perrin in the head, throwing him back into the room.

Schenkman stepped inside.

"Joe?" called Weil from his bedroom. "Who is it?"

Schenkman began moving toward the sound when Perrin's hooker made an appearance. She took one look at the body on the floor and one at the man with the gun, then began to scream.

Phht! The Browning jerked again, and the girl crashed into a glass table covered with half-empty drinks.

Schenkman kept moving toward the other bedroom.

"Joe?"

Schenkman threw open the door in time to catch Craig Weil slipping on a robe. His girl was standing by the bed, lighting a cigarette. When they saw Schenkman, they both opened their mouths in surprise.

Phht! Phht!

The girl slammed against the wall and fell to the floor. Weil spun around and collapsed onto the bed.

The intruder stood there for a few moments as the rock-'n'-roll music coming from the stereo system filled the house. Blood began to seep onto the bed beneath Weil's body.

Schenkman put away his gun. Then he produced a regulation-size Bowie knife from a sheath attached to his belt on the left side of his waist and coolly slit Weil's throat, ear to ear.

Always let 'em know that this was Union business.

Schenkman went back into the living room and did the same thing to Perrin. He then cleaned the knife on the white sofa and returned it to its sheath.

As Schenkman left the house he encountered no one on the street. He walked back to Maltman, down the hill, and hopped into his car. The killer drove onto Sunset, headed west, and disappeared.

Wilcox's Ericsson rang. He removed it from his pocket and made a big show of flipping it open.

"Yeah?"

He listened for a few seconds.

"Right." He snapped it shut and put it back into his pocket.

"You know that lawsuit?" Wilcox asked Essinger.

"Yes?"

"It's been dropped," Wilcox said.

Essinger paid the bill and the two men got into the black limousine for the short ride back to the studio. He felt better, but he couldn't shake the feeling of impending doom.

The car went through the gates of Côte d'Azur Studios and passed the site of the tragic fire that had occurred four months ago. The place had been cleaned up, but the lot was practically deserted. Production had ceased after the disaster. Essinger hoped that it would begin again soon.

They got out of the limo in front of a stately villa that was used for administrative offices. Wilcox followed Essinger inside and into the producer's office. Essinger went straight to the cabinet and poured himself a double bourbon. He sat at his large glass-top desk and fingered a press packet for *Pirate Island* while Wilcox helped himself to a glass of vodka. The press packet was full of publicity photos. A gorgeous black-and-white head shot of Tylyn caught his attention; unconsciously he held it in his hands as he spoke, running his fingers along the edges.

"Thank you," he said to Wilcox.

Wilcox waved at him. "Nuthin' to it. When the Union wants somethin' done, it gets done, that's all."

The killer took a sip of his vodka and continued. "Now. It looks like the Union just did you a favour, right? Now you gotta do the Union one in return. That's the way it works. We scratch your back, you scratch ours, you know."

"I understand. We've been through all of this."

"Right. I, uhm, need to check your tattoo. Orders," Wilcox said, stepping behind the desk. "Stand up and turn this way."

Essinger sighed, stood, and turned his head. Wilcox pulled a cylindrical object out of his pocket and hit a switch. A tiny light shone on the end.

"Look over my shoulder," Wilcox commanded. The film producer did as he was told as Wilcox looked through the object into Essinger's right eye.

"Look up."

Essinger felt the slight warmth from the light on the ophthalmoscope.

"I'm no eye doctor, but I think you have an infection," Wilcox said. "Your eyes are bloodshot."

"I sometimes get conjunctivitis," Essinger said.

Wilcox switched it off and said, "Fine. It looks good. The procedure didn't hurt, did it?"

Essinger shook his head and sat down. "No, that doctor

of yours made me very comfortable," he replied. "But I think you're right. I need to go and see my own eye doctor. I probably have an infection again. My eyes keep watering." He rubbed his eyes and squinted.

"Well, don't cry too much," Wilcox said. "After our little job today, you should be able to rest easier." He moved to the couch and sat down.

"So!" Wilcox said. "You're one of us now."

Essinger swallowed. "I am honoured," he said with a touch of sarcasm.

"*Le Gérant* has a lot of faith in you. If the outcome of the project is a success, and it will be, I assure you, then the benefits for all of us will be pretty damn great."

"I know."

Essinger already knew the gist of the plot. In twenty-five words or less: A lot of people would die, and he was going to help kill them. That was it. That was the pitch.

He took a sip of his drink and reflected on this, all the while looking into Tylyn's marvellous, catlike eyes. She was so beautiful. . . . How could she have left him? She was his treasure, his most valuable possession. . . . Now she was gone.

The more Essinger thought about it, the more he felt angry. She was going to pay, like everyone else.

"Have you heard from her?" Wilcox asked.

Essinger was momentarily startled. "What?"

"Your wife. Have you heard from her?"

"Why do you want to know?"

Wilcox looked at Essinger and said, "Look, pal, she's a part of this thing whether you like it or not. Now. Have you heard from her?"

"No. We're to meet soon to discuss the separation and the so-called 'ground rules' for when we begin shooting."

Wilcox could see that the man was in torment over the woman. He liked to push his buttons.

"Do you think she will divorce you?"

"She wouldn't dare," Essinger said. "Not yet, anyway. Not while there is a movie to be made. It's a *trial* separation."

"I thought I saw a photograph of her in the newspaper, or some magazine. She was with some rich guy from America. A producer or director or somethin'."

Essinger sighed. "One of the benefits of a separation is that it entitles you to date other people without guilt."

Wilcox was enjoying this. "She seems to like her new-found freedom. She doesn't need you, you know. She's independently wealthy, right? You know, I think she's dating a *lot* of other people."

"Would you shut up?" Essinger snapped.

Wilcox laughed. "That's good! Jealousy is a perfectly healthy reaction."

"What are you, my therapist?"

"No, but I'm just trying to point out that you shouldn't have any doubts about what we're about to do, that's all." Wilcox stood and went back to the bar to pour himself another drink. Then he went over to the desk and held out his hand. "Are we on the same page?"

Essinger took a moment before responding. He had given Tylyn a starring role in *Pirate Island* because it would be great for the picture. But he did it mainly because he knew that she wouldn't dare divorce him before the movie wrapped. Wilcox was right. Tylyn was indeed dating again, modelling more than ever—her face and body seemed to be on every billboard in Europe. She was attracting the attention of every available bachelor in the world.

Essinger felt the rage building inside. He quickly slipped Tylyn's photo back in the press packet and took a drink.

To hell with her, he thought. When this was all over, she would be dead.

Essinger turned to grasp Wilcox's outstretched hand, and the deal with the devil was made.

4

The Hydra

James Bond strolled into his office at SIS feeling refreshed and alert. In fact, he was fitter than he had been in two years. He had spent six months after the Gibraltar affair working hard to get back into shape. He had fully recovered from a serious head injury, improved his motor skills by doubling the repetitions in his daily workout routine, and sharpened his reaction time by participating in role-playing and puzzle-solving challenges offered by the firm.

When he got to his floor, he swiped his identity card and went through the sliding glass doors to the communal area shared by the various personal assistants. He was surprised by the presence of a young man sitting at the desk that had seen a succession of temporary secretaries since the death of his own assistant a while back. He looked to be about twenty-five, was tall and thin, had blond hair, and wore glasses. Although he had a baby face, there was something about the young man's demeanour—and even in his eyes—that immediately struck Bond, even before the fellow spoke. Bond recognised the look, for this man had seen some life-or-death action somewhere.

"Good morning," Bond said.

The young man blinked and said, "Oh, hello. You must

be Commander Bond." He stood and held out his hand. "I'm Nigel Smith. I'm your new personal assistant."

"Are you?" Bond shook his hand. The boy had a firm grip.

"Yes, sir. I was recently transferred out of the Royal Naval Marines. I had requested MI6, so they put me here. I understand you've been looking for someone for quite some time."

Apart from his days in the Navy, Bond had never had a male personal assistant before, and he wasn't sure that he liked it.

"That's right, and no one's worked out," Bond said. "You're not with the secretarial agency?"

"No, sir, I was placed here under orders. The Ministry. Sir."

Was this M's idea? Was she trying to punish him by giving him a male assistant? Was it some kind of *message*?

Bond sighed and decided to make the best of it. The young man seemed capable. And since Bond had some rather outdated views on relationships with women in the workplace, it was probably for the best.

"Are you experienced with this sort of thing?" Bond asked.

Nigel shrugged and said, "I'm a quick learner. I do all the usual things—computers, typing, filing, phone, dictation, copying, posting, message taking, and takeaway ordering. What I won't do is fetch your tea, clean up after you, or lie to your wife."

"I'm not married."

"I know. Just telling you how it is, sir. Actually I'm quite familiar with your CV, sir, and I must say that it's a pleasure to be working for you."

"Why were you transferred out of the marines?"

"Injury, sir. Bosnia. Got a piece of shrapnel in my back. Land mine. Lost a kidney. Was discharged on a medical, but I didn't want to leave the business, so to speak."

That explained the young man's rather hardened exterior. He obviously had the discipline of a naval officer and some tough experience to go with it. Bond was beginning to like him.

"What was your rank?" Bond asked.

"Second lieutenant, sir."

"Well, welcome aboard," Bond said. "By the way, I detest tea."

"I'm not too fond of it myself, sir."

"And what *do* you drink, Lieutenant?"

Smith shrugged. "A soft drink suits me just fine, sir. Now, I've left something on your desk that I'm sure you'll want to have a look at. I know you're on the Union task force. I brought some material the Ministry just received from Mossad concerning *Le Gérant*. I think you're right, sir."

"Right?"

"That you believe *Le Gérant*'s real name is Olivier Cesari."

Bond was taken aback by Smith's knowledge of the case.

"I've read your reports, sir," Smith added.

"I see. Well, I'll have a look at what you brought. And please stop calling me 'sir.'"

"What would you like me to call you?"

Bond replied, "I'm sure you'll be calling me all sorts of names before long, but you can start with 'James.'"

Nigel smiled. "Very well, James. Call me Nigel. I'm sure we'll get on fine."

Bond nodded and slipped into his private office. Along with the usual memoranda and interoffice mail, there was an envelope and a videotape. Inside the envelope was the documentation for the tape, which had apparently been shot in the Rif Mountains of Morocco by a Mossad agent eight months ago.

He sat down and spent ten minutes catching up on bureaucratic paperwork and returning e-mails, then used the computer to open the most recent files on the Union. Thanks to his efforts, and to the endeavours of countless intelligence and law enforcement agencies around the world, a profile of the Union's leader, *Le Gérant,* had been pieced together.

He was believed to be one Olivier Cesari, a blind man who was half Berber and half Corsican. His father, Joseph Cesari, had made a small fortune in the perfume business in France. It was possible that Olivier had been born in the Rif Mountains and raised in the Berber culture there until he was eight. At that point, Olivier's father came from Corsica and took the boy away from his mother. Olivier spent the next ten years with his father, living in both Corsica and mainland France. Olivier attended university in Paris, studied law and then economics, but after his graduation in 1970, no records of his subsequent movements exist. It was as if he had disappeared off the face of the earth.

Joseph Cesari had been dead since 1973, a homicide victim in Paris. Bond noted that the man's throat had been sliced, ear to ear. The senior Cesari's estate passed to his son, and in 1975 everything was sold—for a lot of money. Olivier Cesari was never present at the proceedings; it was all done through lawyers and private financial advisors. That was the last time anyone had heard a word from Olivier Cesari.

Why is he hiding? Bond wondered. *Where did he go?*

When Bond was in Morocco on a recent operation involving the Union, the SIS contact in Tangier claimed that he had known Olivier Cesari in Paris, and that he was certain that Cesari and *Le Gérant* were one and the same. Bond believed him.

He pressed a button on the desk. The wall above the lateral filing cabinets slid open to reveal a television. Bond put the videotape in the VCR and sat back to watch.

It was an interview with a Berber tribesman, a man in his

sixties. His head was wrapped in a bulky turban and he wore a *jellaba*. He spoke Berber, but subtitles translated the words into English.

The man told a fascinating story. He described a man of near-mystical powers who came to live with his people for a while, probably thirty years ago. He was something of a folk hero—a man who had lived with the tribe as a young boy, but who had gone to the West to make his fortune. When he returned successful and wealthy, he rejoined the tribe and lived as they did—in the mountains, in tents, away from splendour for a few more years. He was very generous with the money he had made in the West—he gave it away freely to those who performed services for him.

The tribesman described the man's powerful charisma, how he could persuade any of them to do something. The fact that he also paid very well didn't hurt. Eventually he organised groups of loyal followers to do his bidding. Then one day he left, just as mysteriously as when he arrived.

The people from the Rif who knew him called him "The Blind Prophet," for he had an uncanny ability for sight when he physically couldn't see. The man *was* blind, the tribesman explained. Yet he could move around easily in places he had never been before, somehow sensing the placement of objects around him. He was able to identify people he knew simply by their being in close proximity to him. He had prophetic dreams that he described to the tribe.

After the man went away the last time, "The Blind Prophet" became a legend among their people. They still hope that he will return someday.

Bond switched off the tape and returned to the computer. That explained where Olivier Cesari went when he disappeared from Paris. He went back to Morocco to see his mother and live with her people once again. But for how long? Just a few years? Probably no more than five, Bond guessed. Then Cesari left again, and that's where the trail ended. That meant that the last known appearance of Olivier Cesari was at least twenty years ago. If this "Blind Prophet" really was *Le Gérant,* what had happened to him in the intervening years? According to what historical records they had on the Union, the organisation was taken over by *Le Gérant* within the last ten years. What was he doing during the ten years before that?

Bond wanted more information on the Cesari family. He punched in a password that allowed him into the database that MI6 shared with the D.G.S.E. Bond searched through the files until he recognised Mathis's coded identity number on something filed two months ago. He opened it and found that it concerned the fire at the Côte d'Azur Studios in Nice—something Bond had tried hard to forget. The investigation had slowed to a standstill, but the French police had cleared studio owner Léon Essinger of any criminal activity regarding illegal arms. The French government had been forced to issue a public apology to Essinger. Mathis had noted that Essinger received a substantial payoff from an insurance company to help rebuild the damaged sections of the studio—so much, in fact, that major renovations were being performed on other parts of the lot as well.

Bond picked up the phone and punched in the number to Mathis's direct line. After several pips, the line was switched over to an assistant, who informed Bond that Mathis was away on leave and had been gone for two months. Bond left a message for Mathis to contact him, hung up, and then dialled Miss Moneypenny.

"Penny, dear, can you fit me in this afternoon?" Bond asked when Moneypenny answered.

"I suppose we'll never know unless we try, James," she said, suppressing a laugh.

"Look here, you naughty girl, I wanted to have a word with M."

"Oh, James, do you really think I'm naughty?"

Bond laughed. "Penny, you have a knack for cheering me up. When I retire and am old and arthritic, will you marry me?"

"In a heartbeat, James," Moneypenny said. "I thought you'd never ask."

"Well, I don't plan on retiring anytime soon, so don't get yourself worked up."

"Oh, I know better than to do that. Now, what can I do for you?"

"M. Can she spare a few minutes?"

"She's locked away in her office, but she's already mentioned that she wants to have a word with you. Why don't you come up at three o'clock?"

"Thanks, Penny. I'll be there."

He hung up and smiled. The ongoing flirtation he had with Miss Moneypenny was sometimes worth every bit of the hell he went through for Her Majesty's secret service.

M looked up from a report that was marked "For Your Eyes Only."

"Come in, Double-O Seven," she said. "How are you?"

"Fine, ma'am, thank you." He closed the door behind him and sat in the black leather chair across from her desk.

"And how's the new assistant working out?" she asked.

"I've only just met him, but fine, so far," he replied.

"Good, then I assume he can stay where he is?"

So he had been right about it being M's idea! Bond smiled and played the game. "He seems efficient enough."

"Very well. I'll have Miss Moneypenny contact the Ministry. I suppose it's late enough in the afternoon—would you like something to drink?"

"If you're having something . . ."

She swivelled in her chair and poured two small glasses of scotch and handed one to him. "Now, what can I do for you?"

"Probably not much. I think I just wanted a sympathetic

ear," Bond replied. "I'm very frustrated with the lack of progress with the Union."

She nodded. "I can understand that. I'm frustrated too. We all are."

"What's happening with Yassasin?" he asked.

Nadir Yassasin, one of the Union's top commandants and its strategist, had been sitting in an English prison since the Gibraltar affair.

"Still awaiting a trial, I'm afraid," she said. "Hasn't said a word. Interrogation is fruitless."

"I'd like to have ten minutes alone in a cell with him. I guarantee to make him talk."

"I'm sure you could, but that's not possible. Funny how once you've become a prisoner you seem to have more rights than the common person. They protect that man better than if he were Winston Churchill. At any rate, I'm glad you brought this Union business up. I think it's time that you move on. I can't afford having my best people floundering. I've decided to give you a new assignment."

Bond sat up. His pulse sped up automatically, a near Pavlovian reaction to the word. Perhaps he did need to get away from all of this academia and get back into the field, but he didn't feel that the time was right.

"Ma'am? A new assignment? Do you think—"

"—that it's wise?" she finished. "I don't know. We're concerned about the reports coming in from Japan. Have you read the classified document on this man Yoshida?"

"I read the cover summary but haven't had a chance to read the full report," Bond said. "Goro Yoshida, a billionaire, the head of a conglomerate of industrial and chemical engineering firms in Japan and a suspect in organising terrorists?"

"That's right. Foreign intelligence suspects that he may be involved with acts of terrorism against the West, mainly America and Britain. The American embassy was bombed recently, but no one was hurt. Two people were hurt at the British embassy bombing, one was killed."

"What do we know about him?" Bond asked.

"Only that he's extremely wealthy and commands the loyalty of a number of followers who would die for him if he asked them to. A few years ago he left the running of his company to others and now lives in some remote part of Japan. We're not sure what his political ambitions are. He may have ties with the *yakuza*."

"Not much to go on, is there?"

"No, it's all on a hunch from the Americans. They believe that he could be raising some kind of army of terrorists. He's said to have very strong views on Japanese nationalism. He has been very outspoken about the way in which traditional Japanese culture and tradition have been corrupted by Western influences."

"And you want me to find him and see what he's up to?" Bond asked.

"That was the idea."

Bond shuffled in his chair. "Ma'am, with all due respect, I don't think I should leave the Union case. We *are* making progress, although I admit it's slow. I would like to dig deeper into Olivier Cesari's family background. The French provided us with a little, but I need to get back in touch with Mathis at the D.G.S.E. The last time I spoke to him, two months ago, he said that he had a couple of interesting leads. He's obviously on the trail of something big."

"Or he's dead," M said.

The words cut him like ice. Bond sat back in the chair and admitted, "That's possible too."

M took a sip of her drink. Bond continued, "If I know Mathis, then he'll be extremely thorough this time before blowing any whistles. Ma'am, if I could have two more weeks to follow up some loose ends—at least allow me to locate Mathis—then, if I've learned nothing new, you could put me on the Yoshida assignment?"

M drummed her glass with her fingers as she held it.

"Give me one good reason why I should do that," she said.

Bond thought a moment and said, "Because the Union have been too quiet. The New War has screeched to a grinding halt, as you will have noticed. In fact, we've had no Union activity that we know of since the incident in France. It can only mean one thing."

"What's that?"

"They're planning something."

M continued to drum her glass.

"I'm sure you are familiar with the myth of the Hydra," she said. "Every time one of the heads was cut off, two more would grow in its place. That's rather a good analogy for the Union, don't you think? It seems that no matter how many times we've foiled their plans—that business in the Himalayas, or the affair in Gibraltar, for example—they always come back even more powerful than before. The FBI estimates that they have grown at a rate of 150 percent in two years. That's frightening."

"All the more reason why we need to concentrate everything we have on finding their leader, this *Le Gérant*. For once we have a very good lead on who this man might be— Olivier Cesari—and if the French aren't going to look into this man's background and try to find him, then somebody should."

"Very well," M said. "Two weeks. If you can produce substantial information regarding the whereabouts of this man, or any evidence of new Union activity, then you can stay on the case."

"Thank you, ma'am."

She stood and took the decanter of scotch. She refilled her glass and then did the same to Bond's.

"Besides," she said, "I hate them as much as you do."

5

The Tattoo

Nadir Yassasin was being detained at Her Majesty's pleasure in HMP Belmarsh, a Category A local prison that had become operational in 1991 in the London Borough of Greenwich. A Category A prisoner is one whose escape would be highly dangerous to the public or the police, or to the security of the state.

Despite the lack of freedom, the Union's most accomplished strategist found prison life not at all what he expected; in fact, he found it to be relatively pleasant. It didn't hurt that he was treated as a celebrity criminal, receiving special consideration when it came to his cell, his interaction with the general population, and personal activities. He was in the Seg Unit, separated from the rest of the prison, which suited him fine. His "peter," the cell he lived in, was comfortable for the most part, and he had been afforded certain luxuries such as books, a television, and no pad mate. When he went to the hotplate for meals, the other prisoners perceived him as someone mysterious and exotic. A senior officer was assigned to him when he was out of his cell, more for Yassasin's protection than for keeping the peace.

The authorities had attempted to interrogate him about the Union for seventy-three days straight, but Yassasin never bent. Short of torture, there was no way that they were going to extract any information from him. Yassasin was thankful that he was in a civilised country. He had seen what the prison systems in some of the countries he had been to were capable of.

Yassasin finished a surprisingly satisfying bowl of vegetable soup in the hotplate, then stood and motioned to the SO that he was ready to go back to his cell. SO Evans, a burly bald-headed man from a working-class background, followed Yassasin out of the room as the other prisoners watched and whispered. The two men passed the latrine and Yassasin stopped, saying that he had to go.

"I'll wait here," Evans said.

Yassasin went inside and found himself alone. He looked into the mirror at his tall, dark reflection and decided that prison life had not done too much damage to his physique. He had not lost much weight, nor gained any for that matter.

Yassasin stepped to the wall of urinals and prepared to do his business when he felt a change in the air behind him. There was a rush of wind, and out of the corner of his eye he saw a Red Band—a uniform indicating that the wearer was a trusted prisoner who served as a messenger or escort without supervision in certain areas of the prison. Yassasin tried to turn in time, but something metal slammed against the side of his face. He felt as if lightning had struck him as everything went black, pain enveloped his head, and he crashed to the floor.

Belmarsh's health care centre was a good one, designated Type 3, which meant that there were inpatient facilities and twenty-four-hour nurse cover. Sixteen of the thirty-eight available beds were filled—one by Nadir Yassasin, who had suffered a severe concussion and damage to his right eye.

SO Evans had caught the Red Band responsible for the

attack. He was revealed to be a prisoner who had wanted to prove to his peers that he was capable of violence. He had used a metal wastepaper basket as a weapon. Apparently, when the prisoner received Red Band status, he had been denigrated by the general population and had become an outcast. He was simply trying to gain favour with his friends again. The prisoner was stripped of his Red Band, received CC (confined to cell) for a week, and charged with assault.

Two days after the attack, Yassasin's headaches had improved but he was still having problems with his vision. An ophthalmologist was brought in from the outside to examine him as the prison doctors observed. SO Evans, feeling somewhat responsible for Yassasin's condition, was present as well.

The doctor used a Keeler binocular indirect ophthalmoscope with a 20-dioptre lens to peer into Yassasin's eyes after using a dilating solution on them.

"There are still some ruptured blood vessels back there," the doctor said. "That probably accounts for your vision not being perfect. I think it should get better with time. I also—wait, hold on . . ." The doctor peered closer at something in the right eye. "You have some kind of lesion on the retina. It appears to be laser scarring. Have you ever had any surgery on your eyes?"

Yassasin hesitated, then said no.

SO Evans asked, "What did you find?"

The doctor shrugged. "It's some kind of lesion on his retina . . . the same kind that is made by lasers. This one is not in a vital spot that would affect vision. It's almost as if it was put there on purpose, as some kind of signature. That's not unusual. I'd swear this is some kind of . . . design. Whatever it is, it was put there by man. It's not congenital."

The doctor put it in his report as the SO looked at Yassasin and frowned.

• • •

After the lights were out that night, SO Evans slipped past the nurses' station and moved quietly down the hallway to the main ward. The snores there were monstrously loud, worse than on the landings. All the better, Evans thought as he walked slowly and softly past the occupied beds.

Nadir Yassasin was sleeping quietly. He was lying on his back, head propped up on the pillow, with his arms resting gently on his chest. He might have been a corpse in the morgue, ready for viewing by family members and friends.

Evans took a pillow from one of the empty beds and stood over Yassasin. He reached into his pocket and removed a six-inch switchblade. Evans looked around him to make sure that no one was watching, then quickly flicked the blade open. In three expert moves, he thrust the knife into Yassasin's throat, pulled it across, slitting it from ear to ear, and forced the spare pillow down over the victim's face. Evans held the pillow there, muffling the gurgling sounds and soaking up the blood. After a minute of minor struggling, it was over. Even Evans was surprised by how quietly he had done it.

He cleaned the knife on the pillow, put it back into his pocket, and turned to leave, lingering in the hallway long enough for the nurse to turn her back once more. The SO scooted past the desk and out of the health care centre without anyone knowing he'd been there.

The murder of Nadir Yassasin sent shock waves through SIS. The governor of Belmarsh was up in arms, steadfastly defending the security of the prison. A thorough investigation turned up next to nothing. The nurses on duty at the time of the killing claimed complete ignorance of the event. None of the other patients in the health care centre knew anything had happened until the next morning. It was as if Yassasin had been killed by a ghost.

The ophthalmologist's report crossed M's desk not quite

a week later. After she had read it, she called Bond immediately.

She thrust the folder into his hands as soon as he walked into her office.

"Read this and tell me if it rings any bells."

Bond sat down and read it twice. Both times he was struck by the discovery of the strange lesion on Yassasin's right retina.

"When I was in Spain last year," he said, "Margareta Piel inadvertently mentioned something about an 'operation' that Union members had to undergo, part of an initiation, I gather. Could this be it?"

"That's what I was thinking," M said. "I remembered that from your debriefing."

"Can we get a picture of this lesion? The doctor states that it's some type of pattern."

"I'm sure we can," M replied. "I have an idea—suppose that whoever killed Yassasin wanted to keep him from talking or something."

"A Union man—on the inside?"

"Why not?" M asked. "It's happened before. I've already had a couple of chats with Belmarsh's governor. Yassasin apparently had very little contact with other prisoners. The assault in the latrine was a fluke. Prisoners don't have access to the health care centre without authorisation."

"It had to have been a guard," Bond said. "A warder, someone on staff."

"Precisely."

Bond thought a minute. "If our theory is correct, this perpetrator would have the same lesion on his retina."

M nodded. "I'm going to ask the governor to hold mandatory eye examinations for the entire staff. Let's see if it smokes anyone out."

• • •

It was a tough two days. The governor had ordered the eye examinations on the pretext that they were part of a new medical regime that all civil servants, policemen, and government employees throughout England had to go through. Only three members of Belmarsh's staff refused the exam. One was a nurse who was told that she would be fired if she didn't submit to the test. She had second thoughts on hearing that and went through with it. The second was a warder who was planning to retire in five more years. He had been afraid that the authorities would find out that he was practically blind in one eye and would have to take an early retirement. Once the truth came out, he had the exam and was transferred to desk duty with his pension intact. The third holdout was SO Evans.

After extensive questioning, Evans could not come up with a satisfactory reason why he shouldn't have a simple eye exam. In the end, he agreed to do it. Dr. David Worrall, the ophthalmologist, was brought in and he confirmed that SO Evans also had the same, unique scarring on his retina.

The next day, Dr. Worrall was summoned to the SIS building on the Thames. Chief of Staff Bill Tanner ushered Worrall into M's office, where he found himself confronted by M, Bond, the Belmarsh governor, and two representatives from the Ministry of Defence.

"Dr. Worrall," the governor began, "we don't mean to alarm you, but you've stumbled upon something that could very well be a matter of national security."

"I guessed that it was about the retinal scarring I found on those men," Worrall said.

"That's correct. Could you please tell us, in laymen's terms, what it is you found?"

Worrall removed a colour photograph from his briefcase. On first glance, it seemed to be a pink blur with a long dark spot in the middle, but on closer examination, one could see that the spot was a geometric pattern. It looked

like three pyramids in a row, the middle one inverted so
that the sides of the pyramids fitted together:

"This is the tattoo that was on Mr. Yassasin and Mr.
Evans's retinas," Worrall said. "Believe it or not, marks
like these are made by some retina specialists when they
perform laser surgery. It's done with an Argon laser set at a
very low wattage, say point one, and the mark takes up no
more than five hundred microns—which is quite small.
These lasers are used to perform all sorts of things—cor-
rective surgery and the like. I know of at least two doctors
who like to carve their initials on the retinas after they're
done. Like an artist signing a canvas."

"Doesn't that affect the vision?" M asked.

"Not if it's in the right place," Dr. Worrall answered.
"You see, there are areas on the retina that constitute a person's so-called blind spots. We all have them. They're tem-
poral to the area of sharpest vision—the macula. A doctor
can see these areas by looking with an ophthalmoscope. As
long as the tattoo is not placed anywhere near the macula
or the optic nerve, then vision wouldn't be affected at all."

"Thank you, Doctor," the governor said.

After Worrall had gathered his things and was escorted
out, M asked, "What the hell does it mean?"

Bond took the photograph and studied it. "It could be
something very simple. It's an illustration of a 'union'—
note how the three objects fit together nicely. One is inverted, and yet it belongs with the others."

"Why would Union members have that? On their *eye*,
for God's sake," M continued.

"The criminal mind works in mysterious ways. Perhaps
I had better talk to this Evans fellow," Bond suggested.

"So far he hasn't said a word," the governor said. "When
he was put into a holding cell, he made a phone call. He re-

fused help from any lawyers, but said that someone was
coming to help him from France."

"Then I had better talk to him before that," Bond said.

Thus, a few hours later, Bond found himself alone with
SO Evans in a holding cell at Belmarsh. He spent thirty
fruitless minutes asking questions and receiving no answers. Finally, Evans asked for a cigarette.

"If I give you one, you'll tell me what I want to know?"
Bond asked.

Evans shrugged. "No Etonian pencil-pusher from SIS is
goin' to push me around," he said.

Bond leaned forward over the table. "Look. You have a
couple of options here. The first is that you'll tell me everything I want to know, and it'll be at your own volition. The
second is that you'll tell me everything I want to know, and
it'll be at my volition. Which is it to be?"

"You don't scare me. You can't touch me," Evans spat.
"I know my rights."

"Rights?" Bond asked. "What rights? Have you been
charged with anything?"

"No."

"And you've sent your lawyer away, is that correct?"

"That's right."

"You think the Union are going to come and rescue
you?"

Evans shuffled in his chair. "Don't know anythin' about
no Union. I jus' know someone's comin' to get me out of
here."

In a lightning-fast move that toppled his chair and created
a deafening noise that echoed loudly in the room, Bond suddenly jumped up, grabbed the man by his shirt, and roughly
pulled him to his feet. "Listen to me. As far as I'm concerned, you have no rights," he said through his teeth.
"You're not a prisoner here. You have no lawyer present. We
know you have no family, so no one would miss you. You're
going to be charged with murder. You're withholding infor-

mation that is vital to national security. If you think the
Union are going to save you, think again. I don't give a damn
about you. I enjoy squashing vermin like you." Bond locked
Evans's head in his arm and began to apply some pressure.
"I could break your neck with a twist of my arm, you know.
The sound it makes—have you ever heard it? A man's neck
being broken? There's this tremendous pull and then a sudden SNAP! If it's done hard enough, the spinal cord is sev-
ered. If it doesn't kill you, then you're paralysed for the rest
of your life. Would you like to hear what it sounds like?"

"N-n-no, lemme go!" Evans cried in terror.

Bond released the man and he fell back into his chair.
Evans was shaken by the sudden ferocity Bond had shown.
He could now see that there was genuine cruelty lurking
within the man standing over him. Evans, relying on the
experience he had gained working at a prison, recognised a
natural-born killer. In the flash of a second, the man from
SIS had completely changed his demeanour. Instead of the
soft blue eyes he had seen earlier, they were now cold and
steely. The mouth had curved into a grimace and the scar
on the right cheek was more prominent.

Jesus, Evans thought. *Why didn't I see this before?*

"How . . . how about that cigarette?" he whispered.

Bond sat down across from him and removed the gun-
metal case from his jacket inside pocket. He offered Evans
one of his specially made cigarettes and then produced his
Ronson lighter.

Evans took a couple of puffs and blew out the smoke,
obviously taking comfort from the tobacco. "This is good,
where d'you get it?"

"It's imported. Now . . . do we have an understanding?"
Bond asked calmly, but maintaining the level of menace in
his voice.

"What do you want to know?" Evans smiled.

"The tattoo in your eye. Tell me all about it."

Evans cleared his throat. "All Union members have it.

Once you've been accepted, it's like you get a membership card, only it's on your eye. It's sort of a secret handshake, like. Each new member receives some money just for joinin', so nobody minds."

"Who does the procedure?"

"Depends on where you're located. I had mine done in Paris. There's a doctor there—I *don't* know his name, I swear—he does it for most of the Union people in Europe. He travels around."

"But why? Why a tattoo on the eye?"

Evans shrugged. "I wish I knew. Really! No one really knows. It's an order handed down from the big boss, that fellow they call *Le Gérant*. He has some kind of fascination wi' eyes."

"Have you met him?"

Evans shook his head. "I don't know anyone who's met him, except maybe that Yassasin fellow. But he never talked about the Union. He never talked at all."

"Why did you kill him?"

Evans hesitated. "I . . . I was ordered to."

"By whom?"

"I don't know. I get my instructions by phone. It's just a voice. It comes from France. That's all I know."

Bond stood and began to circle the room. "So you reported to your superiors in France that Yassasin's tattoo had been discovered. And they told you to eliminate him before he could talk, is that it?"

Evans nodded. "Yeah, that's it."

"And what did you get out of it?"

"A little money."

"How much?"

"Two thousand quid."

"That's not a lot."

"It's a lot to me. You ever work for the bleedin' government?" Bond shot him a look, and Evans realised his mistake. "Sorry," he muttered.

"One last question," Bond said. "Do you know where *Le Gérant* is now?"

Evans shook his head. "All I know is that the headquarters used to be in Morocco, but it isn't anymore. They moved to Europe somewhere. There's a Paris branch, but I don't think he's there. I believe that's where my instructions came from. That branch controls all of the activity in Europe and the U.K."

Bond circled the room one more time, quietly, staring at Evans, daring him to leave out something. After nearly two minutes of nerve-racking silence, Bond was satisfied that the man was too scared not to talk.

Bond moved to the door and said, "Thanks, old chap," and signalled for the guard to come and let him out.

The Kuril Islands form a chain of about thirty large and twenty small volcanic islands in extreme East Russia, separating the Sea of Okhotsk from the Pacific Ocean. They extend between Northeast Hokkaido, Japan, and South Kamchatka Peninsula, Russia. Settled by both the Japanese and the Russians in the eighteenth century, the islands at that time belonged to Japan. After the Yalta Conference during World War II, the islands were given to the USSR and today remain the property of Russia. Japan, however, has maintained a claim to at least some of the islands. No peace treaty had ever been concluded between Japan and the former Soviet Union, mainly because of the dispute over these "Northern Territories." As a result, there is also no peace treaty between today's Russian Federation and Japan.

Thus, the Kuril Islands remain a mysterious no-man's-land with regard to the two countries. While they are governed as part of Sakhalin Oblast, Russia, in many ways they are still culturally tied to Japan. The islands are heavily forested and contain many active volcanoes. Hunting, fishing, and sulphur mining are the principal occupations

of the inhabitants, among whom are the Ainu, a primitive
race indigenous to the area.

At approximately the same time that James Bond was
interrogating SO Evans in Belmarsh prison, a black
Kawasaki BK117 helicopter landed on one of the disputed
Kuril Islands, called Etorofu by the Japanese and Iturup by
the Russians. The helicopter was big enough for ten passengers, but today it carried only one. He had flown in from
Tokyo, after having made a series of very long flights that
began in Calvi, Corsica.

The helipad was on private property hidden amongst the
trees. The owner was associated with a mining operation
that worked a nearby quarry; but if people at the firm were
questioned, they would have no knowledge of who that
owner might be.

The helicopter touched down on the strip and its passenger looked out of the window at lush, green trees and a
colourful mountain looming in the distance. Was it a vol-
cano? He didn't know and really didn't care. He wanted to
get his business done and go back to Corsica, where he felt
more at home. He wasn't suited to acting as an errand boy
for the Union.

Emile Cirendini, carrying a briefcase, stepped out of the
vibrating chopper and was met by two armed Japanese
dressed in fatigues. One barked a greeting to him that he
didn't understand, but he held out his hand and said, *"Bonjour."* The Japanese guard said something else and pointed
to a jeep a few yards away. Cirendini wondered why Japanese people always sounded as if they were angry when they
spoke.

Cirendini, a slightly overweight but otherwise healthy
man in his fifties, was something of a giant compared to the
two Japanese guards. He was a little over six feet tall, had
short grey hair, a thick moustache, and deep brown eyes.
He climbed into the back of the jeep and felt relaxed for the
first time in twenty-four hours. But then one of the guards

turned to him and said something. He held out an eyemask, the type used on transatlantic flights for people who want to sleep on the plane.

A blindfold? Cirendini took it and shrugged. He had been warned that something like this might occur. He put it on and the jeep began to roll.

The ride was bumpy as the vehicle drove over unpaved, rough terrain. Cirendini's backside was already sore from sitting so long in the aeroplanes; this certainly didn't help.

They drove for nearly twenty minutes. When the jeep finally slowed to a stop and the guard removed Cirendini's blindfold, they were in front of a modest army barracks. Cirendini looked around him and saw that he was in some kind of military camp. He could see a field where men were running through obstacles and conducting target practise. Camouflage netting covered several buildings. A group of soldiers were marching in formation. It looked like basic training for the Japanese army.

Cirendini knew that it was far from that.

After he was thoroughly searched, he was led into a dugout covered in camouflage netting. Steps went down into the darkness; a ten-metre passage emptied into a spacious, well-lit receiving room that was ornately decorated in traditional Japanese style. A sliding paper door opened as a guard ushered Cirendini into the next room.

But the guard stopped him and admonished him for something.

"What?" Cirendini asked.

The guard pointed to Cirendini's shoes.

"Oh, right," he said, removing them.

Cirendini was led into a room where a man was sitting on the floor at a low table, having dinner. A central ceiling fan provided a cool breeze and the smell of incense was strong. The man appeared to be in his fifties. He was handsome, had black hair sprinkled with grey and dark eyes. He was adorned in a colourful kimono.

"Mister Cirendini," he said in English, bowing slightly. "Please sit. Have some *sake*. Forgive me if I don't get up."

Cirendini felt ridiculous sitting at the low table. His size seemed to dwarf everything in the room. A servant poured a cup for him and left them alone.

"You have a beautiful place here, Mister Yoshida," he said.

"Thank you. We try to keep it that way. The Russians have been most hospitable in allowing me to stay here. One of these days the island will be Japan's again. But for the moment, they are being quite reasonable. I suppose it helps that I pay handsomely for the use of the land."

Goro Yoshida took a sip of his *sake* and picked up his chopsticks to resume eating the sushi that was before him. "Would you care for something to eat?"

Cirendini was not fond of uncooked food. "No, thank you. I suppose we should simply get down to business."

Yoshida dabbed his mouth with a napkin and said, "Very well."

Cirendini opened his briefcase and removed a piece of paper. The text was written in English, only a few lines long. He handed it to Yoshida, who took it and read it carefully.

Then, without a word, Yoshida reached inside his kimono and took out a *hanko*. He stamped the piece of paper with a flourish.

"I will make the money transfer this afternoon," Yoshida said as he handed the paper back to Cirendini.

"Thank you," he said. "*Le Gérant* sends you his best regards."

"Tell him that it is a pleasure doing business," Yoshida said with an insincere smile.

Cirendini replaced the paper in the briefcase and stood. A guard opened the sliding door on cue. Cirendini walked out of the room, was blindfolded again, and taken back to the helicopter for another long series of flights back to the Mediterranean Sea.

6

The Sailor

After learning that "Pierre Rodiac" used a yacht owned by the Corsican mafia man Emile Cirendini, Mathis took the ferry to Calvi to investigate further. When he had looked into the CL-20 theft from the air force base in Solenzara, Mathis had made several useful contacts. One of them was a man who worked on the marina in Calvi, which was one of the island's main shipping headquarters. Locals called him "The Sailor," and Mathis was unable to find out his true name. Nevertheless, the Sailor liked wine and money, in that order.

When the Sailor saw Mathis again, he smiled warmly and shook his hand.

"Hello, my friend!" he said. He was a large man with long, curly black hair. His teeth were yellow and a front one was missing. He smelled strongly of fish and wine. "Come to spend more money on me?"

Mathis laughed and said, "I would be happy to if you are willing to have a little chat."

The Sailor put down a crate of salmon on ice, rubbed his hands, and said, "Let's go to the bar over there." He pointed to a pleasant-looking establishment with tables outside. Mathis appreciated the fact that the wharves in Corsica were well maintained, clean, and for the most part, in close proximity to the tourist shops and restaurants.

It was the middle of the day. The sun was shining brightly in a clear blue sky, and the view from the harbour was always impressive. On one side spread the vast Mediterranean. On the other was a panorama of rugged mountains. Mathis noted that the highest peak still had a bit of snow on it. Corsica was indeed a place of hardy landscapes and a strong people to populate them.

All manner of small crafts were docked at the harbour, and there was room farther down the marina for larger cruise ships. Pierre Rodiac's Princess 20M was docked there as well.

The two men walked to a small café with outdoor seating facing the sea. Mathis ordered a bottle of Domaine de Culombu, a rich red Corsican wine, and asked the Sailor if he wanted lunch. The Sailor wasn't about to refuse. After a few minutes, a plate of scorpionfish with lobster sauce was placed in front of him. Mathis had langoustines grilled with basil sauce. Both dishes were Corsican standards.

"So, what brings you to our little island this time?" the Sailor asked.

"Do you know a man named Emile Cirendini?" Mathis asked.

The Sailor's smile vanished. He looked around to make sure no one was listening. Then he shrugged and nodded. "Yeah, I know who he is."

"What can you tell me about him?"

"I believe you already know," the Sailor said. "Right?"

Mathis came clean. "I know that he's a shipping magnate but that he has ties with the mafia here."

"That's right! The old Union Corse," the Sailor said. "You don't hear much about them these days. The mafia today is not the same thing. At least in name it isn't."

"I know. Tell me, is Cirendini still involved in illegal activity?"

"How would I know? I'm just an honest fisherman. But I hear things, you know."

Mathis slipped the man a wad of francs. "I know that his shipping establishment is not far from here. Can you tell me anything interesting about him or his business?"

The Sailor pocketed the money so quickly that he might have made a good magician's assistant. "Yes, I can. I know that he imports and exports beverages, mostly to the mainland of France. That's his main business. He ships other goods, too—machine parts, electronics, that kind of stuff. All day long, every day. What he ships at night, that I don't know."

"At night?"

The Sailor raised his eyebrows. "Sometimes ships come and go in the dark of night, and they don't use any lights, either. Like he's *hiding* something."

"That's interesting. How do they keep from crashing into the rocks? The coastline is awfully treacherous around Corsica."

"Aha!" the Sailor exclaimed, building up to his punch line. "It's because there is a secret entrance to the shipping centre. Through a cave on the coast!"

"You've seen it?"

The Sailor nodded. "I can tell you where it is. It looks like a harmless, natural cave, but it's large enough for a medium-sized boat to enter. Boats can slip in and out without the police noticing. I believe that there is access to the inside of the headquarters from the cave."

"That's excellent. Thank you," Mathis said. He ordered after-dinner drinks, a strong spirit called *eau de vie de Corse*. "I have one more question."

"Go ahead."

"Do you know who sails on that yacht?" Mathis pointed to the Princess.

The man hesitated, then asked, "The blind man?"

Mathis nodded.

"The yacht is owned by your friend Cirendini," the Sailor said. "But the blind man and his bodyguards use it.

They take it out every Thursday night. I don't know where they go."

"Do you know the blind man's name?"

The Sailor shook his head. "A fancy car brings him here and picks him up when he returns."

"Do you know where they go from here?"

"South. That's all I know."

"I've heard that he has a business address in Sartène."

The man shrugged. "I wouldn't know. Sounds like you know more about him than I do."

Mathis smiled. "I don't know nearly enough, my friend. Not yet, anyway."

Mathis found Cirendini's shipping establishment east of Calvi, close to Cap Corse, the peninsula that jutted northward from the island. It was close to the small port of St. Laurent, a prime spot for diving enthusiasts.

Called simply "Corse Shipping," Cirendini's outfit was a large warehouse perched on the cliff overlooking the water. A dirt road went from the main two-lane paved highway to the building. A small gravel parking lot contained four cars. The building was once an old asbestos mine that had been closed years ago. Mathis eventually learned that Cirendini had bought the property and renovated it.

The most unusual thing about it was the freight lift built on the side of the cliff that went down to the docks. Cargo could be placed on the lift at the building level and lowered to the ships waiting below.

Mathis drove his rented Renault Mégane along the coast road that wound through the high cliffs. He went around a bend and pulled over to the side of the road, in a spot designated for snapshot seekers. From here, he could get a scenic vista of Corse Shipping, the cliff it was perched upon, and the docks and coastline below.

There it was, the cave that the Sailor had told him about.

Mathis took some pictures with his miniature belt buckle camera.

He drove back to Corse Shipping and parked his car. He went inside and found a middle-aged woman at the front desk. He could hear the sound of machinery back in the warehouse.

"May I help you?" she asked.

"Is Monsieur Cirendini available?"

She shook her head. "He is away on a business trip."

"Oh," he said. He produced a card and a fake identification that he had made up. "I'm with French Customs. I'm doing routine inspections of shipping establishments in Corsica. I had an appointment to take a look at your facility."

The woman frowned. She checked a book and said, "I don't have you down. When was the appointment made?"

"Weeks ago. It's all right, I don't need Monsieur Cirendini to show me around. I can just have a quick look inside. I won't be long. It's all very routine, I assure you."

The woman was obviously intimidated by the badge. "All right, go ahead."

Mathis went past her through big double swing doors into the warehouse. There were stacks of crates, boxes, and barrels all over the place. Large tarpaulins covered piles of goods. Another area held smaller packages and parcels. Some men were busy loading items onto forklifts. They looked at him suspiciously, but he went about his business as if there was nothing wrong.

One area contained dozens of pressurised soft-drink canisters, the type used in bars and restaurants.

Mathis noticed a caged area full of debris—probably rubbish waiting to be hauled away and destroyed. There were, however, many empty crates and boxes with shipping labels and markings still intact. He slowly made his way over to it. When the men weren't looking, he crouched to his knees to get a better look at what might have been contained in the crates and boxes inside the rubbish cage. He moved around to the other side of the cage to get a better view.

"What are you doing?" boomed a voice behind him. Mathis stood and was confronted by a huge, burly man with no shirt. His chest bulged with muscles and his skin was shiny with sweat.

"I'm an inspector," Mathis said confidently. He flashed the man his badge. "Do you have the key to this cage?"

The man was astounded at the question. "What? Yeah, I have it. Who the hell are you?" Mathis sized him up as the slow-but-strong type.

"I told you, I'm an inspector," Mathis said as he walked away. "I'm finished now, I was just leaving. Thank you very much."

Mathis walked away and shot around an eight-foot-high stack of cargo before the lumbering giant had time to react. "Hey you!" the man called, starting after him. Mathis pulled his weapon and flattened himself against the cargo. As the worker came around, Mathis swung the butt of his Smith & Wesson at the man's face. There was a huge *crunch* as the metal collided with flesh and bone. The giant fell backwards like a brick, out cold.

Mathis peered around the cargo stack to make sure no one had heard. He then searched the man's pockets and found a set of keys. He quickly went back to the cage, examined the lock, and determined which key would be most likely to do the trick. He inserted it into the lock—and it worked.

Mathis squatted to examine the crates more closely. He prised off the top of one and found that it was empty, as expected. He rummaged through the boxes and came across a group of four ordinary wooden crates that were painted with a familiar French military green. And that's when he noticed it. On the corner of a crate, barely visible, was a marking that stated *"Propriété de l'Armée de l'Air."*

Solenzara? It had to be!

Mathis left the cage and locked it behind him. Instead of putting the keys back, though, he decided to throw them in a dustbin. He calmly walked past the still-unconscious big man, smiled at the receptionist as he went past, and left through the front door.

Mathis had chosen to stay at the Hôtel Corsica, on the road between Calvi and the airport. It was a secluded, recently renovated three-star hotel.

When he got to his room, he took some hotel notepaper from the desk and sat down to write. Using a code that he had devised with Bond, Mathis wrote a short but direct message. He folded the paper, put it inside an envelope, and then addressed it to Bond at SIS in London. The next thing he did was pack and prepare to leave.

He went back downstairs to the lobby and checked out. He asked the receptionist where the nearest post office was. She replied that she could post a letter for him, so he left the envelope with her and went outside with his bag to his car.

Mathis drove into Calvi, past the looming citadel containing the old town, and parked his car a block away from the marina. He got out and walked to the docks to look for his friend. He found the Sailor on a yacht, scrubbing the floor.

"*Bonjour,* my friend!" he said.

"*Bonjour,*" Mathis said. "If an Englishman comes here looking for me, please help him out. I'm going down south to see if I can find this Pierre Rodiac."

"No problem. I hope he likes Corsican wine as much as you and I do. By the way, I asked around about this Rodiac. I got some funny reactions from a few people. They told me not to stick my nose into his business. Apparently he comes from a very traditional Corsican family, one that abides by *vendetta.*"

Indeed, Corsica was the birthplace of the vendetta. Every gift shop on the island sold a selection of knives, for these were the weapons of choice among Corsicans. There was even a style with a long narrow blade and a thin wooden handle called Vendetta Corse, named after the centuries-old tradition.

"Rodiac supposedly lives near Sartène, but not in the village," the Sailor continued. "He goes there often enough for one to think that he lives nearby, maybe on a farm or something between villages. I would ask about him at restaurants and bars, I think."

"That's good advice, Sailor, *merci*."

"So you're really going to Sartène, eh?" the Sailor whispered. "Be careful who you talk to. The people in that town take their Corsican heritage very seriously."

"Thanks for the advice," Mathis said. He shook hands with the Sailor, wished him luck, and left Calvi.

7

The Assignment

M had retracted her threat to take Bond off the Union case after he had obtained information about the retinal tattoo, and, furthermore, she had given him another three weeks to find something more concrete about it and its relationship to Union membership. In the meantime, details of this bizarre Union "signature" went out to all the major intelligence and law enforcement agencies in the world. M was confounded by the Ministry's decision not to provide the information to ophthalmologists. Without them, she thought, there was little hope in identifying Union members.

Bond put in another call to René Mathis but learned from his assistant that his colleague was still away on leave. Christ, Bond thought, how long a leave was he allowed to take? Frustrated, Bond sat at his desk at SIS and wondered what the hell he should do now.

"Have you tried working with the Paris station on finding him?" Nigel Smith asked him.

"I never liked working with the Paris station," Bond said, grumbling.

"Do you know the new station head?"

"No," Bond replied.

"He was assigned to the post during the last year. The

entire operation is under new management, so to speak. Bertrand Collette's his name."

"I've never met him."

"Well, I know him," Nigel said. "We studied together at Oxford."

"He's French?"

"That's right. He spent a year at Oxford. Smart fellow. Very good with computers, the Internet, that sort of thing. Why don't I give him a call and see if he can find out anything about Mathis."

"Be my guest," Bond said, but he was sceptical.

When Bond arrived for work the following morning, Nigel stopped him.

"I heard from Bertrand in Paris," he said. "He dug around the D.G.S.E., collecting on some old favours. Mathis walked out of his job two months ago. This story that he's 'on leave' isn't true. He more or less resigned; I suppose the official line is that he's on 'indefinite' leave. He was on a case involving a possible Union-related theft of a new highly explosive material from a French air force base in Corsica. Some stuff the Americans cooked up, called CL-20. However, according to his last report to his chief, he thought he may have found a lead regarding the whereabouts of none other than *Le Gérant*."

Bond asked, "Where is he now?"

"That's the problem. No one really knows. He was last seen in Monte Carlo."

"Monte Carlo?" Bond rubbed his chin. "Good work, Nigel. Keep working on tracking him down."

"I will."

Bond stepped into his office and noticed the blinking red light on his phone. He picked up the receiver, pressed the message button, and heard Miss Moneypenny's voice.

"M wants you as soon as you get in, James."

Bond punched the buttons and got her on the phone. "I'm on my way up, Penny."

He found M with Bill Tanner in her office.

"Morning, Double-O Seven," she said.

"Good morning, ma'am."

"Stroke of luck, I think," she began. "I've had a call from my opposite number at the D.G.S.E. It seems that they were contacted by an ophthalmologist in Paris who was once in the French secret service but has since retired. When he was an agent, his cover was an eye doctor, so when he retired from the service he simply went back to private medical practice." She nodded at Tanner, who continued the briefing.

"It seems that due to a bureaucratic error, this French doctor still receives reports sent to him by the D.G.S.E., so he read all about the tattoo. It interested him a great deal because he had seen the tattoo on one of his patients. He reported it right away."

"Who's the patient?"

"We don't know," Tanner said. "They won't tell us. I think after the debacle in Nice a few months ago, they're not too interested in having us around."

"Whose side are they on, anyway?" Bond asked, shaking his head.

"I want you to go to Paris," M said. "You're to get in touch with our new Paris Branch head and work with him. You're to conduct the investigation with discretion. We don't want to upset our French friends . . . too much. But as far as I'm concerned, Double-O Seven, this is a war and we have to conduct it like one. Find out who this patient is and follow it through to wherever it leads you."

Bond told her what he'd learned about Mathis. She agreed that the information was important. "Keep on it," she said. "Who knows, maybe the two paths will cross at some point. Please make your arrangements with Miss Moneypenny and stop by Q Branch on your way out. Major Boothroyd has something for you."

•   •   •

"Ah, there you are, Double-O Seven," Boothroyd said as Bond walked into his office in Q Branch. He closed the door to keep out the noise from the workshop.

"You wanted to see me, Major?" Bond asked.

"I did, Double-O Seven, I did. Come in." Boothroyd got up from behind his workbench, went over to a table, picked up something inside a cloth bag, and brought it back to Bond.

"When this business with the retinal tattoos began, M asked me if I could come up with something that intelligence agencies could use to aid non-doctors in searching for these things. You're going to test the prototype. Go ahead, open it."

The bag contained an object that was small enough to fit in Bond's palm. Boothroyd's latest invention was heavier than he had expected.

"A camera?" Bond asked, turning it over to examine all sides.

Boothroyd seemed insulted. "It's not— Oh, well, I suppose, it *is* a camera, it's a camera as *well,* and it takes damned good pictures, too, if I do say so myself . . . but that's not what it *is,* Double-O Seven."

"It's not?"

"No, it's an ophthalmoscope."

Bond looked at him blankly.

"You know," Boothroyd continued, "what eye doctors use to look through your pupils and examine the inside of your eye."

"But it's a *nice* camera," Bond insisted.

"Would you pay attention, Double-O Seven?" Boothroyd huffed. "Yes, it's an ordinary camera except when you depress this button . . ." He pointed to a tiny one located on the bottom of the device. Bond pressed it, and the camera shot a thin bright beam of light from its lens.

"Do you know how to examine someone's eye, Double-O Seven?" Boothroyd asked.

"I'm afraid not, Major," Bond said, looking through the camera viewer at a blurry room. "I read your tutorial about it, though."

"Well, that would have given you a rudimentary overview of how it's done. I'm pleased to hear that you bothered to look at it. Come closer to me with the device, Double-O Seven," Boothroyd said.

As the major's face came into view, the highly magnified images of flesh and hair surprised Bond.

"Focus on my eye, would you?" Bond got closer and found the major's eye. "The device inside is a Welch Allyn Coaxial-Plus ophthalmoscope with all the usual features such as superior optics for easy entry into undilated pupils, opacity settings, and twenty-eight lenses. Just be careful that you don't flick it over into the red zone."

"Why not?"

"Because that's the laser. It's not terribly powerful, but at very close range, say, two to three feet, it will cut through thin metal. At a distance you might be able to blind someone temporarily by pointing the beam at his eyes."

Bond instinctively found the correct dials to change lenses. As he advanced the selections in single dioptre steps, the major's eye began to exhibit remarkable clarity. Bond went into the pupil, and into the inside of the eye.

Boothroyd continued, "The camera is also equipped with a handy listening device. You pull out the earpieces from the sides and there's a suction cup—"

"Don't move, major," Bond said as he pointed the light at the back of Boothroyd's eye, turning it into a strange, organic cavern. The blood vessels carved into the orange retinal walls were dark and red.

Boothroyd obliged him but continued talking. "The device is equipped with a halogen bulb. Should last a long time. I also threw in a bonus—a UV filter that allows you to look at fingerprints!"

"Major, when was the last time you had your eyes checked?" Bond asked, focusing on an odd blood vessel.

"Why?"

"You have a blockage of a small vein. It's not too near the light-sensitive area on the retina, but if the obstruction grows you might have a problem like retinal vein occlusion."

"*Thank* you, Double-O Seven, but yes, I know about that little vein. It's been like that forever."

Bond shut it off and said, "In that case, Major, then I'd say you have the eyes of a child."

"I'll take that as a compliment," Boothroyd said, taking the camera away from him. "Look here, if you release this mechanism, the ophthalmoscope separates from the camera housing." He pressed it, and a cylindrical metal object the size of a lipstick ejected from the bottom. Boothroyd held it to his eye and turned on the beam.

"I see, so that you can use it as a legitimate ophthalmoscope instead of a camera," Bond said.

Boothroyd lowered the scope and said, "I don't believe you've *ever* used any of our equipment legitimately, Double-O Seven."

8
The Ally

Bond emerged from the Eurotunnel in his Aston Martin DB5, the one he had purchased from SIS when the company had auctioned off some of the company cars a few years ago. The extras had been removed and the cars were sold to the highest bidders, and Bond had outbid Bill Tanner on this classic favourite. It still ran smoothly.

Bond had his eye on the new Aston Martin DB7 Vantage and was hoping that Q Branch would purchase one for use as a company car. But for now, the reliable DB5 was good enough. It still provoked the occasional stare from other drivers and could impress a girl or two.

He had made the crossing from Folkestone and entered the French traffic at Coquelles, some five kilometres southwest of Calais. Deciding to take the coastal road, Bond pulled into moderately heavy traffic on the A16 and drove towards Boulogne-sur-Mer. He eventually went through Amiens and headed south towards Paris.

Bond loved France, but he wasn't particularly fond of Paris. He found the French countryside gorgeous—its greener-than-green fields and hills, marked here and there with farms and villages, never failed to give him a sense of uncommon tranquillity. He occasionally chose to visit Royale-les-Eaux on the north coast when he wanted to get away from England for a weekend without having to fly all the way to Jamaica to Shamelady, his winter retreat. He also enjoyed parts of the south of France, simply because he adored the Mediterranean.

Paris, on the other hand, he had never warmed to. His attitude probably harked back to his first visit to the city at the age of sixteen, when he had lost his virginity and his notecase in one evening. Although the sex had been explosive, the experience of discovering that he'd been taken for a ride had left a permanent bad taste in his mouth. As he grew older, Bond refused to buy into the myth that Paris was "the most romantic city in the world." No, his feelings for Paris hadn't changed with maturity. He still felt that the city had sold its soul to the tourists. Traffic was horrendous (he wouldn't have driven had he not thought that he might need the car later), and the women, while certainly beautiful, tended to be more aloof and haughty than in other European countries. They were almost as bad as the girls in London!

Bond smiled as he admonished himself for that one.

He got into the city by midday and drove deep into the centre. As he made his way to the Ninth Arrondissement, where the *belle époque* splendour was, mercifully, only partially dominated by the busy traffic and pedestrians, he noticed a large billboard featuring an astonishingly attractive girl. It was an advertisement for a new line of women's clothing called Indecent Exposure, which seemed to flaunt the fact that whoever wore the clothes was actually wearing very little. The girl on the billboard was dressed in nothing more than a drape that ingeniously fastened onto a collar, swept around behind her back and under the right arm, across her breasts, flowed around her waist and back to the front, where it ended, tied at the side of her left hip. What she may have had on underneath was left to the imagination. But it wasn't what she was wearing that struck Bond. It was her stunningly beautiful face. She had dark brown hair cut short and layered, amazing brown eyes that penetrated his solar plexus even from this distance, a sensuous mouth with full, red lips, a fresh complexion, and an attitude that dared anyone to look at her and not be mesmerised.

Perhaps there *were* some French girls worth pursuing! he thought.

Bond had never had a taste for fashion models. While many were extraordinarily gorgeous, he found that they lacked a certain presence of mind that was a prerequisite for him. Good sex was one thing and was fine for one night, but he also liked someone he could talk to if there was going to be any kind of longevity.

He quickly forgot about the billboard girl as he drove past the magnificent Opéra Garnier in Place de l'Opéra, the setting for Gaston Laroux's famous horror story, made a sharp right onto Rue Scribe, then pulled into the drive of his hotel.

Bertrand Collette at Station P had arranged for Bond to stay at the elegant Grand Hotel Inter-continental, certainly one of the finest hotels in Paris and probably in Europe. It was convenient since Station P, the Paris branch of Britain's secret service, was located close by.

In his younger days, Bond had preferred to stay at a hotel near the Gare du Nord, but it was long gone. The Intercontinental was expensive and chic, certainly not a place Bond would stay on his own, but since the company was paying for it . . . why not? He might as well enjoy the luxury. After all, this was *the most romantic city in the world!*

The six-story hotel was deemed the "best and most comfortable" of all known hotels when it first opened in 1862. Home of the equally prestigious Café de la Paix, the hotel was recently renovated so that its former elegance and architectural splendour were restored. Bond thought that all the superlatives were well earned as he walked into the brown and beige lobby. Its dark brown wood panelling gave it a decidedly masculine look, which he appreciated. The airy Restaurant La Verrière and lounge was directly across from Reception under a glass roof, adorned with potted plants and furniture of assorted colours. This atrium effect was quite striking. His suite was just as pleasing, done in beige and maroon.

This will do nicely, he thought as he tipped the porter. He quickly unpacked a few things and got on the phone to Collette.

The head of Station P spoke good English and sounded enthusiastic. He suggested that they meet in the hotel bar. Bond stripped, took some time to stretch and perform callisthenics, had a deliciously hot shower in the all-marble bathroom (after five minutes he switched the water over to ice cold), then dressed in a collarless black cotton shirt, a grey jacket, and deep-grey pleated slacks. Thirty minutes later, he sat down at one of the green marble-top round tables in the small but comfortably refined Le Bar.

Bertrand Collette entered the place, looked around, and spotted Bond smoking a cigarette in the corner.

"*Bonjour, Monsieur Bond,*" he said, offering his hand. Bond shook it, noting the firm grip.

"*Bonjour,*" he said. Since Bond spoke fluent French, they conversed in Bertrand's native language. "Please sit down. What are you drinking?"

Bertrand shrugged. "Gin and tonic, thank you."

There was no waiter, so Bond got up and ordered the drinks from the bartender and got a vodka martini for himself. Sitting again, he offered Bertrand a cigarette.

"No, thank you, I don't smoke. I just drink like a Frenchman."

Bond laughed. "With all the wine you people consume here, it must be very hard on the alcoholics in this country."

"We're all alcoholics, but we just don't admit it. Instead, we go to our meetings, stand up in front of everyone, and say, 'My name is Bertrand and I am a Frenchman.'"

Bertrand was of medium height, blond, and thin. In some ways he reminded Bond of his Texan friend, former CIA agent Felix Leiter. Bertrand was clean-shaven, but he had nicked himself and had a small piece of tissue stuck to his cheek.

"How do you like working for Britain?" Bond asked.

"It's fine. The pay is good. I have many friends in high places here in France, so I am capable of providing your country with good information."

"So what have you learned recently?"

Bertrand leaned forward and kept his voice low. "I'm still trying to track down Monsieur Mathis. He seems to have disappeared. I do hope he has not come to a bad end."

"Me too," Bond said. "We've known each other for years."

"I thought so. Don't worry, we'll find something soon. I have a friend in Monte Carlo who can find out things discreetly. The good news is that I've found out the name of the eye doctor who unearthed the tattoo. His name is Didier Avalon and his office is over by the medical university."

"Can we see him today?"

"We can certainly try. He has patients today, so he should be there this afternoon."

"Good. Listen, you wouldn't mind if I take your picture, would you?"

"Pardon?"

Bond held up the special camera. "Just look into the lens there and say cheese."

Bertrand wrinkled his brow. "I don't like having my picture taken." But he let Bond go ahead. The beam of light struck his eye and he flinched. "What the hell . . . ?"

"Don't move," Bond said, adjusting the lenses.

"Are you doing what I think you're doing?"

"Hold on . . . got it. All right, you're clear," Bond said, shutting off the ophthalmoscope.

"Where did you get that?"

"It's a prototype, but don't worry, they'll be in all the stores for Christmas. Let's go and see that doctor."

Dr. Didier Avalon's office was on Rue de l'Université in the Seventh Arrondissement, very near the Université de Paris Faculté de Médecine. It was inside one of the two-century-old stone buildings that were prominent in the area.

"A lot of doctors are around here," Bertrand said as they parked his Citroën against the curb.

"What makes you think he'll talk to us?" Bond asked.

"Don't worry. I have credentials."

They went up the stairs to the first floor and found the doctor's waiting room. Three patients—an elderly man and two middle-aged women—were there, calmly looking at magazines. Bertrand told the receptionist that they were there on "police business" and needed to see Dr. Avalon right away. She went away, came back a minute later, and told them to wait a few minutes.

The doctor wasn't long. A nurse called Bond and Bertrand into the back, where Avalon had his private office. Like most European doctors, he also lived on the premises.

Dr. Avalon was in his sixties and had short white hair, a full white beard, and glasses. Bond thought that he might make a good Father Christmas if he were fatter.

"How can I help you?"

Bertrand gave him a card. "Bertrand Collette, with the D.G.S.E. We spoke on the phone this morning?"

"Yes?"

"This is my colleague from England, Monsieur Bond."

"How do you do?"

Bond shook his hand.

They sat down. Bertrand continued. "I promise not to take up too much of your time. I realise that you've already talked to some of my colleagues. Monsieur Bond and I are on an international task force, and we have reason to believe that the tattoo you found is indeed criminal in nature."

"Well, I thought it was. You don't get that kind of thing too often," Avalon said. "What happened to the other man I was talking to? Monsieur . . . oh what was his name? I have his card here . . ."

Bertrand quickly said, "He's still on the case here in *Paris,* but I'm handling it from an international standpoint. Two different committees, so to speak. Too much bureaucracy, if you ask me."

Avalon nodded as if he understood. "What would you like to know?"

"Just tell us what you told my colleague."

Avalon shrugged. "Well, a patient came in complaining of conjunctivitis. I examined him. He did have conjunctivitis, and I prescribed an antibiotic ophthalmic solution for him. However, when I used an ophthalmoscope on him, I noticed a lesion at the back of his retina. I looked at it more closely and saw the pattern. Have you seen it?"

"Of course," Bertrand answered.

"Well, then, you know what I'm talking about. In this business it's not unusual for some doctors to make a mark with a laser when they operate—something like a signature. I don't do it myself. Anyway, I saw that this one was fairly elaborate. When I asked him about it, he became very defensive. I used to be in the D.G.S.E., you see, and before that I was in the *gendarmerie.* I was trained to recognise when someone was lying, or acting suspiciously. This patient was definitely acting suspiciously. He wanted to leave immediately and even became abusive, telling me to mind my own business and such."

Bond asked in French, "He was a regular patient?"

"No, he was new. I wasn't his regular eye doctor."

"May we ask who your patient was?" Bertrand inquired. The doctor hesitated. "That's confidential, you know. I told your colleague the other day only because I got a court order to do so."

Bertrand assumed a stern demeanour and said, "Dr. Avalon, that court order stands with us as well."

Avalon seemed surprised. "It does?"

"That's right. So please, it's best if you tell us everything."

Avalon didn't seem too put out by it. "Very well. He's someone pretty famous. That film producer, the director . . . you know, Léon Essinger."

Bond blinked. *Well, well!* he thought. Why was he not surprised?

Bertrand feigned astonishment. "Really? Léon Essinger?"

"That's right. He normally lives and works in Nice, but he has an office here at one of the television studios. Said that he was working on something here in Paris and couldn't go back to Nice just yet. Why, what's that tattoo really mean?"

Bertrand said, "Dr. Avalon, I'm afraid that's classified information. Just know that you did the right thing by coming forward to report it. So, Doctor, will you be seeing Monsieur Essinger again?"

"Only if his condition doesn't improve. Those eye drops usually work, so I doubt he'll be back."

"Can you think of anything else to tell us?" Bertrand asked.

Avalon shook his head. "That's it, I suppose. I was afraid that perhaps I was overreacting, but I knew about Monsieur Essinger's—well, I knew about his reputation with the law, you know."

Bertrand nodded. "Yes, he's been on our list for some time. Well, thank you, Doctor, you've been most helpful. We won't take up any more of your time."

As they walked back to the car, Bertrand said, "I'm way ahead of you. Essinger's office is at France Télévision, southwest of the city centre. He just rents space there. His main office is in Nice."

"I've never met him, but I know who he is," Bond said. "Do you remember what happened at his studios in Nice a few months ago?"

"I sure do. The D.G.S.E. and the police took a beating for that one. Terrible tragedy. I wonder what Essinger is doing in Paris now. Making a movie?"

"Whatever it is, I think it's time for me to have a screen test," Bond said.

9
The *Mazzere*

Mathis found the old woman after a circuitous drive from Calvi, down through the centre of the island to Sartène, in the southern portion of Corsica.

Sartène is called "the most Corsican of Corsican towns." Legend has it that it is actually the birthplace of the vendetta because there is a long history of feuding families in the village. It is an austere, silent place perched on a mountain overlooking the gorgeous, green Rizzaneze valley. The inhabitants are very religious, and they take their Catholicism to extremes. Sartène is famous for a centuries-old tradition that is reenacted annually. Every year on Good Friday, the entire town turns out to watch the spectacle of the Procession du Catenacciu, in which an anonymous, barefoot penitent is chosen and covered from head to foot in a red robe and cowl. He is then made to carry a large cross through the town while dragging heavy chains, followed by several more penitents (some dressed in black, others in white) and priests.

Mathis was amazed that the gift shops sold postcards depicting the Procession du Catenacciu, and tourists could even buy souvenir videotapes of the event. He wondered why any tourists would want to come to Sartène in the first place. It was a shadowy, severe town where even the stone buildings seemed to look upon strangers with suspicion. The atmosphere was oddly oppressive for no tangible reason.

Mathis left the gift shop and walked down the cobblestone street to the Place de la Libération, the town square. He sat down at an outdoor table in front of one of the four restaurants that surround the square and ordered Pietra, the Corsican beer. Directly across the square was the town's pride and joy, the Église Sainte Marie, a church built in 1766 and the centre of activity in Sartène.

For a midafternoon, the town was awfully quiet. Where were all the people? Didn't they work? It was unnerving. Mathis felt strangely paranoid, as if he were being studied and talked about from behind closed doors. "Have you seen the stranger? He has been in town two days, asking questions, taking pictures. Who is he? What does he want?"

When he had first arrived in the village, he had gone straight to Pierre Rodiac's business address that had been provided to him by Dominic in Monte Carlo. Unfortunately, the building turned out to be abandoned. A shopkeeper next door said that no one had used the place in months. Next, Mathis visited the local *gendarmerie*. He showed the policemen his credentials and said that he was looking for a man named Pierre Rodiac. The men grew silent. After a moment, one of them said that they had never heard of the man.

Rodiac obviously had some sort of power over the people here.

Mathis had prepared photos of Rodiac from the shots he had taken at the casino, so he spent the rest of the day visiting the shops and restaurants and showing the picture to the proprietors. "Have you seen this man?" Every time he was met by silence and negativity.

Now, as he sat and sipped the cold beer, Mathis wondered what his next step should be.

"I may know someone who can help you."

The voice was the restaurant owner's. Mathis had spoken to him a day earlier and shown him the photo, with no positive result.

"Oh?" Mathis asked.

"May I sit down?" the proprietor asked.

"By all means."

The man sat down and leaned in close to whisper. "Go into the church and look for an old woman dressed in black."

"Aren't they all old women dressed in black?" Mathis asked.

"Yes, but this one stands out. She wears a lot of jewellery and dresses like a gypsy from the old days. She has a scarf on her head and is very old."

"How can she help me?"

"She is a *mazzere*."

"A what?"

"Most people do not believe in the *mazzeri,* but they have existed on Corsica for centuries. Their gifts are passed down through the generations."

"I don't understand."

The proprietor looked around again to make sure no one was listening. Mathis thought that the man was being overly cautious, for the street, the square, and the restaurant were completely empty.

"*Mazzeri* are otherwise normal people who have the 'gift' of foretelling someone's death. This happens during a dream in which the *mazzere* assumes the body of an animal that ventures into the wilderness to hunt for prey. The prey is another human who is also in the form of an animal—but the *mazzere* can recognise its human identity. The *mazzere* kills the animal and returns home. Some time later, the person represented by the dead animal in the dream usually dies—by disease, misfortune, or whatever. People respect and fear the *mazzeri,* because they don't want to hear if they're being dreamed about!"

"Fascinating," Mathis said, humouring the man.

"The *mazzeri* also have other gifts. They tend to know things that normal people don't. They are very wise."

"And you say this woman is one of these *mazzeri*?"

"Yes. You can ask her about this man you're looking for. Maybe she knows him somehow."

"Thanks," Mathis said, then added, "I have never heard of this superstition."

The man frowned and stood. "As you like," he said, and walked away.

Mathis paid for the beer and walked over to the church. He went inside and was simultaneously impressed and disconcerted by the ultrarealistic depictions of the Crucifixion that surrounded the sanctuary. The cross and chains used in the Procession du Catenacciu hung on one of the walls as well.

There were about two dozen old women in the church, all in black, chanting softly to themselves. Mathis thought it was in Corsican, but he might have heard a Latin phrase or two. He scanned the faces and had no trouble picking out the woman. She appeared to be in her eighties and was sitting apart from the rest of them.

He waited until they were finished with their worship. The women stood and started to mingle and chat as they left the church. The one old woman didn't speak to anyone else and started to leave alone. Mathis stopped her.

"*Pardon,* madame, may I please speak with you?"

She looked at him with suspicion.

He introduced himself and showed her his card. "I have been told that you might be able to help me. That you have certain . . . 'gifts' . . ."

The woman looked at him hard and said, "I don't know what you're talking about," and she attempted to push past him.

"I can pay you," he said. She stopped. "Handsomely."

Her eyes flickered as she turned back to him. "I only talk about my 'gifts' in the privacy of my home. Come and see me there." She gave him an address and told him to come after dinner. Without another word, she moved toward the door and left.

Hours later, as the sun was setting, Mathis made his way through the narrow streets and up a hill into the old town. He found the address and knocked on a large wooden door. It creaked open, and the woman invited him inside.

She introduced herself as Annette Culioli. Her home was modest, containing very little furniture, but was decorated with all kinds of plants and flowers. There were several cats of different shapes and sizes roaming about. For someone preoccupied with death, Mathis thought, she certainly surrounded herself with a lot of life.

Madame Culioli led him into her parlour and asked him to sit down at a small round table. She asked if he wanted any wine.

"That would be lovely," he said.

She went into another room and returned with a bottle of the locally made red wine, Fiumicicoli. She poured two glasses and sat down.

"How may I help you?"

Mathis showed her Rodiac's photo. "I'm looking for this man. Have you ever seen him?"

She took the photo and studied it. A look of fear passed across her face. She handed it back and said, "Yes, I know him. But only in my dreams."

"Can you tell me anything about him?"

"Why do you want to find this man?" she asked.

"Because he is a bad man," Mathis replied.

She nodded. "He is a blind man."

"I know."

"He is of two worlds. He is part Corsican. His other half is very different." She got up suddenly and went into her bedroom. She returned, clutching a Bible. She crossed herself and sat down again.

"In my dreams he is always the wolf," she continued. "But the wolf isn't blind. It can see better than anyone else. In my dreams, I am the wild pig. I have run into the wolf several times out in the *maquis*. He protects his territory. We have fought, but I admit that I have run away from the fights for fear of being killed in the dream. It is bad luck to die in a dream."

Mathis knew that *maquis* was the term used to describe the Corsican wilderness.

"Where is his territory?"

She closed her eyes, as if trying to recall the dream. "Statues. Statues with faces. Old statues. And castles made of boulders. Prehistoric castles."

Mathis thought that he knew what she was talking about. The island was well known for its prehistoric archaeological sites, especially in southern Corsica near Sartène. The sites at Filitosa, Cucuruzzu, and Capula contained objects that matched her description. The phallic stone statues with carved human faces, or menhirs, dated back to the era of primitive man, and archaeologists were still pondering their significance and purpose.

"Do you think this man lives near Sartène?" he asked.

"The *mazzeri* stick close to home in their dreams."

"Are you saying that he is a *mazzere* too?"

She nodded. "He is. And he has other powers as well. He is dangerous. He is a man to be feared."

Mathis handed her a wad of bills and stood. "Thank you, madame."

She took the money, bowed her head, and said, "May God go with you." She crossed herself again, stood, and led him to the door.

The explosion at the British Embassy in Tokyo occurred at five-thirty in the morning, while the city was still asleep. In hindsight, embassy officials were thankful that the bomb hadn't gone off during peak hours of daylight. It could have been disastrous. As it was, there was only minor damage to one of the outside walls of the building at No. 1 Ichibancho. It was the second bombing attempt within three months.

The explosive had apparently been inside a van, and a suicide driver had driven the vehicle toward the front gates. The bomb had gone off on impact, completely destroying the van and its driver and blowing a hole in the gate large enough for the flames to spill inside the grounds of the embassy.

For hours after the explosion, Japanese and British officials had attempted to determine who was behind the attack. There were no claims of responsibility, but a source close to *The Times* suggested that it had been the work of Goro Yoshida's followers.

No one could prove it, though.

10

The Studio

On the afternoon of the following day, Léon Essinger sat in the office that he rented from France Télévision. He was staring at the associate producer of *Pirate Island,* refusing to believe what he had just heard.

"The boats will cost *how much*?" he asked, doing his best to contain his rage.

"Three times as much as we estimated," the young man said, swallowing hard.

"Get out of my office!" Essinger yelled. "What kind of producer are you? Your job is to bring the picture in *under* budget, not *three goddamn times over*!"

"I'm sorry, sir, I'll see what I can do," the associate producer stammered and quickly left the room, shutting the door behind him.

Essinger sighed and put his head in his hands. It was all becoming too much. Everything was piling up, and he was fighting for air. There was the film, the most important thing, of course—that had to be a hit or his career was finished. There was Tylyn, his treacherous wife, the bitch who had left him for "more independence." There was the Union and what he was mixed up in with them. He wished that he had never heard of them.

His secretary, a woman named Madeleine, stuck her head in the door. *"Pardon, Monsieur Essinger . . ."*

"What is it?" he snapped.

"You said I could leave early. . . ."

"Fine, go on. Get the hell out of here." He waved her away.

She made a face as she closed the door.

Essinger reached for a bottle of bourbon from a cabinet behind the desk. He always kept alcohol in his various homes and offices. He noted that he needed to have Madeleine stock up on the Paris office stash. There was just enough for a double.

The phone rang, startling him. He let it ring again as he poured the bourbon and took a large sip. By the fourth ring, he was ready to answer it.

"Oui?"

"Léon."

Christ! he thought. It was Tylyn.

"Hello, darling," he managed to say.

"How are you?"

"Fine. And you?"

"Fine," she said. "Listen, tell me again about this press thing in Monte Carlo."

He breathed easier. He thought she was going to bring up the subject of divorce. He had been dreading it for weeks.

"It's just a press junket, darling," he said. "All the major players on the film will be there. I'm counting on you to be there as well."

"All right," she said. "It's just that . . . well, you know . . . these reporters seem to only want to know one thing."

"And what is that?" he asked.

"Whether or not you and I are splitting up for good," she said.

"Are we?" he asked.

"Léon . . ." she said with a note of disappointment in her voice. "We agreed that we weren't going to talk about it while the film is in production."

"You brought it up, darling."

"Oh, never mind. I'll see you soon," she said.

"So you'll be there? I know how you hate press functions. But you can't be a star without letting the media have a piece of you. I would hate to pull contract on you—"

"I'll *be* there, Léon! Now, I have to go."

"Take care of yourself," he said with a just a touch of sarcasm.

"That's exactly what I'm doing," she said, and hung up the phone.

Essinger slammed the receiver down. "Bitch!"

He fumed for a moment.

She was *enjoying* herself! She was having a *good time* being alone and away from him. She *liked* this independence of hers.

It was over, he told himself for the millionth time. There was no goddamned hope.

The *Pirate Island* press packet was laid out in front of him. The actors' head shots were in a pile of their own. Essinger thumbed through them until he came to Tylyn's.

God, she was beautiful.

After a few seconds' hesitation, Essinger slowly ripped the photograph in two.

He breathed deeply and started again.

He ripped it into quarters. He tore it again. And again.

When his wife's picture was in puzzle pieces, he scooped them into his palm and dropped them into the dustbin.

Essinger got up, gathered his things, walked out of the office, and locked the door behind him. He was ready to go back to Nice and get busy.

It was the only way to bury the pain.

• • •

Bertrand Collette dropped James Bond off in front of the France Télévision building at Esplanade Henri de France. He looked at Bond and said, "Right, you go in and ask for Isabelle Vander, with public relations. You have the press card I gave you?"

"Yes, Bertrand," Bond said. He couldn't help but be amused by his French companion. Collette had nicked himself shaving again and was now wearing two tiny bits of tissue on his face.

"Call me on your mobile when you're ready for me to come back," he said. "I'll be close by."

Bond got out of the car and looked up at the metallic, marble, and glass building that served as the centre for France's stations 2 and 3 as well as other entertainment concerns. Security was very tight at the thoroughly modern, fairly new complex, just as it was at the BBC in London.

He was wearing a dark blue suit and tie, the Walther PPK tucked neatly underneath his armpit. The plan was that Bond would pose as a reporter from a popular British magazine called *Pop World*. It was a legitimate publication that focussed on the entertainment industry, fashion, and pop culture. SIS had connections with the magazine, but this was the first time Bond had used them for a cover. Nigel Smith had overnighted the fake credentials to Bond's hotel and now he was in business. Bond just had to play the role convincingly.

Bertrand had set up a meeting with the studio's public relations department. Bond was a visiting journalist doing a story on various European television production companies. The studio people were pleased to offer him a tour of the facilities.

The centre lobby was a large atrium with glass walls. One could look up and see into the various floors on both sides. Several security guards were in the lobby—at the entrance, on the way to the lifts, and near the reception desk.

Bond checked in at the desk, where they asked for his identification. He gave them a false passport. In return he was presented with a key card that allowed him access past the lobby to the lifts. He was told that Mademoiselle Isabelle Vander would meet him there.

Bond swiped the card under the watchful gaze of the guard and went through the revolving glass door. He waited a minute or two for Mademoiselle Vander, who stepped out of the lift and approached him.

She was probably in her thirties, an attractive woman with blond hair pulled back into a bun. She wore glasses and a business suit.

"Monsieur Bond?" she asked.

"Yes?"

"Hello, I am Isabelle Vander," she said in English. They shook hands. Hers was soft and warm.

"Why don't you follow me?" She led him into the lift and they went up two floors. "Is there anything in particular that you're looking for?"

Bond wanted to say, "The fourth floor," because that's where Essinger had his office. Instead, he feigned interest in the television studios. She brought him onto the second floor, where the main soundstages were set up for television news programs, a game show, and a soap opera, respectively. The game show was currently taping with a studio audience, so they had to be relatively quiet as they walked through the backstage area. Apparently it was some kind of dog show, for contestants had brought their pets with them to perform on the programme. Bond and Isabelle stepped around three owners—one with a chow chow, one with what looked like a black Labrador mix, and one with a Tibetan terrier. Isabelle stopped to pat the dogs and whisper baby talk to them. She and Bond peered through the scenery to see an owner attempting to entice his Great Dane to dance. When the dog finally stood on his hind legs and circled to the music, the audience applauded.

Isabelle led Bond out of the studio and into the control room, where the *réalisateur* was busy directing cameramen and barking orders to assistants. Bond removed a small notepad from his jacket and jotted down some words so that he would appear authentic.

At one point they passed by the washrooms.

"Oh, excuse me, may I go in here for a moment?" he asked her.

"Certainly. I'll wait for you down at the end of the hall, in that alcove by Makeup."

"Fine," he said, then ducked into the Gents. He waited a moment, then peered out the door. The hallway was clear. He slipped out, went straight to the lift, and took it to the fourth floor.

Once there, Bond found his way to Essinger's office, which was closed and locked. He stooped down so that he could access the false heel in his right shoe, a standard field accessory provided to all Double-O agents. Inside was a set of sophisticated lockpicks that were guaranteed to open ninety-seven percent of the world's doors. He began to try them one by one.

The lift bell rang, indicating that someone would be walking his way at any moment. Damn! He tried another pick.

He heard the lift doors open and quickly stuck another pick in the lock. The door swung open and he jumped inside just as footsteps could be heard approaching at the end of the hall.

Bond waited until he heard the person walk by, and then he flicked on the lights. He went through the empty outer office into Essinger's private office. There were piles of papers on the desk, but they were neatly organised by subject. A quick glance revealed that some dealt with a new motion picture that was about to begin production, another pile dealt with details of a screening of Essinger's newest film at the upcoming Cannes Film Festival, and another concerning what appeared to be miscellaneous expense records for Essinger's company.

Bond took a look at the expenses first. There were the expected bills for office rental, utilities, and employee payroll. There were extensive bills from various catering services, mostly a beverage firm called "Marseilles Bottling Company." Something struck him as odd about the invoice. Apparently Essinger had arranged to import canisters of soft drinks from Corsica, using a firm called Corse Shipping. Why would he want to import them from Corsica? Weren't they made in France?

Bond turned to the production pile and examined it. A new film, *Pirate Island*, was scheduled to begin shooting in less than a week. Locations included Corsica and several spots on the Mediterranean. There were details on the cast and crew, the budget, insurance, and a production schedule. Bond removed the camera that Boothroyd had given to him and focused the lens on the production schedule. He snapped pictures of it and of the cast and crew listings. *Who knows?* he thought. *Perhaps there are some known Union people working on the film.*

Bond glanced at the pile of film festival material. Essinger's film *Tsunami Rising* was going to premiere at Cannes in approximately two weeks. There were notes indicating that the production of *Pirate Island* would halt for two days so that Essinger and other members of the cast and crew could attend the screening. The same director who shot *Tsunami Rising* was at the helm for *Pirate Island*, and the two films also shared the same leading actor.

A trade ad announced the screening as an "out-of-competition, gala charity event" that would benefit various causes. Someone had scribbled in ink on the ad, "Royal family?" in French. Clipped to the ad was a note from Essinger's secretary that read, "Léon—still waiting on confirmation of attendance by Monaco and Britain."

Meanwhile, Isabelle Vander became impatient waiting

for "Monsieur Bond" on the second floor. He had been in the washroom for nearly fifteen minutes! What was keeping him? When a production assistant walked through, she stopped him and asked if he wouldn't mind having a look in the men's washroom to see if the visitor was all right. The assistant came out a moment later and said that the bathroom was empty.

Perplexed, Isabelle walked up and down the halls looking for her charge.

Bond spent another five minutes going through the filing cabinets and desk drawers but came up with nothing interesting. He wasn't sure if anything he'd seen in the office was useful. There was nothing that indicated that Essinger might be involved in any criminal activity. The search was fruitless.

He moved toward the door and noticed the wastepaper basket beneath the desk. On a whim, he looked inside and saw the torn pieces of photograph. He dumped them out on the desk and attempted to sort them. Bond could see that the photo was once the face of a woman, but there were too many pieces for him to complete the picture now. He scooped them up and put them in his pocket.

Isabelle gave up looking for Monsieur Bond and went back to her office to report a missing visitor. The security staff were alerted to watch out for an Englishman who was wandering about unescorted.

Bond turned out the office lights and opened the door a crack to look outside. The hallway was empty. He stepped out and shut the door behind him, automatically locking it. He straightened his tie and walked toward the lift. He pressed the button and waited. When it opened, he was confronted by a security guard.

"*Bonjour,*" Bond said.

The guard reacted, recognising him as a visitor. He started to say something, but Bond raised his right arm and punched the man in the nose. He fell backwards into the lift, out cold. Bond got inside with him and pressed the ground-floor button. Unfortunately, someone on two had called the lift and it stopped there.

When the doors opened, Bond shot past a group of men and women, all studio employees. One of the women screamed when she saw the unconscious guard.

Bond ran down the hall and saw the studio that Isabelle had shown him earlier. He rushed in, closing the heavy door behind him quietly. The dog show was still going on. The audience was laughing and applauding at the antics of the chow chow, which was jumping through a series of hoops set on the stage. Two cameras were moving around the action, capturing the best angles for the programme. Bond moved around the scenery to try and get out another way, but one of the production assistants stopped him.

"Who are you? What are you doing back here?"

Bond waved his visitor pass. "I'm doing a story on your studio—"

He was interrupted by a loud bark. The black Labrador mix was behind him and looked as if it would take a bite out of him. Its owner whispered, "Hush, Spike!" but the dog must have sensed that Bond was an intruder. It barked again and growled.

"I was just leaving," Bond said to the assistant and started to go out through the door, but the dog broke free from its master. Bond held up his arm to prevent the sixty-pound dog from leaping onto his chest. The animal collided with him, and Bond hurled it back. It yelped and barked furiously at him.

"Hey!" the owner cried.

Then the Great Dane that was on the show earlier and had been watching the Labrador from the sidelines decided that it, too, would get into the act. It leaped from sitting position, taking his owner by surprise. The dog jumped on Bond, knocking him to the ground.

"Security! Security!" the assistant called into his head-set.

The Great Dane grabbed Bond's right forearm with his huge jaws and held it tightly. Luckily, Bond's clothing was thick, but he could feel the teeth pressing against his skin. Then the Labrador bit into his leg. Bond kicked hard, throwing the dog off, and then rolled as forcefully as he could with the Great Dane's head locked in his arm. The huge dog did a somersault over his body and landed unharmed on the floor. Bond leaped to his feet and ran the most convenient way—onto the set.

The chow chow had just jumped through a hoop as Bond emerged from the backstage area. His appearance surprised the dog in midair, throwing off its concentration. It landed right in Bond's arms.

The audience roared.

The director in the control room went nuts. "Who is that? What is he doing?"

The stage manager was calling frantically into his head-set. "Security!"

By now the Great Dane and Labrador had jumped through windows in the stage setting, which resembled the back of a house. Bond tossed the chow chow at them and ran toward the audience. The three dogs crashed into one another, yelping with rage.

The stage manager attempted to tackle Bond, but he tripped over one of the camera cables. Bond plowed into the seats, causing the audience to panic. The dogs were right behind him. Suddenly the entire soundstage erupted into chaos.

The members of the audience jumped out of their seats and ran toward the exits, crowding Bond from making an escape. Three production assistants tore off their headsets and chased after Bond. One of them grabbed him, spun him around, and threw a punch and missed. Bond, who had carefully avoided hurting anyone except the guard, saw that he had no choice but to defend himself. He hit the man in the stomach, causing him to bend over. Bond then brought his knee up into the man's face. That took the fight out of him. When the other two saw what had happened to their colleague, they hesitated. After a moment's stare-down, they backed off, then directed their energy elsewhere by yelling at the audience to remain calm.

But the dogs weren't afraid at all. They were barking furiously and knocking over the chairs in an attempt to catch Bond, who picked up one of the metal folding chairs and used it to hold them at bay, much like a lion tamer in a circus.

Then four security guards pushed their way through the soundstage entrance into the mass of people clambering to get out. One of them had a gun.

Bond tossed the chair at the dogs, temporarily blocking their advance, then ran back onto the stage. One of the camera cables went up into the catwalk some thirty feet above the floor. Bond jumped and grabbed it, then quickly pulled himself up, hand over hand.

"Stop him!" the stage manager cried. "This is expensive equipment!"

By the time the guards had reached the stage, Bond was on the catwalk. He had to crouch because the ceiling was so low, but he ran quickly to the nearest exit. He almost tripped over some lighting instruments attached to the grid, but he caught himself on a metal beam and used it to swing over a rail onto another catwalk that was nearer to his escape route.

There was a gunshot from below, and a bullet whizzed past him.

"What are you doing?" the stage manager shouted at the guard. "Don't use that in here!"

Bond went through the little door into a lighting control room. It was full of electronic equipment, patch boxes, and dimmer switches. He scanned the wall quickly and found the main power level. He pulled it, plunging the sound-stage into darkness. Then he climbed out of the light booth and found himself in a small corridor on the fourth floor. Apparently the soundstage was two stories tall.

He made his way to the stairwell and went inside. He was alone. Bond pulled out his mobile and punched in Bertrand's number.

"Oui?"

"Bertrand, get over here quick. I'll meet you on the street."

"Is there trouble?"

But Bond hung up. He ran down the stairs two at a time all the way to the ground floor. He stopped to catch his breath, then opened the door to peer outside. It was the lobby, and it was bustling with activity. Guards were looking this way and that, and visitors were being kept from entering the studios.

Now what?

A group of two dozen Italians were making a fuss. They all had tickets to be in the audience of a talk show. A guard was telling them to stand back against the wall until the "problem" was taken care of. A stroke of luck—the guard ushered the Italians back against the stairwell door. As soon as the guard had turned his back, Bond slipped out of the door and joined the Italians. They were so busy chattering among themselves that they didn't notice the extra person.

He waited there for about five minutes, as there was no easy way to break away from the group and get across the atrium to the front doors of the building. Finally, a woman approached them and spoke in Italian. "I'm very sorry, but we have to cancel the show today. We can reschedule you to come back tomorrow."

One of the men protested angrily, but a woman in the group attempted to calm him down. They all began to walk toward the front doors, and Bond merely blended in.

"What do you think is going on?" one of the visitors asked him in Italian.

Bond shrugged. "Someone probably lost a dog," he replied.

The group filed out of the building. Bond got into Bertrand's Citroën and said, "Drive like hell."

Station P was located within a legitimate business on Rue Auber, not a ten-minute walk from Bond's hotel. Internet Works, as it was called, was an e-mail café where customers could check their e-mail or surf the net. The place also served snacks, coffee, and soft drinks. They were open from six in the morning until midnight. Bertrand told Bond that they did *very* well.

"SIS lets me keep the money I make in the business, so I do okay," he said. "If I wasn't an agent, then I wouldn't mind running an e-mail café as my sole occupation."

"It's always important to be happy in one's job," Bond said with exaggerated enthusiasm.

Collette laughed as they walked into the back office of the café. With a flick of a switch, a false wall slid open, revealing something a little more private. All of Collette's communication equipment was inside. The room was full of radios, a couple of computers, and filing cabinets.

"Something to drink?" Collette asked Bond as he opened a small cupboard.

"Please." Bond sat down at one of the desks and dug into his pocket for the pieces of photograph that he had taken from Essinger's office. He spread them out on the desktop, faceup, and began to put the puzzle together.

Collette set a glass of red wine in front of Bond. "Jigsaw puzzles, James?"

"Something like that," Bond said. There were thirty-two pieces, and he nearly had it done.

Those magnificent eyes, Bond thought. He'd seen them before. But where?

Thirty seconds later, the picture was complete.

Who *was* this girl? Bond knew her from somewhere. She was strikingly beautiful. She had a face that he had seen in a magazine, or on television—and then he remembered. She was the girl from the billboard Bond had noticed when he drove into Paris.

He was drawn to the mischievous half-grin on her face that projected a dynamic self-confidence. This girl knew that she was beautiful and loved it. There was also intelligence in her almost catlike eyes. The brown hair was cut short, just covering her ears and giving her a fringe. It was styled with a bit of layered shape that caressed her incredible face.

"Do I win if I know her name?" Collette said.

"You certainly do," Bond said. "Who is she?"

"That's Tylyn Mignonne," he answered, pronouncing her Christian name to rhyme with "smilin'." He waited until Bond registered surprise, but got no reaction.

"Tylyn *Mignonne*," Collette said again. "The famous model and now actress?"

Bond shook his head. "I don't keep up with that world. Tell me about her."

Collette chuckled. "Be careful, James. She is married to Léon Essinger."

"No!" Bond said, aghast.

"It's true, *but* . . ." Collette paused for dramatic effect. "They're separated."

"So there's still hope. Do you have any tape?" Bond asked. Collette laughed again and got a roll of transparent tape out of his desk. Bond carefully taped the pieces of the photo together as Collette spoke.

"That's not her only claim to fame, you know," he said. "Ever heard of a Hollywood filmmaker named Jules Pont?"

"Yes." Bond knew who he was. Again, he paid little attention to the show business world, but Pont was a well-known French film director–turned–producer who had emigrated to America in the forties, made a number of popular and successful films in the fifties and sixties, created his own studio in the seventies, and then died. Some of Pont's comedies from the sixties were considered cinema classics.

"Tylyn's his daughter."

"Really?"

"Mignonne was her mother's maiden name, and that's how she goes professionally."

"So," Bond surmised, "she's probably a very wealthy girl."

"She is indeed," Collette said. "She is the heir to the entire Pont fortune."

"Which must be considerable. His studio is still running in Hollywood, isn't it?"

Collette said, "It sure is. Doing very well, too."

"Tell me about her."

Collette shrugged. "All I know is what the public knows. As she grew up, her parents brought her several times to France. She is an only child. Her parents were fairly old when she was born. She started modelling as a child and became a famous face before she was twelve years old."

"I had no idea," Bond said. "I don't think I've ever seen her before coming here."

"You need to read more women's magazines," Collette said. "Anyway, she achieved supermodel status by the time she was eighteen. She has her own clothing line, too. It's called Indecent Exposure. Pretty sexy stuff it is. Recently she has started trying to be an actress. She's made a few films in France, one that was a big hit worldwide."

"What about the marriage to Essinger?" Bond asked as he finished repairing the photo. He looked at her again.

"They got married about four or five years ago. It was fairly soon after he came back to France."

"Why in the world would a girl like her marry him?" Bond asked.

"He's a celebrity, too. Has money. He's an artist. Don't all those show business types stick to each other like glue? It's a very incestuous world."

"I suppose so," Bond said. "She's in Essinger's new movie, so apparently there are no hard feelings."

"Is she? I would bet that Essinger cast her for the publicity. She's hot right now, and he's capitalising on it. That blockbuster she was in before was made by Essinger before they were married."

"Are they going to divorce?"

"Even the tabloids don't know," Collette said.

"I wonder . . ." Bond said.

"What?"

"If they do divorce, I wonder if Essinger will be upset about not being related to the Pont family fortune anymore."

11

The House

Bond was convinced that Essinger was somehow involved with the Union's latest plot. Why would he have the tattoo if he weren't? What could they possibly want with a movie producer?

The night after Bond's visit to the television studio, he sat down in his hotel room at the Inter-continental to study the photographs he had taken in Essinger's office. Collette had blown them up to a readable size and they were as good as if they had obtained photocopies of the actual documents.

Bond studied the production schedule for *Pirate Island*. Even though it was difficult to say what the movie was about since he lacked a script, the locations gave Bond a pretty good idea that it was an action-adventure film to be shot mostly on water. The cost for special effects and second-unit work was over half the complete budget. Bond found a sheet listing the salaries of principal players in the film—the stars, the director, and the crew. Stuart Laurence, the star, was being paid $4 million. Tylyn Mignonne was being paid $1 million. The director was Dan Duling, who had directed Essinger's previous two pictures. He was being paid $1 million as well.

Bond saw something strange on the sheet, and at first he

thought it might be a smudge. The second-unit director and special effects coordinator, a man named Rick Fripp, was being paid $5 million! More than anyone else on the picture. A London address was written beneath his name.

Bond got on the phone to London and spoke to Nigel.

"Hello, James, how is everything?"

"Fine, Nigel," Bond said. "Listen, can you look up a name for me? He's a movie special-effects man, name of Rick Fripp. There's a London address." He read it aloud and asked Nigel to have him vetted.

Bond rang off and continued to look through the photographs. The taped-up picture of Tylyn Mignonne was set to the side, and he couldn't help glancing back at those bewitching eyes. He picked up the photo and sat back in the chair. Could she be involved in anything with the Union? Surely not. But one never knew. . . .

The phone rang. It was Nigel.

"James," he said. "I ran Rick Fripp through the computer. He has a record. He served six years for manslaughter. Was released four years ago. Before that he had a long arrest record, mostly for petty crimes. There was an armed robbery charge, but he was acquitted."

"How is it that he can stay in the motion picture business?"

"I don't know. I suppose he's good at what he does. His record states that he is an expert in explosives, pyrotechnics. His work on films is primarily in that area."

"Thanks, Nigel. I'll be back in touch."

Bond hung up again and left the room. He went downstairs, bought a newspaper, sat in the Restaurant La Verrière, and had some strong black coffee. He thumbed through the news, noting that the bombing at the British Embassy in Tokyo was still a mystery. It had been a long time since Bond had been in Japan. He wondered if a trip to the Far East might not be in his future.

He continued through the paper and happened to come

across the entertainment section, something he rarely looked at. His heart skipped a beat when he saw the photo, a full quarter-page in size.

There she was, Tylyn Mignonne, dressed in a tantalising wrap similar to the one she was wearing on the billboard. It was an advertisement for Indecent Exposure clothing. Next to the ad was a "personality profile" on Tylyn, accompanied by several other photographs depicting stages of her career: catwalk shots, head shots, and fashion shots.

He read with interest that Tylyn had attended university in Paris after growing up in Hollywood with her famous father and mother. She elected to remain in France and become a model. After several very successful years at modelling, she tried her hand at design and created Indecent Exposure. Now her clothing line was sold all over Europe and she was hoping to open a retail store in America in the coming year.

Her acting career was jump-started with a small role in a French art film that had received good notices at the Cannes Film Festival a few years ago. A larger role for the same director followed that, and it proved to be a popular "foreign film" in America. Hollywood became interested, and she eventually made an American blockbuster that did well internationally.

Although she hadn't made any films for a couple of years, now she was poised to costar with Stuart Laurence in *Pirate Island,* a film to be produced by her husband, Léon Essinger.

There was no mention that they were currently separated.

The article went on to say that Tylyn enjoyed riding as a lifelong hobby. In fact, she owned a stud farm in the south of France, near Antibes. She was quoted as saying that she always went there, to her "home away from home," when she wanted to escape the hectic life of a supermodel and actress. Now twenty-nine years old, Tylyn said that she was actually looking forward to her thirties and that she hoped to correct some of the choices she had made in her personal life while in her twenties.

Bond looked at the Indecent Exposure ad again. It stated that there was an exclusive fashion show taking place the next day at the Louvre.

Bond grabbed his mobile and called Bertrand Collette.

"Internet Works," the Frenchman answered.

"I need a favour," Bond said.

"I will do my best. What is it?"

"There's an Indecent Exposure fashion show at the Louvre tomorrow at noon. Can you get me in? Maybe arrange for *Pop World* to interview Tylyn Mignonne?"

Collette laughed. "My friend, I think you have been struck by a thunderbolt. I will see what I can do."

Bond rang off and smiled. He hadn't looked forward to meeting a girl this much in a long, long time.

Mathis had parked the rental car on the side of the road, carefully climbed over the barbed-wire fence, and walked in the darkness toward the thick trees. Using a specially built penlight with a high-intensity beam, he made his way through the thick of the *maquis* and found the menhirs.

In the moonlight, they were indescribably eerie. The limestone statues were phallus-shaped and stood between four and six feet tall. On the heads were rudimentary carvings of human faces. Erosion had smoothed them down considerably, so much so that what little carving had been done to the stone was barely visible. They were similar to the menhirs that could be found at the prehistoric site of Filitosa, one that was open to the public.

This one wasn't.

Before leaving the D.G.S.E., Mathis had equipped himself with topographical and survey maps of Corsica. He had studied them carefully, pinpointing where the archaeological sites were located in relation to Sartène. He could

see what pieces of land were privately owned and what was
owned by the government or by villages. There were indeed a few patches of privately owned property north of
Sartène and eastward on the road toward Levie. The prehistoric sites of Cucuruzzu and Capula were in that direction as well. Mathis figured that it was highly probable that
other prehistoric artefacts existed on the private properties.
After all, the Filitosa site was inhabited and still owned by
the same family who had discovered it.

Which lot was *Le Gérant*'s?

After making inquiries at the Cucuruzzu/Capula guest
services centre, he had learned that a strange rich man had
taken over a nearby property and had built a house there.
The land had been in one family for generations.

Mathis had waited until nightfall, then had driven close
to where he thought it might be. Sure enough, a gate with a
sign, *"Privé,"* and a barbed-wire fence kept animals and
the curious out. An unpaved road led from the gate up a
hill, into the dense brush. Somewhere back there was a
house.

Now, out of breath from the exertion of climbing the hill
and fighting the thick foliage, Mathis finally came upon a
clearing. There it was, some thirty metres away—a large
two-storey building, the silhouette of which, in the dark,
looked like yet another Corsican old-town citadel. There
were ridges in the high walls, but the roof was flat, like
those of homes in Morocco. Lights were on in two windows. Dark outlines of the mountains surrounding the
property imbued the locale with a foreboding omnipres-
ence. What was especially unusual was that the house was
surrounded by a second wire fence. Mathis couldn't see the
posted signs clearly, but he wagered that the fence was
electrified.

He crept out of the woods and into the clearing. He
couldn't see that anyone was about, so he kept going.
When he made it to the second fence, which did indeed dis-

play warnings for "electrical shock," he lay flat on the ground to catch his breath again. From there he could see that the building was made of stone and wood and seemed to reflect no particular style of architecture, except, perhaps, a blending of Arabic and French, like exquisite palaces in Tangier. The Malcolm Forbes Museum came to mind.

What should he do? Should he call someone and report his findings? Or should he try to get tangible proof that *Le Gérant* really lived here? If only he could catch sight of him.

Mathis crept silently around the fence, eventually coming to the side of the house where vehicles were parked. A garage was open and the Rolls-Royce was sitting inside. A 4×4 and two other cars were parked in the drive.

He could hear voices approaching.

Two men stepped out of the garage and lit cigarettes. They spoke in Corsican, looking up at the clear, star-studded sky. Mathis shrank into the shadows, willing himself to be as still as one of the menhirs that surrounded the property.

Then Mathis's heart nearly stopped when he heard the sound of a car coming up the road toward the house. It would surely turn into the drive to park there with the rest of the vehicles. The headlamps would have to pass over him to do so.

He leaped to the ground just as the car, a sleek Porsche, pulled around, brightly illuminating the area. It stopped near the two men. Mathis looked up from the ground and saw another man get out of the Porsche.

"Bonjour, Antoine," one of the smokers said.

Antoine, a small, wiry man, greeted the two men and said something that made them laugh.

And then—horror!—Mathis noticed that a guard was patrolling the outside perimeter of the electrified fence and was headed his way. If he didn't move quickly, the man would surely notice him in a few seconds!

Mathis stayed perfectly still in the grass. The guard walked slowly, scanning the trees, looking away from the house. Closer . . . closer . . . then the man's boot grazed Mathis's side.

"What the—?" the man mumbled, momentarily off balance.

Mathis pushed the guard and did his best to get up and run.

"Stop!" he heard the man shout.

Mathis ran as hard as he could towards the trees, but the weight he had put on in recent years was a hindrance. Out of the corner of his eye, he could see that the guard was behind him, pounding the ground with large, muscular legs.

Ten more metres! Mathis ignored the pain in his chest as he mustered all of his energy, but it was useless. The guard tackled him and they fell hard on the ground. The impact knocked the wind out of Mathis.

The guard turned him over and slugged him hard in the face, stunning him.

He recovered his senses as they were dragging him to the house. Mathis attempted to struggle and get away, but the three of them held him. A quick kick in the ribs took the fight out of him.

He was brought inside and taken to a spacious room equipped with nothing more than benches, chairs, and cabinets. It was some kind of waiting area, probably for the guards. They threw him on the floor.

A door opened and a man entered the room. He stood silently until Mathis was able to look up.

It was Pierre Rodiac. A.k.a. Olivier Cesari. A.k.a. *Le Gérant*.

"Monsieur Mathis," the blind man said. He didn't look at Mathis, of course. He simply stared straight ahead, his dead eyes focused on nothing in particular. "Welcome. You were successful in tracking me down. Yes—I knew you were following me the first time we were in the same room together in Monte Carlo. Don't you think that *Le Gérant* would know? Tsk-tsk . . . I thought you were smarter than that, Monsieur Mathis. The question is, who else knows that you are here?"

"Everyone," Mathis whispered. "They all know."

"Liar," Cesari said softly. "You have left the D.G.S.E. and are working as a renegade. The only person you are in contact with is a close friend of yours. Someone who works for another intelligence agency. Someone I would love to meet. Do you think you could arrange an introduction?"

"I don't know what you're talking about."

"Oh, I think you do," *Le Gérant* said. "Mister James Bond . . . your friend and ally. Do you think you could direct him in our direction? Perhaps send him a note? Yes?"

"Go to hell," Mathis spat.

Le Gérant laughed. He circled Mathis, never once reaching out in front of him to make sure he wouldn't walk into anything. He knew exactly where the furniture was.

"Antoine?" he called.

"Yes, monsieur," Antoine said. He was standing by the door.

"There is a walking cane next to the bookcase over there. Would you throw it to me?"

Antoine found it. It was a black cane with a silver wolf's-head handle. Antoine threw it, and *Le Gérant* caught it in midair. He never once flinched or moved his head. His hazy eyes were focused on the nothingness straight ahead of him.

"Now," he said to Mathis, "you are going to cooperate, isn't that right?"

"Never," Mathis said.

The cane came down hard on Mathis's back.

Le Gérant took two steps around Mathis and let the cane fly again. Mathis curled into a ball, attempting to ward off the blows.

"Take him outside and soften him up," *Le Gérant* said. "And then we'll let Dr. Gerowitz have a look at him."

The three men dragged Mathis outside. *Le Gérant* left the room and walked down a white, plain corridor until he came to his own quarters, which were tastefully furnished with elegant furniture, a stereo system, bar, and other amenities of comfort. He sat down after pouring himself a cognac and putting on his favourite piece of music, Rimsky-Korsakov's *Scheherazade*. He closed his eyes as the lovely strains of the violins filled the room.

The music didn't quite drown out Mathis's screams.

12
The Girl

The spectacular I. M. Pei pyramid entrance to the Musée de Louvre never failed to impress Bond. While it had its critics, the incongruous nature of a pyramid made of glass and steel tubing, surrounded by a structure that saw its origins in the thirteenth century, was the most impressive thing about it. The juxtaposition was not lost on Bond.

The museum was closed to the public on Tuesdays, so all special events were held on that day. The fashion show was scheduled to begin at eleven-thirty in the morning. Bond arrived at the Louvre entrance at eleven-fifteen dressed smartly in a dark grey Savile Row suit. He joined the gathering crowd in the roped-off section in front of the pyramid to wait for the doors to open. A large banner across the entrance proclaimed: "Indecent Exposure—NOW!" The words were written in script over a faint reproduction of Tylyn's eyes. Bond thought that he might recognise them anywhere now.

The others in the crowd were journalists, fashion photographers, and members of the elite who were lucky enough to receive an invitation. Several groups with television cameras were also prepared to descend into the museum for the event.

The sun was shining brightly, bouncing off the pyramid

glass into Bond's eyes. He turned to avoid the glare and noticed several museum security guards conversing with another man in a dark green security uniform that was
obviously from a different company. Bond couldn't hear
what they were saying, but the man seemed to be trying to
talk his way into the show. The museum guards were shaking their heads and looking at his credentials. After a moment, though, they allowed him over the barrier. The man
went through the doors and disappeared inside the pyramid.

Finally, at eleven twenty-five, the guards removed the
rope and ushered the people inside, checking invitations as
they walked through. Bond got inside and stepped onto the
escalator that descended into the spacious, bright reception
area. The stage and catwalk had been set up just beyond the
circular staircase that led to the ground floor. Numbered
folding chairs surrounded the catwalk, which jutted out
towards the CyberLouvre, the boutiques, and the Carrousel
du Louvre. Bond thought it was a rather odd place for a
fashion show, but apparently the museum was a popular
spot for such events.

Shostakovich was booming out of portable speakers set
up around the runway. A white tent, where the models
could change and prepare to make their appearances, had
been erected at the head of the catwalk and behind the
stage. Another banner with the words "Indecent Exposure"
hung over the curtained opening on the stage.

The audience was buzzing with the excitement in the air.
Bond, too, felt twangs of anticipation as he found his seat,
two rows back from the centre of the catwalk. Not bad.

At eleven-forty, the lights dimmed slightly and spotlights operated by men on pedestals hit the curtain on
stage. The audience applauded as the music switched to a
sensuous, rhythmic jazz-rock piece accentuated by heavy
bass and drums.

A tall blond model stepped through the curtain wearing

nothing but a black brassiere, panties, and high heels. Bond thought that she looked more like a courtesan than a fashion model, but he wasn't complaining.

The expressionless girl walked down the catwalk as the cameras flashed around her. By the time she swivelled to head back to the tent, another girl, a shapely black woman, had emerged wearing a red brassiere and panties, but she had added a garter belt and stockings. The next girl, a brunette, had added a silk robe that flowed behind her as she walked. Each successive model added another piece of clothing. Bond got it—the girls were "dressing" before the audience's eyes. The sixth model in the set was fully dressed in a magnificent transparent evening gown that provided hints of all the various undergarments the other models had worn. The six girls returned to the catwalk and gave a slight bow, then slipped back into the tent.

The music and lights changed. It was time for something dramatic.

When she stepped out of the curtain, the audience went wild with applause. Bond actually felt his heart rate increase.

Tylyn Mignonne was arguably the most beautiful girl he'd ever seen, and he had certainly seen many. She was tall, naturally, with long legs that seemed to move like those of a sleek gazelle. Her dark brown hair was still cut short, the fringe swept to the side to reveal a bit of forehead. She was not terribly thin, like many models. She had a fine figure, a firm one that exhibited the physique of a girl who got a lot of exercise but managed to eat well, too. Her breasts were not particularly large, but, in Bond's mind, they were perfectly adequate handfuls.

She was wearing the wraparound he had seen her in on the billboard, and it revealed much more than it concealed. The rounded, shiny tops of her breasts reflected the lights, and her undulating, flat stomach was completely bare. The wrap covered her waist and hips but just nearly screened the cleft between her legs, which were naked down to the high heels.

As Tylyn walked down the catwalk, the men in the audience whistled and cheered. She responded with warm smiles and waves. Her strong presence, her charisma, and her self-confidence immediately struck Bond. Unlike the other models, who remained relatively humourless and stone-faced throughout the show, Tylyn was obviously enjoying every second. She loved being under the spotlights, having the flashes go off nonstop around her, and receiving the attention of the men in the audience. She had a rapport with the people that the others didn't attempt to create. Bond liked that. He had assumed that models never interacted with the audience while on the catwalk. However, she would pause every now and then to greet someone she knew, squatting down to give them a hug or accept a long-stemmed rose.

Tylyn completed the walk and went back into the tent as the show continued with a new set of fashions, beginning with the blonde in a chemise/panties combination. Bond now understood the allure of fashion shows and why they were always hot tickets. They were indescribably sexy, even when the models were fully dressed. There was something about watching a beautiful woman display herself to a crowd—not like a stripper, who teased her audience with nothing left to the imagination. She was a girl with a secret, a woman who tantalised men with the fantasy that she *might* be willing to show them something. She was the one in charge and would decide when and where that would happen.

The Indecent Exposure line was just what it promised—chic clothing that was sexy and revealing, yet tasteful enough to wear in public. Bond could imagine that much of it would be worn to things like celebrity parties, awards dinners, and the like. This wasn't run-of-the-mill boudoir wear. Tylyn was indeed a clever designer.

The entire show lasted about twenty minutes. Bond had counted ten different models who had changed clothes at least three times each. Tylyn, the last woman on stage, ended the event by leading the rest of the girls out onto the catwalk together. She received thunderous applause and cries of "Bravo!" as she accepted a bouquet of roses from two of the models.

A cocktail reception was held afterwards in the Restaurant Le Grand Louvre, a small room next to the café. Glasses of champagne were handed out to every guest, along with a goody bag of Indecent Exposure promotional materials. Waiters circulated the room with plates of canapés as members of the audience mingled. The models joined the crowd a few moments later.

Bond stood to one side and waited until Tylyn made her entrance. When she finally did, she was dressed simply in black Capri pants and a white silk blouse that was open at the midriff and tied above her navel. Bond liked women in Capri pants because they showed off their calves and ankles whilst keeping the rest of the legs tightly outlined but under cover. He watched her with interest as she greeted people, kissing their cheeks and allowing hers to be pecked. She warmly embraced several members of the press, playing the consummate public relations rep for her company. She might as well have been royalty.

As far as Bond was concerned, she was.

Finally, he edged his way towards her and caught her eye. She looked at him and smiled brightly, momentarily distracted by his dark, good looks.

"Bonjour," she said.

Bond greeted her in French. *"Bonjour.* It was a lovely show. I'm from *Pop World* in England. The name's Bond. James Bond."

"Oh yes, Mister Bond, we're supposed to do an interview, right?" she said, making no attempt to hide the fact that she was pleased.

"That's right."

"Let's see, where could we . . . ?" She thought a second, and then said, "Would you like to talk over lunch? I'm starving, and these crackers and things won't do the trick."

"I'd be delighted," Bond said.

"Great! Let me finish here and perhaps we could take a walk, find a café nearby?"

"Take your time, I'll be right here."

She gave him a nod and a little wave, then turned to the others who were dying to speak to her.

Bond stepped back and picked up another glass of champagne. Out of the corner of his eye, he noticed the security guard in the green uniform standing near the emergency *Sortie* sign.

The man was looking at him, but when Bond's eyes met his, he turned and walked out of the room.

They left the Louvre under the scrutiny of the paparazzi and fans. Bond shielded his face the best he could as the cameras went off. He was uncomfortable being in the limelight like this and hoped that their picture wouldn't be on the front page of a gossip paper. "Tylyn Dating Mystery Man" . . . It was all he needed.

Nevertheless, he couldn't help but feel a slight thrill at being in the company of such a glamorous and high-profile woman. Normally he would have shunned the prospect. He didn't want notoriety, for in his business, it could be dangerous. Too many times the women he had grown close to had met with . . . bad luck.

But as they pushed through the crowd and walked onto Rue de Rivoli and then turned east, they lost the crowd and were on their own.

"That's better, isn't it?" she asked, keeping a fast pace. She spoke in English now, but Bond noted that it was the American variety. "You never think you're going to get rid of them, but surprisingly you always do."

"How can you stand it?" Bond asked. "It would drive me mad."

She shrugged. "I'm used to it. It's part of the life, I suppose. You have to give up certain things, a bit of your privacy. . . . Where would you like to go?"

"It's your city," he said. "But I do know a little place not far from here." Paris, of course, was heavily populated with sidewalk cafés.

"Lead on, sir," she said with a smile.

He escorted her to Rue St. Honoré and farther east until they came to a café called Le Petit Mâchon. It was a charming, quiet place painted yellow and brown. The day's specials were listed on a blackboard that stood on the sidewalk with the small square tables. Tylyn and Bond were greeted warmly by the hostess, who allowed them to pick a table at the end, away from the other parties.

Bond ordered them two kir royales made with champagne and crème de cassis for aperitifs and then took a moment to enjoy looking at her fresh, vibrant face. He hadn't realised how long her eyelashes were until now.

"So, Mister Bond, what would you like to talk about?" she asked with a knowing smile.

"You, of course," he replied. "How do you manage to juggle so many different careers?"

She laughed. "I don't see it that way. It's all one career, really, isn't it? Fashion design is probably my first love, and of course I like to model. It's how I made my name. But I want to branch out, get more involved in film."

"I understand you've got a starring role in a new picture?"

"That's right. It's called *Pirate Island*. My—well, my husband is producing it. We're separated, though."

"Léon Essinger, right?"

"That's right. Anyway, it's a chance to act with Stuart Laurence, whom I adore, and it's probably going to be a big movie. The director is someone I like. He's very good.

I think it will be a boost to my career. I've only made one other movie in Hollywood, and this one will bring me more work there, I hope."

"What kind of part is it?" Bond asked, writing down her answers on a small notepad.

"It's an action-adventure story set in the future," she said. "It's about pirates on high-tech boats. Stuart plays the hero, a man who's trying to save his island from being taken over by the pirates. I play his 'woman.' " She chuckled. "There will probably be a lot of bodice ripping. I'll get to do a little of the action, but they've hired a real stuntwoman for the hard stuff."

"Tell me what you remember of your father," Bond said.

"He was always there for me when I was a little girl. He encouraged me to go into modelling, and he got me my first horse when I was six."

"What was it like to grow up with such a famous father?"

"I never really paid it any mind. He was just 'Daddy' to me. I mean, I knew he was famous and that he made all these great films and had Oscars and all that, but when I was little I just thought that's what all fathers did. He died when I was pretty young. It wasn't until I was a teenager that I fully appreciated the contributions he made to the business."

"What does knowing you're the heiress to a vast Hollywood fortune do to your psyche? It must make you deliriously happy."

She laughed. "I'm usually deliriously happy, most of the time anyway, but that's not the reason why. I never think about the money my family has. I've gone out and made my own money, you know. When I model, I'm paid well. I don't just model exclusively for my own company. If the offer is good, or if it looks like fun, I'm there."

"What made you leave Hollywood?"

"I'm French, aren't I? I was tired of California. I feel

more at home here. I suppose if my acting career takes off I'll have to go back, but then there are plenty of actors who manage to work and not live in Hollywood."

"How did you get your name?" Bond asked.

"Tylyn? Well, it's not French, is it?" She laughed. My mother was expecting a boy, and she already had 'Timothy' picked out. Naturally, when I came out it was a surprise to everyone! She had to scramble to come up with a name for a girl that began with a T. She put 'Ty' and 'Lyn' together and came up with 'Tylyn.' "

Bond thought that she was an amazing girl. She was outgoing, articulate, and intelligent. He could feel her energy and *joie de vivre,* and it was infectious.

"Tell me about your hobbies. What does Tylyn do when she's not working?" he asked.

"Horses. And then there are horses. Oh, and I also like horses," she said, then laughed. "You know I breed them? I love horses."

"I knew that. It's in the south of France, right?"

"Yes, it's a small equestrian centre in Mougins, near Antibes. I live there when I'm not in Paris. I keep a small staff there who run things when I'm gone. I breed horses and sell them to various riding schools and so on. When I'm really stressed out I like to go there and get on Commander, my favourite horse, and ride for hours through the forests."

Bond mused that he knew a certain commander who would like a ride.

"How much time do you get to spend there?" he asked.

"More than you might think. I have a flat here, but if there's nothing happening at the Indecent Exposure studio, then I go to Mougins. I have a workshop there and can work on clothing design if I need to. Oh, here's a card with the address. . . ." She reached into her handbag, found a card, and handed it to him. "You should come around and take a look. You might find it useful for your article."

Bond glanced at the card and pocketed it. "Thank you. I might enjoy that. So other than horses . . . ?"

"I read a lot. There's always a book by my bed. I love mysteries and thrillers. I like to dance. There's nothing more romantic than a man who can dance. I enjoy sports, but I'm not very good at anything but riding."

"You were educated in California?"

She nodded. "Through high school, but then I went to college here. I studied languages here because for some reason in America they don't stress that. I think it's important to speak other languages."

"What else do you speak?"

"Besides French? English, German, and Italian. Some Spanish and a tiny bit of Russian."

"Impressive," Bond said.

She shrugged it off. "It's no big deal. What about you? Have you always been a journalist?"

Bond smiled to himself. "No. I used to be a civil servant. But my life is quite uninteresting compared to yours."

"Have you ever considered modelling?" she asked. "You have *killer* looks."

Bond almost laughed. "No, I've never considered it. But thanks, I think."

"No, really, you have this dark dangerous look that women just eat up," she said, reaching out to touch his hand. "But you probably know that already."

The blond waitress interrupted them with the meals they had ordered. They both had mixed green salads with veal, croutons, tomatoes, and goat's cheese. Tylyn had *côte de veau à la crème d'estragon* for the main course; Bond had *quenelles de brochet fraîches à la crème d'étrilles,* pike with crab sauce. They shared a bottle of Pouilly-Fuissé, which Bond found slightly disappointing, but it was adequate. The food, though, was superb.

As the waitress walked away, Tylyn giggled to herself. "What's funny?" he asked.

"I just remembered a blonde joke. Want to hear it?"

"Certainly."

"A blonde's boyfriend gave her a mobile phone for her birthday. When she was out of the house, he decided to call her and see how it worked. She answered and was thrilled. 'Hi, honey!' she said. 'The phone works great! But how did you know I was at the hairdresser?' "

They both laughed and continued eating.

She ate like a man, Bond thought. She wasn't dainty at all, but all she had to do to retain her femininity was blink those lovely eyes with the deliciously long lashes, pucker her lips when she was tasting something, and smile—which she did a lot. In fact, she laughed quite a bit, and Bond liked that. It seemed that everything amused this girl. She was damned attractive.

Careful, Bond told himself. She was way too famous to get involved with. Veer the conversation toward business. Find out more about her husband . . .

"You know, I'd like to interview your husband. He seems like quite the character," he said nonchalantly.

She snorted. "Léon? He's a pig. Why would you want to talk to him? I'm much more interesting." She laughed again.

"I have no doubt about that," Bond said.

"Besides, he rarely meets the press these days," she said. "Ever since the trouble he had in America. You know about that . . ."

Bond nodded.

"I suppose we're still friends. After all, I'm going to act in his movie," she said.

"Then I take it that the separation is temporary?"

For the first time she frowned. "I don't want to talk about that. Léon and I have an agreement not to talk to journalists about our separation."

"Fair enough. When do you start shooting?"

"In a couple of days. In fact, I'm going to have to leave

soon, I hope you don't mind. I have to catch a plane to Nice in a few hours. I want to spend tomorrow at my home in Mougins. I need a good ride before I start work the following day."

She gave him a look that Bond could have sworn was an invitation.

When he didn't respond, she continued. "The next day we have to meet in Monte Carlo for some awful press event. I usually hate talking to the press, but somehow I don't mind talking to you." She laughed again so adorably that Bond wanted to hug her.

"Anyway," she said, "we start shooting the day after the thing in Monte Carlo. In Corsica. If you want to drop by the set, I think I could swing it."

She was after him! Bond thought. That was three times that she had been the aggressor. He simply couldn't resist this girl.

"Perhaps you'll see me in Monte Carlo," he said.

"I hope so." She wiped her mouth with the napkin and said, "This was fun. Did you get everything you needed?"

"Yes, for now anyway, thank you."

"I must run." They both stood, and she held out her hand. It was soft, warm, and heavenly. "Thanks very much for the lunch. I hope to see you again, Mister Bond."

"Call me James."

"All right, James. *Au revoir.*"

And she was gone.

Bond sat back down and ordered coffee. He watched her back as she hurried up the street and waved for a taxi.

Somebody pinch me, Bond thought. She was simply too good to be true.

As he gazed out over the street, he noticed the gym across the road. And there he was—the man wearing the dark green security uniform was inside the gym, looking at him from the window. The same man from the Louvre.

What the hell do you want, you bastard? Bond thought to himself. Was he a flunky for Léon Essinger? Perhaps keeping tabs on his wife?

The man turned away and disappeared as Bond raised his coffee cup in salute.

13
The First Visit

The letter that René Mathis had written to James Bond had an unfortunate unscheduled trip. The receptionist at the hotel in Calvi had forgotten about it and didn't mail it until two days after Mathis had given it to her. Then a careless letter sorter in the Calvi post office accidentally dropped the envelope into a bin that was meant for mail travelling to Italy.

When Andrea Carlo, a postman in Milan, came across the letter more than a week after Mathis had sent it, he was in a destructive mood. His wife had just given birth to their sixth child, and he was worried about how they were going to make ends meet. His boss at the post office was a stingy crook, and he had aspirations to quit his day job to become a writer.

He looked at the envelope and decided to play a little joke. Instead of dropping the letter into the bin meant for the United Kingdom, he put it in the one targeted for America.

It was only a matter of good fortune that when the envelope arrived in New York three days later, an efficient postal worker caught the error and immediately dropped it in the bag en route to the U.K.

Unfortunately, the letter would arrive at MI6 nearly two weeks late.

• • •

The day after his lunch with Tylyn Bond checked out of his hotel, left a voice message for Bertrand, and drove south out of Paris. He took the A6 towards Lyons, a journey that he always enjoyed. He began to feel much better about France after he had left the bustling metropolis of Paris. It was a pleasure to go cross-country.

After passing through Lyons, the country's second-largest city and the home of Interpol, Bond got on the A43, which in turn became the A48, to travel southeast into the mountains towards Grenoble. He probably could have avoided the French Alps by taking a detour south of Lyons, but Bond enjoyed the scenery. Grenoble was situated in a broad valley and surrounded by spectacular mountains— the Chartreuse to the north, the Vercors to the southwest, and Alpine peaks stretching east to Italy.

As he left Grenoble and headed towards the Côte d'Azur, Bond noticed a dark green van gaining on him. Bond increased his speed, passing several cars, but the van's driver insisted on keeping up with him.

Fine, Bond thought. Let's see who this is.

Bond slowed down so that the van was soon right on his bumper. The van could easily pass him if that's what the driver wanted to do. Sure enough, after a few moments, the van pulled into the left lane and sped past Bond. It was difficult to see inside, for the windows were tinted. But what surprised Bond was that the side of the van displayed the words "Securité Verte." Bond was fairly sure that this was the agency that employed the man he had seen at the Louvre and at the gym across the street from the sidewalk café yesterday.

The van was now in front of him and the driver decreased his speed. Now it was Bond's turn to tailgate.

What sort of game were they playing?

Bond threw the car into lower gear and pulled into the left lane, almost wishing that the car still contained some of

Boothroyd's extras. He accelerated and pushed past the van, then swung back into the right lane. He then increased his speed and moved way ahead of the van very quickly. The driver didn't show any inclination to follow him this time, leaving Bond perplexed as to what all that was about.

As he was approaching Grasse on the N85, Bond pulled over to fill up with petrol. It was a self-service facility, so he got out, swiped his card for five hundred francs, and stood holding the nozzle while he surveyed the road.

From nowhere the green van appeared and pulled into the service station. It stopped at the pumps directly across from the Aston Martin. The passenger door opened and the man Bond had seen at the Louvre stepped out. Bond thought quickly, analysing the situation and looking at all his options should the man try anything.

He was large and tanned, with curly black hair and the broken nose of a boxer or wrestler. He still wore the security guard uniform. Up close, Bond thought that he looked vaguely familiar, someone from the deep past.

"Monsieur," he said, then continued in English. "My boss would like a word with you."

Bond kept his hand on the petrol nozzle. "Is that so?" he asked. "And who might that be?"

"If you would be so kind as to follow us, he is waiting."

"Sorry, I was taught to never go anywhere with strangers," Bond said.

The man sighed. "I'm afraid I must insist," he said. He started to draw a gun, but wasn't fast enough.

Bond pulled the nozzle out of his car and doused the man with petrol, simultaneously bending to the side and kicking out with his left foot. The gun went flying. Bond dropped the nozzle, then gracefully spun around and kicked the man in the face with his right foot, knocking him to the ground. Bond then reached into his pocket, grabbed the Ronson lighter, and flicked it on.

The man lay sprawled on the pavement, looking up at Bond in terror. His shirt was soaked in petrol.

Bond held the lit Ronson in front of him and said, "Want to play catch?"

The man shook his head.

Bond reached down and picked up the gun. It was a Smith & Wesson .38. He emptied the cylinder and tossed the empty gun to the man. "Go on. Get the hell out of here. And tell your boss that if he wants to see me, he should make an appointment like anyone else."

Bond casually returned to his car, put the cap back on his tank, and got inside the Aston Martin. He pulled out of the service station, squealing the wheels as he sped out onto the highway.

That had felt good. Bond relished the electricity of danger. It was the best stimulant on the planet. He basked in the sensation for a while in silence, waiting for the van to reappear behind him. Surely they would continue the pursuit, and Bond was looking forward to a confrontation.

As expected, a few minutes later the van was behind the Aston Martin again. It was gaining on him, but Bond threw the car into low gear and shot ahead. He swerved in and out of traffic, putting some distance between him and the van. Soon he came upon another vehicle travelling slowly in his lane. It was another green van, identical to the Securité Verte van that had been following him all day.

He decelerated so that he wouldn't come too close to it. However, the van behind had gained on him. Now he was boxed in between the two.

If only he had the car's machine guns! Just a rocket or two!

The road made a sharp bend between two mountains, forcing the vehicles to slow down. Bond gripped the wheel and decided to take a risk. He pulled out into the left lane and stepped down hard. The Aston Martin roared ahead of the first van and was about to shift back into the right lane when a third green van appeared in front of him, headed straight for the car.

Bond slammed on the brakes and spun the wheel to the right, knocking the first van hard so that it veered off the road and scraped against the rocks on the side of the mountain. Bond managed to pull over to the right as the oncoming van zoomed past him. The road continued to curve around the mountain, leading right into a tunnel. Bond accelerated again, hoping to lose them there. But as he approached the tunnel, he saw two sets of headlamps come on, aiming right at him.

There was no way out.

Bond screeched to a stop just outside the tunnel. He flipped open the compartment that held the Walther P99, grabbed the gun, and waited to see what they were going to do. The three vans, one slightly disabled, pulled up behind him. The doors opened and several armed men got out. Two were carrying submachine guns. The man with the doused shirt gestured with his reloaded Smith & Wesson for Bond to get out of the car.

Bond aimed the Walther at the man's head as he got out of the Aston Martin.

"I'll take at least one of you with me," he said.

"We don't want anyone hurt," the man said. "Please, Mister Bond. Our boss is right inside the tunnel."

Bond didn't want to take his eyes off the security guard, but he dared to glance into the darkness. One of the cars inside started its motor and inched out into the sunlight. A black stretch limousine pulled up between Bond and the security guard, and then the window glided down.

The man in the back of the limousine had a brown, crinkled face shaped like a walnut.

My God! Bond thought.

The man had aged. The black hair had turned completely white, but the dark eyes hadn't changed at all.

It was really he, the head of the Corsican mafia, Marc-Ange Draco. Bond's father-in-law.

Bond was flabbergasted, completely speechless, standing outside the Aston Martin on a road somewhere in France and facing a man he thought he'd never see again.

"Don't look like you've seen a ghost, James, it's really me," the man said, smiling.

"My God, Marc-Ange, I . . . we all—heard you were *dead! Years* ago!" Bond said in a half-whisper.

Draco laughed. It was a laugh Bond remembered from another time.

"Merely rumours," Draco said happily. "You'd be surprised what disappearing can do for you if you want to get away from it all. That's what I did. I got out of circulation for a while and no one ever saw me—so everyone *assumed* I was dead. How long has it been, James?"

"Forever," Bond said. There was a brief awkward moment as the two men were suddenly at a loss for words. Then they embraced as family.

When they parted, Draco asked, "How have you been, James?"

"I'm fine, Marc-Ange, and you?"

The smallish man shrugged his unusually broad shoulders. "Not bad."

There was another uncomfortable moment. Bond had never made a point of staying in touch with Draco after Tracy's death. After all, the man was a criminal. But the main reason for not doing so was that it brought back painful memories of a woman he had loved and lost.

Draco finally said, "Come sit in the limousine and let's talk."

Uh-oh. Bond felt a pang in the pit of his stomach. *Are today's events a repeat of what happened long ago?* The first time Bond had met Marc-Ange Draco, he had been forcefully taken to the man. Draco's charm had disarmed Bond, and they ended up talking as friends. Then Draco asked

Bond for a "favour," and what a favour it was. He wanted him to marry his daughter, Tracy.

What was Draco going to ask him *now*?

It was cool in the air-conditioned interior, which was done up in expensive leather and sported a well-stocked bar. Draco still lived in his own brand of splendour.

"I know what you're thinking, James," Draco said. "You're wondering if I'm still in the, uhm, *business*. Once again, I must implore you to stay behind the Herkos Odonton with regard to what I'm about to tell you."

Bond smiled. "Herkos Odonton" was an expression Draco used to mean that the listener must keep what he heard a secret.

"The hedge of my teeth," Bond said, literally defining the term.

Draco twisted to the bar. "Drink?"

"Please," Bond said.

Draco dropped a couple of ice cubes into each of two Waterford pint glasses, then picked up a bottle of I. W. Harper bourbon and poured a generous measure into each glass. He set the drinks, a siphon of soda, and a flagon of iced water on a small tray table that unfolded between them.

They clicked glasses and said, "Cheers," together.

"But before I get to business, first tell me about yourself, James. I follow your career, you know," Marc-Ange said. "I have my sources. You continue to be a credit to your service. I congratulate you."

"Thanks," Bond said. "I suppose I'm fine. There's nothing to tell. I haven't changed much."

"No, you haven't," Draco said. "The years have been kind to you. Me—I just keep getting fatter. For a while it was the hair. My hair kept getting whiter. Now it's completely white. So I complain about my weight now."

While Draco intended his comments to be humorous, Bond detected an intangible sadness about the man. The earlier laughing had been abrupt and was finished with quickly. The boisterous, interminably optimistic Marc-Ange Draco he had known years ago was different now. Bond surmised that he had undergone some kind of tragedy.

"So you want to know if I'm still a crook, yes?" Draco asked.

"If you'd care to tell me, Marc-Ange," Bond said.

"Very well," Draco said, taking a sip of bourbon. "The short answer is 'yes,' I am still a crook. Now would you like the long answer?"

"That's up to you."

Draco paused to down his entire glass, then poured himself another. Then he spoke slowly and earnestly.

"After Teresa's de—uhm, after Tracy's *murder,* I withdrew from public life. The organisation was run by my lieutenant, Ché-Ché—you remember Ché-Ché, James?" He pointed to the man outside with the broken nose. No wonder he had looked familiar to Bond! Ché-Ché le Persuadeur had been a longtime associate of Draco's. Ché-Ché had changed his shirt and cleaned himself up, but he didn't look particularly cheerful.

"Now I do," Bond replied. "Tell him that I hope there are no hard feelings."

"Don't worry about it. He did a fine job while I . . . went into hiding. I was not a happy man, James, I admit it. The loss of Tracy was quite overwhelming. At first I blamed you, and I was angry with you, but common sense prevailed. I completely understand that it wasn't your fault. And you exacted revenge for us both, and for that I am grateful. In many ways, it was my fault. I pushed her into the arms of a man who lived on the edge in his profession. Like me. But never mind that, it's the past.

"Around the time that rumours of my death began to circulate, there was trouble within the Union Corse. One of my lieutenants, Toussaint, left to form a rival syndicate.

There was a war. I decided to let them fight it out, just to see who was stronger. I stayed completely away, which is why everyone thought I was dead except my most trusted associates. I have only a handful of them these days."

Draco offered Bond a cigar, but he refused, preferring to smoke one of his own specially made cigarettes provided by Tor Importers. They contained a unique blend of Balkan Yenidje and Turkish Latakia tobaccos that Bond craved, especially with bourbon.

Draco lit his cigar and continued. "About nine years ago, my life turned around. I climbed out of my depression. I met a woman—a girl, really . . . she was French—and we fell in love. It didn't matter that she had barely come of age. We got married in Corsica."

Draco wouldn't look at Bond now. Instead, he gazed out the car window at the French countryside.

"We had a child together. A daughter. James, I had found a new lease on life. I didn't want to be a crook anymore. I let Ché-Ché run everything, while I was happy again for the first time in as long as I could remember."

Bond saw the bomb coming before Draco dropped it.

"Earlier this year, they met with . . . an accident," Draco said in as steady a voice as he could. "My wife and daughter. Together. Killed. So I have been in mourning for the last several months."

"I'm sorry, Marc-Ange," Bond said. He didn't know what else to do.

Draco nodded, his eyes brimming with moisture. "Since then, yes, I have returned to my work. The business is not what it was. We don't call ourselves the Union Corse. My small group of men still run a Corsican mafia, if you really want to call it that. For me, it's just business."

Bond knew that Draco meant the "business" of common racketeering crimes—prostitution, money laundering, gambling, smuggling, and sometimes murder.

"Don't get me wrong," Draco said. "I own some legitimate businesses as well. A security agency, as you can see, a real estate company, a chain of tobacco shops . . ."

"So it was you who had me watched yesterday in Paris," Bond said. He gestured to the green security vans.

Draco shrugged again.

"What happened to your other men?" Bond asked.

"Ah! That's why I invited you to have a talk with me. Toussaint and his merry followers joined a little organisation you know as the Union."

Bond felt a sudden burst of adrenaline. Of course! Draco had his fingers everywhere in France. As the Capu had once found a clue pointing to the whereabouts of Ernst Stavro Blofeld, Draco could possibly help Bond again.

"Marc-Ange, can you tell me anything about them? Do you know where their headquarters are?" Bond asked.

"Don't be so impatient, James," Draco said, smiling. "No, I don't know where *Le Gérant* is, but I certainly *know* him."

"Do tell," Bond said.

"His name is Olivier Cesari. I knew his father well. Joseph. He was one of my lieutenants in the old Union Corse."

Bond raised his eyebrows. "I thought he was in the perfume business."

"He was. That was his day job. He did quite well with it, too. In fact, our organisation financed his start-up. But he was also on my team and was quite useful. Joseph Cesari certainly passed on his ruthless qualities to his son. Whatever he wanted, he got. Anyway, I was quite close to both the father and the son. I adored young Olivier, and when he grew up, I could see that he was a fine, intelligent young man, despite his affliction of being blind. Now he is the head of the most powerful criminal organisation in the world. He swallowed up my entire business after the war had torn us apart. The Union now operates where we used to. My small band of associates and I have had to work more in France rather than Corsica and have had to look for other means of doing business. So far, we have just squeezed out a living. Olivier Cesari keeps challenging my, er, territories. He has gone from being like a relative to becoming my worst enemy."

"This is extraordinary," Bond said.

"That it may be. But true. So I am offering you, James, the chance to work together again. I want to find *Le Gérant* too. I know that he appears in public now—he has been seen in Corsica and in Monte Carlo. As I said, I don't know exactly where he is, but my sources tell me that he lives somewhere in Corsica now, and that's where the headquarters are located. I am still working on finding out where it is. In the meantime, I know for a fact that Olivier Cesari goes to the casino in Monte Carlo every Thursday night to gamble. He uses an alias, Pierre Rodiac."

Bond said, "Coincidentally, I'm going to Monte Carlo tomorrow, and tomorrow is Thursday."

"Precisely," Draco said. Draco beamed. "I thought that bit of information might be useful."

"Have you ever heard of a man named Léon Essinger?" Bond asked.

"Of course. Famous movie producer with a lot of legal problems," Draco said.

"I'm pretty sure he's involved with the Union."

Draco waved his hand and grimaced. "Forget it. You're—how do they say it in America?—you're 'barking up the wrong tree' with him."

"He is a Union member. I have proof."

"He may very well be. I wouldn't doubt it if the Union was helping him with his legal woes. Essinger is small potatoes. Go after the big fish."

"Perhaps you can help me with a related problem," Bond said. "I'm searching for a French colleague of mine, René Mathis. He disappeared not long ago while on the trail of *Le Gérant*. In fact, he was last seen in Monte Carlo."

"I know Monsieur Mathis, James. We met in the old days. I will see what I can find out for you. If he did find the Union headquarters, though, I doubt very seriously that he's still alive."

Bond nodded grimly.

"I'll be in touch," Draco said. "I'll also be watching your back, although you probably don't need my protection."

"Thanks," Bond said. "It will be interesting to meet Cesari face to face."

Draco reached into his pocket, pulled out a business card, and handed it to Bond. "Here is my number. You can call me from anywhere in the world if you need to find me."

Bond pocketed the card and said, "Thank you."

"And now, I have another piece of information I need to impart to you." Draco took another drink.

"What's that?"

"The Union have just made a business deal with the Japanese terrorist Goro Yoshida."

14

The Horses

Bond arrived in Mougins as the day turned from late afternoon to evening. He had consulted a road map and found the little road that led to Tylyn's home, which was located a few kilometres east of the village. He would have missed the turnoff had it not been for a small sign that said *"Ferme Equestre—Privé."* Bond turned the DB5 onto the dirt road, rumbled over cattle grids, and drove the three kilometres to the house.

It was a lovely property in the forest, not far from Antibes, where the landscape was ideal for horse riding. The impressive main house looked like an inn, with two storeys and numerous windows. It was mostly made of a dark, rustic wood and would not have been out of place in the American Midwest. Two smaller buildings of similar construction stood near the house, probably related to the horse business, and a large barn was behind. Bales of hay were stacked in front of the open barn doors, along with a forklift for loading and other equipment.

Bond pulled into a gravel parking area in front of the house and got out of the car. From here he could see a path that led through the trees to the stables, which were built inside a large pen. The stables were quite large with blue-and-white-striped roofs. There was probably room for at least ten horses. The paddock provided plenty of space for the horses to exercise outside.

A sign near the front door proclaimed *"Ferme Equestre—Pension—Entrainement—Stages—Competitions."* Bond knocked and waited until he heard footsteps on the other side. A frumpy woman in an apron answered it.

"Oui?" she asked.

Bond explained that he was looking for Tylyn and that she had invited him.

The housekeeper chattered a bit, then pointed towards the stables. Bond thanked her, turned, and strolled down the path through the trees.

As he reached the paddock, he saw her. She was atop a beautiful Selle Français that was prancing around the fence. He was as fine a specimen as Bond had seen, with upright shoulders, a strong neck, compact body, and what appeared to be powerful hindquarters. The French saddle horse was completely brown except for white "sock" markings above its hoofs and a white "star" marking between its eyes. It was equipped with a black Western saddle and bridle.

Tylyn was attired, in part, in traditional dressage clothing—a canary waistcoat, white shirt with white stock, white breeches, and black dress boots with spurs. All that was missing was a black tailcoat and top hat.

Bond stood and watched her as she took the horse around the paddock, performing various manoeuvres—spins, rollbacks, flying lead changes, and sliding stops. It was obvious that Tylyn was a pro. She handled the horse with self-confidence and a firm command, yet she was gentle and loving, speaking to him in French.

He finally made his presence known by stepping forward and standing by the gate. As Tylyn made another lap around the paddock, she saw him and beamed.

"James! What a surprise!"

"I decided to take you up on your offer to show me your home. I hope you don't mind," he said.

"Not at all! I was just giving Commander a little exercise. Perhaps you'd like to go riding? I was going to take him into the forest."

"I'd be delighted, although I'm not quite dressed for it."

"Don't be silly. You don't need to look like a jockey. Unlatch the gate there, and come on in. We'll see if we can find you a horse that's not too wilful."

Bond opened the gate and closed it behind him as he walked into the paddock. Tylyn trotted the horse to him and swung her leg over and off. She landed on her feet and tied the reins to a pole. She murmured in the horse's ear and stroked him, saying that she would be right back.

"Did you drive from Paris?" she asked as they went into the stables.

"Yes, I parked in front of the house."

"That's fine. After our ride, I hope you'll stay for dinner. Chantal is a very good cook."

"That would be lovely."

There were several horses in the stables—black ones, white ones, brown ones. Tylyn ultimately picked a chestnut French Trotter.

"This is Lolita," Tylyn said. "She's fairly young, but she's well behaved. How are you on a horse?"

Bond shrugged. "I know how to make them go, turn, and stop. Changing gears can be tricky sometimes, but parallel parking is relatively simple."

Tylyn laughed. "I think you'll do fine." She deftly put the bridle and bit on the horse and led her out of her quarters. The horse nuzzled Bond as he patted her strong neck.

"Oh, Lolita likes you!" Tylyn said. "Actually she likes men, period. She's a little flirt."

"Then I'm sure we'll get along just fine," Bond said.

"Come on, help me saddle her up."

•　　•　　•

It was the glorious time of day. The sun was setting with finality and the remaining half hour of daylight took on a mystical orange glow. Deep amongst the pine trees it was darker, but the light and shadow provided the two riders with a breathtaking scenic trip through the forest.

Bond conceded that she was a better rider than he was. In fact she was, quite simply, amazing.

Tylyn didn't have to show off. Every perfectly timed and flawlessly executed move that she made with the horse seemed effortless; it was completely natural to her. The horse was so well attuned to her commands that they truly acted as one entity, as if she were the upper half of a centaur.

Bond didn't embarrass himself, though. He met the challenges with finesse. At one point, Lolita hesitated before jumping over a fallen tree. Bond had to urge her three times to go for it, and by then, Commander was nearly half a kilometre ahead. Tylyn weaved in and out of the trees at a frightening speed, but Bond did his best to keep up. Even though Tylyn's horse was definitely stronger, faster, and more familiar with his rider, Lolita, Bond thought, was doing a damned fine job obeying him. As far as he was concerned, she was a terrific horse.

He caught up with Tylyn by a brook near the opposite edge of the forest. Commander was having a drink. Tylyn smiled broadly.

"How do you like her?" she asked.

Bond let Lolita trot over to the water so that she could drink as well.

"She's marvellous," Bond said. "A little shy at first, like most first-timers, but she became enthusiastic once I took control."

Tylyn laughed. "That's what I like! A man who associates riding with sex."

"Isn't that what everyone associates it with?"

"Only the right people." And with that she pulled on the

reins. "Let's go, Commander!" Immediately, the horse bolted from the water and cantered back into the woods.

Bond sighed. "Come on, Lo, we had better go too." He had to pull on the reins twice to get her to move.

It had grown considerably darker. Bond couldn't see a thing, but Lolita trotted around the trees using her own sense of guidance.

"Tylyn?" he called.

In the vague distance, he heard Commander whinny.

"Go," he said to Lolita, urging her forward into the gnarly black and grey maze.

They were foolish to have stayed out past dark, Bond thought. Tylyn should have known better, unless it was her *intention* for him to follow her somewhere. Could it mean that she was a member of the Union, or that she really liked him?

Bond hoped that it would be the latter.

Commander whinnied again, and Lolita picked up speed. The horse did remarkably well navigating through the obstacles. At one point, she came too close to a tree and skinned her left hindquarter but kept going.

He found Tylyn's horse riderless, obviously distressed.

"Tylyn?" Bond called.

There was nothing. Just the sounds of the night.

"Tylyn?" he shouted again.

Then he heard the soft moan. It came from a clump of bushes to his left. Bond got off Lolita and tied her to a tree, then approached Commander, who was acting quite skittish.

"Easy, boy," Bond said soothingly. "Give me your reins . . ."

The horse hesitated and jumped away from Bond twice before he could get close enough to grab them. Once he did, the horse calmed down and allowed Bond to tie him to a tree next to Lolita.

Bond raced to where the moaning came from and found Tylyn, sitting up, rubbing her face.

"Ohhh," she said, dazed.

"My God, are you all right? What happened?" Bond knelt beside her, but it was too dark to really see what was wrong with her.

"Commander tripped and I went flying," she said. "It's my fault. I shouldn't have been racing him in the forest after dark. It's just that he *enjoys* it so."

"Are you hurt?"

"My eye hurts. There's something in it—I can't get it out. I might have a bruise on my left arm and shoulder, where I landed, but it's mostly my pride that's hurt."

"Can you stand? We should probably get out of here."

"I think so, it's just . . ." She stood and kept rubbing at her eye. ". . . my eye really hurts. I can't open it. Do you have a flashlight, by any chance?"

"Yes," he said. "Sit down again." She did so, and Bond pulled the camera out of his jacket pocket.

He held it up to her and said, "My camera has special photographic lenses that work with certain kinds of built-in light sources. I'm going to use one on you, all right?"

"Sure, just get that awful thing out of my eye!" It was obvious that she was terribly uncomfortable but doing her best to maintain composure. Her beauty aside, it was Tylyn's willpower and spirit that continued to impress him.

He looked through the camera and flicked on the light. Tylyn's face was illuminated in a halo-like circle that centred on her eye. She was squeezing it shut.

"You're going to have to try and open your eye, Tylyn," Bond said. "Otherwise I can't see anything."

"Oh, all right, damn it," she said. "Help me, just go slow."

He put down the camera and used both hands to gently rub her face around her eye. With his fingertips, he gained a hold on the skin surrounding her eye and slowly began to flex his fingers, pulling open her eyelids.

Tylyn cursed like a man.

He held her eye open with his left hand while he reached for the camera with his right. He held it up, flicked on the light, and shone it over her eye.

It was teary and red, all right, and Bond immediately saw the cause. In the anterior corner of her eye was a foreign object—a splinter, perhaps.

"Just hold still, Tylyn, I see it," he said. "You're going to have to hold your eye open, all right?"

"Okay," she said, and replaced his fingertips with her own, forcing the eye to stay open.

Bond put the camera in his left hand and removed the heel of his right shoe. The escape materials that Q Branch had provided were about to come in handy once again, for inside the kit was a pair of tweezers. As it was dark and Tylyn was probably in too much pain to notice, Bond retrieved them and focused his attention on her eye. He shone the light into the pupil and examined the retina. He looked up, down, to the sides—she had no Union tattoo.

With a quick and deliberate move, Bond reached into the corner of Tylyn's eye with the tweezers and grabbed the offending splinter. He pulled it out smoothly and quickly, then surreptitiously replaced the tweezers. Tylyn felt no pain, just an overwhelming sensation of relief.

"Oh, *merci beaucoup!*" she cried, and impulsively threw her arms around him and kissed him once on the mouth. This took both of them by surprise. Then time seemed to stop as Bond and Tylyn concurrently worked out how they were going to react to that kiss. Should they laugh about it and move on? Should they say nothing? Should they do it again?

Bond leaned in and kissed her longingly, and Tylyn let him do it.

•   •   •

They emerged from the forest an hour later, after the sun was well on its way to the other side of the world. Their clothes were dishevelled and there were twigs in their hair, but there was no other damning evidence of what had occurred between them. They had wrapped themselves in a blanket that Tylyn had kept fastened to her saddle, and there on the ground they had made noisy, animalistic love. For her, it was a catharsis of sorts, as she had been mostly celibate since her separation. For Bond, it was the culmination of an intense desire that he had felt since he had first become aware of Tylyn's existence.

As they approached the house in silence, walking their horses and holding hands, Bond wondered again if he should take this any further. For one thing, he was being dishonest with her. He was no journalist. He would have to come clean, tell her what he really did for a living. He wasn't sure if he was ready to do that.

They had salade niçoise and wine by candlelight in her home, where they sat at a round table in the dining room and looked out large French windows at a garden that was barely illuminated by the outdoor bulbs. A mixed-breed dog and a tabby cat sat quietly in the room with them, eyeing the couple intensely. Tylyn had put on a Billie Holiday CD, and it created a pleasant, mellow mood.

They spoke of horses, of how her business with them barely turned a profit but that she enjoyed it so much that she could never abandon it.

"I raise horses for riding schools, mostly. I sell them in France and some in Spain, too. I won't sell to racers—I'm not sure I like that," she said. "And never to circuses unless I personally know the people in charge of the animals."

"Why do you want to act, Tylyn? You have so much already," Bond said. "Your horses, your clothing company, your modelling career . . ."

She laughed. "I know, I know, it isn't as if I have nothing to do all day long. Why does anyone want to act? It's a

thrill. It's a new direction. I'm ready for new directions."
She sighed. "And tomorrow it all begins."

"What time do you have to be in Monte Carlo?"

"Pretty early. I'll be up before the sun."

"Then I shouldn't stay and keep you."

"Don't be silly," she said, starting. She put out a hand
and laid it on his. "Don't go. Please?"

Bond looked into her magnificent eyes. He knew, as did
she, that something had happened—not just the physical
pleasure that they had experienced in the woods, but an
awakening, the opening of private doors that were rarely
unlocked. Poetry and mythology had cast labels on the
phenomenon throughout history: "love at first sight,"
"finding one's soul mate," or "falling head over heels."
Bond never set much store by such romantic notions, but
he did know that there was something palpable between
them.

Bond turned his hand over, took hers, and said, "I hope
you're not on the rebound from your husband."

She shook her head. "It isn't. Well, maybe it is. I don't
know. You're not the first man I've slept with since we separated. You're not the first man I've slept with since we
were *married*." For the first time since he had met her, Tylyn allowed Bond to glimpse her vulnerability. She said
soberly, "Léon was not good for me. At first I thought he
was, and the first couple of years were happy. But he has
his dark side, you see. Me, I always look on the light side
of life, whereas he always looks on the black side. I was
more of a possession to him than a wife. And I think he always wanted to get his hands on my family's money, even
though he knew he couldn't get near it."

"Did you have a prenuptial agreement?" Bond asked.

"Yes, and the deal was that he got nothing. He knew
from the beginning that my money would always be my
money. He never had a problem with that. He wouldn't get
anything unless . . ."

"Unless what?"

"Well, unless I died or something. Then he would inherit it all. But after we're divorced, that's no longer a consideration."

Bond said nothing. He stroked the back of her hand with his thumb.

"I guess I'm not the marrying type," she said. "I'm too much like one of those horses out there. I like to ride with the wind and go wherever it takes me."

"You can say that again. I've seen it up close!"

She looked at him hard. "Have you ever been married?"

Bond was always reserved when it came to talking about that chapter of his life, but this time the question threw him more than usual. She must have seen the walls go up, for she immediately said, "I'm sorry. That's none of my—"

"Yes, once," he replied. "It was another time, another place."

She nodded. "I suppose you have to talk about my marriage in your article?" she asked softly after a pause.

Oh yes, the article. How was he going to get around that?

"I don't have to mention it at all," he said.

"Good, because if you'll keep it off the record, I'll tell you something."

"You have my word."

She took a sip of wine, then said, "I'm going to divorce Léon. He just doesn't know it yet."

"Don't you think he has a pretty good idea that you will?"

"He's deluded," she said. "He believes that the separation is indeed a trial one, and that we'll be back together as soon as filming starts. He probably cast me just so he could keep some kind of hold on me, but I'm going to prove to him, and to the world, that I'm quite independent now. I'm not going to say anything until after filming is completed, but he's going to have to give me a wide berth over the next few weeks. In fact . . ." She looked at Bond with inspiration in her eyes. "Will you come and visit me on the set?"

"You really want me to?"

"Yes! Oh, it would help my cause enormously, you see. Léon will see that I am *not* his wife anymore, and it will make my decision to divorce him that much easier for him to swallow. Will you?"

Bond smiled. "I might."

"I can see that I'm just going to have to persuade you," she said, standing and pulling on his hand.

"Where are we going?"

"It's time for dessert."

"Dessert? Where?"

"In my bedroom," she said, leading him out of the room.

Bond woke to the sensation of a soft weight on his legs. He shifted beneath the sheets and saw that Tylyn's tabby cat was sitting on his thighs, on top of the covers.

Tylyn's side of the bed was empty, but there was a note on the pillow. Bond moved, nudging the cat to jump off the bed. He sat up and read the note:

Dear James, make yourself comfortable. Ask Chantal for anything. I've left my mobile number. I hope to see you soon. Kisses, Tylyn.

Naked, he slipped out of bed and found his clothes on a chair across the room. Once he was dressed, he left the bedroom and found his way to the dining room, where Chantal was already laying out breakfast for him: a feast of fresh scrambled eggs, a plate of assorted fruit, and yoghurt. It couldn't get any better than that.

After thanking Chantal profusely, Bond got in his car and left Tylyn's home. He drove east, towards Monte Carlo.

All he could think about were the sounds she had made last night in bed.

Put her out of your mind! he willed himself. His usual method of detachment that normally protected his heart from the tumultuous hazards of romance was simply not working this time. Could this be love?

Whatever it was, he thought, he was hooked. The pursuit was on.

15

The Casino

Tylyn had checked into the Hôtel de Paris in Monte Carlo in the morning. She spent three hours in the spa, swimming pool, and beauty salon, then had something to eat. She was preparing for the press reception that afternoon when there was a knock on the door of her suite.

"Who is it?" she asked in French.

"Léon."

She frowned and sighed. "What do you want?"

"I want to talk to you for a minute. May I come in?"

Shaking her head, Tylyn put on one of the hotel's terry-cloth robes over her underwear, unlocked the door, and opened it. Essinger stepped inside and kissed her on both cheeks. She returned the greeting, but only perfunctorily. He was dressed sharply in a silk white shirt with full, puffy sleeves, opened at the neck. His black trousers were tight around his buttocks.

"You look like one of the Three Musketeers," Tylyn said.

"Rather pirate-like, don't you think?" he asked, smiling. "I thought it fit with the theme of our movie." He set a shopping bag on a table.

"What do you want? I'm busy getting ready."

"We have another press conference in Nice tomorrow before we set sail for Corsica."

"Oh, no, Léon, do we have to?"

"You're required by contract to do publicity, darling, so, yes, you have to. And . . . I'd like you to accompany me."

She shook her head. "I'll go, but I'm not accompanying you, Léon. We had an agreement. This is strictly business, this movie. You wanted me in it, and I wanted to be in it, and I'm working for you, but I'm no longer living with you."

He tried to grab her arm and pull her towards him. "But Tylyn—"

She broke free and walked away from him. "No 'buts,' Léon. Where is the press conference tomorrow?"

"At the harbour, in front of our cruise ship. After the conference, we set sail."

"All right, I'll be there. Now go away."

He went to her and tried to take her into his arms. "Tylyn, don't be this way."

She turned to him and said, "Léon, how many chances did I give you? How many times did I say, 'If you don't change I'm going to leave'? How many times have you been caught with some young girl in your bed?"

"You're no saint either, Tylyn. I seem to remember catching you as well."

"No, I'm not a saint, but I'm not a liar. And I don't hit my lovers," she said, rubbing her cheek. There was no longer a mark there, but the memory of it would remain with her always.

"Tylyn, I *have* changed," Essinger pleaded. "When we're together again, after the separation, you'll see."

"Oh, Léon . . ." She was tempted to tell him that she had no intention of getting back together, but it just wasn't the right time. "Please go."

"I see," Essinger said, releasing her. "You have another lover, is that it?" She recognised the change in the tone of his voice. It meant trouble.

"What are you talking about?"

Essinger went over to the shopping bag he had brought, reached inside, and pulled out a new copy of *Paris Match*. He turned to a page and showed her.

There were shots of the Indecent Exposure fashion show in Paris, including several flattering ones of Tylyn. Down at the bottom of the page was a photograph of her and Bond, leaving the museum. Bond had his face covered with his hand so that it was difficult to identify him. The caption read, "New Romance in Store for Tylyn?"

"Who is this man?" Essinger asked.

"Just someone I met. He's a journalist, for God's sake, Léon," she said. "He's with an English magazine. We had an interview scheduled and we went out for lunch to talk. It was arranged by my manager."

Essinger wasn't sure whether or not to believe her.

"You'll probably get your own chance to meet him," she continued. "I've invited him to the set. He's doing an extensive article."

"The set?" Essinger snapped. "All press of that sort must be cleared through Dana in publicity!"

"Then he'll come as my guest!" Tylyn said. "Now get out!"

"I think you should stay away from him," Essinger said.

"You can't tell me what to do anymore, Léon."

He grabbed her roughly by the shoulders. "Listen to me, you little— *Oww!*"

Tylyn snapped her knee into his groin. He let her go and doubled up, falling onto the couch.

"I'm sorry, Léon," she said. "You seem only to understand things when they're directed at your wallet or at your genitals. Now I'm going back into the bedroom to finish getting ready. As soon as you've recovered, please let yourself out."

With that, she left him in agony. After the door slammed shut, Essinger muttered to himself, "You'll get what's coming to you, you just wait and see."

After a few minutes, he rolled off the sofa and slowly got to his feet.

Bond phoned Bertrand Collette when he got to Monte Carlo midafternoon.

"I need you in Nice by tomorrow morning," Bond told him. "And bring Ariel with you." He was referring to something that Q Branch had shipped to several foreign stations a few months ago for testing purposes.

"Ariel?" Collette asked. "What for?"

"Essinger's film is shooting on water. She might come in handy."

"That won't be easy. I have to find a . . . What do you call it in English? A proper . . . hitch."

"Do your best, Bertrand," Bond said. "Just be at the harbour in the morning."

After checking in with Nigel in London, Bond spent the rest of the day keeping an eye on the casino and doing his best to avoid Tylyn's press reception, which was at the Hôtel de Paris, next door. He thought it best not to appear too eager.

Later he ate dinner alone, put on an Armani dinner jacket, and stood outside the casino to smoke a cigarette and contemplate what might happen that evening. Was he really about to meet *Le Gérant* in person? Mathis had done so and had discovered something significant. Apparently whatever he had found was important enough to affect his disappearance.

The Monte Carlo casino was one of Bond's favourites. He knew the general manager and several staff members personally. He had both won and lost great sums of money at the casino over the years. Forget what anyone says, Bond thought. Gambling was not fun and games—it was serious business. Lady Luck could be a cruel mistress.

As he walked inside the elegant casino, Bond reminded himself that although he would be using the company's money, a limit on the amount available had been imposed this time and he couldn't afford to lose more than three hundred thousand francs. A tidy sum, but nowhere near the maximums in the *privé* rooms. He hoped that his prey would not be playing for the kind of extremely high stakes that could result in his being wiped out in one hand.

After his passport was checked and he had made the transaction for chips, Bond went into the main room. For a Thursday night, the casino was crowded early. There must have been a ship of tourists in town. From the looks of them, Bond guessed that they were Americans.

He took a moment to admire the elaborate paintings on the ceiling that represented the four seasons, then went into the *Salon Privé*. A crowd had gathered at one of the *chemin de fer* tables, so Bond stepped over to see if this was where the action was tonight. Sitting at one end was a man wearing dark glasses.

So . . . was this *Le Gérant*? At last?

Bond scanned the rest of the faces. There were two bodyguards behind the blind man. A smallish bookeeper type sat next to him and acted as his eyes. There were three other players sitting at the table—an Arab in a turban, an elderly German man, and a fat, ugly American with a smelly cigar. The American, in particular, was in a foul mood. The blind man had taken him to the cleaners.

A group of at least ten other men, representing several nationalities, were standing around the table and observing.

As for the man who might be *Le Gérant,* he was broad-shouldered, muscular, and tanned. His dark hair was slicked back, a little too oily. The man looked to be physically fit, and Bond guessed that they were around the same age.

The croupier announced that the bank stood at a hundred thousand francs.

"Banco," Bond said.

They all turned to look at the newcomer.

Le Gérant said, "Ah, new blood. Welcome, monsieur. Please sit down." Without moving his head, he raised his hand and snapped his fingers. One of the casino employees stepped up with a leather-covered chair and placed it at the other end of the table for Bond.

Bond sat down and placed his chips in front of him. Immediately he felt the indescribable rush that went with high-stakes gambling. How many times had he been in this position, facing a ruthless opponent over cards? This was life or death played out on a green felt-covered table. Would tonight lead to death for one of them?

As the croupier counted the chips, Bond stared at the blind man. He never shifted his position; he kept his head straight, as if he were staring through solids into the next room. A slight smile was beginning to form on the man's face.

The cards were dealt. Bond received a three and a four. Seven—not bad.

The bookeeper whispered in *Le Gérant*'s ear after looking at his two cards.

Bond waved to signal that he didn't want another card. The hand was played out. Bond revealed his seven.

Le Gérant turned over a two and a six.

"Bad luck," the elder gentleman said to Bond.

"Yeah, join the club," the American said.

The bank stood at two hundred thousand francs. It was all that Bond had left. Was this the moment of truth? Would it be all over in two hands?

The croupier announced the bank's amount, challenging anyone present if they wanted to wager. If they had chosen to do so, several players could have combined forces to bet against respective parts of the bank. But no one desired to risk even a small part of his funds against a man who seemed unbeatable.

"Banco," Bond said, which meant that he was betting against the entire bank alone.

Le Gérant smiled. "I think this game is about to get interesting, eh, Julien?"

The bookkeeper whispered, *"Oui, Monsieur Rodiac."*

Le Gérant slipped the cards out of the shoe. Bond had a two and a queen, which was not encouraging. He watched the blind man as Julien peeked at their cards. He whispered to *Le Gérant,* who registered no reaction whatsoever.

Bond asked for a third card, the one that would decide the fate of the game. The croupier handed it to him on the paddle and flipped it over.

A seven. Bond had a total of nine. He was careful not to show any emotion, but inwardly he breathed a sigh of relief.

Le Gérant remained stone-faced, but the shock on Julien's face was evident. He had to draw a card. As he did so, Julien whispered in his ear, and after a second or two, he turned over the hand.

A total of eight.

The crowd gasped. The blind man's luck had suddenly turned!

If Bond's perceptions were correct, then *Le Gérant* had known that he was going to lose. Bond had seen it in his demeanour. The man had realised it before he had drawn the third card. What was his secret?

There was a moment's pause as the bank and shoe was turned over to Bond. He was now a hundred thousand francs wealthier than when he had started.

Le Gérant said, "I hope you will allow me a chance to win my money back, Monsieur Bond."

The man knew who he was! But how?

"Of course," Bond said, doing his best to retain his cool. "I wouldn't just win and run."

Was he completely blown?

"Banco," *Le Gérant* said.

The bank was worth four hundred thousand francs.

The identification had rattled Bond a bit, but he summoned his concentration and managed to deal the cards from the shoe with panache. It was important to appear confident and relaxed. Julien glanced at the cards and whispered in his employer's ear. Bond looked at his hand. He had a king and a five, which put him on shaky ground. A total of five could go either way.

Le Gérant sat a moment, pondering his hand. Should he draw? Finally, he nodded. Bond slapped a new card onto the table and the paddle carried it over to the blind man. Julien looked at it and whispered, then turned it over. An ace.

Damn! Bond was not allowed to draw. The rules stated that the dealer had to stand on a five if he dealt an ace as a third card to his opponent.

Le Gérant flipped over his cards, revealing a five, a ten, and an ace. Six.

He had won back the entire bank.

Bond turned over his cards. The crowd murmured enthusiastically, some shaking their heads in sympathy for Bond.

He shrugged it off and smiled to the crowd. "Easy come, easy go," he said.

But he was completely broke, so he set down a couple of chips he had held in reserve for a tip, stood, and said, "*Merci, monsieur.* I hope we will meet again soon." He passed the shoe back to the other end of the table.

Le Gérant smiled and said, "I'm sure we will, Monsieur Bond. It was a pleasure."

Bond walked away and went to the bar. He ordered a martini and nursed it while he reflected on what had just happened.

Le Gérant had swatted him away like a fly. Bond had never been bested so quickly. The man had been dealt a five and a ten, which gave him a total of five (since tens were worthless). However, he was entitled to draw on a five or not. He had chosen to do so. Had he not done so, there would have been a tie.

Was it luck? A good guess on *Le Gérant*'s part?

Bond could see where the legends about the man having a sixth sense might have come from. He certainly had a sense of power about him. He was confident, good-humoured, and obviously wealthy. This could really be the man who controlled the largest and most notorious criminal organisation on the planet.

Bond walked out of the casino towards the Hôtel de Paris. It would be a while before *Le Gérant* finished for the night. He might as well look into other matters that were weighing heavily on his mind.

As he entered the grandiose lobby with its marble floors, high domed ceiling, stained-glass windows, and a bust of Louis XIV, Bond felt a touch of apprehension. What was preoccupying his thoughts now was seeing Tylyn again. She was in the hotel somewhere. Should he phone up to her room? Was pursuing this girl really wise?

"James?"

His heart skipped a beat when he heard the voice. Bond turned, and there she was, an angel in a low-cut red dress, one that he had seen in the fashion show. She looked her best, which was saying a lot.

"It *is* you!" She beamed happily, embracing him.

"Hello, Tylyn," he said, kissing her cheeks. "Last night was lovely, do you know that?"

She nodded. "You don't have to tell *me*. I'm so glad you're here! Oh, but James, I'm leaving for Nice very soon. In an hour, I think. A car is picking me up. What are you doing here?"

"Looking for you, of course."

"Well, I wish you had come sooner! I was *so* bored at dinner this evening. I had to eat with the other actors, the director, and . . . well, Léon, too. I could have done without that."

"How was the press conference?"

"Nothing new there. A lot of patting each other on the back. More like a pep talk than a press conference. 'Aren't we great? Look at us, we're about to make a cool movie!'"

"Would you like to have a drink?" Bond asked.

"Let's go for a walk instead, what do you say?" she suggested.

"That sounds wonderful."

They walked behind the casino on Avenue de Monte Carlo, past the Bar Américain, and down broad stone steps to the gardens and terraces of the casino. This was an ideal lovers' walk, as the gardens overlooked Monte Carlo's harbour and were stocked with all kinds of exotic flowers. It was a beautiful night; the sky was clear and the stars were out in force. The Mediterranean lay flattened out before them in the darkness, reflecting the moon on its surface. There were several other couples strolling through, as well as groups of tourists. All were exquisitely dressed, ready to partake of an evening's gambling at the casino.

The harbour down below was well lit and busy. One of the yachts there belonged to *Le Gérant*. Which one was it? As they walked, Bond noted that there was easy access to the marina from the gardens by means of a lift.

Tylyn spoke of her day and how she had missed Bond's presence. "I don't normally do that, you know," she said. "I realise that we, well, we jumped into bed on the first date and all, and I just don't want you to get the wrong idea about me."

"I don't believe it's possible to have wrong ideas about you."

"You're sweet." She leaned up to kiss him, but she didn't have to go far. She was nearly as tall as he was. "I wish I knew more about you."

"Tylyn . . ." he said.

She put her hand to his mouth. "No, don't. Not now. I know we're probably rushing things. Let's not. I'm not ready for a serious relationship, you should know that. Let's just take things day by day, all right? I'll learn about you in due time."

Bond nodded and kissed her again. She looked past Bond and frowned.

"Damn," she said.

"What?"

"It's Gérard, one of my husband's flunkies."

Bond casually looked behind him. A large man in a suit was some ten yards away, talking into a mobile.

"Your husband has you followed?" Bond asked.

"It doesn't surprise me," she said. "Look, I hope you're not going to disappear. Léon already suspects that I'm seeing you. I think a little jealousy is good for him. Will you come to the set to visit me?"

"You're just using me," Bond said, teasing her.

"No I'm not!" She laughed, and pushed him. "Well, okay, maybe I am, a *little*. But I like you, too, James. I really do. Do you believe me?"

"Yes, Tylyn, and I like you, too. Let's give Gérard something to report to his boss."

With that, he kissed her passionately, holding on to her as if she were the last woman on earth. Tylyn lifted one leg behind her, bent at the knee. They stayed locked in the embrace for well over a minute. When they looked up, Gérard was talking animatedly into the phone.

"I must go now," she said. "I'll be at the harbour in Nice tomorrow at ten-thirty for another press function. Then we set sail. Léon has chartered a cruise ship to carry the cast and crew out to sea. You're welcome to join me."

"I, uhm, have to *work* sometime, Tylyn," Bond said. "But I'll see what I can do. Besides, I'm not sure that I can stay away from you now."

She kissed him again, said goodbye, and ran towards the stairs. She turned, waved to him, then went up to the hotel.

Bond began to stroll back toward the casino when he heard a man's voice.

"Hey."

Bond turned to see Gérard standing with his hands on his hips.

"Bonjour, monsieur," Bond said, and attempted to move on. Gérard reached out to grab Bond's arm.

Bond reacted quickly by snatching Gérard's wrist, twisting the man's arm under and around to his back, and applying sufficient pressure to induce a good deal of pain.

"Why don't you mind your own business, my friend?" Bond whispered, then shoved the man to the ground. He then straightened his bow tie, brushed off his jacket, and continued to walk up the stairs to the Place du Casino.

Bond waited at the bar until *Le Gérant* was ready to leave. He and his entourage cashed in the blind man's impressive pile of chips, placed the cash inside a silver metal briefcase, and left the building. Bond followed them at a safe distance as they walked through the gardens to the lift. He noted that Julien would take *Le Gérant*'s arm to guide him only occasionally. Most of the time *Le Gérant* was able to navigate the gardens without help and with no walking cane.

The party took the lift down to the harbour level, where they boarded a luxurious Princess yacht. Bond took a seat at the marina bar and ordered another martini. He watched the yacht's crew come and go, loading various bags from a van that was parked by the dock. After twenty minutes had passed, Bond saw two men appear on deck and walk across the bridge to the dock. One of them was Léon Essinger, and he was carrying the silver metal briefcase. Was it still full of money?

Bond recognised the other man, too, as someone very high up in the Union's bureaucracy. What was his name?

Of course—he was Julius Wilcox. The ugly one. The *commandant* with the reputation for being the cruellest man in the world.

Bond removed his camera from his jacket pocket and snapped a photo of the two men with the Princess in the background. Along with the retinal tattoo, this was further proof that Essinger was in bed with the Union.

He watched as the two men went up the stairs toward the casino, presumably to their car.

Now what? Bond asked himself as he lit a cigarette and stared at the dark sea. There were two courses of action open before him. One was to pursue *Le Gérant,* find out where he went, and ultimately discover where the Union's stronghold was located. The other was to stay close to Essinger and determine what the Union was up to. The latter was easily the more attractive, simply because of Tylyn's presence. Would both paths ultimately converge into one? Did it really matter which way he went?

While anyone else might have flipped a coin to help him decide what to do, Bond merely blew smoke rings in the air and chose to go with his gut.

16
The Movie

Nice was one of Bond's favourite places in France. Considered the capital of the Riviera, it was a fashionable but relaxed city. Standing at the edge of the port, Bond could see one of the relics of this earlier era, the Château d'Anglais, a pink tiered building at the top of Mont Boron. Nice has one of the prettiest harbours in France, mostly because it is clean and surrounded by the hills and brown and yellow apartment houses, the spectacular veterans' monument cut into the cliff facing the water, and the lovely expanse of Mediterranean.

The harbour was busy on this bright and sunny day. Camera crews were set up in front of a dock where the *Starfish*, a large luxury cruise ship, had put into port. A large banner with the words "Pirate Island" had been hung over the side of the ship, announcing to the world that this was Hollywood come to the Mediterranean.

A long table covered by a white cloth had been set up on the boardwalk near the ship's dock. There were microphones on top of the table, awaiting the film's stars and major players. A crowd had already gathered and was becoming impatient.

Bond lit a cigarette and stood apart from the group, keeping his eye peeled for anything unusual. Right on time, a familiar face appeared in front of him.

"I just want you to know, *Mister* Bond, that I had *hell* getting here with your ridiculous contraption," Bertrand Collette said. Once again, the French agent had nicked himself shaving and his face was decorated with two small pieces of tissue.

"Bertrand," Bond said, "have you ever considered using an electric razor?"

"Very funny." He pointed to a small boat at the other end of the harbour. "I secured a boat for our use. It's nothing fancy, but it was still expensive. An Outlaw Sportsboat with a ninety-five-horsepower engine. Will that do?"

"How fast does it go?"

"They told me up to forty-five miles per hour."

"Fine," Bond said. "Thanks. And where's Ariel?"

"She's in the horse trailer I had to rent, along with the *four-by-four* I had to rent to haul her! I must say, I would hate to be the accountant at MI6. He probably suffers from a bad heart."

Bond laughed. "In truth, he does. Now, listen. This press conference is going to begin in a few minutes. I'm going to do my best to get invited along for the first couple of days of shooting. I have a feeling that it won't be too difficult."

Collette shook his head, smiling. "How do you do it, James? She is one of the most desired women in the world! You bastard!"

Bond shrugged and went on. "What I'll need you to do is follow the production company out to sea. I believe they'll be going to Corsica first. Bring Ariel in the boat. I may need her for some reconnaissance. I'll keep in touch by mobile. All right? Am I working you too hard?"

Collette shook his head. "I'm fine. Actually, this is the most excitement I've had since I took on the job for your government. Just do me a favour."

"What's that?"

"Next time you kiss Tylyn, please pretend that you're me."

The conference began soon after Collette went to arrange things with the boat. Léon Essinger, Stuart Laurence, Dan Duling, and Tylyn Mignonne got out of two separate black limousines and were ushered to the press table by security guards. Tylyn looked gorgeous. She was wearing black Capri pants again, and a colourful halter-top that made excellent use of her perfect breasts. As she passed by Bond, she greeted him warmly and gave him a big hug. Essinger, who was right behind her, glowered at them both.

Once they were all seated, a publicity director started the proceedings by introducing the participants and turning over the mike to Essinger.

"Thank you," he said in English. "We are all very excited and happy to be here, for today we begin production of my new film, *Pirate Island.* My good friend Dan Duling is directing from a brilliant script by Robert Cotton. We have a superb team of special-effects people. Our stunt coordinator is one of the best in the business, and he is with us today. Rick? Where are you?"

A stocky man with red curly hair stepped out of the small group of people behind the table. He waved to the cameras. Essinger handed him the microphone. "Rick Fripp, ladies and gentlemen," he said.

Fripp took the microphone and spoke in a thick Cockney accent. "'Ullo, it's a pleasure to be 'ere. I just want to say that *Pirate Island* will have the best damn stunts ever in a motion picture. If there were an Oscar for stuntwork, it would be ours. I guarantee it. You're gonna see things you've never seen before, even in 'Ong Kong movies. And the explosions! Wait until you see the explosions in this picture! We're gonna blow things up real good, I tell ya, real good indeed. 'Alf the bloody budget is going to me and my stuff, so we're puttin' it all on the screen. I'm the best, y'see, that's all there is to it." He handed the mike back to Essinger and stepped away.

What an arrogant ass, Bond thought. The man oozed smarmy egotism, and if anyone on the crew was a possible Union agent, it was most likely him. He had a criminal record, he knew explosives . . .

Stuart Laurence, the lead actor, said a few words next. He was a handsome, virile type, an American who had made a number of popular action films. He was definitely the biggest box office draw connected with the picture. Tylyn spoke after him, saying that she was grateful for the opportunity to be in a big-budget film financed by Hollywood but made by a French production company.

The reporters began to ask questions. The first one was directed at the producer. "Monsieur Essinger, will you ever be going back to America?"

Essinger shrugged. "Hollywood has its charms, but I like working in my native country. Besides, if I went back there, my next picture would have to be a prison movie."

He got some laughs out of that.

"Can you tell us about the screening of your newest picture at Cannes?"

Essinger smiled. "I'm glad you brought that up. *Tsunami Rising* will have its world premiere in eight days' time, the second night of the Cannes Film Festival. We will suspend production on *Pirate Island* for two days so that many of us can attend the screening. Mister Duling directed it, and Mister Laurence is the star. It will be a very special charity event at Cannes, a screening out of competition, of course. I've just had confirmation that Prince Edward and his wife Sophie from the U.K. will be attending, and Princess Caroline of Monaco will come. It will be a splendid evening."

That explained the notations Bond had seen in Essinger's office in Paris!

After the conference, Tylyn found Bond and hugged him again. The cameras flashed, much to Bond's chagrin. "You're coming with us, right?" she asked him.

"I wouldn't miss it," Bond said. "If you'll still have me."

"Are you kidding? Come on, I'll introduce you to Léon."

She led him past the reporters to where Essinger was talking to Fripp.

"Léon," she said, interrupting, "I'd like you to meet Mister Bond."

Essinger poured on the charm. *"Bonjour, monsieur."* He shook Bond's hand. It was firm but a little sweaty. Bond noted that the man's body odour was particularly strong. Or was the smell coming from Fripp?

"So I understand you'll be joining us for a few days?" Essinger asked.

"Yes, and I thank you for allowing me to do so," Bond said.

"Don't thank me," he said, "thank Tylyn. *She*'s the one who wants you here. Have you met your fellow countryman, Mister Fripp?"

Bond shook hands with the stuntman. The grip was strong and vicelike. The freckle-faced Fripp smiled, revealing two missing teeth.

Yes, the body odour was Fripp's.

"How do you do?" Bond asked.

"Fine, mate. It's a pleasure," he replied.

"Tylyn, I suggest you take your friend and get aboard," Essinger said. "We set sail in thirty minutes."

"Let's go," she said to him.

Bond grabbed a small bag that he had brought with him, then walked up the ramp with one of the world's most desirable women.

The *Starfish* was a floating hotel. There were rooms for fifty people, and the cast and crew took all of them. Accompanying the *Starfish* were several smaller craft carrying production equipment, costumes, and other supplies needed to support the production.

She docked at Calvi that evening. Under orders from the

producer, late-night partying was discouraged. First call was to be at the marina early the next morning.

Bond and Tylyn had a quiet dinner in town at one of the many sidewalk cafés off the main street. They had thin, crispy pizzas with a bottle of the local red wine. Afterwards they strolled among the tourist shops, looking at the extensive displays of Corsican knives, T-shirts with the symbol of Corsica, "the moor," on them, and other arts-and-crafts souvenirs.

When they had grown weary of walking through the village, she turned to him without warning and asked that they go back to the ship. *"Faisons l'amour,"* she said.

That night they made love in her cabin aboard the *Starfish,* basking in the warmth of each other's skin. It wasn't as wild and savage as that first time in the woods near Tylyn's horse farm. This time it was languorous and unhurried. The ebbs and tides of their pleasure were extended over several hours before they finally fell asleep in each other's arms, sometime after midnight.

The next morning the crew reported to the set on the harbour at sunrise. Art directors had been working through the night "aging" the marina. Set pieces had been added to create the illusion that the harbour was the handiwork of a future civilisation, after the "apocalypse."

The harbour looked nothing like it had the previous day. All contemporary boats had been removed and replaced by strange, ultramodern seacraft.

"Oh, look, there's my stunt double," said Tylyn as they arrived.

She pointed to a woman who was conversing with Rick Fripp. She was the same height and weight as Tylyn, and she had the same hairstyle, but the face was nothing like her. In fact, Bond thought she had the face of a bulldog.

Bond followed Tylyn over to them.

"Hi, I'm Tylyn," she said.

The woman introduced herself as Betty and shook Tylyn's hand. She also had an English accent. Up close, Bond noticed that Betty was covered in scars.

Rick Fripp said, "Betty's one of the finest stuntwomen in the business. She'd take a bullet if the script called for it."

Betty said, "I *have* taken a bullet. It's not fun."

"Was that for a movie?" Bond asked.

"No, it was when I was arrested for armed robbery," Betty said.

What *was* this? Bond wondered. Did all stunt people have to spend time in prison before they were qualified for their profession?

Filming got under way after Stuart Laurence arrived. The scene involved Stuart's character, a fellow named John Duncan, and Tylyn's character, a woman named Sandra Jurinic, bartering with a boatman. Just as the deal was made, they were attacked by a group of pirates who had surrounded the dock. John and Sandra managed to fight their way out of it, jumped on a boat, and escaped.

There was a bit of dialogue between Stuart, Tylyn, and a character actor playing the part of the boatman. The director, Duling, gave them minimal instruction and made a master shot from a wide angle. After a short break, they did four additional takes with more coverage. Bond watched from the sidelines, paying more attention to Rick Fripp than to the action. In his opinion, though, Tylyn did a more than respectable job in her short scene. She had a commanding presence, a good voice with strong timbre, and she looked absolutely marvellous.

After lunch, the shooting continued with the fight sequence. The "pirates," dressed in an odd mixture of period swashbuckler costuming and space age slickness, were choreographed to jump out of a Trojan horse–type boat docked at the pier. As they took "John" by surprise, all sorts of mayhem erupted, including exploding grenades, fistfights, gunfire, and a hair-raising leap onto a travelling boat. Rick Fripp took over the direction and Bond was fairly impressed with his ingenuity and expertise. Perhaps the fellow was legitimate after all. Had he given up his bad-boy ways for good?

Bond doubted it.

Tylyn rehearsed the link between the earlier dialogue scene and her character's fight sequence. She was allowed to throw a couple of punches and kick one of the pirates, but the more complicated and difficult moves were given to Betty. After the director called "Cut!" Betty would step in, find the mark where Tylyn had been standing, and take over.

When Tylyn was off camera, she stayed close to Bond.

"I wish they'd let me do more," she whispered. "Those moves aren't that difficult. I think I'm more limber than her anyway."

"They can't afford to have you get hurt, Tylyn," Bond said. "Besides, what would we do if you injured your back?"

She jabbed him in the side with her elbow, but she laughed. "Come here, you," she said, pulling his head to hers. She kissed him deeply, in front of everyone.

When she let go, Stuart Laurence said, "I hope you'll kiss *me* like that in our love scene, Tylyn."

Everyone laughed and whistled, and Bond, for the first time in his life, felt a bit embarrassed. He didn't like to flaunt his romances in public. He considered it in bad taste. Still, he was so taken with Tylyn that he went with the spirit of the moment.

Léon Essinger, on the other hand, was not pleased. He muttered to Fripp, "Journalist indeed. I hope he's getting one hell of a story."

In the small Chicago suburb of Buffalo Grove, Illinois, a national fast-food franchise was just changing its menu from breakfast to lunch. A steady crowd had been pouring in since the early hours, and the staff was prepared for the noon rush.

The smell of grilled hamburgers filled the restaurant as a potpourri of people formed queues to order food. There were mothers with their toddlers, men wearing greasy overalls from the road work up the street, and employees from the strip mall shops.

None of them noticed the Japanese man sitting alone, quietly eating his meal. After all, the dining area was already crowded. When he had finished, he slipped out of the chair, deposited his rubbish in the bin, placed his tray on the appropriate counter, and left the premises. He was so inconspicuous that no one saw him leave a paper bag under his table.

The explosion that occurred fifteen minutes later blew out two walls and killed forty-two people.

The FBI spent the following three days at the site, attempting to piece together what had happened. They had very few clues, and not one of the surviving witnesses was able to identify the Japanese man. No one even remembered seeing him. In his preliminary report, the investigator in charge suggested that a radical anti-Semite had placed the bomb, for the village had a large Jewish population. But he was just guessing; there was no evidence to support this hypothesis.

It was a week later when the FBI head office in Quantico, Virginia, received an anonymous note that mentioned the bombing in Illinois. It was written in Japanese, claiming that followers of Goro Yoshida were responsible for the crime. It had been perpetrated as a strike against the "decadent and sin-ridden West."

The note also promised that the best was yet to come.

17

The Trawler

The next day, the production moved out to sea. The art directors had completed the preparation of a major action scene set some five miles out from the northwest coast of Corsica. The focal point of the scene was a large, disabled tanker that was rigged to be aflame when the scenes were shot. Other abandoned vessels were scattered about, floating on the water or halfsubmerged. A high-speed boat chase would occur in and out of this area.

The *Starfish* sailed to the point, followed by the smaller boats carrying the equipment. One particular ship interested Bond, and that was a trawler carrying all of Rick Fripp's equipment. It was the largest of the accessory boats, and it also seemed to be the best guarded. The cast and crew had strict orders to stay away from it, ostensibly because there were explosives aboard. Bond had decided early on that he would have to get a look inside it.

Tylyn had the day off, but they were stuck on the *Starfish*. The cast had the options of swimming in the ship's indoor pool, trying a little scuba diving in the sea, amusing themselves in the ship's cinema or game room, or simply relaxing on deck. Tylyn chose to lounge on deck, and Bond joined her. He watched over the rail as Fripp and his team sped from point to point in speedboats, supervising the rigging of the special effects.

Bond eventually found a moment to move away from Tylyn and make a call on his mobile.

"Bertrand?" he asked when it was answered.

"Hello, James. I hope you slept better than me."

"What do you mean?"

"I'm in this little sports boat, remember? And Ariel isn't the most obliging of roommates. She takes up the entire back end of the boat. There's no place for me!"

"Sorry about that, Bertrand. Listen, we're approximately five miles out from the coast, do you see us?"

"I've been trailing behind, no problem," Collette said. "I'm keeping a safe distance."

"Good. Tonight I'm going to attempt to get over to Fripp's equipment trawler. Get some sleep today and I'll contact you after midnight."

"Over and out, James."

The day progressed uneventfully. Bond and Tylyn sunned themselves on deck and had dinner in the ship's dining room, segregated from the rest of the cast and crew. The rumours were flying about the couple, and Essinger, for one, was not happy about it. But Tylyn and Bond were oblivious to the gossip. Even though Bond was acting on a pretext, he found that he was enraptured with Tylyn. When two people are in the throes of courtship, when joy and sensuality overwhelm them, when they cannot possibly be happy if they are not with their new partner—then they are blind to everything around them.

As they walked back to her cabin after the late meal and bottle of champagne, Bond was lost in his thoughts. He had purposefully sought out Tylyn in order to get close to the film production. His aim had always been to investigate Essinger. However, he had done very little spying and much more lovemaking. In some ways, he felt guilty about

it. Was he doing his job? Was he learning anything new
about the Union? On the other hand, he felt perfectly entitled to enjoy himself with this wonderful girl. While he had
experienced the love of many women, he rarely reciprocated with more than his body. This was one of those uncommon occurrences when he had to admit that he was
falling in love. He was treading on dangerous ground, to be
sure. Once again his brain attempted to warn him that Tylyn was far too famous for him to be involved with. And,
once again, his heart told him otherwise.

When they were in bed, naked and entwined, Tylyn took
his right hand and slowly licked and sucked on each finger.
"You have such strong hands," she said. "Make love to me
with just your hands."

Bond obliged her by first massaging her feet. He kneaded
the heels, pressed hard on the bottoms of the big toes,
rubbed the arches, and gently applied pressure to the soft
spots below her ankles. Carefully, tantalisingly, he worked
his way up each leg, one at a time, working the muscles and
sending waves of pleasure up her spine. Bond purposefully
avoided her sex and moved to her waist and hips. He massaged her there for a while, then navigated to her shoulders.
He took each arm and squeezed the muscles all the way
down to her fingers. He pressed his thumbs into the fleshy
mounds in her palms.

As she moaned softly, closed her eyes, and parted her
lips, he gently massaged her eyebrows and forehead. He
rubbed her temples and cheekbones, then reached back and
pressed on various points in the back of her neck.

Finally, he took a breast in his hand and used his thumb
and forefinger to stimulate the nipple. When it was erect,
he slowly and gently twisted it, pulled it, twisted it, pulled
it . . . Tylyn squirmed under him as he alternated between
the two breasts. Then, keeping his left hand on one breast
and continuing the nipple stimulation, he slid his right hand
down to the mound between her legs. Her hair was soft and

thin there. She was wet, and his second and third fingers
slid inside easily. Tylyn moaned loudly and arched her
back as he used his thumb to circle the erogenous zone at
the top of her vulva. He kept up this rhythm for several
minutes, using her natural lubrication to slide his thumb up
and down and around her clitoris, while keeping his two
fingers deep within her. Tylyn's breath increased, and her
moans became louder until her stomach tensed and she
gasped. Bond felt her contract spasmodically around his
fingers as she writhed on the bed.

Later, after she had caught her breath and calmed down,
she snuggled next to him, and said, "Don't you dare leave,
James. Don't you dare."

She reached down, grasped him, and proceeded to return
the favour.

But leave he did.

Much later, after Tylyn was sleeping soundly, Bond
woke himself with that internal, trained alarm clock that allowed him to do so at any time, day or night. All he had to
do was set his mind to it before falling asleep. It was second nature.

He slipped out of bed without disturbing her and dressed
in his swim trunks, black trousers, and a black T-shirt. He
grabbed the camera and strapped it to his waist, along with
one of the new Walther P99 Tactical Knives that he had
brought along in his bag. It had a five-and-a-half-inch
blade and fitted neatly into a nylon sheath clipped to the
belt. Bond then grabbed the spare key to Tylyn's cabin,
slipped out of the room, and locked the door behind him.
He crept down the hallway, purposefully avoiding the lifts,
and took the stairs to the lower levels of the ship.

There were two gangplanks from the *Starfish*. Because
cast and crew had to be able to get to various points in the
water, a portable dock had been built at the site. Several
speedboats and sports boats were anchored there, ready to

shuttle people to their desired locations. Two gangplanks led from the *Starfish* to the dock, one for passengers, and a larger one for crew with cargo to load or unload.

Bond went for the cargo area, not wishing to be seen by someone who still happened to be up. It was fairly well lit, but completely quiet. There was probably a night watchman somewhere, but Bond didn't see him.

He moved into the room, stepping slowly until he was able to peer around some stacks of cargo near the open loading door. The sky was dark, but the bridge and dock were well lit with strung bulbs. The water splashed and splattered next to the opening, rocking the bridge slightly.

There he was—a lone guard in a security officer's uniform, sleeping in a chair. He was armed, sitting right at the entrance and snoring like a sawmill.

Bond's training had included many hours of practising stealth, and he was particularly adept at it. His instructor had said that Bond "moved like a cat." He was able to walk, run, jump, swim, strike, and kill without making a sound. This ability was essential for someone in his profession to stay alive.

It was this skill that allowed Bond to run and take a shallow dive into the water without waking the guard.

The water was much colder than he had expected, but it felt invigorating. It made his senses come alive, totally alert and ready to work.

He swam slowly but steadily toward the trawler, which he estimated to be about a hundred metres away. No problem. By conserving his strength, he was able to pace himself and arrive at the trawler in ten minutes. When he got there, he found that the trawler had a similar entrance arrangement with a portable loading dock floating outside of the opening.

It was well lit inside, and Bond thought that he heard voices. He climbed out of the water onto the dock, then slithered on his belly to the side of the opening, hugged the wall, and looked inside.

There were two of them. One was a security guard and the other was none other than Rick Fripp. They were laughing about something. Then Bond heard Fripp say that he was going to bed.

Uh-oh, Bond thought, *that means he will be coming this way and hopping into one of the boats tied to the platform.* Bond shrank into the corner between the hull and the platform, but Fripp never showed. Bond looked inside again and saw that Fripp had left the room through a door leading to another part of the trawler. *Where did he go?* Bond wondered. *Wasn't he sleeping on the* Starfish *like everyone else?*

The guard, left alone, began slowly and self-consciously to pace the floor with his hands behind his back, lost in thought.

Like a cheetah, Bond bolted and rushed at the guard, striking him in the back of the neck with a spear hand. The man noiselessly crumpled to the floor.

The place was like a warehouse, with crates and boxes stacked all around. Bond examined each pile and determined that most of it was legitimate production equipment. In one section, set apart by a rope, were crates of explosives. Bond took a look at them, assuring himself that there was nothing illegal there. He noted that they came from an address in Corsica rather than France. The label read "Corse Shipping," which Bond remembered as being listed on the manifests he had seen in Paris.

A door was behind the crates of explosives. He listened at it, hearing nothing. Bond tried to open it, but it was locked. No time to go back to the guard and find the key on him.

He unhooked the camera from his belt and turned the dial to the laser setting. He squatted so that he was eye level to the lock, then aimed the camera lens at it. He pushed the shutter button and the bright white-blue laser shot into the metal. Bond held the camera steady until the lock was melted through. He shut off the laser and tried the door. It opened. Bond replaced the camera on his belt and went inside.

It was a small workshop. Tools were fastened to the wall, and there were two worktables where small pieces of props or machinery were assembled or repaired. On one table were the parts of what looked like a mobile phone. Bond knew that in fact it was some kind of radio transmitter. He leaned in closer to examine its exposed guts and found the tiny antenna.

Bond examined the other table and found two small crates with lids nailed on. The sides were marked with the warnings to "handle with extreme caution." Again, "Corse Shipping" labels were plastered on the tops. Bond unsheathed his knife and used it to pry open one of the crates.

Carefully packed amongst straw and padding were glass containers filled with a white crystalline material. It almost resembled cocaine, but it was much too sparkling for that.

Could this be the CL-20 that Mathis was looking for? The stolen explosives from the French air force base? If so, then they had ingeniously used the film production as a means of smuggling it out of Corsica.

He heard a door creak inside the warehouse. Bond cursed softly and moved back away from the table, flattening himself against the wall by the door.

It opened a few seconds later, and Rick Fripp walked in. Bond didn't hesitate. As soon as the man had cleared the doorway, Bond locked his fists together and brought them down on the back of the stuntman's head. Fripp fell to the floor, groaned, and attempted to rise. Bond kicked him with his bare heel in the back of the head. Fripp jerked forward and dropped into unconsciousness.

Bond took another look around the room to see if there was something he might have missed. Then he had a moment of inspiration.

Why not? He went to Fripp's body and pulled his head up. Bond removed the camera again and held it in front of Fripp's face. With his left hand, Bond opened Fripp's eye and turned on the ophthalmoscope with his right.

Fripp groaned, beginning to stir. What was that bright light in his eye?

Bond focused it into Fripp's pupil and found the retina.

Fripp moved slowly and moaned even louder. The muscles in his face started to resist Bond's fingers. His hands started to move. Any second he would recover sufficiently to be able to knock Bond away. So far, though, Fripp had not focused on Bond's face. He had not been recognised yet.

Come on! Bond willed himself. *Find it! Is it there?* The light scanned the retina, skipping over the red blood vessels and the macula until . . . yes! There it was, the Union tattoo.

Fripp regained his senses enough to groan with confusion. "Huh?" he mumbled as he looked at Bond, unable to focus his eyes.

Bond said, "Don't worry, Mister Fripp, you don't need glasses. I'm afraid your frequent headaches are being caused by something else."

With that, he grabbed Fripp's curly hair and casually banged his head hard on the floor, knocking the man out again.

He stood and left the workroom and stepped quietly past the still-unconscious guard. As quietly as he had come in, Bond dove into the water and swam back to the *Starfish*.

Twenty minutes later, he crawled onto the bridge and peeked into the opening. The guard was still sound asleep. Bond stole past him and out of the cargo area, dripping water and unfortunately leaving a trail.

He moved into the corridor toward the stairwell, and almost made it when a voice stopped him.

"You! What are you doing?"

Bond turned to see none other than Julius Wilcox, the ugly Union killer.

"You're all wet! Who are you? What the hell are you doing?"

"Just felt like a swim," Bond said, then ducked into the stairway. He ran up the stairs to the next level and waited to see if Wilcox would pursue him. There was no sound. Bond kept going until he got to Tylyn's level. Using his key, he swept into her cabin, where she was still sleeping like a princess. Bond removed the wet clothes, hung them over the shower stall, dried off, and got back into bed.

Before falling to sleep, Bond decided that he would phone Collette in the morning and have him position Ariel. He would then prepare to leave the *Starfish* for good. As Julius Wilcox must have recognised him, his life wasn't worth a penny.

"Wake up, you fool," Wilcox said, banging on Essinger's door.

When it opened, Essinger, his eyes full of sleep, said, "What do you want? Do you know what time it is?"

Wilcox pushed Essinger back into his cabin, entered, and shut the door. He pulled Essinger up by the pyjama collar and growled, "Do you know who that is that's sleeping with your wife?"

"Yes, he's some kind of journalist from England."

"What's his *name*?"

"Bond, I think. James Bond."

Wilcox released Essinger, shoving him to the bed.

"What's the matter with you?" Essinger spat.

"That man is an SIS *agent,* you idiot! We know him! We've had dealings with him before."

"You're joking!"

"You fool, why didn't you have him checked out when you learned that your wife was dating him?"

"I didn't really know she was *dating* him," Essinger said huffily. "That was only evident once they got *here*."

"We have to take care of this immediately," Wilcox said.

Essinger sat up. "I'll do it. There will be a lot of dangerous stunt work at the shoot tomorrow—er, today. Accidents can happen. They're inevitable."

Wilcox nodded. They had an understanding.

18

The Getaway

Bond and Tylyn were up bright and early, but the production crew were awake before dawn. The spectacular boat chase for *Pirate Island* would begin filming today, and Rick Fripp had estimated that the entire sequence would take a week to shoot. Tylyn was needed only for close-ups, for Betty would be doing the rough stuff. The rusty tanker had been set on fire and was already burning on "low." On Fripp's orders the gas could be increased, turning the tanker into an inferno.

"It's full of explosives," Tylyn told Bond. "They've been rigging explosives all over the water. It will truly be something to watch."

They stood at the rail of the *Starfish,* observing the preparations. From what Bond could see, last night's little mishap hadn't affected Fripp's working capacity.

The entire "setting" was an area of approximately a kilometre in diameter. Dotted within the setting were the various disabled boats, the tanker, and other obstacles that would figure in the chase. There were four Fountain powerboats that had been outfitted to participate in the scene: two forty-seven-foot and two forty-two-foot Lightning sports boats.

Stuart Laurence joined them, for a stuntman was doing

most of his scenes in the chase as well. "Those are among the best racing boats in the world," he explained. "They bought a fleet of powerboats from Reggie Fountain's company in America—you know, he's a champion boat racer— and then the production designer created those futuristic hulls for them."

"How fast do they go?" Bond asked.

"Usually they're at the seventy to eighty miles per hour mark, but Fountain has outfitted them with extra boost that increases that speed. The two forty-twos have twin engines that'll push the speed up to one hundred and fourteen or so. The other two have triple engines that will kick the speed up to one hundred and twenty," Laurence said. "I'd love to get behind the wheel of one, but the insurance company won't let me. All the shots of me at the helm are done at, what, forty miles an hour?"

"I love speed," Tylyn said. "I've never been in a boat going that fast, but I'm sure I would find it thrilling, not scary."

"It's pretty dangerous," Laurence said. "Look, they've got rescue teams and a medic in ready." He pointed to a group near the portable dock with another powerboat displaying the international Red Cross symbol.

Two bulky men whom Bond recognised as a couple of Essinger's flunkies appeared on the deck and approached them. One of them was Gérard, the fellow he had met in Monte Carlo.

"Monsieur Bond?" Gérard asked.

"Yes?"

"Monsieur Essinger would like a word with you. Could you follow us?"

Aha, here it was. Well, better now than later.

Bond smiled broadly and said, "How nice. Tylyn would you like to accompany me?"

"Just you, monsieur," Gérard said.

Tylyn squeezed his arm. "He probably wants to do an interview after all. Don't worry, he won't bite. Much."

Bond kissed her cheek and went with the men to the lift. Gérard walked in front, while the other man, a rough-looking man with a hawk nose, took up the rear. They took it to one of the higher levels, where Essinger had his luxury cabin. They escorted him to the door, and Hawk Nose knocked. A voice replied, "Come in."

Gérard opened the door and held it for Bond. Bond carefully stepped inside, followed by the two goons. Hawk Nose quickly shut the door behind them.

Two more bodyguards—one wearing a baseball cap and another with an eyepatch—were standing in the middle of the room. They were both holding metal tactical side batons. A blow by one of those with the appropriate force could break a man's skull.

Gérard suddenly grabbed Bond from behind, pinning his arms to his sides. Hawk Nose moved around in front to frisk him, removed the Walther, then punched Bond hard in the stomach. Bond winced but had sufficiently tightened the muscles in his abdomen to lessen the blow. Springing into action, he jumped up and kicked Hawk Nose in the chest, knocking him back into Baseball Cap. Bond then brought back his foot hard, digging his heel into Gérard's shin. Gérard yelped and let go. Bond swung around and spear-handed the man in the neck, crushing the trachea.

A bolt of pain shot through his left shoulder. Eyepatch had hit him with the baton. The pain was so great that Bond fell to his knees, clutching his shoulder with his right hand. Eyepatch raised the baton to strike again, but Bond put his weight on his good arm, levered himself on the floor, and kicked out at Eyepatch's legs. The man lost his balance and fell into Baseball Cap, who was also attempting to hit Bond with his baton.

Hawk Nose leaped onto Bond and began to punch him, but Bond rolled and managed to get on top. He slugged

Hawk Nose hard, then used a split second's reprieve to reach for the PPK that had been dropped on the floor. But Eyepatch was too fast. He kicked the gun out of Bond's hand, sending it flying across the room.

The baton came crashing down again, barely missing Bond's head. He had sensed it coming and moved an inch to the side; but still, the metal rod smashed into his neck and skinned his ear. He fell over but used the momentum to roll toward his gun.

"Hold him!" Eyepatch shouted.

Baseball Cap and Hawk Nose jumped on Bond and attempted to do just that. Bond deftly swept the Walther into his hand and rolled onto his back. He squeezed the trigger twice, blasting holes in Baseball Cap and Hawk Nose's chests. Hawk Nose catapulted into Eyepatch, who caught and held the screaming man in front of him for cover.

Bond fired again. The bullet zipped through Hawk Nose's shoulder but missed Eyepatch. But this gave Bond the time he needed to get to his feet.

Eyepatch, covered in the other man's blood, dropped the baton and reached for a Smith & Wesson that he had beneath his own jacket. Bond shot again, this time putting a bright red hole through Hawk Nose's neck. This one penetrated Eyepatch's shoulder. He yelled and fell back, dropping Hawk Nose and the handgun. Bond didn't stay to see what kind of damage he had done. He turned, jumped over Gérard's body, and ran from the room.

Bond took the stairs two at a time. He emerged on the dining level and darted through the restaurant, where a few of the cast and crew were having coffee. They gasped as they looked up and saw that the side of Bond's head was covered in blood and he was carrying a gun.

Bond heard a gunshot behind him and everyone in the room screamed. Bond leapt behind an empty table and pushed it onto its side. Peering over it, he saw that Eyepatch had followed him down. There was blood sopping through his jacket on his left shoulder, but he was fit enough to fire his gun. Eyepatch shot at the table, blasting a hole through it, too close to Bond's face for comfort.

Bond jumped from the table and ran through swinging double doors into the kitchen. Another bullet shot past him, ricocheting off the wall. As he ran through, Bond swept a dozen metal pots and pans off a counter with his arm, knocking them all over the floor behind him and creating a terrible racket. The cook was horrified and shouted something to him in French. Bond went out the back exit just as Eyepatch burst in, hampered by the clutter on the floor.

As he came out of the kitchen, Bond ran into none other than Tylyn.

"James?" she said, panicked. "What was that noise? My God, your face! What's wrong?"

But he kept running.

"James!" she called after him.

He reached the deck rail and looked over it, down to a lower level. It wasn't too far, so he climbed over it. Before dropping down, he met Tylyn's eyes and said, "I'm sorry. Someday I'll explain."

Bond let go of the rail and dropped twenty feet to the next deck, crashing into a chair to break his fall and startling several people who were reclining in the sun. He got to his feet and rolled, then got up to run again. Tylyn ran to the rail above and called to him. "James!"

Then Julius Wilcox appeared from nowhere and was at her side, aiming a gun at the running figure on the deck below.

Tylyn, enraged, pushed the ugly brute. "What are you *doing*?" Wilcox reacted with a snarl and shoved her to the deck.

Bond ran to the edge and looked down at the water below. The portable dock was on this side, thank God. He climbed over the rail and prepared to dive into the Mediterranean. He holstered his gun and tore off his jacket.

Wilcox aimed and fired just as Bond performed a neat swan dive, sailing forty feet to the water.

He swam hard for the dock. Already the guards had been alerted and were swarming down the *Starfish*'s various staircases and ramps, ready to intercept Bond. But he made it to the dock first. He climbed out of the water, ran to the first 47 Lightning powerboat, untied it, and jumped in. It took him a few seconds to examine the controls and start the engine.

The boat's engines created a huge wake and a tremendous roar that could be heard over the entire setting. Bond manoeuvred the boat away from the dock and steered it towards Corsica. However, two thirty-eight-foot Lightning sports boats manned by guards came around the tanker and were headed in his direction. Bond made a hook, turning the boat sharply to the left. He sped back toward the centre of the setting, where the director and stunt crew were just beginning to shoot part of the chase.

Duling called "Action!" as Rick Fripp sat at the controls inside a 42 Lightning sports boat near the burning tanker. He had access to the trigger mechanisms for every explosive he had planted. Two "pirates" in costumed 42 Lightnings sped out from another direction and started to chase a disguised 29 Fever piloted by Betty and Stuart Laurence's stunt double.

The guards made it to the dock and jumped into two of the remaining boats. They revved up noisily and took off after Bond, who was headed directly for the centre of the action.

Bond bore down on the accelerator, increasing his speed to almost a hundred miles per hour, sped into the scene, and started to gain on Betty's boat.

Duling shouted, "Hey! What's going on? Who is that?"

The guards' boats jumped into view and then the gunfire began. Bullets shot across the water, breaking the surface with dozens of jabbing spurts.

"This wasn't in the rehearsal!" Duling shouted into his walkie-talkie.

The assistant director asked if he wanted to cut.

Duling replied, "No! Keep the cameras rolling. This looks great!"

Bond sped forward, overtaking Betty's boat, but it wasn't long before Wilcox and one of the guards appeared in another powerboat. They zoomed in from the side, seemingly out of nowhere. Wilcox was now armed with a submachine gun. He let loose a barrage of ammunition at Bond's craft, shooting several holes in the side and into the engines. The boat kept going, though, straight for one of the "derelict" boats that had been constructed for the movie. Bond increased his speed and prayed that he could remember how to perform a particular manoeuvre. He turned the wheel and his boat did a marvellous barrel roll, jumping out of the water and somersaulting at high speed in midair. The Lightning barely missed the top of the obstacle and then landed on its hull with a splash.

Everyone on the *Starfish,* who had by now appeared on the various decks to watch the scene, applauded. What a terrific stunt! Who was that driver? Excellent action choreography! It looked so real!

Fripp, now in communication with Wilcox by walkie-talkie, barked instructions to his pyrotechnics people, stationed in small rowboats at various stages in the setting.

"Yes, damn it!" Fripp shouted. "Fire them now! I don't care if he's too close!"

Bond steered his boat towards one of the obstacles, hoping that it would provide some cover from the gunfire. He got within thirty metres of it, when it suddenly exploded with intense force. Bond hit the deck as shrapnel and burning debris flew over his head. Without looking he made another hook to the right so that the boat wouldn't sail right into the burning mess. Once he was clear, he stood and gained control of the boat again.

Fripp shouted more orders into his walkie-talkie. Explosives had been rigged in the water at various intervals to simulate cannonballs hitting the surface. These began to go off as Bond sped over them.

Christ! Bond thought. *It's like going over a minefield.* He had to get out of the setting as quickly as possible, but he was surrounded on all sides now. The other boats were closing in, and there was nowhere else to go.

"Ha!" Wilcox shouted. "We've got him now."

Bond looked around for an escape route. The only possible place to go was into the burning tanker. Bond turned the boat towards it, prayed that Collette had followed his instructions, and stepped on the gas. The engines roared as the boat shot toward the tanker.

"This is better than I had hoped!" Wilcox said. Fripp thought the same thing, for he shouted more orders into his walkie-talkie.

"Yes! Blow the tanker! Blow it now!" Wilcox yelled.

Fripp pulled the lever.

Bond knew that he had to reach full speed before attempting this particular move, and he didn't have a lot of room to do so. He accelerated, gripped the wheel, and concentrated on the water ahead of him. The speedometer was at 112. The tanker was metres away.

No time left. It had to be now.

Bond hit a wave with perfect timing and performed a flawless "stuff," a stunt in which a boat dives completely under the water.

The Lightning disappeared under the surface just as the tanker blew to pieces. It was a deafening explosion, causing all the spectators in the area to flinch and hold their ears. A huge fireball erupted as the tanker broke into a dozen pieces. Monstrous clouds of black smoke poured out of the wreckage.

Tylyn, aboard the *Starfish,* screamed as she saw Bond's boat vanish into that maelstrom. The other people gasped,

certain that they had just seen a stuntman killed in action.
Dan Duling was aghast and speechless. The tanker was destroyed and he never got the right shot. And who *was* that
guy in the boat?

The next ten minutes were pure chaos. The rescue boat
and medic sped to the scene to look for Bond, but they
found nothing. His Lightning surfaced on the other side of
the tanker, but Bond wasn't in it. The dive underwater had
saved the craft from being destroyed, but it had been
streaked and scraped by burning metal.

They searched for thirty minutes. Bond's body was
nowhere to be found. Had he been vaporised in the blast?

Wilcox pulled his boat over to where Fripp was stationed.

"Do you think that got him?" Fripp asked the ugly man.

"It looks like it, doesn't it?" Wilcox replied. "Let's keep
looking and make sure."

A half hour later, Essinger had Wilcox in his office aboard
the *Starfish.*

"What the *hell* gave you the authority to blow up my
tanker? We *needed* that for the goddamned *movie!*" Essinger said through clenched teeth.

"Relax," Wilcox said. "The Union will cover your costs.
We've been after that guy for a long time. Besides, I
thought you said that *you* were going to take care of him."

Essinger fumed. "He . . . he got the better of my men."

"Apparently."

"It seems he got away from *you,* too, Wilcox," Essinger
spat.

Wilcox didn't reply. He merely stepped close to Essinger
and clutched the man around the neck with a strong grip.
He squeezed, cutting off Essinger's oxygen and sending
bolts of pain into his throat.

"Listen, friend," Wilcox whispered. "Don't *ever* talk to

me like that again. If you do, I'll rip out your larynx and make you eat it. Do we understand each other?"

Choking and turning blue, Essinger managed to nod.

"I can't hear you."

"Ye—es—ss!" Essinger stammered.

Wilcox released him, and the producer fell to his knees. The ugly man moved away and heard commotion in the corridor outside.

"Get up, someone's coming," he said. "Be cool, Essinger."

Wilcox managed to stand just as Tylyn, near hysterics, burst into the cabin.

"What the *hell* is going on?" she demanded. "James is dead! Your goons just *killed* him!"

Essinger, a consummate showman, did his best to assume a calm demeanour, cleared his throat, and said, "My 'goons,' as you call them, were merely trying to catch him, darling. I've been meaning to tell you something about your friend, Mister Bond."

Tylyn couldn't comprehend her husband's seemingly unconcerned attitude.

"What the hell are you *talking* about?"

He had to clear his throat and rub it again. "You see, dear," Essinger continued, "Mister Bond isn't a journalist. He never was."

"What?" she snapped.

"He's a criminal, Tylyn." He held her by the shoulders, attempting to talk sense into her. "He wanted to sabotage our production. He's one of those industrial spies who work for other movie companies. He was hired to cause *Pirate Island* to shut down. That's why he got close to you—so he could be in proximity to inflict a great deal of damage. I just got off the phone with Rick. He says that the tanker is destroyed and we never got the shot we needed for the movie. That's going to cost us a lot of money."

"I don't believe you!" she screamed. She turned to

Wilcox. "And *you*! Who the hell *are* you?" She turned back to her husband. "Who *is* this man, Léon? Why has he been hanging around you so much? He doesn't *work* for you, does he?"

"Mister Wilcox is a . . . financial advisor," Essinger said. "Now, darling, we must try to forget this and get on with making a movie."

"To *hell* with your movie!" Tylyn shouted. "James is *dead*!"

Essinger almost shrugged. "I know, it's a pity. Luckily we're insured. But that will teach the other studios not to go messing with Léon Essinger, eh, darling?"

"You're a liar!" she said with venom, struggling to get out of his grasp.

"It's true, Tylyn," he said. "The man was a killer. A hired gun. Whatever he promised you or told you, they were all lies. I'm sorry."

Tylyn broke away from him, put her arms around herself, and sobbed. Essinger moved toward her to comfort her, but she backed away, shouting, "Leave me alone!" She turned and ran out, tears streaming down her face.

After a moment, Wilcox said, "She could hurt us."

Essinger spat, "She won't be with us long."

Wilcox paused before suggesting, "You might need to make sure that she attends the screening in Cannes. At this point there's no guarantee that she will."

Essinger, still upset about Wilcox's threat, the loss of the tanker, and his wife's reaction to the spy's death, merely nodded.

"I've already taken care of that," he said.

As soon as the boat dived beneath the tanker, Bond used his arms and legs to springboard his body out of the boat. The trick was to stay suspended in the water so that the boat passed beneath his body without hurting him. Then, as soon as it was clear, he had to dive as deeply as he could to avoid the impact of the blast.

An impact it was. The force of the explosion was like a sledgehammer, slamming into Bond with a fist of fury. Completely dazed, he floated motionless for a few seconds, then began to drift up towards the mayhem.

Snap out of it! Bond shouted to himself. *Swim!*

Summoning every ounce of strength in his battered body, Bond willed himself to paddle with his arms to halt his ascent. Then he straightened, aimed his nose downward, and swam towards the bottom of the sea.

Bond opened his eyes to the stinging, murky water. He swam harder, forcing his body to work on automatic while he concentrated on finding what Collette had conveniently dropped in the water on the perimeter of the setting just before sunrise.

He reckoned that it was a good forty or fifty metres to the landmark, or rather, the watermark. A buoy floated inconspicuously at the perimeter on the north end of the setting, and that's where he and Collette had decided would be the safest place for Collette to bring his boat and get as close as possible to the *Starfish*.

Bond's lungs were burning like hell. How long had he been holding his breath? A minute or two? He had to have air soon. But was he still too close to the tanker?

When he thought that he had swum at least twenty metres away, Bond had no choice but to risk it. He surfaced and gulped a glorious breath of air and immediately dived back underwater. Bond hoped everyone would be focused on the tanker and would not have noticed him.

The oxygen energised him. He kept swimming toward the buoy, confident now that he would make it. The tide was much stronger than he had expected, but with a steady stroke he eventually reached the target. When he was able to grasp the side of the buoy, Bond surfaced again and took some breaths. Resting momentarily, he looked back at the chaos. Boats were zipping this way and that, the perimeter was covered in black smoke, and he could hear a lot of shouting.

How would he explain this to Tylyn? he wondered. Would he ever see her again and *have* a chance to explain?

Possibly not, thought Bond. And what good had he accomplished? What had he learned? Not much, only that they were carrying what he believed to be the stolen CL-20. Reporting it to the authorities was useless, for the Union would surely take care to hide it better. They were obviously attempting to smuggle it somewhere, probably into France. What he needed to do was regroup and formulate a new plan of attack. He had to discover what they were up to before he could credibly blow any whistles.

With a heavy heart, he turned his back on the destruction and began to work his way around the buoy with his hands until he was on the side facing the open sea. There, tied onto one of the buoy's handholds, was a rope, pulled taut into the water. The weight at the other end was not so much as to topple the buoy. Bond took another breath and descended the rope, hand over hand, until he came to the magnificent machine tied at the bottom.

Ariel was a K-10 hydrospeeder, an innovative self-propelled diver propulsion unit that had recently been developed in America and was now being sold as an aquatic novelty to Caribbean holiday resorts. Bond had first seen one in Belize, where a diving colleague named Gaz Cooper sold and demonstrated them. Q Branch had licensed the technology and built a hydrospeeder with a few extras.

It was basically an underwater bicycle with a built-in rebreathing system. It was the size of a small motorcycle, but with no wheels. Instead it had two short wings that jutted out near the bow. The two motors were aft. The diver sat on a curved seat and leaned forward until his chest was resting on the top of the hydrospeeder.

Bond took the rebreather first and inserted it into his

mouth. The lovely oxygen flowed when he turned the valve. Collette had been thoughtful enough to leave a face-mask tied to one of the controls. Bond put that on next, doing his best to flush out the water. Then he sat on the vehicle and started it. Finally, he untied the rope and he was off.

A man riding a hydrospeeder could stay underwater for nearly two hours. Seated on the vehicle, a diver's body hydrodynamically completed the form of its design as his hands were used to manipulate the independently operated wings that controlled pitch and roll. The feet pushed on independent motor controls for the left and right motors, varying the yaw and speed. Embedded in the hydrospeeder was an oxygen tank. The vehicle had an electrical engine, delivering about two thousand watts for two hours. Dive data were available at a glance on the dashboard, which was flat in front of the diver's face.

Normally, it could travel up to five or six knots, but Major Boothroyd had increased that speed to ten with the aid of a turbobooster he had installed in between the two original motors. Other extras included twin harpoon guns in the front, a mechanism for releasing small mines in the water below the vehicle, smoke screen capability, superior high-intensity headlamps, and a second rebreather, although the hydrospeeder wasn't really built for two. Like most of the vehicles made by Q Branch, Ariel was also equipped with her own tracking signal and a self-destruct feature.

Bond studied the compass on the dashboard and the blinking light that marked the GPS coordinate of his destination. It would take him an hour to get there.

The hydrospeeder gracefully moved through the water, some fifty feet below the surface. It was an exhilarating feeling. He had enjoyed the thrill when he had first tested the hydrospeeder in Q Branch's tank at MI6. Now, out here in the wide-open sea, he was able to give her a full workout. He could roll and spin, dive up or down, or ascend and descend in a straight vertical line.

There were plenty of fish around, mostly grouper and painted comber, gliding along with Bond over the sponges that grew plentifully on the surfaces of rocks. The famous Corsican vibrant red coral was also abundant in the area. The bottom was covered with various types of seaweed. Some of it was brown, a lot of it was green, and a portion was red. As always, the alien landscape of an underwater vista never failed to mesmerise Bond. He was in his element.

Two dentex, carnivorous fish related to the sargo, appeared and swam behind Bond. Although they probably weren't dangerous, he didn't want to take the chance of one becoming curious and taking a bite out of him. He pushed a button, and dark black smoke poured out of the hydrospeeder's tail. It was enough to scare off the fish.

The vehicle sped out of the dark cloud and sailed over a bed of ascidians, which resembled soft tubes and grew in violet and red with a little black here and there. They undulated back and forth, suggestively beckoning to Bond with their oval, open lips.

The GPS signal indicated that he was close. Bond began his ascent slowly, for even on a hydrospeeder, a diver had to compensate for the changes in pressure. On the way up, a beautiful rainbow wrasse swam near him and studied him curiously. It seemed to be congratulating him for making it. Eventually Bond saw the dark shape of Collette's boat above him and rose to the surface.

19

The Infiltration

Nigel Smith looked at the piece of mail that had arrived for Bond. The envelope was addressed, by hand, to "Commander James Bond." Whoever had written it had also used 007's subtle security code—a semicolon after the name and commas after every line in the address except the last one. This meant that the contents were "friendly" and/or "personal" and went straight to the addressee, going through only the obligatory X ray upon its arrival in the post at MI6 without being opened.

There was no return address, save for a single "M" with a circle around it.

Nigel knew that it wasn't from M. Could it be . . . ?

He was dying to open it but thought it best to contact 007 first. Nigel picked up the phone and dialled Bond's mobile number.

It went unanswered.

Bond had lost his mobile during his getaway from the film set. He was lucky to have his Walther, the Q Branch camera, and the clothes on his back.

After loading Ariel onto the Outlaw and docking at Calvi, he and Collette spent the remainder of the afternoon resting at the Hotel Corsica, coincidentally the same establishment where René Mathis had stayed. Its location on the outskirts of town suited Bond nicely, just as it had his French cohort.

"Bertrand, let me borrow your phone, would you?" Bond asked after he had napped, showered, and put on some clothes that Collette had brought with him. Collette tossed his mobile to him and Bond dialled MI6.

Nigel was very relieved to hear from him.

"I was beginning to wonder what had happened to you," he said. "I was just about to leave the office."

"Everything is fine, I think. Bertrand Collette and I are in Calvi trying to decide how to proceed."

"Well, perhaps I have something that will help you. You have a letter here from an 'M,' and it's not our inimitable chief. It was sent from Corsica, but it somehow got lost in the mail and just arrived here today."

"Christ, that's from Mathis!" Bond said. "What does it say?"

Nigel opened it and read it aloud. "'James—I have tracked our friend to Corsica. I am going today to see if I can find his home. Corse Shipping near St. Florent is full of cobwebs, especially the cave below the cliff. If you do not hear from me in a few days, find the man they call the Sailor at the marina in Calvi. René.' "

"Full of cobwebs" was a code that meant the place was dirty—that is, occupied by the opposition.

"What is the date on the letter?" Bond asked.

"Hmmm . . . over two weeks ago."

"Oh, no. Thanks, Nigel. I'm going to look into this."

After he rang off, Bond and Collette looked at a map and pinpointed St. Florent and the best way to approach it.

"Corse Shipping figures in whatever Essinger is doing with the Union," Bond said. "The firm was mentioned in documents I found at his office in Paris. They've been providing catering services and the like. I also saw the name stamped on the crates containing explosives for the film in

Fripp's trawler. If that was really the stolen CL-20 I found there, then Corse Shipping had its hands on that, too. I think we should take a look at the place."

"I figure we can take the boat and approach the place by sea, what do you think?"

"We'll go tonight, after dark," Bond said. "But first there's a man at the marina I have to see."

Bond went alone to the harbour. He asked someone where he might find "the Sailor," and the man pointed to a sail-boat tied to the opposite side of the dock. Bond went over there and found the Sailor asleep on his boat.

"Pardon?" Bond asked, waking him.

"Huh? Who is it?"

Bond explained that he was looking for a Frenchman who may have befriended him a few days ago.

"Oh yes, Monsieur Mathis," the Sailor said, climbing out of the boat and standing on the dock. "Would you like to buy me dinner, too?"

Bond shrugged. Why not? "If you can help me, I'd be happy to do so."

Over pastis—a strong anise-flavoured aperitif—and a couple of pizzas the Sailor explained that Mathis had been asking about Emile Cirendini and the mysterious blind man known as Pierre Rodiac. The Sailor said that Mathis had traced Rodiac to Sartène and had gone down that way over two weeks ago. He hadn't heard from Mathis since.

"Did he say anything about Corse Shipping?" Bond asked.

"Apparently this Rodiac fellow has dealings with Emile Cirendini. Cirendini owns the boat Rodiac uses to travel to the mainland." He pointed to the Princess. "That's it. I know that your friend went to Corse Shipping to snoop around. I don't know what he found."

Bond bought the man a bottle of wine and bid his *adieu*.

• • •

After the sun set, Bond and Collette took the Outlaw back out to sea and sailed east towards Cap Corse. They passed St. Florent and soon found Corse Shipping on the coast. It was a forbidding place, perched high up near the coastal highway.

"There doesn't seem to be much activity right now," Bond said, studying the coastline with binoculars. "All the lights are off."

Then he saw the cave.

"Bertrand, pull in a little closer. Do you see that cave there?"

Collette threw the engine into gear and headed to shore. "That must be what Mathis was talking about. I'm taking Ariel into it," Bond said.

Collette stopped some fifty metres out, dropped anchor, and cut the lights. It took them a few minutes to drop the hydrospeeder in the water and for Bond to change into a black wetsuit. He put on the face mask and jumped in.

"If I'm not back in an hour, call the marines," Bond said.

He climbed aboard Ariel and started the engine. Breathing regularly with the self-contained oxygen unit, Bond dived, manipulated the controls, and began travelling towards the cave some fifteen feet below the surface.

The inside of the cave was dark and ominous when he brought Ariel to the surface. Bond flicked on the high-intensity headlamps and pointed the hydrospeeder at the back of the cavern. At first glance, it appeared to be a natural cave big enough for a small tugboat. After a bend in the tunnel, the water passed between two stalagmites that stood like sentinels guarding whatever was beyond. Keeping low, Bond noticed that some machinery had been attached to the stalagmites. They were electric eyes, placed four feet above the surface. Trespassers would be caught before they could go any further. Bond submerged again and propelled Ariel forward through the passageway until he came to a larger cavern that was probably man-made.

Sure enough, there was a dock there. Several speedboats were tied to it, as well as a craft that looked similar to a coast guard's patrol boat, but without markings.

Bond tied Ariel to a post on the dock and climbed up. Barefoot, but armed with his gun in a waterproof holster, his knife, and the camera, Bond stepped across the dock to metal doors that presumably led to a lift. There was an elaborate alarm system incorporated in the doors, so he pulled the camera from his belt and activated the laser once again.

He aimed it at the alarm box and made two quick cuts across the mechanism, burning it out and deactivating it. Bond replaced the camera and tried the doors. They opened freely.

A wide hallway led to a freight lift. It was open cage style, with a sliding mesh gate for a door. How noisy would it be? Bond slid open the gate, got inside, and pressed the top button. The machinery whirred and clanged, but it wasn't as loud as he had feared. Still, it was possible that the noise would alert someone.

He took the lift to the top level, deep inside the Corse Shipping complex. It opened to the warehouse, which was full of crates, boxes, and barrels. He stepped out and got his bearings. He could see the outside lift, the one that faced the sea, on the other side of the warehouse. To his right he found the exit leading to the complex offices. He peeked into the brightly lit corridor and heard voices somewhere down the hall. Should he risk going farther?

Careful not to make a sound, Bond inched down the corridor until he found the office the voices were coming from. Next to it was another office. Bond listened at the door, heard nothing, tried the knob, and opened it.

There was no one in the office. It contained a worktable and a desk. Bond switched on the light and locked the door behind him. He removed the camera from his belt again and pulled out the two earpieces that were attached to thin, flexible tubes. Bond flicked a switch on the bottom of the camera, out of which he pulled a stethoscope-like suction cup, also attached to a flexible tube. He licked the cup and stuck it to the wall, then put the earpieces in his ears.

He could hear the conversation clearly, and, in fact, recognised one of the voices.

"Now that the bastard is dead, we don't have anything to worry about," Julius Wilcox said. "What a mess. They'll have to completely rebuild that damn tanker and film the sequence all over again. Essinger is pretty upset. But at least we got rid of the spy."

"Let's hope so. We've come too far to abort the project," the other man said. Emile Cirendini, perhaps?

"Oh, we won't abort, believe me. Once *Le Gérant* accepts a client's money, he goes through with the project, no matter how risky. Besides, this one will be a piece of cake. All of the parts are coming together nicely. Are you on schedule?"

"As soon as the detonator is completed, we'll be ready," Cirendini said. "I'll have the entire assembly shipped out by the usual method to the studios in Nice."

"Excellent," Wilcox said.

"Have you spoken to *Le Gérant*?"

"Yes, a few minutes ago. I'm sure he'll be staying put at his house until the project is completed."

"If you ask me, he's been very careless lately."

"How do you mean?" Wilcox asked.

"Gambling at the casino in Monte Carlo. Going out in public. It's not going to be long before someone figures out who he is."

"*Le Gérant* can do whatever the hell he wants to do. Nothing the Union have ever done can be traced back to him. He's perfectly clean. The man's a goddamned genius."

Bond glanced around the room while he listened. On the floor next to the worktable was a stack of large film cans, the kind that contained 35mm motion picture prints. Bond took a look inside the top one and saw that it was empty. Next to these were empty pressurised soft-drink canisters, the kind seen in bars with hoses attached to them. A means of smuggling, perhaps? On top of the worktable was an odd-looking device that Bond was almost positive was the detonator Cirendini was talking about. By examining the pieces and the various small boxes that the parts came in, Bond determined that the device contained a servo receiver connected to an electric detonator manufactured by a Canadian company. It was a high-strength unit designed for use in explosive initiation applications where there was no need for a delay between charges.

It was something that anyone could purchase over the Internet.

What the hell were they planning to blow up? What was the significance of the film cans? What about the soft-drink canisters? This must all be related to the radio transmitter he had seen on Fripp's trawler. Was Fripp assembling the transmitter to these devices, the receiver, and detonator?

Bond was tempted to smash the pieces with the butt of his gun then and there, but he froze when he heard a knock next door.

"What?" he heard Cirendini ask. There was activity outside the door.

"Monsieur, there is a strange boat not far from the cave. It's been there for half an hour."

Damn! They've seen Collette's boat.

"Well, get out there and find out who it is. Use your discretion," Cirendini said. "If you think that it's warranted, kill whoever it is and get rid of the boat."

"Yes, sir."

No time to lose. Bond pulled the suction cup from the wall, replaced the earpieces, and hooked the camera back on his belt. He listened at the door and waited until he heard the guards walk away.

The corridor was clear. Bond slipped out of the office and made his way back to the warehouse without being detected. He carefully looked inside the swinging doors before entering and saw that three guards inside were blocking his way to the lift.

So far, no one knew that he was there. If he could cause a diversion . . . ?

Bond drew his gun and peered inside again. Along one wall were stacks of more soft-drink dispenser tanks. Perhaps these were full of pressurised soda? Bond took a bead and fired. One of the tanks burst, spewing cola in a steady, high-pressure stream.

The guards immediately snapped out of their reverie. One of them went over to the tanks to see what had happened. The two others walked towards the swinging doors, certain that the gunshot had come from that direction. As soon as they were two feet from the doors, Bond swung them open as hard as he could, hitting them both in the face. Bond spun inside, elbowed one guard in the stomach, leaned to the side, and kicked the other guard in the chest. He then grabbed hold of the first guard's arm and threw the man over his back into the second guard. They toppled to the floor.

Bond ran to the lift before the third guard could stop him. He got into the cage, slammed the gate shut, and pushed the button for the lower level. The third guard drew a handgun and fired down into the lift as it descended. Bond hugged the metal wall, just beyond the guard's aim. In just a few seconds, the lift had disappeared to a lower level.

Then the alarms went off.

When the lift got to the bottom, Bond could see several guards lining the corridor that led to the cave-dock. Luckily, they were facing the opposite direction and the alarms had covered the noise of the lift descending. Nevertheless, it was a thirty-foot gauntlet that he had to run through in order to get out of the place.

Bond waited a few seconds before opening the gate. He knew that timing was everything. Gun in hand, he sprang out of the lift and ran like the devil, firing shots above the guards' heads. The men immediately jumped for cover behind the boxes and crates that lined the corridor, too surprised to react in any other way. By the time Bond got to the door he had disarmed earlier, one of the guards had found the wherewithal to fire back. Bullets zinged around Bond's head, boring holes into the metal door. He dropped to the floor, rolled, and shot back at the several guards running towards him. He hit the two men in front and they fell back into the others. That gave Bond the time he needed to get to his feet and open the door.

The "patrol boat" was gone. Bond rushed to the edge of the dock and was relieved to see that no one had discovered Ariel tied there underwater. He quickly got aboard, untied her, and submerged.

Bond used minimal lighting to navigate his way out of the cave and into the open sea. Once he was clear of the cavern, he cut the lights and surfaced.

Oh no! Cirendini's patrol boat was alongside Collette's Outlaw, which was on fire and sinking fast. He heard the men on the patrol boat whooping and hollering as a burning figure, obviously bound, fell over the side of the Outlaw into the water.

Bond quickly dove again and sped at top speed toward the wreckage. It took him nearly three minutes—far too long, he feared. He put on the high-intensity lamps and swerved the hydrospeeder back and forth, searching frantically for Collette's body.

There! The lifeless figure was floating towards the bottom, a weight attached to his feet. His arms were bound behind his back. When Bond got close enough with the vehicle, the illumination revealed that his friend was badly burned.

Bond cut the engine and slipped off Ariel so that he could grab Collette. He immediately shoved the second rebreather into the Frenchman's mouth. Bond laid him over the hydrospeeder, started her up, and began to ascend.

When they broke the surface, Bond did his best to revive Collette. He removed the rebreather and laid Collette on his back over the vehicle. He then performed mouth-to-mouth resuscitation and CPR.

"Come on, Bertrand!" he whispered. Bond glanced up and saw that the patrol boat was headed back to the cave. They hadn't seen him. The burning Outlaw had all but sunk completely.

Bond continued working on Collette for another three minutes, but his friend showed no signs of life.

Damn it! You're alive! I know it!

Bond blocked out everything around him and concentrated fully on Collette. He didn't believe in miracles, but he prayed for one now.

Was yet another ally going to die while serving with him? Bond had seen it happen too many times. It seemed to be a curse. He brought death wherever he went, which was why he preferred to work alone.

Come on, damn it!

When Collette unexpectedly coughed up water, Bond thought that there might really be a God.

20

The Second Visit

Bond ditched Ariel in the bay off St. Florent and rode in the ambulance with Collette back to Calvi. Although the coastal port didn't contain a hospital, it had an emergency treatment centre affiliated with the main hospital in Bastia. The Antenne Médicale d'Urgence handled all but the worst cases on site; otherwise a patient would be sent to Bastia by helicopter or ambulance. It was a small facility with three patient rooms, a treatment room, and an administration office.

A doctor and nurse took Collette into the treatment room and remained there for nearly an hour. Bond paced the small waiting area, feeling ridiculously helpless. Finally, the doctor emerged and approached Bond as Collette was wheeled into one of the patient rooms.

"Your friend has suffered many second-degree burns and a few third-degree burns. We've done what we can tonight, but he'll have to go to Bastia in the morning and spend some time in their burn ward," the doctor said.

"But his chances of recovery are good?" Bond asked.

"Yes, after some skin grafting and rehabilitation. He's very lucky to be alive."

"Should he go to Bastia tonight?"

The doctor shook his head. "It wouldn't do him much

good to move him again so soon. We call this the eighth floor of the Bastia Hospital. Our care here is just as good, and we can watch him tonight. Why don't you go home and get some sleep, monsieur? We'll be transferring him tomorrow around eight o'clock. You can check with the Bastia Hospital staff after eleven to see which room he's in."

"Thank you," Bond said. "May I see him?"

"He's heavily sedated," the doctor said. "But I suppose it's all right. If he's asleep, don't disturb him."

Bond went into the room, which looked like any other hospital room in the world. Bertrand Collette was on his back, legs and arms bare and suspended. The skin was ugly and charred and was covered with a greasy ointment. His face was covered in bandages.

He bent over Collette's face and thought that he might be asleep when the Frenchman whispered, "The things I do for England . . ."

Bond laughed softly. "I'll make sure you get an O.B.E. for this, Bertrand."

Collette groaned and said, "They really got me, didn't they, James?"

"It's not so bad," Bond said. "The doctor says you'll recover completely. It'll take some time, but you'll be fine."

"And I'll look like the Phantom of the Opera. What will people say?"

Bond said, "Just tell them that you cut yourself shaving."

That made Collette laugh.

"I'm going back to the hotel," Bond said. "Then I suppose I'll go to Sartène tomorrow. I'll give you a call when I can."

"James?"

"Yes?"

"Merci."

Bond patted the top of Collette's head and left the room.

• • •

It was nearly two in the morning when Bond got back to the Hotel Corsica. Weary and discouraged, he took the stairs to the second floor and made his way to his room. As he put the key card into the lock, though, he sensed that something was amiss. Years of experience had fabricated in him a kind of organic radar, something inexplicable that pricked his nerves whenever trouble was around the corner—or behind a door.

Bond drew the Walther, dropped to a squatting position, and flung it open.

Marc-Ange Draco sat facing him, an open bottle of bourbon at his side.

"Marc-Ange!" Bond said, standing. "I might have shot you."

"No, you wouldn't have," Draco said. "Your reflexes are too good. You would have seen that it was me before you pulled the trigger. Just as you did. Come inside."

Bond entered and shut the door. They were alone.

"Marc-Ange, what the hell?" Bond asked, holstering the Walther.

"Sit down, James," Draco said. "Have a drink with me. I'm well ahead of you. I think you need one, too, no?"

"As a matter of fact," Bond said, pulling up a chair. They sat around the coffee table that was a piece of standard furniture for the rooms.

Draco poured a tall glass of bourbon for Bond and handed it to him. *"Salute,"* he said, and they clicked glasses.

After the lovely fire coated his throat, Bond asked, "Now tell me, Marc-Ange, how did you find me?"

"Tsk-tsk," Draco said. "Surely by now you know that I have eyes and ears all over this island. There are some people, you know, who believe that you are dead."

"Mmm," Bond said, taking another sip. "I suppose it won't be long before they realise that I'm not."

"I think you can bet on that. I apologise, James, but it appears that you were right about Léon Essinger. He *is* involved with the Union."

Bond said nothing.

"But I still think that he's not your primary concern," Draco said. "Our friend, *Le Gérant,* is hiding somewhere in the vicinity of Sartène."

"I know," Bond said. "I got a message from Mathis. It came rather late, I'm afraid. I'm going south after sunrise to look for him."

"Ah, I may be able to help in that regard," Draco said. "Since you last asked, my eyes and ears have been watching out for your D.G.S.E. friend. It seems that he was indeed last seen making inquiries in Sartène. After my man paid a very large bribe to a restaurant owner there, we learned that Mathis was directed to speak to a *mazzere* who lives in town."

"What the hell is that?"

Draco explained the legend of *mazzeri* and how they could foretell deaths in dreams.

"That sounds like a load of rubbish to me," Bond said.

Draco shrugged. "Being Corsican, I should take offence at that, but I tend to agree with you. I am very superstitious, to an extent, but I don't see dead people. At any rate, Mathis's trail stopped there. I was about to send my man to talk to this *mazzere,* but I figured that you would want to do that yourself."

"Do you know how I can find him?"

"Her. Her name is Annette Culioli." He gave Bond the woman's address.

They sat in silence for a few minutes, savouring the strong bourbon.

"The Union are up to something with Essinger's film production company," Bond said. "I found evidence that they've got some explosives. Something stolen from an air force base."

"Is that all you know?"

"Unfortunately, yes," Bond said. "Not enough to blow the whistle. I found what looked like a radio transmitter in the possession of Essinger's special-effects man. I think I found pieces of its companion receiver at Emile Cirendini's place last night, and it was attached to a detonator."

"But for what?"

"I don't know. Yet."

Draco said, "Emile Cirendini used to be one of my most trusted colleagues. I gave him a lot of power in the old Union Corse, but he misused it. He defected years ago. Now he's with *the* Union. We are enemies, to say the least."

"Well, he's in this up to his neck," Bond said. "The Union are using his shipping firm to transport materials."

Draco nodded. "I tried to shut him down years ago, but the Union is much stronger than my little band of rebels. He damned near shut *me* down. I'm lucky to be operating at all on this island."

Again, Bond noted that Draco seemed unusually morose. His father-in-law had definitely changed. The once boisterous, life-loving pirate was now merely a shell of his former self. He seemed to be a broken man, someone who had been through too many tragedies.

"How many times have you been up against the Union?" Draco asked.

"What do you mean?"

"In an actual skirmish. Say, in a year."

"This past year? It's like the cold war all over again," Bond replied. "We hit one of their safe houses, they hit one of ours. They've been a thorn in our side for a few years now."

Draco looked concerned. "Tell me, have you had any particular fights with them in *France* this past year?"

"Yes," Bond said. "Just after New Year, I was helping Mathis with a case in Nice. The D.G.S.E. thought that the

Union were hiding arms at Essinger's film studios there. They set up a raid. It went . . . wrong."

"You were there?" Draco asked.

Bond nodded. "We had bad intelligence. They were waiting for us. If I hadn't have shot those barrels of petrol—but then they would have got away if I hadn't. I don't know how much you know about it."

"There was a fire," Draco said bluntly. "Several innocent people died. It was all over the news. Of course I know about it."

Bond nodded and took another drink. They were silent again for a long time. Bond sensed that Draco wanted to say something else that weighed heavily on his mind. Instead, though, the broad-shouldered man stood abruptly.

"I must apologise again, James," he said. "I have become much too antisocial since the deaths of my wife and daughter. Forgive me. I had better leave you now so that you can get some rest."

"Don't go on my account, Marc-Ange," Bond said. "Is it something you'd like to talk about?"

"No," he said. "I *don't* want to talk about it at all." Draco held up his hands. "It is late. Good luck with your *mazzere*. I hope you find your friend. *Adieu*."

Without further ceremony, Draco walked out of the room without the obligatory embrace, or even shaking hands.

Odd, Bond thought. The man was very depressed. Not the old Draco at all.

Bond finished the glass of bourbon and crawled into bed. He was fast asleep in less than a minute.

When Tylyn Mignonne awoke the next morning aboard the *Starfish,* the emptiness and pain she felt in her heart were as heavy as ever. She clutched her pillow, and moved over to bury her face in the other one. She could still smell Bond on it.

Had she loved that man? she asked herself. Or was he merely, as he had playfully suggested, a rebound partner?

Whatever, she thought. The pain was real. She missed him.

Tylyn didn't believe a word that Léon had said about Bond. A film studio spy? Was he kidding?

She was convinced, however, that Bond was not who he said he was. He really wasn't a journalist. Was he some kind of policeman? Had he been investigating Léon? She knew that her husband had been involved with underworld types in the past. But Léon only associated with criminals, he wasn't one himself. That ugly man, Wilcox, now *he* was a crook if ever there was one. He looked as if he could easily kill someone.

The police had spent a day at the set, making inquiries. They had asked her many personal questions about Bond, but it was obvious that they didn't know who he really was either. The investigator in charge told her that the magazine he supposedly worked for, *Pop World,* confirmed his employment, but that was as far as they went. Since the body was never found, and from all the statements they took from witnesses, it appeared that neither Essinger nor anyone involved with the production was responsible for what had happened.

Oh, James, what did *happen?*

Had he been using her to get close to her husband? But his affections had seemed so real. Had she been a fool?

There was a knock on the door.

"Go away, it's too early," she called.

"Tylyn, I have some news for you!" It was Léon.

"Tell me later."

"I think you should hear it now."

She got out of bed, put on her robe, and opened the cabin door. He was dressed in "captain's" gear, smiling with exuberance. It made her want to throw up.

"What do you want?" she asked.

"I've just received word from Cannes," he said. "You have been asked to present the cheque to the charities on the night of our screening!"

She frowned. "What?"

Essinger was clearly taken aback by her lack of enthusiasm. "The screening at Cannes! At the end of the week. Remember? We're screening *Tsunami Rising* at a charity event."

"I wasn't planning on attending, Léon," she said. "That's your movie, not mine."

"But think of the publicity we can generate for *Pirate Island* if you're there. Prince Edward will be there! Princess Caroline will be there!"

"Oh, Léon, don't give me that crap. You just want me there so you can pretend I'm still your wife."

"You *are* still my wife."

"Not for long, Léon."

He stepped inside and shut the door. "What do you mean?"

"Get out of my cabin."

"What do you mean?"

"I didn't want to tell you until after we finished shooting the film," she said. "But I think we should divorce."

Essinger said nothing, but she could see his lower lip begin to tremble.

"Come on, Léon, you know it would be best," she said.

"I could fight you on this, Tylyn," he said finally.

"I was hoping that you wouldn't. It would be easier on us both if you didn't."

Essinger moved away, his back to her. "Then do this favour for me," he said.

"What?"

He turned to face her and put his hands on her upper arms. "Present the cheque at the screening. Show the world that we're still friends. It will do you good. You need to be there. Please."

She sighed. "You're saying that there will be no contest in the divorce if I agree to do that?"

He nodded.

"All right," she said.

He started to embrace her, but she held up her hands. "But everything else still stands. Our relationship from now on is strictly business. I don't accompany you, I don't sit with you, we are not photographed together."

"Very well."

"Now get out of my cabin."

"You're not still upset about that man Bond, are you?" he asked.

"Upset? *Upset?*" She turned on him, livid. "You and your thugs *killed* him! I don't care what you say he was, it didn't give you the right to do what you did."

"We didn't kill him! He brought it on himself!"

"Get out. I don't want to discuss it."

Essinger said, "Fine. I'll see you on the set later." He turned and left the cabin, slamming the door behind him.

Tylyn was furious.

That man was up to something. She knew him too well. He had something fiendish in the works, but she was too distraught and too involved in the film to attempt to find out what it was.

If only James were with her. He had possessed a kind of strength that she had found addictive.

But now she would have to forget all about him.

21
The Prisoners

"You are the second man to come looking for the dream wolf."

Annette Culioli set down a glass of red wine on the table and stood for a moment, looking at Bond with trepidation.

He thanked her for the drink and said, "Madame, I assure you that my intentions are honourable and that the main reason I look for this man is because my friend may be in danger."

"He *is* in danger," she said, sitting down across from him. "The dream wolf told me so."

"Oh?"

"As I mentioned to your friend, the wolf and I are competitors in the dreamworld. However, be that as it may, we also converse from time to time. Even though he is a wolf, I can understand what he says."

Bond thought that the woman was on a plane of existence somewhere on the far side of Jupiter, but she was undoubtedly sincere in what she had to tell him. While he didn't believe one bit in the mumbo jumbo of dreamworlds and the human-animals that inhabit them, he sensed that the basic details of her stories bore some resemblance to the truth. As long as she didn't break out tarot cards or a crystal ball, Bond thought, then he might be able to take her seriously.

"I cannot say where your friend is," she went on to say.
"The dream wolf has him in his den."

"Do you know where that is?"

"All I know is that he lives amongst the menhirs."

"The menhirs?"

"The ancient statues."

Right, Bond thought. He knew about Corsica's famous
prehistoric sites and the ancient dwellings and artefacts
that were plentiful in the southern part of the island.

"And this wolf," Bond asked, "do you think he is the
blind man I spoke about earlier?"

The *mazzere* nodded. "The wolf can see, though. He can
see very well. I interpret this to mean that the blind man
can also see very well in his own way. He is a formidable
person, someone who has great powers of intuition and
control. He dominates my dreams when he is in them.
Sometimes I cannot escape him. One day he will kill me in
my dreams, and that will be the end of my life on earth."

Bond had heard the old adage that if one dreamt of dying
oneself, then it surely would bring about a real death. He
never believed it, but he had never dreamed of his own
death. Not that he could remember.

"Is there anything else you can tell me?" he asked her.
"Anything that might help me find my friend?"

"Look for the menhirs that are not on public property,"
she said. "Look in the vicinity of Cucuruzzu and Capula,
but not as far east."

"*Merci,* madame," Bond said. He stood and turned to
leave, but she stopped him.

"Monsieur, I warn you," she said. "This man is the devil.
Even though his eyes do not see, he can look into your
soul."

Bond nodded and left the house.

He stepped out onto the cobblestone streets of Sartène,
still mystified by the strange, austere atmosphere of the

place, and walked back to where he had parked his rented car.

Bond would have preferred to have his Aston Martin with him, but, having left it in a car park in Nice, he was forced to rent a vehicle from Europcar in Calvi. They had given him a modest Renault Mégane 1.6 16V. It was brand-new, with less than five thousand kilometres on the clock, and Bond was pleasantly surprised by its performance.

After having driven it down the island to Sartène, he now left the village and travelled north again until he reached the D268 towards Levie, on the way to the tourist sites of Cucuruzzu and Capula. Filitosa had been another possibility, but he ruled it out after studying his maps. From what the old woman had said, the most likely place for *Le Gérant*'s home was the stretch of road that traversed several lots of private property.

Unwittingly retracing Mathis's footsteps, Bond overshot his mark and found the reception area for the Cucuruzzu and Capula sites. He turned around and went back towards Propriano, drove a few miles, and suddenly had to stop when a small herd of wild pigs crossed the road. Huffing and snorting, the pigs took their time, unafraid of the giant, four-wheeled machine bearing down on them. As Bond waited patiently, he looked to his right and noticed the roof of a white building on a hill in the distance. It was barely visible from the road here, seen through a small opening in the trees; if he had been a few feet forwards or backwards, the foliage would have blocked it. Bond threw the car into reverse, made a U-turn, and drove back towards the Cucuruzzu and Capula centre.

He parked the Renault in the gravel car park, locked it, and began to walk the two or three kilometres back down the road. The sun had nearly set, but there was enough light left to forgo using a torch—for now, anyway.

But by the time he had reached the spot where he had

seen the pigs, it had grown quite dark. Bond carefully climbed over the barbed-wire fence and made his way through the thick brush towards the building.

It was as dense as a jungle until he came to a clearing of sorts. In the moonlight, he could see the building some forty metres away. A dirt road led to it through the trees from the main road, but there appeared to be yet another tall wire fence around the perimeter of the property. There were lights on inside, and he could vaguely see vehicles behind the house.

Had Mathis come this way?

Bond moved around the clearing, looking for a spot with more cover that might allow him to get closer. He made a half-circle around the property and came upon the menhirs.

On first sight, they were quite ominous. Phallic and imposing, the ancient stone statues had eroded faces that stared into the forest, protecting the grounds from God knew what. After finding the first one, Bond saw that they were spaced evenly around the perimeter of the land.

Finally he realised that the clearing circled the entire grounds. He would have to cross the exposed, open area to get to the second fence. Bond focused on a tree that stood alone on this side of the fence and made a run for it. He was there within seconds. He flattened himself against the trunk and peered around. There was no one about. He was safe for the moment.

Up close, Bond could see that the second fence was electrified. It was made of thick horizontal wires and was eight feet tall. Every ten feet or so were warning signs that were quite clear in their meaning. He studied the fence and could find no other easy access, but then he looked up at the tree he was hugging. At least three branches hung over the other side of the fence. Bond climbed the tree and inched himself onto a limb.

From this vantage point, he could see guards patrolling the grounds. There were two at the electric fence gate on the main dirt road leading to the house. Another man was in front of the home, and he figured that there were probably more on other sides of the structure.

Bond dropped to the ground, landing softly on his feet in the grass. He kept still and silent to make sure that no one had noticed him, then began to walk in a squatting position, like a monkey, towards the house.

Where would the best place be for him to gain entry? Should he take out one of the guards? What the hell was his plan?

Admitting to himself that he didn't have one, Bond kept going, hoping that an opportunity would present itself.

He was nearly at the house when a guard came around the corner with a large dog on a lead. It appeared to be a German shepherd. The man was talking to it in Corsican, urging it to do something. The dog sniffed the ground for a bit, pulling the man closer to where Bond had flattened his body on the ground. The guard stood with his back to Bond, patiently waiting for the dog to finish his business. Bond lay perfectly still, willing the dog not to pick up his scent. At this point, he wasn't sure how bright the moonlight really was. If the guard looked this way, would he be seen?

The dog continued to sniff the ground. The guard tugged on the lead and said something. The dog refused to move. It began to growl softly.

The man questioned the dog, and it barked.

Bond cursed to himself. *Pull the dog away, man!*

The guard tugged on the lead, ordering the dog to come along. It continued to growl, but it finally moved. They walked together back towards the house, and Bond was able to breathe again. He waited a minute after they had disappeared around the corner, then raised himself.

Bond rushed to the side of the house and drew his Walther. Creeping along the wall, he came to the corner and peered around. It was the front of the house, brightly lit, with two guards standing in front, conversing. One of them was the man with the dog.

Perhaps the other direction? Bond thought. Maybe he could get in through the back, where the vehicles were parked.

He retraced his steps along the wall until he came to the next corner and looked around. All clear. He kept going, inching along the wall and ducking under the windows.

When he got to the next corner, Bond sensed that he wasn't safe. He looked behind him and out towards the electric fence, but he couldn't see anything that might be a threat. He listened carefully and thought that he heard panting around the corner of the house.

He cautiously took a look. Sure enough, three German shepherds were not six feet away, their leads tied to a pole near bowls of food and water.

That way was no good either. What was he going to do? He couldn't give up. If Mathis was inside, he owed it to his friend to do something.

Bond began to doubt the wisdom of storming the building alone. He should have called London, asked for backup. Did he think he was so invincible that he could walk into the Union headquarters alone and get away with it? The insanity of what he had done was suddenly all too clear. Then again, Bond justified, he knew that he probably hadn't much time. If Mathis wasn't already dead, then he was surely suffering. It wouldn't be the first time that he had walked blindly into a situation like this. He worked better by himself anyway. He had always believed that when he was killed, he would be alone, on a mission such as this.

A short bark interrupted his agonising thoughts. There was a whine from one of the dogs, and he heard the sound of a lead scraping across the ground.

One of the animals walked out to the length of his lead

and was in plain sight of Bond. It turned, sniffed the air, and saw him.

The ensuing barks from all of the dogs were so loud that they must have alerted the entire island to Bond's presence.

Bond broke into a run, electing to get out rather than fight his way inside. But as he was running, he realised that he wouldn't be able to get over the electric fence here. The tree branches that he had used before were too high to reach on this side of the fence. Frantically, he scanned the fence for the best possible means of escape and finally chose to run towards the main gate. He would shoot the guards if he had to.

The barking grew louder. The three dogs had been set loose and were chasing him across the clearing. They were strong, well-trained animals, and they were gaining on him much faster than he would have liked.

He heard shouts from the house as the guards began to give chase as well. Bond forced himself to run faster, but now the guards at the gate were headed towards him, guns drawn.

One of the dogs leaped onto his back, effectively tackling him. Bond fell to the ground as the animal tore into his shoulder with its strong jaws. The Walther exploded once and the dog went limp, but by then the other two beasts had reached him. Instead of jumping on him, though, they squatted on either side of him, growling and barking, threatening to attack if Bond moved so much as an inch.

The guards surrounded him. One of them ordered him to drop his weapon, and he did so. A guard approached him carefully, pulled off the dead dog, then kicked Bond squarely in the ribs.

It took four men to drag Bond, kicking and struggling, into the house. They brought him in through the back, a servants' entrance of sorts, next to the garage where three or four vehicles were parked. Bond noticed a Rolls-Royce and two 4×4s, but he didn't have much of a chance to get a very good mental picture of the area.

Here, the inside of the building was nondescript. The stone and plaster walls were white with no decoration of any kind. It was a room where the guards and servants could put their things, as there were cabinets, coat hangers, and shelves, but the only other pieces of furniture were benches. Once they were in the room, two men held Bond upright, while another guard, a rather short but wiry fellow, stood in front and unleashed three hard blows to Bond's solar plexus. With the wind knocked out of him, they dragged Bond through a wooden door and down a bare corridor.

Bond must have lost consciousness for a moment, for the next thing he knew, he was being strapped into a black leather chair that resembled something a dentist might have in his office. Bond's arms were secured to the arms and his legs were locked into cuffs at the base. The room was small and there was a stand next to the chair with a slit lamp biomicroscope and other medical devices attached to it. An instrument counter with a sink was near the chair, next to the wall.

What the hell was a doctor's office doing in this house?

Once Bond was secure in the chair, all but one guard left the room. The silence was unnerving.

He was still reeling from the blows to the stomach. The little man had known exactly where to hit him.

"Don't even think about offering me a bribe," the guard said in English.

Bond managed to say, "Sorry, I'm out of dog biscuits anyway."

The guard backhanded Bond across the face.

At that moment, a middle-aged man wearing a white coat and thick eyeglasses entered the room.

He said, "Good evening, I am Dr. Gerowitz." He spoke in English, but the accent was decidedly Eastern European. "I need to examine your eyes."

What the hell? Bond thought.

"Please look into the light," the doctor ordered.

Bond turned his head, refusing to cooperate.

The doctor sighed. "Either you do what we say and we get this over with painlessly, or we try other methods. I assure you that we will get the same results no matter what."

Bond reflected on his situation and decided that perhaps it would be better if he acquiesced. Bond turned back to the doctor as a light shone into his eyes. The doctor was using an ophthalmoscope, larger than Bond's, certainly without Boothroyd's additions, but very bright all the same.

After a few seconds, the doctor switched off the light. "He does not have the tattoo," he said to the guard in French.

"Did you really think he would?" the guard replied.

The doctor addressed Bond in English. "That's all for now. You can go." The guard stuck his head out the door and called his cohorts. The other three men came back in the room. One held a Glock to Bond's head as the others unstrapped him.

They took him down a hall and ordered him to walk down a flight of stone steps. The basement was cold and damp, furnished with a desk, lockers, and a cabinet.

The small guard who had hit Bond in the stomach earlier was sitting at the desk. He got up and addressed him in English.

"I am Antoine," he said. "I am head of security here. Take off all your clothes, please."

Bond didn't move.

The little man, who was probably no more than five feet tall, lashed out with his fist so quickly that Bond had no time to tighten his stomach muscles. He doubled over and fell to his knees.

The little bastard was strong, Bond thought, but his skill was in knowing where the vulnerable targets on a man's body were and repeatedly assaulting them.

"I will ask you again," he said, calmly. "Remove your clothes."

Bond got to his feet and did as he was told. He watched as another guard placed the Q Branch camera, his knife, the Walther that they had taken from him earlier, and the rest of his clothes into a locker. Another man handed him what amounted to prison clothes—grey loose-fitting trousers and a short-sleeved shirt with no pockets. They felt like pyjamas with too much starch.

The next thing they did was shackle his ankles. There was a chain about two feet long between the two cuffs, allowing Bond to walk but not run. Next, they cuffed his wrists together in front of his body. The chain between these cuffs was only two inches.

"Follow me, please," Antoine said. He opened a wooden door behind the desk and walked into a dark stone hallway that smelled musty and mouldy. A guard followed behind Bond, urging him forward with the barrel of a gun.

At the end of the hall was another heavy wooden door. Antoine unlocked it and held it open. The other guard shoved Bond through the door. He fell hard on the wet, stone floor. The door slammed shut and was locked from the other side.

It was fairly dark in the room, and the smell of urine and excrement was strong. A little light came from a single low-wattage bulb on the ten-foot-high ceiling. Straw lay about the room, but there was no furniture.

It was a dungeon, pure and simple.

As Bond's eyes grew used to the dimness, he noticed a dark shape on the floor next to the wall. It started to move, and then it sat up.

It was a man.

"Is someone here?" he asked in French.

"René?" Bond asked.

The man gasped. "James?"

Bond rushed to the man and knelt. It was really Mathis, alive and well! He, too, was shackled in the same manner.

"My God, René, are you all right?"

Mathis uttered a slight, sarcastic laugh. "I guess. It's good to hear your voice. But it appears that you are in the same predicament as me."

"I'm afraid so," Bond said. Then he noticed that Mathis was waving his head around strangely.

"What have they done to you, René?" Bond asked.

Mathis swallowed and nearly choked. "I, uhm, I can't see a damned thing, James. They have blinded me."

22

The Ordeal

Bond felt a sinking feeling in his chest. Were they going to blind him too?

"What happened?" he asked Mathis.

"They used a laser, an eye laser, one of those things that eye doctors use to correct your vision," Mathis said. "It was horrible. They prolonged it over several days, burning me a little bit at a time. I didn't begin to lose my sight until three or four days after they started. Now I'm completely blind. Forever." He sighed. "I don't know why they did it. I certainly didn't know anything. They never really asked me any questions, except . . . well, they asked about you."

"Me?"

"They wanted to know if you would be coming this way to look for me."

"And?" Bond asked.

"After several days of torture, I told them that you would probably find me. They were waiting for you," Mathis said. "I'm sorry, James."

Bond put a hand on his friend's shoulder. "It's all right. They would have found out that I was coming by other means, I'm sure."

"Yesterday a guard said that you were already dead, but I didn't believe him."

"I think my little visit to Corse Shipping last night may have put an end to that particular rumour," Bond said.

"Cesari. *Le Gérant*, he's obsessed with eyes. I suppose it's because he's blind, too, but who knows? He keeps an eye doctor here on the premises."

"I've already met the good Dr. Gerowitz," Bond said. "He checked me for the retinal tattoo."

"That's another indication of *Le Gérant*'s fixation with eyes," Mathis said.

"A deranged mind works in unusual ways," Bond said. "Look, don't worry. I'll get us out of here, somehow. Perhaps another doctor can help you . . . someone in Paris . . . ?"

"It's impossible, James," Mathis said. "There is no way out. They have a guard outside the door at all times. We have to sleep, eat, and shit in here. It's a pigsty. Every day they come for you and torture you a little bit."

"Then that's when I'll make my move," Bond said.

"I wish I could have more confidence," Mathis said. "I'm afraid they have broken me. As for finding another doctor, that's of no use, too. My retinas are completely scarred."

Bond heard a rustling sound in a dark corner, near the straw.

"What the hell is that?"

"Oh, that's our only regular visitor," Mathis explained. "He comes in through a hole in the wall, scrounging for food."

Bond peered closely at the pile of straw and saw two red eyes. When the shape moved, he saw that it was a large, grey rat.

Bond jumped at it, but it didn't scamper away in any hurry. The animal moved with little concern for the two humans in the cell with it. After sniffing the straw one more time, it slipped into a crack in the stone wall.

"The food isn't too bad," Mathis said. "They've been

leaving a couple of meals a day, mostly stuff you can eat with fingers. No utensils."

Bond felt sorry for Mathis. His friend had lost his vitality and will to survive.

"Listen, René, I think the Union is about to do something big," Bond said.

"Tell me what you know," Mathis said. Bond related how he had discovered the substance he suspected to be CL-20, the detonator, and radio transmitter.

"From what you describe, that sounds like CL-20, yes," Mathis said. "It's quite volatile. The Americans developed it as a rocket propellant, but some fool in the military decided that it would make an excellent explosive. What do you think the target is?"

"I don't know," Bond said. "But it's pretty clear that they're using Essinger and his movie production to smuggle the materials out of Corsica. I imagine that they will end up somewhere in France."

The sound of boots on the stone floor outside the door interrupted them. Keys rattled and the door opened.

Antoine and three other guards entered, guns drawn.

"You," Antoine said to Bond. "Let's go."

He got up and went with them, coolly and with no resistance.

After they had strapped him into the examination chair, one of the guards released a catch on the headrest. Hidden attachments for straps protruded from its sides with a click. Two guards held Bond's head as a third man strapped it down tightly. Two sliding panels were fitted onto the headrest and pushed inward, holding Bond's skull like a vice. These were tightened considerably, preventing any movement of the head.

Then all of them left the room, abandoning Bond to the eerie, antiseptic stillness of the place. A cold chill ran up

Bond's back when he thought about what was going to happen.

Le Gérant entered the room alone and shut the door behind him. Keeping his head motionless, the mysterious Pierre Rodiac, a.k.a. Olivier Cesari, sat down on a swivel chair next to the desk. He was wearing sunglasses, dark trousers, and a short-sleeved polo shirt. He looked as if he were ready for a game of golf.

"No, I'm not your physician, Mister Bond," the man said, smiling. "I never got my doctorate, you see. Welcome. We've been expecting you."

"*Le Gérant,* at last," Bond said. "I should have killed you in front of everyone in the casino."

"But you didn't, now, did you?" Cesari said. "That's exactly where you and I differ, Mister Bond."

Bond waited for him to go on.

"You lack vision, Mister Bond," Cesari said, shaking his head. "You are a victim of your own stubborn, compulsive ways. You are a very good gambler, Mister Bond, I grant you that; and you have great courage when it comes to taking chances. However, you have no idea what the outcome will be for anything you undertake. To you, it's all a risk. Life is one big game. On the other hand, I never bet. I only act when I know with certainty what the consequences will be. And I usually do."

"What are you planning, Cesari?" Bond demanded. "What's the CL-20 for?"

Cesari chuckled to himself. "I'm impressed, Mister Bond—or should I say, Agent Double-O Seven? I didn't think you had uncovered so much."

"Cesari, if I fail to report, you're going to have the entire Ministry of Defence at your doorstep. They'll find you. We all know who you are now. It won't be so easy to blend into the scenery anymore."

"By the time you fail to report and they *do* find this lovely house, I'll be gone. I never stay in one place very

long, you know that. I rather like it here, though. It would
be a pity to leave. I spent some of my younger years in Corsica, you see. This was my father's ancestral home."

"Stick to the subject, Cesari. What about the CL-20?"

"I remind you, Mister Bond, that I am sitting *here* while
you are sitting *there*. You are not in any position to tell me
what to do, are you?" *Le Gérant* had quickly lost his good
humour and was snarling.

He paused a moment to calm down. "I finally have the
great James Bond in my hands. It's a moment that I thought
would have given me more satisfaction. Instead it's just,
well . . . predictable."

Bond decided to gamble. "What is Goro Yoshida paying
you? What does he want from the Union?" he asked.

"Ah, Mister Yoshida," *Le Gérant* said. "Let's just say that
he made the Union a very good offer. You must remember
that the Union does not take any sides in a matter. We are
not a political organisation. What Yoshida wants to accom-
plish is of no importance to us."

"How many people will die this time?" Bond asked.

Le Gérant shook his head. "That doesn't concern me."

"How can it not? Are there innocent people involved?
For God's sake, Cesari, what are you planning?" Bond per-
sisted.

"I think you know, Mister Bond. You just haven't put it
all together yet. We've even spoon-fed some clues to you
so that you would follow your nose here, right where I
wanted you. Out of the way of our project. You have the
uncanny knack of ruining our plans, and I didn't want you
near our latest one."

Bond thought a moment. All the pieces seemed so dis-
connected: detonators from Corsica, explosives from
America, transmitters from France, a movie company carrying the parts . . . Was there something happening soon
that involved crowds of people?

Then it hit him. "Cannes," Bond said. "You're going to blow up the film festival."

"Well, that's a bit of an exaggeration, Mister Bond," *Le Gérant* said. "Let's just say that we're providing the fireworks at a special screening with a lot of VIPs, exactly two evenings from tonight."

Christ, it was the charity event that was going to be attended by Prince Edward and Princess Caroline! Now it made sense. The pieces all came from different places. The explosive was stolen from the air force base in Corsica and then smuggled by the film company out to sea and ultimately to France. The detonating device was assembled at Cirendini's shipping firm and smuggled to the film set. Final construction of the bomb or bombs would probably be completed by Rick Fripp, the explosives expert, under the guise of "special effects" work on the film.

"Why? Why kill off a bunch of celebrities at a charity function? What's the point?" Bond asked.

"It's Yoshida's idea of a major strike against the West," *Le Gérant* said. "He believes that the festival symbolises the decadence of the West. He has a big problem with that. The stroke will also damage Japanese companies who are colluding with the West in the film industry. You know and I know that when famous entertainers die, it makes the news. Attacking the entertainment industry will hit the West where it hurts the most. People in the West love their celebrities more than their politicians. It will be a shocking, history-making terrorist strike. And the Union will carry it out."

"You're insane, Cesari," Bond whispered. "What happened to you that made you so indifferent to human life, to human feelings?"

Le Gérant was silent again, contemplating the question. Then he said, "Why should I reveal anything to you about myself? I must admit that there is no question in my mind that you are a superior human being and deserve a certain amount of respect. While I possess the greater intellect, you are undoubtedly the finest specimen of a man that I have ever encountered. You are a killing machine unlike any other. I wish that I could tempt you into working for the Union, but I won't bother asking. I know what your answer would be."

Bond told him where he would put his offer if given the chance.

Le Gérant smiled. "We are not too dissimilar, Mister Bond. We are both passionate about our work and our beliefs. We strike back at those who try to hurt us. We are cunning and skillful, albeit in different ways. You were orphaned at an early age, Mister Bond. I'm sure that has something to do with it. You see, I had a difficult childhood, too."

Bond, unable to move his head and limbs, listened with fascination to the story that Olivier Cesari began to tell.

"My father was a Corsican, born and raised in Sartène by strict Catholics who attempted to beat religion into him. When he was nine years old, his parents were killed as a result of a vendetta. He depended on the old Corsican mafia, the Union Corse, to raise him. He grew up to be a brutal and sadistic man, but someone with a very good business sense.

"Once, when he was in Morocco on business, he raped a Berber girl who lived in the Rif Mountains. She became pregnant and gave birth to me. Some might say that I was born with a disability. I, however, consider my blindness fortunate. Nature compensated by enhancing my other senses. By the time I was seven, I realised that I had mental capabilities that my people considered somewhat . . . mystical."

He paused a moment as if he were savouring the image of a memory, then he continued.

"I lived with my mother in the Rif Mountains until I was eight years old, when my father returned and took me to Corsica to live with him. He ripped me away from my mother and her people and forced me to be almost like a servant to him. Even though I was blind, I had to learn to cook meals, fetch drinks for him, clean the house. My father was prone to losing his temper, so he beat me regularly whenever I displeased him, which was often. We lived in Sartène, but we spent a lot of time in mainland France, especially Paris. My father had a mafia-backed perfume business, you see.

"While being a strict disciplinarian, he also demanded great things from me. In his own way, he loved me, I suppose. He spent a lot of money for an operation to restore the sight in my eyes, but it didn't work. He pushed me to excel in school, in my studies, and in day-to-day challenges I might face. He wanted me to overcome my disability, and in some ways, I am grateful to the bastard for pushing me so hard. Without the extra effort, I might never have risen above my situation.

"As a result, I learned everything I could. I read every book in Braille that I could get my hands on, studied mathematics and philosophy, learned foreign languages, and above all, mastered courses in law and economics. This education, combined with two cultural backgrounds—first growing up in the Moroccan mountains, and then with the Corsican mafia as family—you can see how I might have developed into . . . a precocious young man."

"That's not the word I would use," Bond said.

Le Gérant ignored the barb. "I learned early on that I could predict things," he went on. "My grandfather on my father's side, I discovered, was a *mazzere*. As the ability is hereditary, I ended up with the skill. I could foresee events in my dreams even before I was old enough to understand what they meant. Gradually, though, I turned this skill into helping me with my blindness. I tap the same areas of the brain that are used for dreaming to boost my senses of hearing, tasting, smelling, and touching. As a result, I know exactly where this jar is sitting . . ." He reached over to the desk and picked up a jar of cotton swabs without turning his head. "I can *feel* the space it's sitting in without touching it."

"All right, you've proved you're a circus freak, Cesari," Bond said. "Let's get on with it."

Le Gérant stood and clasped his right hand around Bond's neck and squeezed, cutting off his victim's air supply.

"On my eighteenth birthday, my father was murdered," Cesari said, digging his fingernails into Bond's skin. "His throat was cut from ear to ear, the first appearance of the mark of the Union. I inherited his estate, which was considerable. As it was I who had brought about his demise, I gained a significant amount of respect among his peers, many of whom did not like him any more than I did."

He let go of Bond's throat. Bond gasped for breath.

So the man had committed patricide, Bond thought. That explained a lot.

Cesari sat down again. "I went back to Morocco after that. My mother had died shortly after my father kidnapped me. I lived with her people for several more years, until I was the master of two vastly different cultures. With my money, success, and psychic abilities, I quickly accumulated a following in Morocco. The rest, as they say, is history.

"The dreams continue to this day," he said. "I am always a wolf, hunting prey in the *maquis* of Corsica. Lately, I've been stalking a majestic stag. I'm going to kill it eventually, I know. And when I finally do, I'll be able to confirm that the stag is who I think it is."

He stood once more and placed his hand on Bond's shoulder. "The stag is you, Mister Bond."

He moved away and opened the door. He said something in Corsican, and a moment later Dr. Gerowitz and a guard entered the room.

"You've already met the good doctor, Mister Bond," Cesari said. "I leave you in his capable hands. I think it's high time that the Union receive some payback for all the times you've caused us trouble. Good day."

With that, *Le Gérant* left the room and shut the door behind him.

"What's the matter, Cesari?" Bond shouted. "Too squeamish?"

Bond turned his attention to Dr. Gerowitz, who approached the chair and stepped on a lever on the floor. The seat reclined so that Bond's torso and head were at a forty-five-degree angle from his waist. The doctor then held an eyedropper over Bond's eyes.

"This won't hurt," he said. "It's one percent mydriacil and two and a half percent phenylephrine. The solution will dilate your eyes."

Bond squeezed his lids closed.

"Come, come, don't act like a child," the doctor said. "That's what children do when they see the eye doctor." When Bond refused to open them, the doctor nodded to the guard. The guard forcefully pulled Bond's eyelids apart with his hands. The doctor managed to put a couple of drops in each eye.

"I'm going to leave you for a few minutes while those drops work on your eyes," Gerowitz said as he replaced the eye drops on the desk and left the room. The guard remained in the room, sitting behind Bond where he couldn't be seen.

Concentrate, Bond told himself. He had withstood great amounts of pain in his lifetime, and he could stand this, too. He would fight it every step of the way, and he would endure whatever the sadist could unleash.

To be tortured for torture's sake. That was the worst. At least if the inquisitors were trying to find out something, a victim could always talk and perhaps be granted a reprieve from the pain. But to be at the hands of a sadist who simply enjoyed torturing someone . . . it was a sobering notion.

The twenty minutes that Bond sat helpless in the chair waiting for the doctor to return had to be among the most excruciating moments he had ever experienced. The anticipation of horror could be as bad as, or even worse than, the actual torment.

The doctor came back in the room and said, "Let's get started, shall we? We're going to do a little at a time every day, per *Le Gérant*'s orders. I could blind you with a single stroke of my laser and be done with it, but no, I'm afraid we have to draw it out. Now, to make sure you keep your eyes open . . ."

The guard helped the doctor place terribly painful retractors on Bond's eyes. The devices were reverse clamps that kept the eyelids open. Once they were on, Bond's eyelids were pulled apart and there was nothing he could do to alleviate the discomfort. The guard then stood by the chair and applied drops to Bond's eyes, since he was now unable to blink.

"The drops our friend here is applying will keep your eyes moist while I work. Oh, are the retractors uncomfortable? I could have put some anaesthetic drops in your eyes, but I elected not to. Now, then . . ."

The doctor sat down in the swivel chair and pivoted the Coherent Novus Omni argon laser around in front of Bond's face. He looked through it at Bond's right eye.

"You'll probably feel a burning sensation," the doctor warned. "Usually we anaesthetise the eyeballs before this type of procedure, but . . . oh, well."

The doctor flipped a switch and the laser shot into Bond's pupil. The sensation was bizarre and unnerving; it felt as if a tiny needle had just entered his eyeball and was jabbing the back of it, but it wasn't terribly painful.

"This argon laser is set to point one watts," the doctor said. "As I inch up the wattage, I believe you'll feel a bit more pain."

The pricking sensation indeed began to change. Bond

now felt heat in his eye. It was beginning to burn. He felt his heart racing as he clutched the arms of the chair, completely powerless.

"I'm at point two," the doctor said. "You feel that, don't you?"

Bond breathed in through his teeth, his jaw clenched in agony.

"Now we'll go up one more notch to point three," the doctor said calmly.

Suddenly, Bond's eye felt as if it were on fire.

Bond couldn't help screaming, especially when he smelled his own eye burning.

23

The Rat

Léon Essinger suspended production the day before the screening at Cannes. Everyone had the next three days off so that many of the principals involved in *Tsunami Rising* could be at the event. There wasn't a lot that they could do on the film anyway. With the boat chase sequence completely derailed, the director had spent the last two days on pickup shots. The production was already several days behind schedule.

The *Starfish* pulled into Nice that morning. The cast and crew disembarked and scattered. Tylyn went home to Mougins, Stuart Laurence went to his rented villa in Nice, and Essinger and his team went to the Côte d'Azur Studios.

After Essinger had settled behind his desk, Julius Wilcox and Rick Fripp entered the office. They grabbed bottles of beer out of the portable refrigerator and sat on the sofa.

"Make yourselves at home," Essinger said sarcastically. He was attempting to catch up on paperwork. "I can't believe these expenses. It's going to cost even more than I thought to rebuild that goddamned tanker."

"You worry too much," Wilcox said. "Put that stuff down and let's talk."

Essinger, frustrated, pushed the papers out of the way, got

up, took a beer for himself, and joined the other men around the coffee table.

"Mister Fripp has some news for us," Wilcox said.

Fripp cleared his throat and held up his glass. "The bomb is finished, ready to go."

Essinger didn't say anything until they both looked at him. "What—" he said, "am I supposed to applaud?"

"I just thought you'd be pleased to know," Wilcox said. "Everything is in place to deliver it to the Palais tomorrow. Now we have to talk about our alibis. Mister Fripp and I shouldn't have a problem. It's you, mister big-time movie producer, that I'm worried about."

"What for?" Essinger asked. "I never attend my screenings—everyone knows that."

"We just don't want it to be too conspicuous that you're not at *this* one," Wilcox said. "Please go over the routine one more time."

"Christ, Julius," Essinger said. "After we arrive at the Palais for the screening, I am to be taken ill. I'll drink the castor oil in the men's room before the event begins. I'll make sure several people see me throw up."

"You guarantee it'll make you vomit?" Fripp asked. "If not, I can cook up something that will do the trick!"

"It'll work, trust me," Essinger said. "At that point, I will beg everyone's pardon and leave to have a lie-down. I'll go straight to my hotel room and make sure all the doormen see me."

"You know that the police will question you over and over and over?" Wilcox suggested.

"I can handle it," Essinger replied.

"Very well," Wilcox said. "I'm sure you'll be off the suspect list as soon as Yoshida's people announce that they were responsible for the act."

"Too bad we have to lose so many good people on the film," Fripp said. "Do you have a director in mind to replace Duling?"

"Are you kidding?" Essinger said. "*Pirate Island* will have to start again from scratch. We're losing our lead actor *and* director."

"And lead actress," Wilcox reminded him.

Essinger stiffened slightly. "Yes."

"But your insurance will cover it," Wilcox said. "The entire production is protected. You'll receive a shitload of cash, Léon. From your insurance company and from your wife's inheritance. I wouldn't mind being in your shoes after all this is over, fella."

Essinger took a sip of his beer and nodded. Sure, it would be great. As long as he was able to live with himself.

When Bond awoke that morning, his eyesight had returned to normal. When they had finally taken him back to his cell, an agonising, aeons-long fifteen minutes after Dr. Gerowitz began working on him, Bond's vision was blurry due to the dilating solution he had received. At first he was alarmed that his eyes had been permanently damaged. But as the doctor had predicted, the laser had not harmed his vision. With no small amount of skill, Gerowitz had avoided the crucial sites at the back of the eyeball—namely, the macula and optic nerve areas. Ironically, Bond was thankful that Gerowitz was good at what he did.

The only things that were sore were his eyelids, because of the retractors forcing them open. They felt as if they were made of sandpaper.

"I didn't start noticing a change in my eyesight until the fourth day," Mathis had told Bond. The idea, then, was to torture him psychologically as well as physically. The day-to-day fear of becoming blind was almost too much to take. The good doctor would play havoc with areas in the eyeball that did not affect sight, pricking and burning him for a few seconds at a time without anaesthesia. It was no wonder that Mathis was now so resigned. The ordeal would break anyone.

Bond was determined to find a way to avoid it.

They heard the keys rattle in the door at midmorning. A guard came in with a tray of food—bowls of oatmeal and no utensils. Surprisingly, it tasted good, even scraped out by hand. The meal gave Bond the much-needed energy to formulate a plan.

He ate all but a small amount of the food. He carefully crawled to the hole in the wall and smeared the remaining oatmeal along the floor and into the straw.

Bond then moved closer to Mathis to tell him what he had in mind.

Tylyn Mignonne arrived in Cannes that afternoon and checked into the exclusive Carlton Hotel, *the* place to stay when at the film festival. In the past she had stayed at the Majestic and the Martinez, both first-class hotels, but the Carlton represented the top of the heap when it came to celebrity placement.

There was plenty about the film festival that Tylyn disliked. Mostly she felt that it had become way too snobbish for her taste. The organisers perceived it as a much bigger and more important event than it really was. She was constantly amazed by the lavish attention thrown on the Cannes Film Festival by the international media. There were more reporters and paparazzi at Cannes than there were film industry professionals. And even that inner circle was becoming more and more difficult to break into. She knew two journalists in Paris who were refused press accreditation simply because their publications weren't big enough.

What particularly irked Tylyn was the fans' behaviour. She couldn't believe they could stand in the Riviera sun outside a hotel for hours just to get a glimpse of a celebrity. Even in Hollywood it wasn't that bad.

Because of the increase in media attention and interest from the masses, security had been beefed up considerably at the festival. Tylyn was more aware of uniformed guards everywhere. They were even stationed in front of her hotel, checking to make sure anyone who came in was staying there.

La Croisette, the main street that ran along the beach to the Palais, was already crowded and much of it blocked off from traffic. It was madness to get into a car anywhere near the festival grounds; it was easier to simply walk from one's hotel to the Palais. However, that meant fighting one's way through mobs of fans wanting a photo, an auto-graph, or even a kiss.

As Tylyn lay on the bed in her suite, she decided against going outside. The opening-night screening was in a few hours—some film by a hot American director—and she felt obliged to go. She didn't really want to. If she could have her way, she would stay secluded in her room until tomor-row night, when she absolutely *had* to make an appearance at Léon's charity screening. But she had received scores of interview requests and she was under contract to give a few. She would be busy all day tomorrow up until the time of the screening, so why shouldn't she take today off?

Having made the decision, she phoned her publicist and told her to give away the tickets.

She turned on the television and—surprise, surprise—the programme was coverage of the film festival. There was a clip of Prince Edward and his wife Sophie, Countess of Wessex, arriving in Cannes that afternoon. The reporter said that Princess Caroline of Monaco would be arriving tomorrow for a grand event screening of *Tsunami Rising*. A roster of the celebrities scheduled to attend included a glamorous head shot of her.

She ran through the channels with the remote and even-tually turned it off. She lay back on the bed and stared a hole through the plain white ceiling.

Tylyn had spent the last few days in an uncustomary daze of distraction. At one point during a take, director

Duling had to shout at her to concentrate. She knew that she needed to snap out of it, but damn it, she had a lot of questions! Tylyn *knew* that her husband was up to something and that it had to do with James Bond. She couldn't prove it, but it was the only possible explanation.

And what of James? Who was he really? Had what they experienced in the short time that they knew each other been real? No one could fake that kind of intensity, except perhaps a professional con man. If he had really lied to her about himself, it would break her heart. So far, she had been able to prevent that from happening because she refused to believe that he had been dishonest.

Instead, she concentrated on her memories of him: his steely blue eyes, the cruel mouth that had kissed her so passionately, his strong arms and hands, his expert and generous approach to lovemaking, his smile, his laugh . . .

She missed him deeply.

They came for Mathis at midday. He offered no resistance as two guards led him away, while a third kept an eye on Bond.

He was back thirty minutes later. Even though Mathis was already blind, *Le Gérant* had ordered the torture to continue simply to be cruel. Mathis looked deathly pale and was unable to speak coherently when they threw him down on the cell floor.

"Let's go," Antoine said to Bond.

Bond wondered how long the sadistic bastard was planning on keeping them alive. At this rate, he could torment them forever.

The second appointment with Dr. Gerowitz was half an hour of profound pain. From the moment Bond's head was strapped down and the terrible retractors were placed on his eyelids, he had rarely felt a more powerful sense of helplessness and fear. Not once did the doctor ask him any

questions. Bond was never instructed to give away MI6 secrets. All they wanted, it seemed, was to hurt him.

Hours later, after the blurry vision had diminished, Bond
heard the scratching sounds in the corner of the cell.

"James?" Mathis whispered.

"I hear him," Bond said quietly. He slowly raised himself from the floor and looked.

The rat had just come out of the hole and was sniffing the
trail of now-sticky oatmeal that Bond had left. The rodent
scampered along, scraping up the food and sniffing the
straw around it.

Bond sat up and slowly crawled toward it. The cuffs
around his hands limited his movements, but he managed
to slide along without being too obvious. When he was
within arm's reach of the rat, he stopped and waited. The
animal, chewing on a chunk of oatmeal, eyed Bond but
didn't seem to be afraid of him. In its tiny mind there was a
belief that it was superior to the filthy human that left so
much waste in the room for it to enjoy. The rat knew that it
could bite the hell out of a man, so it didn't feel any need to
be afraid.

With an unexpected lurch and the speed of a cobra, Bond
grabbed the rat with both hands and clutched it around the
neck. He squeezed as hard as he could, fighting the struggling rodent as its claws slashed his hands and wrists. He
slammed the creature against the stone floor and continued
to choke the life out of it. It took nearly a minute, but finally the rat was dead in Bond's hands.

"Are you all right?" Mathis asked.

Bond came back carrying the rat carcass. It was as big as
a squirrel.

"A little scratched up, but I'll live," Bond said. "Ask me
again after I'm done with the really disgusting part."

Before he could have second thoughts, Bond sunk his
teeth into the rat's back. He needed something that the animal had—the only problem was that it was on the inside of

the rat. Since Bond had no knife to cut the damned thing open, he had to take a deep breath and use the only other sharp objects he could find.

It was dark outside when the guard finally brought Bond and Mathis their dinner. The keys rattled in the door, and it swung open.

"All right, stay back and I'll put these on the floor," the man said, but he was surprised when he didn't see anyone sitting in the relatively clean section of the cell. He surveyed the room and saw two bodies in the straw. The man inched forward to get a better look. The one called Bond was facedown. The other one was on his back, and there was blood and what looked like animal viscera all over his face.

What the hell had happened? Had they killed each other?

The guard foolishly stepped closer, just as Bond had hoped he would. Bond lunged with the femur, puncturing the soft layer of skin beneath the guard's chin. The rat's leg bone, while brittle, had been whittled on stone to sharpen it. It served very well as a makeshift weapon—something that could take a person by surprise. The ploy worked beautifully.

The guard dropped the tray of food and screamed, but Bond didn't stop there. He propelled himself at the guard, tackling him. He took hold of the man's hair and slammed his head with tremendous force several times against the concrete floor. A pool of blood appeared underneath his skull.

Bond fumbled for the guard's handgun, drew it, and aimed it at the open doorway just as a second guard came in to investigate the noise.

The gun kicked twice, knocking the guard into the wall. He slid to a heap, leaving a bloody trail on the stone.

Bond turned back to the first guard and searched the

man's pockets. Thank *God* he had the right guard! Bond took the set of keys and just managed to twist his wrist enough to insert the appropriate one into his cuffs. Free at last, Bond unlocked the shackles on his ankles and then freed Mathis.

Mathis took an old rag and wiped the rat's blood off his face. "We fooled him good, eh?"

"Come on," Bond said as he took Mathis by the hand and led him out of the cell.

24

The Breakout

It wasn't difficult to break into the locker where the guards had put Bond's weapons and clothes. He dressed quickly, made sure his Walther was loaded, clipped the camera to his belt, strapped on the knife, and he was ready to go. Mathis stood by with his own clothes, waiting for Bond to help him.

"Come on, René," Bond said. "We had better hurry before someone else comes down here."

"You must go without me, James," Mathis said.

"Don't be ridiculous."

"I mean it, James. I would be a burden to you. By yourself, you just might make it out. If you have to drag me along, I will only slow you down and probably get us both killed."

"You're coming with me. Now get dressed!"

"No, James." Mathis dropped his clothes on the floor. "I insist. Go on. Get out of here. I'll be fine. I'll just go back into the cell and wait for you to bring reinforcements."

Bond knew that Mathis was right, of course. He was loath to leave his friend, though.

"René . . ."

"Go!" Mathis said forcefully. "If you don't leave now, I'm going to start shouting. I mean it." He reached out with his right hand. "Good luck, my friend."

Bond clasped the man's hand and held it firmly. "I'll be back for you. I promise. Your job is to stay alive until then."

"I'll do my best," Mathis said. He smiled for the first time since Bond had been captured. "Now get the hell out of here."

Bond left him and climbed the stone steps to the ground floor of the château. He glanced at his watch and saw that it was after midnight. He silently stepped down the corridor towards the room where they had first searched and beat him. Luckily, no one was about at this time of night. He listened at the wooden door at the end of the hall and thought that he could hear movement.

The element of surprise was his only ace. He lightly tapped on the door and readied himself. When it opened, Bond let go with a solid punch to the guard's face. The man went tumbling backwards into the room. Bond stepped inside, drew the Walther knife, and hurled it at the one remaining guard in the room. The blade pierced his chest with a dull thud. Bond rushed to him and covered the man's mouth before he could scream. Once he collapsed to the floor, Bond removed the knife, wiped it clean on the man's trousers, and made a quick examination of the first guard to make sure that he was still out.

The cabinets here were stocked with a variety of weapons. Bond took three hand grenades and a machine gun, then opened the door slightly to peer outside. Two men were talking to a man at the wheel of a delivery lorry. Markings on the side of the lorry indicated that it was a beverage supply vehicle. The motor was running; either the lorry had just pulled up or it was about to leave. Bond calmly walked outside with the PPK in hand, aimed it at the two men, and said, "Hey!"

When they turned, the Walther recoiled twice.

Bond pointed the gun at the lorry driver. "Get out," he commanded. The driver, eyes wide, jumped out and held up his hands. "Lie on the ground," Bond ordered. When the man was facedown, Bond said, "Don't get up until I'm gone."

He leapt into the driver's seat, threw the lorry into gear, and backed out. He turned onto the dirt road and headed for the electrified fence gate.

Olivier Cesari was sleeping soundly, enjoying a dream in which he had just stalked and killed a young fawn. He possessed such agility and skill as a wolf that Cesari never wanted to wake from these dreams. As in dreams in which people imagined that they could fly, the feeling was so exhilarating that the reality of the waking world was in contrast a complete disappointment. If Cesari could have had his way, he would have remained asleep forever. In his dreams, he was the king of his realm, the master of everything he touched.

And he could see . . .

However, something wrestled Cesari away from his newly killed fawn. He looked up from the dead animal and saw the stag—the one that he had been hunting for months, the beast that represented the British secret agent who had caused him so much misery.

The stag was staring at him, taunting him, and telling him that the war wasn't over by a long shot. Before Cesari the Wolf could run and leap at the wretched creature, the stag turned and bolted.

That was when Cesari woke and knew that James Bond had escaped. He reached for the phone and called down to the basement.

There was no answer.

Bond floored the accelerator, increasing his speed. The guards at the gate snapped out of their complacency and realised that something was terribly wrong with the lorry driver. They both pointed rifles at the vehicle and shouted for him to stop.

Bond ignored them.

The men jumped out of the way at the last second as the lorry burst through the metal gate. The electrified fence, now exposed, burst into flames at the breakpoint. One of the guards got on the radio just as the alarms went off in the complex.

Bond kept driving, eventually reaching the main paved road. Instead of turning right, to head toward Sartène, Bond went left towards the prehistoric sites that he had seen before he was captured.

Within seconds, a Porsche and a Land Rover were behind him. He heard gunshots, but the lorry was so big that Bond couldn't discern if the bullets had hit the back or not. Because of the vehicle's bulk, the damned thing would do a maximum of only fifty miles per hour.

The Land Rover swerved into the left-hand lane and pulled beside the lorry. Bond ducked as a bullet smashed the driver's-side window, spraying shards of glass all over him. Bond drew the Walther and, with his left hand, aimed it out the open window and shot at the 4×4. The vehicle slammed against the lorry in an attempt to force it off the road, but the truck was too heavy. Bond tried the same manoeuvre by turning the wheel sharply to the left and banging the lorry into the Land Rover. The 4×4's tires screeched as it shot over to the far side of the road, scraping against the brush, but the driver managed to bring it back beside Bond. The guard in the passenger seat of the 4×4 aimed again and shot at the lorry. This time a bullet whizzed past Bond's face.

Damn!

Bond stuck his left arm out of the window again and squeezed the Walther's trigger. The round caught the guard in the face. He was thrown back into the driver, causing another near collision. The 4×4 slowed down and moved back into its proper lane.

Off with the kid gloves, Bond thought. He grabbed one of his grenades, pulled the pin with his teeth, and carefully tossed it out the window. It landed and bounced on the road behind him. If his timing was any good at all, then . . .

The Land Rover drove over the grenade just as it exploded. The 4×4 bounced into the air, riding a ball of flame and smoke, then veered to the right, landed on its side, and slid for twenty feet.

The Porsche's driver steered around the burning wreck and kept up the pursuit. He increased his speed and pulled up beside Bond in the left-hand lane. The passenger had a machine gun and proceeded to spray the side of the lorry with bullets. Bond stepped hard on the brakes so that the Porsche shot ahead of the lorry. He then aimed the Walther out the window and shot at the car's tail. He was successful in putting several holes in the boot, but couldn't get a good bead on tyres or anyone inside. Firing a gun with his left hand out of a moving vehicle was not his strongest skill.

Bond remembered that the road curved around a gorge close to the prehistoric sites. He was nearly there. The Porsche had continued on, the driver probably thinking that he would turn around at the next opportune spot. Bond heard more gunshots from the rear and cursed to himself when he saw yet another 4×4 behind him.

He drove the lorry onto the curve that hugged the side of a high bluff. To the left was the gorge, probably two hundred metres down.

Since it was dark, Bond decided that this might be his only means of escape. Keeping his hand on the wheel, he scooted across the seat to the passenger side. He removed his foot from the accelerator, slowing the lorry down to about thirty. He opened the passenger door and prepared to make his move.

He took a second grenade, pulled the pin, and dropped it onto the floor. Then he simultaneously turned the wheel to the left and leapt from the lorry cab. He landed hard on the road, rolled, and quickly made for cover on the shoulder. The lorry weaved unsteadily toward the edge of the gorge.

Come on, Bond willed. Had he forced the wheel far enough to the left?

The lorry's left front wheel went off the road, causing the vehicle's weight to shift and lunge in that direction. Finally, the back left wheel slipped off the road and the lorry was well on its way to hell. It toppled off the bluff and dove nose first into the trees just as the grenade exploded. The lorry exploded in a fireball that lit up the sky. Its bulk carried the vehicle over the tops of the trees as it somersaulted and collided into an outcrop of large boulders.

Bond didn't waste any time. He ran into the trees and climbed the bluff, looking for a safe place to hide above the road. He heard the 4×4 stop and the shouts of the men inside. He stopped to watch as the Porsche returned to the scene. Two men got out of the car and joined the others to examine the spot where the lorry went off the road. One of the men pointed to the wreckage as they pondered what to do. Was the escaped prisoner dead?

One of the men got a torch out of the car and began to shine it over the trees on the right side of the road. They weren't going to leave anything to chance. *Le Gérant* would have their hides if they hadn't searched properly.

Bond kept going. Once he reached the top of the bluff, he headed east. If they were following him, he couldn't hear them. He ran like a dog, tripping over fallen trees, cutting his arms and face on low branches, and tumbling down slopes. Fighting the forest was more difficult than he had estimated. After fifteen minutes, he was completely out of breath and had to stop.

He sat on the ground, willing his heart to stop pounding.

As he breathed deeply, he listened to the night air and heard vehicles not far away. They hadn't given up the search.

Bond got up and continued to run. He rushed through the dense trees, over large rocks, and down a slope until he ran right into the barbed-wire fence that he had been looking for. He cut his hand climbing over it, but compared to everything else he had suffered in the last twenty-four hours, it was nothing but a scratch.

The archaeological site of Cucuruzzu and Capula was a major tourist attraction in southern Corsica. When Bond had been searching for *Le Gérant*'s home, he had studied the area and learned that the site contained stone man-made dwellings that dated from prehistory.

Bond found himself in a forest of chestnut trees. He removed the camera from his belt and flicked on the ophthalmoscope light, which served as something of a torch. At least it illuminated the ground in front of him.

The landscape around him was not only dense with the trees but was also heavily populated by granite boulders of varying sizes. They were in piles in some places, as if a giant had collected them and stored them at various points in the forest. Mostly they were in the shape of large round spheres, the result of erosion. Piled up in this way, the rocky masses created a kind of granite chaos.

Bond climbed over one pile and descended onto the path that tourists used when visiting the site. He breathed easier, knowing that he wasn't going to become completely lost in the dark woods.

Eventually the footpath led him to a shelf bordered on the left by the granite spheres and on the right by a heavy wall of trees. He moved along the rocks past a menhir that presented on one side a bas-relief of a sword disposed vertically, and on the other side very stylised anatomical details of a man. Just beyond the menhir was the prehistoric castle of Cucuruzzu.

The casteddu was an amazing Bronze Age structure

made entirely of stones, ingeniously placed one on another and affixed with lime mortar. At first glance, it might have appeared to be yet another pile of boulders, but closer examination revealed that there was order to the placements. This was a shelter for prehistoric man.

Bond climbed up and over the boulders and down a "staircase" of rocks into the enclosed space. There was no roof in this small castle. Instead, little cavelike rooms had been created out of the rocks. The rooms originally had their own purposes—one or two for sleeping, one for working, one for storing food . . .

Bond crawled into one of the shelters and found it surprisingly comfortable. The flat stone floor was smooth enough to lie on, no doubt made that way by ancient man. A nice, bearskin rug would have made it more pleasant, but at this point Bond didn't care. He was exhausted.

He figured that if he could catch a few precious hours of sleep, he could get out before the site opened for business the next morning. He hoped he could find a ride to Sartène and from there call London and arrange for quick transport to Cannes. That was the most important thing at this point. He had to stop that bomb, and he had less than twenty-four hours to do it. If *Le Gérant* got away, then so be it. With any luck, the guards would give up the search and report that the escaped prisoner had died inside the lorry. The Union leader would then figure that there was no longer a threat of being discovered and stay put.

Lying in the dark hole, Bond was unable to escape a swirl of mental images. There was Dr. Gerowitz adjusting the slit scan machine in front of his face; *Le Gérant* relating his life story; Mathis fumbling for his food in the cold, damp cell; the torn-open carcass of the rat; and the inescapable vision of Tylyn Mignonne's sensuous eyes. Nevertheless, he fell asleep, safe for now, in a shelter built aeons ago by men whose destinies lay in their dreams.

25

The Screening

The sun bounced off the surface of the Mediterranean and struck Bond's eyes like a dagger. He flinched but was thankful that the glare was bright and uncomfortable, for another scenario might have dictated that he be unable to see the light at all.

The Aerospatiale Eurocopter SA 360 Dauphin soared over the sea, having left Calvi twenty minutes earlier. They would reach Cannes in forty-five minutes, shortly before sunset.

It had taken nearly all day for Bond to get out of Corsica. Early that morning he had emerged from the *casteddu* as the birds were dining on worms and insects. He made his way down the footpath, climbed over the fence, and found his rental car in the parking lot where he had left it. As he drove along D268 back to Sartène, he passed the gate leading to the Union's chateau. His thoughts turned to his friend who was still inside. Was Mathis still alive? What had they done to him after they discovered that Bond had escaped?

First things first, he told himself. Bond turned his back on *Le Gérant* for now and focused his energy on stopping the Union's plan in France. When he got to Sartène, he went straight to the *gendarmerie,* presented his credentials, and got on the phone to London. The efficient Nigel Smith immediately made arrangements for Bond to be picked up by helicopter, then transferred him to M. After Bond had explained what had occurred over the last few days and what was about to happen that night in Cannes, she told Bond to sit tight. She returned the call in ten minutes and explained that a British SAS force and a French RAID team would meet Bond in Cannes. The French would pick him up in Sartène and fly him in a helicopter to Calvi for a quick refuel, then on to Cannes. In the meantime, she would work on the American, French, and Russian governments to help put together a strike force to raid the Union headquarters in Corsica, but that would certainly take more time.

Bond suggested that they should forgo contacting the other countries and simply hit them alone. M rejected that ploy as being too politically volatile.

"What about the bomb?" M had asked. "How will you know where to find it?"

Bond had thought long and hard about that. All of the various clues pointed to the pressurised soft-drink canisters. He had seen them at every stage of his investigation—listed on the manifests in Essinger's office in Paris, empty ones in the back room at Corse Shipping, full ones in the warehouse—that had to be the answer.

They were going to fill up one or more soft-drink canisters with the CL-20, attach their homemade detonators to them, and deliver them to the theatre. Then, during the screening, they would be set off with the remote-control device Bond had seen in Corsica.

The trick would be to find the right canisters in time.

The Dauphin picked Bond up on a relatively clear plateau near the *gendarmerie*, and Bond said goodbye to southern Corsica. It was a quick ride to Calvi, but by then it was already late afternoon. To distract him from his own impatience, Bond made a phone call to the Bastia hospital and spoke to Bertrand Collette. His friend had already received a skin graft and was feeling poorly, but he wished Bond good luck and told him not to worry.

Now, as the helicopter approached the Riviera coastline, Bond felt his stomach tighten. While he possessed the ability to remain cool and calm in most situations, on the inside he could feel quite the opposite. His steely reserve was a façade that he had perfected with years of experience. The reality was that he was only human and was susceptible to pain, fear, and anxiety like anyone else. What made him different was how he acted under the pressure.

He knew that the events of the next few hours would be yet another test for him.

Tylyn Mignonne also knew that something significant would happen to her that evening. She didn't normally believe in premonitions, nor did she suppose that what occurred in her dreams might possibly come true.

She had suffered a restless night in the hotel. Awful dreams of burning corpses haunted her when she did actually fall asleep. The projector in her mind kept replaying images of the Hiroshima mushroom cloud, pictures of radiation victims and buildings on fire. At one point in the middle of the night she had woken in a sweat. She turned to grab hold of her lover, James Bond, but then she realised that he wasn't there. He was dead.

As a woman who was usually happy-go-lucky, Tylyn didn't cry very often. But she had held back tears for days, and the dam had finally burst. She cried for twenty minutes, sitting on her bed with her knees to her chest. Afterwards, completely spent, she was able to go back to sleep, but the disturbing dreams continued. One figure kept emerging as the protagonist in them.

James, where are you now? she had called to the void. And there was an answer—his voice, ethereally floating in the air, said, *Be careful tonight, darling.*

Now, as she put the finishing touches to her makeup, she felt apprehensive. It wasn't because she would be required to speak in front of hundreds of people, including members of royalty, but because something terrible was going to happen. The dreams had told her so.

She zipped up the black evening dress that she had designed herself. It was floor-length with a slit that went up to her waist, revealing a long, sexy-smooth leg. She had to wear a G-string instead of panties with the garment; otherwise anyone might see them. Instead, what they got was a flash of bare hip. The neckline was low but tasteful. While her breasts weren't particularly large, they were certainly adequate enough to produce substantial cleavage. The crowning touch was the diamond necklace that Léon had given to her their first Christmas together. She had only worn it once and she somehow felt that tonight would be an appropriate occasion to display it again. She didn't know why.

She decided to walk to the Palais alone, not caring if the paparazzi followed her or if fans demanded a photo or an autograph. She craved the independence, and she needed to remind herself that she was strong and resilient.

As she walked out of the Carlton through the gauntlet of onlookers, she switched on the million-dollar smile and waved as the cameras flashed. Someone yelled, "Marry me, Tylyn!" She blew a kiss to the man, then pulled him out of the crowd. She put her arm through his and asked him if he would walk her to the Palais. Flabbergasted, the young man nearly tripped and fell, but he quickly regained his composure and began a ten minutes that he would never forget.

The Palais des Festivals was a grand structure that contained two cinemas and several floors of meeting rooms, pressrooms, and other facilities to accommodate the huge event that the film festival had become over the years. A wide red carpet adorned the sets of steps leading up to the Lumière Amphitheatre, where all of the major screenings were held. Traffic had been blocked off, and security barriers were set in place to keep the onlookers back.

Evening screenings were always black-tie affairs. Even the most famous celebrity could not gain entrance without a tuxedo. Tylyn had witnessed an incident a few years back in which a prominent, hot young American director was denied entry because he was wearing a turtleneck sweater. He was so enraged that he swore he would never return.

The parade of glamorous people usually began half an hour before the screening. No one was exempt from making the red carpet entrance. Everyone had to do it—the celebrities, the critics, and the invited guests. The festival's organisers orchestrated it that way to make sure that all of the VIPs were seen at *their* event.

Tylyn said goodbye to her lucky escort at the edge of the red carpet, then proceeded to walk up the stairs alone. She continued to wave as the camera flashes exploded around her like fireworks. Other exquisitely dressed guests were also ascending the stairs. She recognised the likes of famous French actors Catherine Deneuve, Sophie Marceau, Jean-Louis Trintignant, Gérard Depardieu, Carole Bouquet, and Isabelle Adjani. Esteemed directors from all over the world were there: David Lynch, the Coen brothers, Roberto Benigni, James Ivory, John Madden, Jane Campion, and Francis Ford Coppola. Tylyn assumed that the royal entourages had either already made their entrances or were being held back until last.

She found Stuart Laurence at the top of the stairs. She joined hands with him, and they both waved to the crowd before going inside.

Tylyn thought the Lumière Amphitheatre was the ideal cinema. Despite the hassles and madness of the film festival, attending a screening at the Lumière was always a pleasurable experience. The acoustics were perfect, and every seat in the house was a good one. She admired the purple and pink décor; the carpet and upholstery were kept in pristine condition, as if the cinema were a royal palace. The stage was black, and there were large white panels in the ceiling that concealed lighting instruments. Usherettes dressed in white dresses with black polka dots greeted the audience as they entered.

Tylyn saw Léon in the lobby. She didn't want to speak to him, but he saw her and gestured for her to come over. Luckily, that ugly man Wilcox wasn't there. She took a breath, then pulled Stuart along with her to greet her soon-to-be former husband.

"Tylyn, you look beautiful," he said, kissing her cheeks.

"Stuart, dashing as always." He noticed the necklace and said, "Darling, you have made me very happy by wearing that."

She shrugged. "I thought I should do something for you. This is your night, Léon. I hope this time you'll stay for the screening."

He shook his head. "I'm sorry to disappoint you, but no, I won't be staying for the screening. I'm way too nervous. In fact, my stomach is about to explode as it is. I feel very sick."

"Take it easy, man," Stuart said, clapping him on the shoulder. "Maybe you should sit down. You *do* look a little pale."

"Oh, I'll be all right, I think," Essinger said, stifling a belch. "We had a little scare this afternoon. I thought the film hadn't made it to the Palais. I used a new security firm to deliver it. They were late, but it's here now, thank God."

At that moment, the level of excitement in the lobby increased tenfold. All heads turned as Princess Caroline of Monaco entered with her group.

"I must greet Her Royal Highness," Essinger said. "Will you excuse me?"

"I'm coming with you!" Stuart said. "Tylyn?"

"You boys go ahead," she said. "I'll meet the princess later."

They left her, and she decided to avoid mingling in the lobby. She would have killed for a glass of champagne, but that would have to wait until the party afterwards. Apparently Léon had arranged for a bash at one of the exclusive beach restaurants nearby.

Pretending not to notice some film critics whom she knew, Tylyn left the lobby and made her way to her seat inside the theatre.

In the projection booth perched directly underneath the balcony, Julius Wilcox and Rick Fripp looked out of the small windows at the ever-growing crowd. Only Fripp was dressed in a tuxedo.

"I can't believe we're doing away with some of the most important names in show business tonight," Fripp said.

Wilcox dismissed the thought with a wave of his hand. "You've seen one goddamned movie star, you've seen 'em all."

"I understand you received some bad news this afternoon."

Wilcox nodded. "I spoke to *Le Gérant*. It appears that our English spy is alive and well. He's probably on his way here. We need to keep a look out for him. Shoot to kill."

"Right," Fripp said. "I could have sworn he had died in that explosion."

Wilcox said, "He'll wish that he had. Apparently he was at Corse Shipping the other night when I was there seeing Emile. We still don't know if he found anything out."

The projectionist entered the room and asked, "What are you doing here? Who are you?"

Fripp flashed his backstage pass and said, "We're with the film, my friend."

He looked at them suspiciously and said, "Oh. Well, maybe you can explain something."

"What's that?"

"The film. I opened all of the cans except for one. It

wouldn't open because there's a lock on it." He pointed to the stacks of metal film canisters on the worktable. All of them were open and the reels removed except for the one that had two padlocks affixed to the sides. The film had been spliced together onto two large reels for the projection system, as was the custom. "As far as I can tell, I've got the entire film loaded. But there's this one can that I can't open. What's inside it? Surely not more film?"

Fripp feigned interest, counted the empty cans, and said, "No, you've got them all. I don't know what this extra one is. Maybe it was stacked with the other cans by mistake. Just leave it and our people will take it back tonight."

"It's marked 'Tsunami Rising, Part Eight,'" the projectionist said. "But according to my notes, there are only seven parts."

"That's correct," Wilcox said sternly. "This eighth can is a *mistake*. Forget about it. Just do your job."

The projectionist looked at Wilcox as if to say, "Who the hell are you telling me what to do?" but the man thought better of it. This man was the ugliest and meanest-looking person he'd ever seen. So he shrugged and said, "Fine."

Fripp and Wilcox left the projection booth and closed the door.

"You think he's all right?" Fripp asked.

"Yeah," Wilcox said. "Better give me the phone now. I've got to get out of here. I ain't wearing a tux."

Fripp gave him a mobile. "Here it is. You know the code."

"I'll hit the buttons one hour into the screening," Wilcox said, "and I won't be calling for a pizza. Are you all set to get out?"

"I'm leaving with Léon," he said. "I had better get downstairs. He's probably drunk his stuff by now."

Wilcox chuckled. "I wish I could be there to watch him puke."

26

The Raid

"I'm Commandant Perriot," the head of the French RAID team said to Bond. "We have assembled twenty men, all armed and ready to go." He pointed to the two military vehicles that were idling near the helipad. The men inside were dressed in camouflage military uniforms and riot gear.

"Have you heard from the SAS team? Where are they?" Bond asked.

The man shrugged. "I just heard that they will be here in ten minutes. Do you want to wait?"

Bond looked at his Rolex. The screening would begin in ten minutes.

"No. Let's go."

They both jumped into the first truck and set off. The Dauphin had landed at the heliport west of the city. It would take them at least ten minutes to get into the Centre-Ville. With the traffic and pedestrian congestion, it might take longer.

"I have radioed the Cannes police," Perriot said. "Hopefully they have cleared the way for us."

"What have you told them?"

"Only that we have information that a terrorist act might occur at the festival this evening. I gave them no details, as per your instructions."

"Good," Bond said. "We don't want them to start evacuating the cinema."

"Why not, may I ask?"

"Because that would tip off the bombers that we know about the plan," Bond said. "If I'm right, the triggerman can set off the bomb at his discretion. It's a radio-controlled device, so he could be anywhere in the vicinity. If we start evacuating, he'll know that the game is over and set it off immediately. Mission accomplished."

"What are we looking for, exactly?" the commandant asked.

"I'm guessing, but I believe the bomb is disguised as a pressurised soft-drink tank," Bond said. "One of those that fits underneath a bar and has a hose attached to it for dispensing soft drinks. I think it's safe to say that it's in the cinema itself."

"Right."

The two trucks reached the Palais just as the last of the guests were ascending the red-carpeted stairs. Several Cannes policemen were gathered at the barrier to meet the RAID team. A young captain saluted Perriot and said, "Everyone is inside, monsieur. Do you want me to evacuate the VOs?" Bond knew that VO was a code that meant *visiteurs officiels*. He pointed to two armoured Rolls-Royces standing nearby.

Perriot turned to Bond. "What do you think?"

Bond shook his head. "Not yet. If they left it would arouse too much suspicion. Let us have fifteen minutes. If we haven't found anything by then, let's see if we can *quietly* get the VOs out of the cinema. As it is, just our appearance in the front of the building is sure to alert the terrorists to our presence."

Bond and Perriot, followed by the RAID team, ran up the steps in full view of the crowd and cameras. Immediately the rumour mill began to churn: *What's going on? Did something happen inside? Is Princess Caroline all*

*right? I heard gunfire! No, you're crazy. It's probably ter-
rorists from the Middle East. It's a publicity stunt.*

A news reporter approached the police captain and asked
what was happening.

"Nothing, just extra security," he said, but he wasn't
very convincing.

"Twenty armed men in riot uniforms?" the reporter
asked. "Come on, sir, the people have a right to know.
They're already talking. Has someone been hurt?"

"No, please move along."

The cinema manager met Bond and Perriot at the entrance.

"Please take us immediately to the bar," Perriot ordered.

The manager looked confused. "But . . . there is no bar
in the Lumière," he said. "The only bar in the Palais is Jim-
my'Z on the third floor of the main building. It's nowhere
near the Lumière Amphitheatre."

"No place where soft drinks are served to the audience?"
Perriot asked.

"No, monsieur," the manager replied. "We keep our cinema clean."

Bond cursed softly. "Then I don't know what we're
looking for," he said to Perriot. "I suggest that we start the
search backstage, in the lobby and in the catwalks. Tell
your men to use complete discretion. As far as the civilians
are concerned, we're just extra security. After all, royalty is
in attendance."

The team burst into the lobby and spread out. Several
men went upstairs, while Bond and others took the corridor
that led along the left side of the house to the backstage
area. The Lumière manager pulled Perriot to the side and
asked, "If there is a bomb in the theatre, shouldn't we evacuate?"

Perriot was explaining the problem with doing so when
a tall American film critic walked by on his way to his seat
after visiting the toilet. He wasn't fluent in French, but he

thought that he understood the words for "bomb" and "the-atre." Alarmed at the sight of the soldiers, he immediately went inside to tell his colleagues what he had heard.

Bond reached the backstage area and peered through the black curtains at the audience. He could see the special sections set aside for Prince Edward, Princess Caroline, and their respective groups, as well as for the celebrities involved with the film.

His heart skipped a beat when he saw her. Tylyn was sitting next to Stuart Laurence. Her diamond necklace caught the houselights and she looked magnificent even from this distance. When was she scheduled to speak? Before the screening?

He scanned the faces for Essinger but didn't see him. It figured. If he were in on the plot, he would have found a way to be absent.

Bond turned from the curtains and rushed behind the huge screen, where the RAID team were busy searching behind and under every object. He looked up and noticed catwalks above the stage where the crew could hang lighting instruments or adjust the screen. He pointed them out to one of the men and directed him to climb the steel ladder and look up there, then he went out the door leading to dressing rooms and backstage offices.

As he stepped into the brightly lit corridor, he heard a voice that he recognised.

"Ohhh, I feel terrible. I really must go."

"Léon, it is such a shame!" a man said in French. "Was it something you ate?"

"It must have been. I just vomited all over the dressing room. I'm very sorry."

Bond peered around the corner and saw Essinger, Fripp, and several other people dressed in formal wear. The one speaking to Essinger was an older, bald-headed man whom Bond recognised as Gilles Jacob, the president of the film festival.

"I had better take Monsieur Essinger back to the hotel," Fripp said. "Come on, Léon."

"But my screening!" Essinger moaned. "I need to be here! Ohhhhh!" He began to retch again and ran into the dressing room. Bond heard him gagging loudly. Everyone in the corridor winced.

"Poor man," Jacob said.

Bond drew his Walther and stepped into view. "Hold it right there, Fripp."

The stuntman froze.

"What is the meaning of this?" Jacob asked.

"Hands up, *now*!" Bond ordered. "Monsieur Jacob, please take your party and step back. Go into the theatre. This is police business."

When they didn't move, Bond shouted, "GO!" They left immediately, frightened to death.

Fripp raised his hands but looked at Bond with a sneer. "You're not going to get away with this, Bond," he said.

"Get your friend out of there and let's go," Bond ordered.

Fripp stepped back two steps but kept his hands raised. "My friend is very ill. Can't you hear him?"

"Stay where you are!" Bond spat. "Where's the bomb?"

"What bomb?" Now Fripp smiled.

"No games. Either you tell me where it is or I'll blow a hole in your head." He pointed the Walther at Fripp's head.

Before Fripp could react, gunfire erupted from the dressing-room door. A bullet barely missed Bond's shoulder. He responded instinctively and ducked, momentarily moving the gun away from Fripp. Essinger had the door ajar and was aiming a gun through the opening. He fired again, but Bond leapt out of the way, slamming against the corridor wall. This gave Fripp the opportunity he needed to run. Bond shot wildly at Fripp but missed him.

Fripp pulled a Browning Hi Power from inside his

tuxedo jacket and fired at Bond, but the bullet missed completely and went into the wall. He continued to run.

Essinger slammed the dressing-room door shut and locked it. Bond levelled his fire at the door, emptying his magazine. When he stopped to reload, Bond shouted, "Essinger? If you're alive you had better talk to me!"

"Go to hell, you bastard!" the man shouted from inside the room.

A RAID officer ran into the corridor. "I heard shots!"

"Help me break this door down," Bond said. Together, they kicked it in and burst into the room. Essinger, his shoulder and arm bloody from a gunshot wound, stood with his hands in the air.

Bond held a gun to his head. "Where's the bomb, Essinger?"

"I swear I don't know," he said, trembling. His face was ashen. "Please, I have to sit down, I feel so sick. . . ." He dropped to his knees.

"Talk, damn it!" Bond shouted, jabbing the gun barrel into Essinger's temple.

"They didn't tell me!" Essinger said. "I swear! They thought it would not be wise for me to know that particular detail."

Bond turned to the RAID man and said, "Take him outside and watch him. I'm going after the other one."

"*Oui*, monsieur."

Bond left the room and ran back towards the stage, where Fripp had disappeared. A moment later, Essinger collapsed. The soldier knelt beside him and slapped his face. "Monsieur? Monsieur?"

He didn't hear someone step into the room behind him. An expert's hand grabbed the soldier's helmet and pulled his head back. In the time it took for the soldier to register that he was being attacked, the knife slit his throat from ear to ear. He fell over, blood gushing from his neck.

Julius Wilcox held out a hand to Essinger and helped
him up. "Come on, let's *blow* this joint."

In the house, the audience was still buzzing, happily waiting for the moment when the festivities would begin. So
far, most of them had not noticed the soldiers running
around backstage. But the film critic who had overheard
Commandant Perriot and the theatre manager told his
friends that there was a bomb in the cinema.

"I think we should leave," he said.

"You're mad," one of his colleagues said. "Sit down."

Unfortunately, a woman sitting behind them heard what
was said and whispered to her husband, "That man said
there's a bomb in the theatre!"

Several rows behind them, in the VIP section, Tylyn
Mignonne was becoming impatient. *Let's get on with it!*
she thought. She was nervous enough as it was. Stuart Laurence had been talking nonstop, but she hadn't been listening: her mind was elsewhere.

She perked up when she saw a man in a tuxedo run from
the wings in front of the huge white screen. He turned and
pointed a gun at something in the wings. It went off, frightening the entire audience.

"My God! It's Rick Fripp!" Laurence said.

No one moved. Was this part of the show? What was going on?

"Something's wrong," Tylyn said. She started to stand,
but Laurence stopped her.

"Wait," he said. "I'll bet Léon cooked up some kind of
preshow entertainment for us."

"I wouldn't bet on it," Tylyn said, but she settled un-
easily in her seat.

Fripp ran into the wings on the other side of the stage
and began to climb the metal circular staircase that led to
the catwalks. Bond had run behind the screen and almost
caught him, but the stuntman performed a surprise karate

kick that kept his pursuer at bay. Bond chased him to the staircase and followed him up. He didn't want to fire his gun for fear of causing a panic.

When they reached the catwalk, the two men were nearly sixty feet above the stage. Bond tackled Fripp, and the Browning went flying. Fripp slugged Bond hard in the face, but Bond reciprocated with blows to Fripp's stomach. The catwalk was very narrow, perhaps three feet wide, so there wasn't much room for them to roll around in. Nevertheless, Fripp leapt on top of Bond and attempted to push him off. Bond locked his foot around a metal beam and grabbed hold of a rail above his head. It was a matter of strength now. Fripp was very fit and obviously was used to working with heavy objects. Bond felt his trunk sliding off the catwalk despite his hand- and footholds.

But Fripp made a fatal mistake when he bent one leg to obtain better leverage. He left himself wide open for Bond to drive his knee hard into Fripp's groin. Fripp yelled, immediately released Bond, and fell back onto the catwalk in pain. Bond punched him in the face and shouted, "Where's the bomb? Tell me!"

Even through his agony, Fripp remained defiant. He spat at Bond and laughed. Bond punched him again and then rolled him to the edge of the catwalk.

"Tell me or I'll push you over," Bond said.

"Let's go together!" Fripp said. In a surprise move, he grabbed Bond's neck and hurled his body over and off the catwalk, dragging Bond with him.

The two bodies fell together ten or twelve feet and collided with a bank of multicoloured strip lights, which halted their fall, but their weight broke one of the support chains holding it up. The entire mechanism fell loose and hung vertically, in front of the screen where everyone in the house could see.

The audience gasped when they saw the two men hanging off the dangling strip lights.

Tylyn recognised Fripp again. The other man—he looked familiar too. She stood abruptly when she realised who it was. "James?" she gasped.

Fripp, fighting to hold on to the swaying bank of lights, grabbed a broken live wire. He screamed as the volts surged through his body and sparks formed a halo around him. He fried for nearly ten seconds before the wire broke and he fell. He landed with a loud thud on the stage, causing several women in the audience to scream. Bond still hung on to the panel, fighting for his life.

The tall film critic turned to his friends and asked, "Now do you believe me?" and then he stood and shouted, "There's a bomb in the theatre!"

27
The Search

The theatre erupted into chaos. The royalty VIPs were immediately ushered out through emergency exits by the efficient Palais security guards and handed over to the Cannes police. The respective parties from Britain and Monaco were then whisked away in armoured cars and taken to safety.

Tylyn was caught in a stampede of people attempting to escape, but she wasn't trying to leave at all. She wanted to get up to the stage.

"James!" she called.

Her voice barely carried over the clamour, but Bond heard her. He had a tenuous hold on the strip light panel and couldn't hold on much longer.

Tylyn forced her way through the crazed audience. A man knocked her over and she was almost trampled, but she crawled into a row of seats and stood on one. The shoulder strap on her dress broke and she could barely keep it up over her breasts. In desperation, she grabbed the nearest man and ordered him, "Tie this!" The man was in such a state of fright that he tied the broken strap around her upper arm without thinking. It did the trick; her dress stayed up.

Tylyn then lifted up her skirt so that she could step over

the seats and get to the stage that way. She held on to the excess material with one hand and used the other to support herself as she climbed over each seat back, row by row.

When she got to the stage, Bond was slipping.

"Hold on, James!" she called. Looking around frantically for something to cushion his fall, Tylyn finally ran to the side of the proscenium and grabbed hold of the bottom of the act curtain. She pulled it towards centre stage, in front of the screen. This formed a hammock-like canopy that curved beneath Bond's feet.

"Jump!" she called. "I've got it!"

Bond let go of the strip lights, fell twenty feet, and hit the curtain. The weight and force caused Tylyn to drop her end, but the curtain provided just enough of a break to his fall. He clung to the curtain and swung with it back to its original place, then dropped to the stage on his feet.

Tylyn ran to him and embraced him.

"My darling!" she cried, kissing him. "You're alive, you're alive!"

"Tylyn," he said, panting, returning her kisses. "You have to get out of here now. There's a bomb in here somewhere. Léon is responsible. I can explain later, but you must leave!"

"I'm not leaving without you!"

"Tylyn, I have a job to do here. I will find you outside. *Please!*" He grabbed her shoulders hard and pushed her away from him. He looked her in the eyes and said, "I love you, Tylyn. Now, please go." Without another word, he turned and ran into the wings to continue the search for the bomb.

Tylyn stood there a second, her fingers to her lips. "I love you too," she whispered.

Bond found the dead soldier in Essinger's dressing room and cursed. He followed the corridor to the end and came upon an emergency exit that probably emptied into the back of the building. He kicked it open and looked outside.

A white van was pulling out of a reserved parking space. As it turned to head towards the exit, Bond saw Julius Wilcox in the passenger seat. Bond leapt down to the pavement and ran as fast as he could.

The van stopped because the driveway was jammed with pedestrians. The panic had spread into the street as the audience came running down the steps. Now there were police sirens blaring all over the Centre-Ville and everything was chaotic.

"Run them over!" Wilcox shouted at Essinger, who was driving. The producer's shoulder was bleeding profusely from the gunshot wound and he was in terrible pain.

"I can't do th—" Essinger protested, but Wilcox had a gun to his head before he could finish the sentence.

"Go, you bastard," Wilcox said. He held the mobile phone in his other hand. "We have to get a few blocks away before I can activate the bomb. The blast will level the entire building and kill everyone around here. Running them over now won't make a bit of difference. Do it!"

There was a loud thump on top of the van.

Essinger looked up, his eyes wild with fright. "There's someone on the roof!"

"Drive, you idiot!" Wilcox shouted.

Essinger stepped on the gas and the van bolted into the crowd. There were screams as three or four people were hit. Wilcox aimed his pistol up and began shooting holes in the top of the van.

Bond, lying on top of the vehicle's roof rack, turned his body this way and that, gambling that the bullets wouldn't hit him. One came too close for comfort, searing the side of his face as it exploded into the sky. Temporarily blinded, Bond held on to the van tightly as it sped into the street.

Inside, Essinger asked, "Did you get him?"

"I don't know," Wilcox said. He set down the mobile,

rolled down the passenger window, stuck his head out, and climbed up in his seat so that he could look. As soon as he did, Bond's shoe smashed into his face. Surprised, he dropped his weapon and almost fell out of the window. Bond kicked him again, but Wilcox managed to slip back inside.

"Knock him off, damn it!" Wilcox yelled.

Essinger swerved the van back and forth in an attempt to swing Bond off the top, but it was no use.

"We have to go faster!" Wilcox said. "Step on it!"

"I can't!" Essinger exclaimed, gesturing to the congestion on the street. "Where the hell do you suggest I go?"

Wilcox reached over and turned the wheel so that the van drove off the street and onto the pavement. Pedestrians jumped out of the way as the van crashed over several restaurant tables and chairs. Essinger took the wheel again and manoeuvred the van off the pavement and into a side street, where it hit a parked police car, scraped the side of a limousine, and continued on into the crowded Rue de Antibes. There the congestion was even worse.

"Oh no!" Essinger said. "There's no place to go!"

"Run them over! Kill them all!" Wilcox shouted.

But by that time Bond had climbed over to the side of the van and was hanging on to the door handle. He managed to plant his feet firmly on the footstep there, then used every bit of strength he had left to slide open the door.

Essinger screamed when he saw that Bond had got inside. Wilcox got out of his seat and threw himself at the intruder, just as Bond managed to draw his Walther. The gun went flying as the two men fell into the back of the van. Essinger did his best to keep the vehicle moving, but when he heard a siren behind him, he panicked.

"The police!" he called back to Wilcox, but his partner couldn't hear him.

Clenching his jaw and closing his eyes, Essinger floored the accelerator and hoped for the best. The van lurched forward, hit three cars parked along the side of the road, then swerved to the other side, onto the pavement, and into a large storefront window. The glass shattered, and alarm bells rang with ferocity. Essinger was thrown forward into the windscreen, which cracked his head and rendered him unconscious.

The crash had little effect on Bond and Wilcox, who had their hands around each other's throats. Wilcox was an agile man, but Bond was the superior fighter. He took a chance and let go of Wilcox's neck so that he could get in two quick punches to the man's face. But Wilcox wouldn't let go. He was squeezing hard, causing Bond to choke and gag.

Desperate now, Bond's right hand groped the floor of the van for a weapon—his missing Walther or anything that might even the odds. He felt a steel rod of some kind and grasped it. It was a tyre iron. Bond swung it hard and fast onto Wilcox's head. The ugly man released his grip on Bond's neck and fell over, dazed. Bond hit him again, but this time Wilcox blocked the blow with his arm. He yelped like a dog at the pain, but that didn't stop him from rebounding. Julius Wilcox was no amateur.

Before Bond could strike him again with the tyre iron, Wilcox kicked him hard in the chest. Bond flew back against the van wall and struck his head on the edge of the door. Wilcox, seemingly immune to the punishment he had received, pounced on Bond and began to pummel him mercilessly. Bond held his arms in front of his face for protection, but the Union killer got through with several powerful blows.

Bond's head slammed against the floor, but through the haze he could see his Walther a few feet away. There was only one thing to do. He allowed Wilcox to continue punching him unrelentingly so that the killer wouldn't notice him moving his hand toward the gun. Nearing unconsciousness, Bond inched his fingers a bit closer . . .

closer . . . and he had it! Holding the barrel against Wilcox's stomach, he squeezed the trigger. The retort was deafening inside the confined metal space as the bullet went through Wilcox's abdomen, exited out of his back, and blew a hole in the van roof. The expression on the killer's face changed from rage to disbelief. He stopped hitting Bond and froze for a moment.

Bond fired again. Blood dribbled from the ugly man's mouth as he coughed twice. Bond rolled him off and got up. Wilcox twitched and jerked for ten seconds, then lay still.

A groan from the front of the van got Bond's attention. Essinger was coming to. Blood streamed down his head, and his tuxedo was soaked from the shoulder wound. Bond stuck the Walther to the back of his head.

"Now," he said, catching his breath. "Where is the bloody bomb?"

Essinger nodded. "All right. Just a second." He was very woozy. "Let me get my bearings."

"Now, talk!" Bond spat, shoving the barrel into Essinger's neck.

"All right!" Essinger reached over to the passenger seat and picked up the mobile phone. "I need to call the man who is supposed to set it off."

"What?"

He showed Bond the phone. "I need to call it off. He has to get the message not to detonate the bomb."

The fight with Wilcox had left Bond disoriented as well. Not thinking straight, he said, "All right. Call him."

Essinger switched on the mobile and punched a number. Then another.

Bond's mind reeled. *Wait a minute!* The detonator was built to receive a radio transmission.

"Go ahead," Bond said, shoving the barrel into Essinger's neck again. "Kill them all."

Essinger hesitated. His finger was poised to hit another button, but the hand holding the phone began to shake.

"Do it," Bond taunted. "Your friends and colleagues, the people who gave you a career, your *wife* . . . Kill them all."

Essinger closed his eyes and coughed.

"But if you do it, remember that I'm not there to die along with them," Bond whispered. "I'm right here."

With a whimper, Essinger dropped the mobile. Bond picked it up and shut it off.

Completely subdued, Essinger wilted in the seat. "It's in the projection booth," he said. "In a film can."

Bond lowered the gun.

"They put the CL-20 in a film can and rigged the thing with a radio-controlled detonator. The can itself serves as the antenna. It was enough explosive to kill everyone in the theatre and probably a good many outside of it." The man began to sob. "I'm sorry. I didn't want to do it."

Bond left him and got out of the van. The police were just pulling up, followed by Perriot and two of the RAID officers.

"Are you all right, monsieur?" he asked.

Bond nodded. He pointed to Essinger. "Take him." He gave the mobile to Perriot and told him where they could find the bomb.

Bond refused to go to hospital, claiming that his injuries were superficial. He had certainly received worse. His face was battered, his eye was swollen, and his ribs hurt, but there was nothing broken. He allowed a paramedic to treat his cuts and scrapes, then walked over to the command centre that had been set up in the British Pavilion next to the Palais. This was a place where U.K. citizens attending the event could have a snack or a drink, check their e-mail, have meetings, or simply relax.

The British SAS team had arrived ten minutes too late to participate in the search for the bomb, but now they were

doing their best to interview witnesses and gather information about what had happened. The bomb had been found
in the projection booth and carefully removed from the
site.

Bond joined the commanders of the British and French
teams in the tent after ordering a beer at the bar.

"Congratulations, monsieur," Perriot said. "You have
done an exemplary job."

"Hear, hear," said the rather stiff man in charge of the
British. He lifted his own glass of beer to Bond.

Bond ignored the praise and said, "I want to know how
they got that bomb into the building."

The Cannes police captain cleared his throat. "We were
just going over that. It appears that the film production
company—that is, Monsieur Essinger's company—used a
private security agency to deliver the film cans. This is
fairly standard procedure. The security personnel had
clearance passes and were able to drive right up to the
Palais and walk inside with the cans."

"Pretty cheeky, if you ask me," the British commander
said.

A young technician with the French police who had been
busy hooking up a VCR to a monitor said, "Excuse me, but
I think I'm ready."

"Ah," Perriot replied. "We have tapes of everyone going
in and out of the building. I got them from the Palais security team. There are cameras set up at every entrance." He
turned to the young man and said, "See if you can find the
service entrance tape. The film was delivered shortly after
six o'clock."

"Yes, monsieur," the lad said, and got busy reviewing the
material.

Bond asked, "So what happens next?"

Perriot answered, "Well, for one thing, we're going to
question every single person associated with Monsieur Essinger. They're being rounded up as we speak. I think that

the real culprits, though, were Monsieur Wilcox and Monsieur Fripp. They are dead, of course."

"I have it, monsieur," the young man said. He switched on the tape and they all turned to the monitor.

The camera showed the back entrance of the Palais, shot from the inside looking out. A Palais security guard was standing by the door checking the badges of everyone who walked in.

"Fast-forward, please," Perriot ordered.

The technician did as he was told until two men with film cans could be seen at the door.

"There. Stop, please."

The tape resumed its normal speed.

When Bond saw who had delivered the film cans, his heart sank. He closed his eyes and rubbed his brow.

"Are you all right, Monsieur Bond?" Perriot asked.

He sighed heavily, and said, "Yes. It's been a long day."

Another young man in an SAS uniform approached him and asked, "Are you Mister Bond?"

"Yes?"

"There's someone here to see you. Outside."

Bond got up slowly, drained his beer, set the bottle on the table, and walked out of the tent. What he had viewed on the television monitor had thoroughly disheartened him, but when he saw who was waiting outside the tent, his spirits picked up.

"Tylyn," he said.

They fell into each other's arms and the entire world was lost to them.

They bathed together and then had a luxurious dinner in her room at the Carlton. Tylyn dressed Bond's wounds and kissed them, then gave him a thorough massage. They made love, and this time it was soft and gentle. Bond noted that their couplings had always been different, both in mood and intensity. He knew that this was a woman with whom he could find variety for the rest of his life.

Afterwards, they lay in bed naked. He smoked a cigarette and she sipped a glass of cognac. Tylyn cleared her throat and said, "I have something to say, and I'm not sure how to say it."

"Then just say it," Bond replied.

"All right." She took a sip and began. "You lied to me, James. You told me you were a reporter, and I believed you."

"Darling, don't you see now why I did that? I was investigating your husband."

"And you used *me* to get to him."

He crushed the cigarette in an ashtray and sat up in the bed. "No. I didn't. At first, perhaps, I may have thought that I might get close to him through you. But after I met you all of that changed. I wanted to be with you, Tylyn."

She sighed. "And this job of yours. You're really a policeman. You carry a gun. You advocate violence."

"I don't advocate anything," Bond said. "Sometimes, yes, I have to use a gun. But only if I have to."

She nodded but didn't look happy.

He reached out and ran a finger along her smooth cheek. "Tylyn," he said. "Don't think about that now. We're both alive. I'm desperately attracted to you, and I hope you still feel the same about me. I'm sorry I deceived you, but I promise to make it up to you. Tomorrow I have to finish this job in Corsica, but I'll be back tomorrow night, and we can spend the rest of our lives together if that's what you want."

"Is that what you want?" she asked.

He hesitated. "I don't know. Perhaps."

"I don't know either," she said. "Let's not think about that."

"All right. Let's just enjoy each other tonight, shall we?"

She nodded and leaned over to kiss him. He placed a

hand on her breast, gently laid her back, and made love to her once again.

Bond rarely dreamed, but he had a vivid one that night.

He was running through the Corsica *maquis,* the thick forest near the prehistoric sites. He was naked, but as he looked down at himself he saw that he wasn't human anymore. He was an animal, some kind of stag.

He ran past the strange menhirs, and several of them turned to watch him go by. One even whispered that he should be careful.

That's when he realised that he was being followed. Looking behind him, he could see the silhouette of a wolf in the distance, running after him. He increased his speed, but the presence of the wolf was overpowering. The beast was getting closer . . . closer . . . until Bond could feel the animal's hot breath on his back.

He heard a horrendous, unearthly snarl as the wolf leapt for him—

And Bond woke up.

He got out of bed, careful not to disturb Tylyn, and took a bottle of Perrier from the bar. He drank it down quickly and sat in a chair to calm himself. His heart was pounding.

Tylyn stirred and noticed that he wasn't beside her. She looked up and saw him. "What's the matter, sweetheart?"

"Would you believe me if I told you that I had a bad dream?" he asked.

She smiled. "Yes. I would." She reached out to him. "Come back to bed. I'll make sure you get back to sleep safely."

He crawled under the sheets and felt her smooth, soft skin next to his. She reached between his legs and caressed him. In seconds, the aftertaste of the nightmare had vanished.

"Fais-moi l'amour, James," she said.

He was happy to oblige.

28
The Showdown

Interpol officials agreed with M that Commander James Bond should be placed in charge of the strike against the Union headquarters in Corsica. During the night, Interpol worked feverishly with the governments of Britain, America, and France to put together a team of professional soldiers culled from the countries' respective armies. The international force totalled twenty-six men, all SAS trained.

Bond learned that he had been chosen to lead the team when he awoke at sunrise. Nigel Smith had tracked him down by phone and told him to report to the airport in Nice at nine o'clock sharp. The ring had disturbed Tylyn's sleep, but she quickly dozed off again. Bond quietly got dressed, left without making a sound, and was picked up by a military escort and taken to Nice.

The meeting took place at a hangar near Terminal One. A French air force captain provided aerial reconnaissance photos of *Le Gérant*'s compound and made suggestions for an approach.

"The element of surprise must work in our favour," he said. "The Union must surely know that we're going to hit them, so what we need to do is make certain that we hit them before they *think* we're going to hit them. They just might be banking on the notion that a raid can't be organised overnight. That's why we're moving so fast. From the satellite films we have obtained, we can see that there has been activity for the last twenty-four hours. We estimate a force of twenty men, but that's difficult to say; at any rate, it looks like they're moving out. If we don't get there quickly, they could be gone before the day is over. The raid is on now, gentlemen, and we want to be hitting targets no later than noon."

Someone asked what the objective was—to take prisoners, or what?

"Shoot to kill anyone that moves, except for two people," Bond said. "There is a hostage in the basement. You'll find his photo in the packet. My squad is going after him. Once the hostage is safe, we can blow the house to kingdom come. Second, everyone must be on the lookout for the blind man, the Union's leader. That photo in your packet was taken recently in Monte Carlo. He is our primary objective and is wanted alive. That said, if the rest of his men meet with unfortunate accidents, I'm not going to blink twice."

The French officer resumed speaking. "We're in three squads. Each squad will assault a different side of the building. Your squad leader will brief you on the specifics. We'll all be equipped with headsets so that we can communicate with each other. We leave in one hour. Good luck."

Bond checked his weapons—the Walther knife and the reliable P99, plenty of extra magazines, a bulletproof vest, and headset. As an afterthought, he clipped the Q Branch camera to his belt. Commandant Perriot approached him and said, "I just want you to know, monsieur, that it will be a privilege serving with you. After witnessing your courage yesterday in Cannes, I would follow you anywhere."

"Thank you for volunteering," Bond said. "Before we leave, I need to make a phone call." He found Marc-Ange

Draco's business card in his wallet and said, "I know some-one who might be able to help us."

Le Gérant got off the phone with one of his most trusted colleagues and told Julien, the bookkeeper, "They are not going to be able to get together a strike force in one day's time, just as I thought. We've been given a reprieve. Tell the boys that they don't have to kill themselves to pack. Instead of being out of here by noon today, we have until midnight tonight. All right?"

"Oui, monsieur," Julien said, and marched out of the office.

But *Le Gérant* had a bad feeling in his gut. Something was wrong. Should he effect his escape now?

He stepped to a window, even though he couldn't see the view of the Corsican mountains around the property. *Remember what the dreams have told you, Le Gérant* said to himself. His last dream was a testament to his upcoming triumph, for in it he had slain the majestic stag. That meant that there was nothing to worry about. He didn't need to run so soon. The dreams had predicted that he would emerge victorious.

And dreams never lied.

The French army loaned them three Aérospatiale (Euro-copter) AS 565 Panthers armed with cannon pods, Matra Mistral AAMs, HOT AT missiles, rockets, and torpedoes. Nine men in each chopper were quite comfortable as they made the journey from Nice to southern Corsica. As Bond looked down at the broccoli-like clumps of trees and the rough terrain of the rocky mountains, he thought again of the phone call he had made earlier and how it would affect the mission.

Never mind, he told himself. *Get on with it.*

The helicopters flew over Propriano and headed east

towards Levie. Bond spoke into the headset, "This is it, gentlemen. Prepare for Phase One."

Every man in each chopper jumped up, checked his equipment, lowered the safety goggles on his helmet, and stood at attention near the open door. They were armed with M-4 A2 assault rifles, handguns, grenades, bulletproof vests, and knives.

"Monsieur Bond?" Perriot said on the headset.

"Yes?"

"I just received word that Assault Team B successfully raided Corse Shipping in St. Florent. Emile Cirendini has been arrested."

"One down, two hundred to go," Bond said.

The choppers neared the property, split up, and flew to respective points of a triangle in the sky. Bond's helicopter would drop the men at the back of the house, where the vehicles were parked. Another would land in front, inside the electrified fence. The third would hover above the building and watch all sides of the property, attacking where necessary.

Bond looked out and saw the house and grounds—the strange hybrid of Moroccan and Corsican architecture, the circular field that surrounded the house and the fence. The gate looked as if it had been repaired.

There were a lot of men outside, especially in the back. A lorry was parked by the house and workers were busy loading things into it. Several other vehicles—4×4s, the limousine, and a few cars—were sitting at the edge of the parking area, yielding the space to the lorry. At least four guards were in front of the building.

By the time the choppers were above the property, the Union men knew that they were under attack. Well trained and prepared, they dropped what they were doing, grabbed weapons, and ran for cover or their defence posts.

"Hit them!" Bond commanded. "Go go go!"

All three helicopters let off rockets. One went straight

for the front door of the house, directly over the guards' heads. The entire façade crumbled in a mass of flame and smoke. The second shot hit the side of the building, where Bond thought the barracks might be. The third rocket hit the lorry that was already nearly full of the Union's equipment. In Bond's opinion, it exploded with satisfying intensity.

The speed with which the return fire began surprised them all. The Union men were disciplined, well organised, and they knew what to do. As many of them were former professional soldiers, each man could be a formidable opponent. An army of them was daunting indeed.

Bond's chopper flew within ten feet of the ground and he gave the order to jump. He went first, leaping out of the aircraft and landing on his feet. The others followed him, spraying the area with bullets. Bond ran for cover behind one of the parked cars and let loose a volley of ammunition at two men crouched behind the limousine. They were armed with what appeared to be Uzis.

Bond unclipped a grenade, pulled the pin, and tossed it over to the limo. It rolled underneath the car. The men saw it and started to run, but it was too late. They were caught in the blast, which was intensified by the limo's exploding petrol tank.

Bond and two British men ran through the flames and into the open garage. They were met with streams of gunfire, so they hit the ground and rolled, firing as they went. One of the British soldiers was struck. His body continued to roll until it lodged against a stack of tyres. Bond and the other man concentrated their fire on the area of the garage where two opponents had found cover behind a 4×4.

On the other side of the house, things were not going so well. The Union managed to blow a hole in the hovering third helicopter with a twenty-year-old U.S. M40 recoilless rifle that had been hidden on the roof of the building. The chopper wobbled in the air for a few seconds before it burst into flame and plummeted to the ground with a tremendous crash. All nine men inside were killed instantly.

"We've lost a third of our force," Bond heard Perriot say in his headset. "We're going to try to take out the gunner on the roof."

Bond shouted to the other man with him, "Cover me!" The soldier sprayed the 4×4 with his M16 while Bond rose and ran like the devil towards the open door to the house. The soldier's bullets punctured all four tyres and riddled the vehicle with holes. This flushed out the two Union men, who made a desperate run for the open air. The British soldier picked them both off easily, then gave Bond the thumbs-up sign as he reached the door.

Bond entered the guards' quarters and found it deserted. He kicked the door to the corridor open and ran down the familiar, blank hallway toward the staircase leading downstairs.

There was no one about—it was too easy. Bond held the P99 tightly in both hands, ready to assume firing stance. He inched to the stairwell and peered down. Stepping quietly, he went all the way to the basement and again found it empty.

He ran to the locked wooden door and banged on it. "René, are you in there?"

"James?"

Bond fired the P99 into the lock, demolishing it. He opened the door, ran inside, and found Mathis standing against the wall.

"Are you ready to get out of here, my friend?" Bond asked.

There was something about Mathis's joyless expression that Bond should have interpreted more quickly, but in his haste to free his friend he had been careless. Still, his reflexes were just fast enough to prevent grievous bodily injury.

The wiry little guard Antoine jumped onto Bond's back

and attempted to plunge a knife into him, but Bond used the man's own momentum and weight to throw him over his shoulder. In doing so, however, he dropped the P99. The gun slid across the stone floor and into the straw in the corner.

Antoine sprung off the floor with surprising agility and lunged at Bond again with the knife, a long and slender Vendetta Corse. Bond twisted and avoided being stabbed, then swung and kicked the Corsican with his right foot. The blow hit Antoine in the chest, knocking him back into Mathis. They fell on the floor, giving Bond the time to unsheathe his own knife.

Antoine got back on his feet and held the knife in front of him.

"You want to dance, my friend, let's dance!" he said. He swished the knife in the air a couple of times. Bond, although adept at knife fighting, knew that he was no match for a Corsican who had grown up with a knife as an extension of his hand.

"René, the gun, over in the corner!" he shouted.

Antoine leaped forward, and Bond barely feinted in time. The blade sliced a bit of the material on the side of his vest. Bond spun and went into a crouch just as Antoine swung the knife over his head. Bond bounced forward with his knife pointed at the little man, but Antoine was like a circus acrobat. He performed a short leap, did a somersault in midair, and landed on his feet behind Bond.

How the hell . . . ?

Before Bond could turn around, the killer slashed the back of his neck with the blade. Bond felt a wrenching sting before falling forward, rolling out of the way, and jumping to his feet.

Antoine stood across the room, grinning, his knife dripping with blood. Bond felt the back of his neck with his left hand. It was wet and there was a painful cut just below his hairline, but luckily it wasn't very deep.

Antoine gestured with his free hand. "Come on!"

Angered now, Bond rushed him with the knife, but Antoine was too fast. The Vendetta Corse hit home and made a nasty gash on Bond's upper arm. Bond twisted and retreated to avoid another slash, but he had backed into the wall—the worst possible position to be in during a knife fight.

Antoine raised the knife by the blade, ready to throw it at Bond. In that split second, Bond considered unsnapping the PPK but knew that he wouldn't be able to draw the gun before the Union man released the knife. He was done for.

A gunshot reverberated in the stone cell, its volume magnified tenfold by the enclosed space. Antoine recoiled as if he had been hit with a sledgehammer between the shoulder blades. The knife fell from his hand as he staggered a couple of steps towards Bond. His eyes glazed over, and then he collapsed with a thud.

Mathis stood behind him, Bond's P99 in his hand.

"I hope that was him and not you, James," Mathis said.

"You did just fine, René," Bond said, immensely relieved. "You haven't lost your aim at all."

"They didn't tell me anything, James, but I knew you were coming soon. They started to pack up last night and move out of here. You are lucky that you got here before they left."

"That's because they thought we weren't going to be ready to hit them until tomorrow. They believed that they had another half day to clear out," Bond explained.

"How is that?"

"I'll tell you later," Bond said. "Do you know if *Le Gérant* is still here?"

"I cannot tell you, James," Mathis replied. "I've been down here in the dark the entire time. As a matter of fact, I would be in the dark no matter where I was, so I'm not the best person to ask."

"Don't worry about it," Bond said. "Let's get out of

here." He took the gun from his friend and led him out of the cell.

On ground level, Commandant Perriot and his squad had successfully taken out the guards in front of the house. They rushed in through the burning opening that had been created by the rocket and were met with heavy resistance inside. Six Union men had barricaded themselves in the foyer, and they shot three RAID officers before the latter could find cover. Perriot ordered one of his squad members, a man carrying a flamethrower, to "barbecue the bastards." The officer readied the instrument and walked through the opening. He loosed with a spray of fire that resembled a dragon's breath. The Union men screamed as they were hit. Four of them panicked and ran, their clothes ablaze. Marksmen shot them as they emerged from the house. The other two were burnt to a crisp where they crouched.

Perriot led the rest of the squad farther inside. It didn't take them long to find the stairs to the roof, ascend them, and assume positions for an assault. Two men bravely volunteered to go up first. They burst through the hatch, firing their M16s as they climbed. The two men manning the M40 pointed it at the hatch and sprayed it with bullets. One of the RAID men went down, but the other successfully hit the two shooters. The rest of the team emerged from the stairs and made a clean sweep of the roof, making sure that no other Union men were hiding there.

Bond brought Mathis out through the back. He signalled his helicopter with the headset; it came down and landed in the field. Bond helped Mathis get inside, told him to sit tight, and gave the pilot the go-ahead to ascend to a safe position.

"Commence Phase Two," Bond said into his headset.

He reentered through the back after verifying with Perriot that his squad was accomplishing its goals. They had lost too many men, but the Union force didn't appear to be as strong as they had expected.

Bond made his way through the war-torn building until he passed the exam room where he had been tortured. Bond kicked the door open and found Dr. Gerowitz cowering behind the exam chair. The man raised his hands and screamed, "Don't shoot! Please! I am unarmed! I was just following orders!"

Bond levelled the P99 at him and said, "I can overlook what you did to me, Doctor. This is for what you did to Mathis."

He squeezed the trigger and gave the ophthalmologist a third eye.

Bond left the room and continued into the bowels of the building. He approached the intersection to another corridor and peered around the corner. Two guards were waiting at the end of the hall in front of a closed, ornate wooden door, their guns aimed in his direction. Bond pulled the pin out of a grenade and tossed it at them. The blast shook the whole house.

He ran around the corner, stepped over the bodies, and kicked the broken door out of the way.

This had to be *Le Gérant*'s inner sanctum. It was an office, elegantly furnished with an unusual mixture of Berber rugs and tile work, yet there was also a Western sensibility to the place. Bond went through a door into a large bedroom that was similarly decorated. No one was there. There didn't appear to be any other way out of the room. He went back into the outer office and heard Perriot in the headset say, "Monsieur Bond, we have set explosives through most of the house. Just let us know when you are ready."

"Not yet," Bond said. "I'm still looking for the golden goose."

He made a cursory search of the desk for any clues that might point to where Cesari might be. Had he already left?

Perhaps he had decided to abandon his home as soon as he had found out that the Cannes project had failed.

He went back into the bedroom and examined the walls. He opened the wardrobe and pushed back the clothes hanging there. The light caught the back wall of the wardrobe oddly, making it appear at an angle. Bond touched the wall, and it moved. It was a secret door, and it was ajar!

Bond opened it, revealing stone steps leading down into darkness. He unclipped a torch that he had on his utility belt, switched it on, and told Perriot where he was going.

"Let me send some backup to help you," the commandant said.

"No," Bond insisted. "I work alone. If I'm not back in ten minutes, that's a different story."

He descended the stairs and found himself in a dark, damp cavern. A path led between two stalagmites into a pitch-black tunnel. Bond entered the tunnel, which, before long, began to twist and turn. Eventually it came to a fork.

Now where?

He gambled and took the path to the right. Soon he ran into a T intersection.

The damned place was a labyrinth.

He went right again and noticed that the cavern floor was sloping down. It grew steeper, and soon the tunnel spread into such a large chamber that Bond couldn't see the other side. As he began to traverse it, he had an overpowering sensation that he was being watched. He stood in one place and turned 360 degrees, shining the torch all around him, but he couldn't see a thing. He took a step, intending to continue walking across the chamber, when suddenly a figure rushed toward him from the darkness. Bond raised the P99 and fired, but a long, metal object slammed into his left shoulder. He dropped the torch, and it rolled down the steep cavern floor and disappeared off a ledge.

The cavern was plunged into total darkness. Bond was

completely blind. With the P99 pointed in front of him, he slowly turned around again, listening carefully.

He thought that he heard something to his right, twisted, and fired the gun.

The hard metal object struck him again in the back. He fell to his knees and felt the rush of air next to him in time to deflect a second blow with his arm. He turned and fired his gun in that direction, but it was no use.

After a moment's silence came the voice. "Here we are again, Mister Bond. We seem to meet under the most unusual circumstances."

Bond shot toward the voice, but then he heard Cesari laugh behind him. Bond twisted again and fired. There was silence, and then the voice came from yet another place in the dark.

"You're in my habitat now, Mister Bond," Cesari said. "You can't see a thing, can you? Neither can I, but as I explained to you before, I *can* see. I know exactly where you are."

As Cesari spoke, Bond could hear his voice moving. He fired the gun into the darkness again, but the laugh came from a different direction.

The club struck him hard on the right shoulder blade.

"Was that your head or your shoulder?" Cesari asked. "Forgive me. I know where you are, but I suppose my aim isn't perfect."

Bond was in agony. If his shoulder blade wasn't broken, it was bruised as hell. He lay on the ground, clutching his arm.

"Have you had any strange dreams lately, Mister Bond?" Cesari asked. "You know what they say: Never dream of dying. It just might come true."

Bond rolled over to face the direction of the voice and spray-fired the Walther. This time he heard an "Oompf" and a sharp intake of breath. Something hit the floor, probably the club Cesari had been using to hit him with. Bond fired again.

He managed to get to his feet and remove the camera from his belt. He ejected the ophthalmoscope cylinder, dropped the camera, and switched on the light. It gave him enough illumination to see shapes within ten feet around him.

There on the floor, a few feet away, he saw Olivier Cesari attempting to crawl away. He had been hit, but it was difficult to tell how badly.

"Hold it, Cesari, I see you now," Bond said. "Give it up. Hands above your head."

Cesari stopped moving and sat down on the ground. He held his side, which appeared to be soaked in blood.

But before Bond could make another move, he felt another presence rushing toward him. A powerful fist hit him in the face and a shoe kicked the Walther out of his hand. He dropped the ophthalmoscope as he fell to his knees.

Two torches switched on, flooding the chamber with light.

He looked up and saw the man known as the Sailor with a torch and a gun pointed right at his head. Next to him were Ché-Ché le Persuadeur, also holding a torch, and Marc-Ange Draco, who said, "You had better raise your hands, James. It's over."

29

The Final Visit

Bond wasn't surprised to see his father-in-law.

The Sailor and Ché-Ché relieved Bond of his weapons, threw his headset on the ground, then resumed covering him.

"I was wondering if you would turn up, Marc-Ange," Bond said. He slowly raised his hands. He nodded to the Sailor. "Your 'eyes and ears,' I presume?"

Draco replied, "Yes, the Sailor has always worked for me. You never cease to amaze me, James. When I got that phone call from you this morning, I thought that you were still in the dark, so to speak. I should have known that you might feed me false information. Stupidly, I trusted you at your word."

"We watched some security camera tapes last night, Marc-Ange. When I saw your security firm, the men in green uniforms delivering the film cans to the Palais in Cannes, I knew then that you were involved."

"Securité Verte," Draco said. "Yes, they were my men. So that's how you caught me. Interesting. Now I understand why you called this morning and asked if I would be interested in helping you with a raid *tomorrow*. You said that it was taking more time than expected for the various governments to put together an assault team. Ha, and then you show up a few hours later and surprise us. Very clever, James. You knew that we would have abandoned ship already had we not believed that we had more time. *Le Gérant* would have been far away from here."

"Why, Marc-Ange?" Bond asked. "Why join up with this poor excuse of a businessman?" He gestured to Cesari, who slowly stood and limped over to the Sailor.

Draco shrugged. "The money was better. Besides, blood is thicker than water. Olivier here is my nephew. His father and I were half brothers. We shared the same mother, you see."

The news was like a punch in the solar plexus. That explained a hell of a lot, Bond thought. Christ, that would make him related, by marriage, to *Le Gérant*! Tracy and Cesari were cousins!

Draco continued, "When Olivier took over the Union from its American founder a few years ago, I was one of the silent investors who helped fund him. Needless to say, my investment has paid off splendidly. As the Union grew in power and size, I was happy to let it absorb the old Union Corse. It was a pleasure to let someone else be in charge for a change. I hadn't . . . been the happiest of men in many years."

It was all clear to Bond now. After the death of Tracy, Draco, once a criminal but a man with principles, had become a bitter, vengeful man. He was a totally different person from the man Bond once called his friend.

"It grieves me, James, to have to do this to someone who is family," Draco said. "You have to die today, my son."

"Marc-Ange, you have the power to walk away from all this," Bond said. "I cannot believe that you would have allowed that bomb in Cannes to kill so many people."

Draco shook his head. "Then you don't understand me at all, James. After what I have gone through, I didn't care what happened to a bunch of rich movie stars. Do you remember me telling you that I remarried and had a child?"

"Yes. You said that they died in an accident."

"It was no accident. My young wife was an actress, a beautiful young woman who had her whole life and career ahead of her. Our little girl, Irene, was a child actress. She had been on the stage a few times. She was making her first motion picture with her mother in Nice . . . when you killed them."

"Me?"

"Last January," Draco said. "The fire at Côte d'Azur Studios. You told me yourself that you had fired the shots that burst the petrol tanks. That fire killed a number of innocent people, James, and I'll bet that you had not one single moment of remorse."

"That's not true, Marc-Ange," Bond said. "I felt terrible about it. I'm very sorry about your wife and daughter, but it *was* an accident. You know I didn't set out to kill anyone inside that soundstage."

"Apologies are not accepted," Draco said. "I am Corsican, and we take blood vendettas very seriously. They can never be broken. I cannot let you kill my nephew, nor can I allow you to wreak any more havoc on the Union. The war is over, James, and you have lost."

Cesari limped to Bond and stared through him. With a sneer, he hit Bond in the stomach. Bond doubled over and fell to the floor.

"Ché-Ché, Sailor, take *Le Gérant* out to the helicopter," Draco said. "I'll wait here with our friend."

"Are you sure, boss?" the Sailor asked. "We can finish him off for you if you want."

"No, go on," Draco said. "Get him to a doctor quickly."

The two men led Cesari out of the cavern after giving Draco one of the torches.

"This tunnel leads to a hidden helipad in the hills behind Olivier's estate. It's a real pity that you destroyed the house. It was worth a lot of money," Draco said.

Bond started to get up, but Draco pointed a Glock at

him. "Even though you're my former son-in-law, James, don't think that I won't shoot you."

"Then do it, Draco," Bond spat. "Get it over with, or do you have any more speeches to make?"

Draco shook his head. "You were always impatient and petulant, weren't you, James? We're going to sit here and wait a few minutes. I have to give Olivier time to get out of here. You see, all of the explosives your little assault team has placed in the house are superfluous. The entire complex is set to blow up in"—he glanced at his watch—"approximately five minutes. It will take out the house, your men, and, unfortunately, this lovely cavern."

"What about you?" Bond asked.

"Oh, I'm cashing in my chips, James," Draco said with a sigh. "My world just hasn't been the same without my wife and daughter. There is no joy for me anymore. I have decided to end my miserable life, and I'm going to take you with me."

Ironically, Bond found himself faced with the opposite dilemma. Could he kill his father-in-law? A man he had admired?

Then it hit Bond. "You were trying to put me in Cesari's clutches the entire time, weren't you? You deliberately misled me, telling me that Léon Essinger wasn't important. Instead, you threw clues at me, advised me, pointed the way to this place so that your nephew could get rid of me as he pleased."

"Yes, but you managed to escape," Draco said. "That complicated matters. We nearly aborted the project, but *Le Gérant* had confidence that it could still be pulled off. Now, then. I suppose I should play it smart and shoot you here and now."

Once again, Bond started to stand but Draco stopped him. "Just stay on the ground, James. I feel safer that way."

Draco didn't notice that Bond had repositioned himself on the cavern floor. He had sat down on the ophthalmoscope cylinder that he had dropped earlier. Bond palmed it and stuck it in the elastic of his sleeve.

"What difference does it make, Marc-Ange?" Bond asked. "If we're both going to die in a few minutes, what's the point in feeling safe?"

"I want to keep you here long enough for Olivier to get away. I don't care what happens to me."

"Then let's have a cigarette," Bond suggested. "I carry fine Turkish—"

"Forget it. You'll only pull out one of your tricks," Draco said. "I said stay down—"

Bond moved as if to reposition himself again but instead switched on the ophthalmoscope's laser and pointed it at Draco's face. The light surprised and blinded him momentarily, long enough for Bond to jump up and kick the Glock out of Draco's hand. The gun slid on the incline but lodged against a rock before going over the ledge. Bond stood, stepped in to Draco, and punched him across the face. The man fell backwards and rolled until he stopped, facedown.

Bond carefully moved down the incline and picked up the Glock. It was a shame that those other two had taken his weapons. He hoped he could catch them in time.

He walked up the incline and started to run in the direction they had gone, but he heard Draco say, "James."

Bond whirled to see Draco with a miniature derringer, something he probably had kept up his sleeve. There was a pop as flame burst from its barrel and Bond felt a sharp, searing pain in his left shoulder. Instinctively, Bond fired the Glock, hitting Draco between the eyes. The former organised-crime boss jerked back and crumpled to the ground like a puppet.

There was no time to think about what he had just done. Bond turned, picked up his headset, and started to run as he spoke.

"Perriot, get all the men out of the château, *now*! It's going to blow in two minutes! Move!"

"I read you, James! Evacuation commencing!" he heard Perriot say.

Bond followed the path through the cave, winding around fallen boulders and what appeared to be still-active formations. The ground was very damp, the air was musty, and there were more stalagmites to contend with. Eventually he came to a solid wall and could find no other way through.

Damn! He must have missed a turn. How much time was left?

He backtracked, studied the walls more carefully, and this time saw an opening to the right that he hadn't noticed earlier. He went through it and could smell fresh air. The light was brighter and natural.

He emerged from the cave on the inside of a hollowed-out hill. The sides of the hill adequately disguised the helipad and stone bunker that had been constructed there. A French Aerospatiale Astazou Alouette III was idling, its blades whirring around in anticipation of lifting off. Bond could see a pilot, Ché-Ché, the Sailor, and Cesari inside the elongated cockpit. Two Union men were supervising on the ground, their backs to Bond.

He aimed the Glock at the pilot and fired just as the helicopter began to rise. The windscreen shattered, and the pilot recoiled and slumped in his chair. The Sailor's face registered surprise as he pointed at Bond. The two men on the ground turned and drew their weapons, but Bond swung his gun toward them and fired first. The guards fell back against the bunker wall and collapsed. Bond continued to fire at the figures in the cockpit, but he ran out of ammunition. He dropped the Glock and ran to the bunker, praying that there would be more weapons inside. Bond kicked the door open and rushed at a third guard inside the bunker. Before the man could react, Bond punched him in the stomach and threw him to the floor. He then kicked him in the chest, stomped on his face, and kicked him again in the ribs for good measure.

Thank heaven! There was a cabinet containing several rifles. Bond used his boot to break the glass doors. He reached in, grabbed a .40-calibre M203 grenade launcher, checked to see that it was loaded, and ran outside.

The helicopter was destabilised, rising by itself. The Sailor had pushed the pilot out of the way and moved into his seat, desperately trying to get the aircraft under his control. The Alouette wavered awkwardly in the air but suddenly regained its balance and hovered some sixty feet off the ground. Bond raised the weapon and aimed at the rotors. He squeezed the trigger and felt a tremendous kick against his shoulder.

The helicopter started to shift direction, as if it were ready to move from its stationary position, just as the grenade exploded over the top of the blades. The flames engulfed the cockpit as the aircraft shook, completely disabled. The fireball appeared to swallow the helicopter whole as the craft shot out of Bond's sight. He could hear the roar, though. The glissando from a high pitch to a low one indicated that they were on the way down.

He not only heard the crash but felt it as the ground shook.

Bond dropped the M203, then quickly climbed to the top of the hill and out onto its exterior. The only traces left of the Union and *Le Gérant* lay in the messy bonfire below.

Not quite thirty seconds later, the world convulsed as the hidden bombs in the house blew. There was a chain reaction, for the Union's bombs set off the explosives that Perriot and his men had been setting. The result was a destructive force nearly three times that which had been intended.

Bond hit the ground and felt the heat pass over him. Pieces of debris fell all around him, and he must have been at least a quarter kilometre away from the house.

In a couple of minutes, it was all over. He could hear the surviving soldiers hooting with joy. Bond got up, held his shoulder, and walked back to the site of the devastation.

The strike team had made it out in time. Perriot helped Bond get emergency medical treatment for the gunshot wound and offered to ride with him to Propriano, the nearest village with decent medical facilities. Bond declined, but thanked him anyway. All told, the Interpol force lost nearly half its men, but there wasn't a single survivor from Union headquarters.

The battle, and perhaps the war, was over.

30
The End

The waiter brought a bottle of Nuits-Saint-Georges, one of the finer red wines. After he had uncorked it and Bond had tasted it, the waiter poured the two glasses and left the couple alone.

It was early afternoon and they were sitting at one of the many sidewalk cafés in the old town of Nice, not far from the flower market made famous in Hitchcock's *To Catch a Thief*. Tylyn had worn sunglasses in the hope of avoiding recognition, but they were no use. An American tourist asked her for an autograph (on a napkin, no less—Bond wondered why anyone would bother), and some giggling French teenagers interrupted them to ask if she really was Tylyn Mignonne.

"If you'd rather leave, we can," Bond suggested.

"No, it's all right," she said. "I'm used to it. People recognise me all the time."

She took a sip of wine and sat quietly. Bond had never seen her so pensive.

"Tylyn?"

"I know," she said. "I'm not saying much. I think it's probably because I have so much to say."

"Then why not just say it?"

She looked away and rested her chin in her hand, elbow on the table, a posture that Bond thought of as "typically

Tylyn." He had seen her do it on a number of occasions, and it made her look more like an inquisitive college student and so *unlike* a model or well-known actress that it was endearing.

"Because I don't know if it's the right thing to say," she replied.

Bond shifted in his seat and poured another glass of wine and topped hers up. The doctor who had extracted the .22 bullet had given him pills for the pain, and the throbbing in his left shoulder was just beginning to subside.

But the pills wouldn't work with affairs of the heart. That kind of pain was more resilient.

"I served Léon with papers today," she said, as if to change the subject. "I'm almost sorry I wasn't there to see his reaction."

"I'm afraid that a divorce is the least of his concerns right now," Bond noted.

"Hmm. How long do you think he'll be in jail?"

"It's difficult to say," Bond said. "Depends on what the final sentence is. His lawyers will appeal, of course, and it could go on forever. But he won't be roaming the streets, that's for certain. He is accused of terrorism against his own country. Pretty serious stuff. He's liable to go to jail for the rest of his life."

"I would like to feel sorry for him, but I don't," she said. She took another drink. "And to think that I thought I loved him once."

"Don't be hard on yourself," Bond said.

"He wanted to kill me," she said. "He knew that bomb would kill me, along with all those other people. He wanted my money, my family's money, whatever he could get—"

"But that won't happen now," Bond said. "Try to put him and what happened behind you. You're an optimistic, life-loving girl. Don't let this ruin your sparkling personality."

She smiled. "You're teasing me."

He reached out and took her free hand. "What's next for you?" he asked gently.

She shrugged and said, "With *Pirate Island* cancelled, my agent will be sending me out for more auditions and such. There are a few scripts that have come in that I need to read. A producer in Hollywood wants me to come out there and be in something. I have another fashion show to plan for next fall. I need to approve a new line of clothing for my company. I have a photo shoot next week. . . . Shall I go on?"

"At least you'll be busy," Bond said. "That's the best therapy."

"And what about you, James? Are you off on another dangerous mission that puts you and your loved ones' lives at risk?"

Bond couldn't help detecting the sarcasm.

"Probably," he said. "And that is as good an opening as any for what I have to say. Perhaps after you hear what I'm going to tell you, you may not need to tell me what's on *your* mind."

She looked at him through the dark glasses, took a sip, and said, "Go on."

"Tylyn, I know you're upset that I deceived you. But now you understand that I was working undercover. If I had not done it that way, Léon and his people might have been successful in killing hundreds of people. You do re-alise that, right?"

She nodded.

"I fell in love with you for a number of reasons," he con-tinued. "However, someone in my profession simply can't turn his back on his job. I have been faced with the choice between Profession and Love before, and whenever I have chosen Love . . . it doesn't work out."

"What are you saying, James? That you can't see me anymore?" she asked.

"Something like that. Another factor is your celebrity status. I can't afford to be recognised. If I were with you, both of our lives would be at risk. You are in the public eye a great deal. My enemies would try to get to me through you. I was married once, Tylyn, and that union proved fatal to my wife. I saw one of my in-laws recently, and that reminded me just how dangerous it is for a woman to fall in love with someone like me. At the same time, I can't be seen in glossy movie-star magazines, accompanying you to awards shows. My life depends on my being anonymous. Do you understand?"

Tylyn smiled, but he knew that tears were forming beneath the dark glasses.

"I had a similar speech prepared," she said. "It basically amounts to the same thing, but for different reasons."

Bond poured some more wine into her glass and encouraged her to go on.

"I don't think I can have a relationship with someone in your profession, either," she said. "It's a profession built on deceit, and I just can't abide that. I'm not sure that I can forgive you for lying to me and masquerading as my lover—"

"I wasn't masquerading," he interrupted, but she put up her hand to stop him.

"I believe you," she said. "But I still can't forgive you. Our love affair was not what I thought it was, and I'm not so sure that it's salvageable. Even if you were to give up your job, which I'm not asking you to do, I don't think we could make a go of it."

Although he knew that everything she said was reasonable, Bond felt surprisingly rejected.

He took a sip of wine and smiled.

"What's funny?" she asked.

"Nothing's funny," he said. "I was just thinking that I haven't been ditched too many times in the past, and I'm not sure how I like it."

"We're ditching each other," she said. "It's mutual, isn't it? I mean, God, James, I would *love* to be with you. I'm mad about you, and I know you feel something similar for me . . . but it would be *insane*! We would drive each other crazy with the demands of our respective careers and end up hating each other."

Bond squeezed her hand and said, "You're absolutely right, darling. I couldn't have said it better."

"But we'll be friends?" she asked.

Bond laughed. "I suppose. As much as that's possible."

She grew silent again, finished her glass of wine, and after a moment said, "I had best be going. I don't want this to be any more painful than it already is." She stood and said, "Please don't get up. Wait here until I'm gone, all right?"

Bond nodded.

She leaned over, took his chin in her hand, and kissed him.

"Take care of yourself, James."

"You too, Tylyn."

She walked away, leaving Bond alone with the wine and his thoughts. The waiter came by and asked if there would be anything else. Bond asked for the bill.

He looked to see where she had gone, but he didn't see her. He took the last drink of wine and sighed. It was time to bury the emotions once again, lock them away in the vault so that they could never escape and unwittingly reveal that he really did have a heart.

He would save all that for his dreams.

Bond left money on the table and stood. Once again he glanced down the street, but she had disappeared. He turned and walked in the opposite direction, retreating into the shadows of his life.

FOR YOUR EYES ONLY

```
TO:      ████████
FROM:    ████████
RE:      ████████
```

In a world ████████████████████████████
████████████████████████████████████
████████████████████████

████████████ where nothing is what it seems
new information is the difference between ████████
life and death ████████████████████
stay informed:
                go to — www.jamesbondnews.com